OPERATION
CERTAIN DEATH

Kim Hughes, GC, is an acclaimed public speaker and a trustee of the Victoria Cross and George Cross Association. Recently leaving the Army, Kim is the most highly decorated bomb-disposal operator to have survived the Afghan conflict. He was awarded the George Cross in 2010 following a gruelling six-month tour of duty in Afghanistan during which he defused 119 improvised explosive devices, survived numerous Taliban ambushes and endured a close encounter with the Secretary of State for Defence. His internationally bestselling autobiography, *Painting the Sand*, has now pathed the way in his transition to fiction writing.

Also by Kim Hughes

NON-FICTION

Painting the Sand

KIM HUGHES

OPERATION CERTAIN DEATH

A Dom Riley Thriller

SIMON &
SCHUSTER

London · New York · Sydney · Toronto · New Delhi

First published in Great Britain by Simon & Schuster UK Ltd, 2021

1 3 5 7 9 10 8 6 4 2

Simon & Schuster UK Ltd
1st Floor
222 Gray's Inn Road
London WC1X 8HB

Simon & Schuster Australia, Sydney
Simon & Schuster India, New Delhi

www.simonandschuster.co.uk
www.simonandschuster.com.au
www.simonandschuster.co.in

A CIP catalogue record for this book
is available from the British Library

Paperback ISBN: 978-1-4711-8359-1
eBook ISBN: 978-1-4711-8358-4
Audio ISBN: 978-1-4711-9173-2

Typeset in Spectrum by M Rules
Printed and bound by CPI Group (UK) Ltd, Croydon, CR0 4YY

MIX
Paper from
responsible sources
FSC® C020471

FRIDAY

ONE

'It's the Rolls-Royce of IEDs.'

That was the first thing that went through my head when I pushed away the coarse sand with my paintbrush, exposing part of the pressure plate. The majority of the Improvised Explosive Devices we came across in this part of Helmand were crude to the point of caricature. 'Chip shop bombs', the Boss called them. I wanted to point out it should be 'kebab shop', but he hadn't yet been on one of those cultural sensitivity courses the army had introduced. Something designed to help win the hearts and minds of the very people who were busy blowing the feet, legs and bollocks off our lads.

What he meant was that they were lashed-together devices, usually a couple of planks of wood held apart by rubber rings which would compress when stood on or driven over. This pressure brought together two pieces of metal – washers or parts of old hacksaw blades – which would complete an electrical circuit, thus causing the detonator to explode, which in turn would set off the main explosive charge buried beneath. Crude, as I said, but undeniably effective. And available in their thousands, thanks to the Taliban's bomb-making factories.

But this one was a Rolls-Royce among Trabants. The wire — proper, heavily insulated stuff, not the usual Iranian crap that fell apart when you touched it — had been properly crimped using US-sourced 3M connectors. Christ, I thought, as I exposed a little more of the circuit, there was even a touch of *solder*. Unheard of. This was how one of those picture restorers must feel when they rub at a corner of a painting bought for five quid at a car boot sale and discover an Old Master. I was dealing with something by a maestro, the Leonardo da Vinci of the Taliban's bomb-makers. I was almost impressed.

As often happened when I paused to take in a situation such as this — one involving a threat to life; *my* life — I had something akin to an out-of-body experience. From my new POV, I was hovering above the rough road where I was lying on the ground. A corridor of yellow lines, like the dashes in Morse code, ran behind me, broken railway tracks leading back to the Incident Control Point (ICP). The spray-painted path showed the route I had cleared with my mine detector, all the way up to where the IED had been buried. I would re-sweep it on my way back to the ICP, too, or the Boss would have my nuts faster than any explosion could.

To my right was a concrete culvert that gave off an horrendous lingering stench. Beyond that a field of fully grown maize sloped gently upwards and gave way to a series of pomegranate orchards. I could see the flash of silver as the sun glinted off the irrigation ditches that criss-crossed this terrain, the only way the local farmers could put some colour and life into the desert. A bird of some description patrolled over the fields. I squinted. A shrike. Possibly a red-tailed shrike. There were several species of these hunter-killers in Helmand. They were called 'butcher birds' because of their habit of impaling the body parts of their prey on thorny bushes. The Spanish call them *El Verdugo* — The Executioner. I always thought *El Verdugo* was a very apt avian symbol for Afghan (like all soldiers serving there, I tended to truncate the name of the country).

It was only two hours after dawn, but the sun was already blow-torching down on me. My back was sodden and sweat was pooling behind my ears. I never knew you could sweat there, or from many other weird nooks and crannies, until I came to Afghan. The precious moisture trickled down my jawline and puddled on my chin before dropping onto the sand, staining it dark for a second before the heat sucked the patch dry once more.

There were flies circling and landing on my lips and I spat them away with the tip of my tongue. These fat black bastards were coming from that ditch to my right that ran alongside the road. There were clouds of mosquitoes swarming over it and it gave off the inevitable smell of human shit, which was the signature fragrance of this part of the world. The ditch was probably used as a sewer by those who normally dwelled in the deserted mud-built compounds that lay ahead, just beyond the T-junction that the booby-trapped road led into. Danish soldiers also serving with ISAF (International Security Assistance Force) had declared the dwellings secure and empty at first light, but even so I felt like I was being watched through the 'murder holes', the firing slits carved into pretty much every wall of the complex. The feeling of being observed by the locals – 'dicked', as we said – was constant and it never left you once you were outside Camp Bastion or whichever Forward Operating Base you were deployed to.

Over to my left, beyond the three circles of red paint that marked other IEDs planted a stone's throw from where I lay, was the Boss, my Staff Sergeant, working on the fifth and – we hoped – last of the cluster of IEDs for the day. He, too, was lying prone, 'painting the sand' with his brush to reveal a pressure plate.

5

I could see he had laid his Sig pistol within easy reach, next to his bag of tricks. Most did that. I didn't. A gun was one more thing to get in the way. I preferred to rely on the infantry that were watching over us for firepower.

I glanced over to see how Staff was getting on with his IED. It was extremely unusual to have two ATOs – Ammunition Technical Officers – in a bomb disposal team. Ours (codename: Blackrock 22) was a pilot scheme to see if splitting the burden of defusing the endless stream of IEDs between a pair of operatives helped alleviate some of the stresses and strains that built up over weeks and months of lying inches from sudden death. It had caused something of an outcry, because it meant other ATOs were stretched very thin indeed. It took seven years or so to train up an ATO. The truth was, as with many things, the army just did not have enough to go around.

'What you got, Boss?' I shouted over to him. He was close enough that I didn't have to use my PRR – Personal Role Radio.

'Same old shit,' he replied. 'You?'

'Yeah. Same old, same old.'

Best not to break his concentration while he dealt with his own device. He would find out soon enough that the mine wasn't that at all.

Not only would I take photographs of the device once I had uncovered more of it, but I'd also try to recover any bits that would prove useful for analysis by our Intelligence people. DNA samples were extracted from any hair or sweat left on the constituent parts and added to our burgeoning database. The Weapons Intelligence Section was particularly interested in anything new or novel and this, my forty-third IED, was certainly that.

I wondered if I'd make the half-century mark. In bombs, not years. But maybe I'd get to celebrate both. It was the end game now. We were leaving, letting the Afghans get on with it. I doubted the IEDs would stop. We just wouldn't be there to defuse them. I'd be at home with Tracey-Jane and the kids. And perhaps I'd come out of the army altogether. Although none of us ATOs were sure exactly how the skills and drills of Explosive Ordnance Disposal could be applied in Civvie Street.

I thought about the bomb-maker again as I continued to brush the sand away. Many of the builders were kids, their small, dextrous fingers deftly putting together pressure plates, filling old shell cases or palm oil cans with homemade explosives. Then crawling out in the dark of night and digging these lethal devices into the ground, when actually they should have been tucked up in bed. The good ones did a great job of making sure the bombs were well covered, that the excess soil was disposed of and that the earth was a uniform colour once again, so the bomb couldn't be spotted with the naked eye.

Something told me this particular technician wasn't a kid though. Staff always said that every bomb had a personality. Or, at least, it reflected the personality of the man – it was usually a man – who had assembled it. This one was neat, fastidious, considered. An adult had put this device together. Someone who took pride in his work, even if that work was to kill the British, Danish and Estonian soldiers who were working this part of the province.

And, apparently, the IED-builders' new job description was to take out the army's bomb-disposal specialists. ATOs had been declared the prime enemy. We were cats to their mice. Or was it the other way around? Anyway, we were told there was a bounty out on us, a reward for the first bomb-maker to kill an ATO. It was hardly a reassuring thought, lying there in the sun, brain boiling beneath my helmet, that there was a price on my very hot head.

Operation Certain Death, that's what we ATOs called a tricky situation. But, given the bounty on us, everything was tricky now.

Stay focused.

Skills and drills, remember. They keep you alive. I looked over at the Boss again. He was concentrating too hard to have spoken. It was in my mind, a replay of the phrase he used over and over again, along with: *The bomb isn't your enemy. Complacency is.*

Even though sudden death was mere inches away, I felt the familiar tingle of excitement, not fear, as I worked at exposing the business end of the IED. Well, maybe there were a few grace notes of dread, the ones that kept you sharp. This was why we signed up for the High Threat bomb-disposal course. We do this because it saves lives, we tell ourselves, it is how we make a difference. The truth is we also do it because it is the biggest fucking buzz on the planet. Until it becomes routine, boring, *easy*. That's when you die.

I took a deep breath and puffed a little air out to shift the salt-craving flies. I glanced back at the ICP, which had been set up between the two Mastiff Protected Patrol Vehicles that had brought us here. Carl, our Electronic Counter Measures man, who was busy jamming any signals that might detonate the bomb, was also taking notes of what we were up to. Around him stood our infantry escort, SA80s at the ready. Lost among them, crouching in the shadow of one of the vehicles, was the slight figure of Moe, our young interpreter or 'terp'. It was hard to tell how young he was because, like all interpreters in Afghan, his face was almost permanently covered by a scarf, so he couldn't be recognised by any Taliban scanning us through binoculars or sniper scope. Recognition would mean certain death for him and his family. That very morning the Boss had given the lad his own *shemagh* scarf, just to make certain he was properly masked up. Now only his dark, sad eyes were visible.

The Boss had told a story about Moe as we bounced to this spot in our Mastiff PPV. This wasn't uncommon. Moe the terp was the butt of many jokes. They made the kid laugh and gave him a sense of belonging to Blackrock 22, rather than just being a mouth-for-hire. You knew you were accepted in the team when everyone took the piss out of you. Sick humour, insults and practical jokes were the glue that held us together.

'*So, Moe comes into the FOB and the Captain says to him: Where've you come from? I came down the Pharmacy Road comes the reply. Are you mad? the officer asks. It's full of IEDs and Waheed, the warlord, is out there. Did you see him? I did, admits Moe. I was about three kilometres away from here when he stepped out and put an AK-47 to my chest. He accused me of being a terp. I denied it. So, he said, drop your pants. I did. Now, take a shit. What could I do? He had the AK-47. I took a shit. Now eat it. What? Eat it? What could I do? He had the AK-47. So, I ate it. He started laughing, but as he did so I jumped on him and wrestled the AK-47 from him. Drop your pants, I said. What could he do? I had the gun. He did so. Take a shit. What could he do? I had the AK-47. Now, eat it. He did so. You ask me if I have seen Waheed the Warlord? We just had lunch together!*'

I chuckled to myself. The last time he had told that joke, it had been Pedro the Bandit. Sometimes I wondered if sending the Boss on a cultural sensitivity course would be a waste of time.

Back in the moment, I used the point of my trowel to break up a tennis-ball-sized sphere of hard sand and swept it away. As I did so, I exposed part of the battery assembly. Now I could see the set-up quite clearly. Still very neat in execution, but still the same basic principles. Switch, detonator . . . *boom*.

It wasn't quite time to start cutting wires, though. Sometimes there was a collapsing circuit, a second system piggy-backed onto the first. So, if you cut the primary or main circuit, the back-up activated and fired the detonator and it was All Over Now, Baby Blue. To be fair, the majority of IEDs I had come across in Afghan

didn't have anything quite so sophisticated as a collapsing circuit – the IRA ones in Northern Ireland were a different matter,
because those fuckers were always trying to catch us out – but it
was worth checking. My life was worth it. I continued to brush,
sweep and excavate further. Stopped. There was something else
down there. Something new. More cable. Running through a
buried plastic conduit. That was new, too. No, not cable. String.

It's a command-pull IED.

That was the last thing that went through my head.

*

'And how does that make you feel?'

TWO

And he was back in the room.

It was suddenly very cold and he shivered, missing the sun on his neck. He felt a surge of resentment, as if he had been woken during a particularly pleasant dream, even though what he had been experiencing was more like a waking nightmare. It was one he always hoped would end differently. It never did. Nick always died.

Even so, it was good to hear his old friend's voice, despite Riley knowing it wasn't real, just some part of his brain unwilling to let Nick go completely. The pain of reliving that day, now more than four years in the past, was almost worth it, just to spend some time with him.

Riley looked around the room, confident he was in the real world once again. Rather than lying in a fly-flecked corner of Helmand, he was sitting in the Psychological Assessment Suite on the third floor of what used to be, in Leicester's glory days, one of the city's many shoe factories. Now it was a series of offices, including the one he was in, which was rented to PAS – Psychological Assessment Services – which specialised in providing detailed reports to employers about a subject's state of mind. Employers like the army.

Outside, the sun had finally replaced the wind-driven rain

squalls that had swept over the central part of England for the best part of a week, which had made spring seem like a very distant prospect indeed. Now, with the gales departed and the sky blue, it looked far more inviting than the rather sterile consulting room, with its retro van der Rohe furniture and one of those curved Arco lamps that people thought turned them into Don Draper.

Staff Sergeant Dom Riley pulled his gaze from the Crittal window and sniffed, trying to clear his sinuses, but the smell was still there. Shit, sand and blood. This olfactory reminder of Helmand could strike at any time. Many a meal had been ruined by an unbidden taste of the foul, penetrating dust that swirled around Afghanistan and the iron tang of the red mist that bombs tended to leave hanging in the air when some poor fucker trod on an IED.

His ears were still ringing, as if the blast that had taken Nick had happened moments ago. Riley realised that the woman sitting in the chair beside him had spoken. Ms Carver. The 'Ms' being very important. Late twenties. Probably very attractive when she didn't wear unflattering black suits and scrape her dark hair back and leave her face looking so scrubbed it was as if she had had one of those derma-peels. Still, Riley supposed she had to have some line of defence against the parade of horny squaddies who came into her office for 'assessment'. Except he wasn't there for any routine mind games. He was there fighting for his job.

'I'm sorry?'

'How does that make you feel?' she repeated.

How the fuck do you think it makes him feel?

Nick, still in his head, still mouthing off. But his dead friend was right. It was a waste of a good man. And it made Riley furious. This, though, wasn't the time or the place to vent his anger. He managed to keep a lid on it, which wasn't always the case. He was a soldier, he reminded himself. Suck it up, leave the politics to others. You fought for your mates, not the big picture. And you sometimes lost your mates in the process.

He was there because of an incident at the Felix Centre at Marlborough Barracks in Warwickshire, where he had been giving a briefing to a group of trainees on the Improvised Explosive Device Disposal course. The students were in the middle of analysing two famous cases, the Pizza Bomber and the Harvey's Resort device, but with Riley having returned from operations in Northern Ireland they were equally keen to learn from real-life experiences in the field. The general public thought that, since the peace process, Ireland was a bomb-free, if not riot-free, zone. They couldn't be more wrong. Old habits die hard. The 'New IRA' bombs in a hijacked pizza delivery van outside the Londonderry courthouse in January 2019 demonstrated that. However, not all the attendees on the course were willing to take his advice. Some were convinced they had nothing to learn from old hands like him. It was because of one of those smart arses that he was having to answer stupid questions in an old shoe factory.

He decided to give Ms Carver what he suspected she wanted to hear. 'I feel scared. Angry. Frustrated. Sad. It's weird. Being inside his head.'

He sensed her stiffen slightly at the last part, like a cat poised to leap on a mouse. Shit, he hadn't meant to say that. Now she was bound to write 'mad fucker' in his file.

'Inside his head how?' she asked.

He found himself answering, despite his usual reticence on the subject of Nick to anyone but army buddies. 'Whenever I think of that day, I'm not an observer. Or a bystander. It replays as if I am him. It is me defusing the bomb, me who sees the command-pull wire, me who . . .'

13

He stopped. Yes, he was Nick Steele except for the fact that his old friend wouldn't have known a shrike from a shitehawk. That bit was all genuine Dominic Riley.

'You get the picture,' he said.

Ms Carver nodded. 'It is a common scenario in cases of PTSD for—'

'I don't have . . . PTSD.' He managed to edit out the word 'fucking' at the last moment.

It was her turn to stay silent.

'And if I have, it's under control. It's got nothing to do with why I reamed out the trainee.' It was lazy labelling. Every soldier who served had to have some degree of PTSD these days. Just like every struggling kid at school had to be 'on the spectrum'. Soldiering was brutal, dirty, often thankless work, always had been. It fucked you up, although the exact recipe was different for every individual. Of course, defusing IEDs as a career added its own piquancy to the mix.

Ms Carver's face showed no response. 'We'll come to him in a moment. Tell me more about being Nick.'

'There's nothing to tell.'

'Can you try? How does this transference manifest itself?'

'Transference?' He knew what she meant. He was stalling for time.

'Being inside his head.'

'It's weird.'

She gave a rare, albeit brief, smile. 'We're used to weird.'

He took a deep breath. In for a penny. 'I can see me. That's what is so strange. I can actually see and hear me.'

'Go on.'

He didn't want to 'go on'. He wanted out of there. But, as that wasn't an option, Riley steeled himself and explained how, as Nick, he could go back to the hours leading up to the incident, back to when he had been listening to off-colour jokes about Moe the terp. It was beyond bizarre that as 'Nick' he could observe 'Dom'. If he thought about it too much it was a total mindfuck. This bizarre Nick/Dom chimera – him but not really him – would relive how they had cleared the lines from the ICP, marking the safe path with yellow spray paint. The laying out of the initial kit (trowel, brush, snips, camera) and making sure that the man-bag containing the other gear – such as the remote-operated 'flying scalpel' to cut wires, det cord and plastic explosive for controlled detonations – was in easy reach. Then he was examining the IED. Discovering that this one was a cut above your normal piece of crap. Brushing, probing. And then ... seeing the command-pull wire.

It meant someone had been lying in wait, maybe just a few metres beyond the rough culvert, ready to tug the cable that would set off the bomb and kill or maim an ATO. Riley often wondered if the string-puller had got the bounty. Because Nick certainly died that day.

'After the blast, I'm back in my skull. I'm watching his final moments. The explosion threw him into the ditch,' Riley said. 'Then all hell let loose from the murder holes in the compounds and the maize field where the bomber must have been hiding. AK-47s, a couple of RPGs.'

'Were you hit?'

'No. I was pinned down. I couldn't move.' He cleared his throat. This still hurt, like a wound that refused to scab over. 'Couldn't help Nick.'

His instinct had been to run straight across to where his friend lay. But he couldn't. He had another set of instincts, army-instilled. Although the IEDs between him and Nick had been clearly marked with the red paint, he had no idea if they were the only bombs on that road. The safe paths were yellow-sprayed corridors and there were only two of those, both leading from the bombs to the Mastiffs and the Incident Control Point. Besides, the air was fizzing with rounds. The infantry crouched by the Mastiffs were returning fire, too. Even crawling on his stomach, there was a good chance of Riley being shot by one or both sides. Or blown up by an unmarked IED. So, against what every neuron in his brain was screaming, he had stayed put.

And then Nick had appeared.

He had pulled himself up out of the rancid sewer by his elbows, enough so that his upper body was visible. His face was relatively unscathed by the blast, but Riley could tell from his expression that his pal was in great pain. Riley yelled at him to get down, but taking cover wasn't foremost in Nick's mind.

'Look after Teej,' he yelled. At least, that's what Riley later decoded. At the time it was closer to a scream of agony, with some fractured words along for the ride. His head had drooped and his right arm disappeared and for a second it looked like he might slide back into the ditch. But he heaved himself further up with his left arm and when his right came into view again, Riley saw that Nick was holding his Sig sidearm. His hand was shaking with the effort, as if it was the heaviest pistol ever invented. He could barely lift it to his temple.

'No, stop, Nick, medics are en route!' Riley had no idea if that was true, but it was likely. No matter whether the call had gone out or not, he had to convince Nick the medivac was on its way. Had to make him believe it was worth hanging on. 'Stay with us, pal. We'll get you out!'

But Nick was no longer listening. The sound of a bullet cracking through bone snapped across the desert floor, striking Riley like the tip of a whip across the face.

THREE

Nottingham's latest shopping and dining plaza, Alan Sillitoe Circus, was officially opened by a (living) local celebrity author on a Tuesday. Conditions weren't ideal, grey and overcast, with persistent drizzle and a snatching wind, but the writer made the best of it with some jokes about football, the Sleaford Mods and D. H. Lawrence, and read part of *The Loneliness of the Long Distance Runner*.

Come the Friday after the unveiling, though, the promised spring had arrived with the new plaza's polished limestone flooring reflecting a thin but welcome sunshine and some of the hardier children stripping off to play among the water spouts that formed the central feature. The Circus was a sweeping circle with two arched entrances opposite each other, the circumference lined with bars and shops. Those who feared yet another parade of chains had been mollified by the council's decision to offer a rates holiday to any locally owned business. So it wasn't all Lush and River Island. The Starbucks was busy, but Notts Coffee was busier, and the most anticipated opening was SteakHolder, modelled on the popular Hawksmoor chain in London, but cheaper and rumoured to be funded by an ex-Notts County footballer.

At ten minutes to midday, in front of the Bugg Bar stood

a white-shirted waiter, a Spaniard who was riding the ripples from the uncertainties of Brexit, proudly surveying his fiefdom of tables, as if he was working on Las Ramblas, rather than an out-of-town shopping centre in Nottingham. He looked over at a glum-looking woman who had been nursing a coffee for thirty minutes, staring off into space.

She was just entering her mid-thirties, but she was already widowed, and was now remembering when she and her late husband – a victim of knife crime during a botched robbery – used to visit the Royal Oak which once stood on this spot. On several occasions during the half-hour she had been on the plaza, she felt as if the old shabby pub was still there, and her husband had merely slipped inside to the lavatory and would be back at any moment; but mostly she felt like an amputee, a victim of phantom-limb syndrome, wanting to stroke and itch an appendage she no longer had.

A young man brushed by her table and worked his way into the centre of the plaza, where he put down his rucksack. He was dressed in light-coloured chinos, deck shoes with no socks, and a grey T-shirt. His hair, thick, dark and luxuriant, almost touched his shoulders.

There were now seventy-one people on the plaza, including six female students – two wearing hijabs – four middle-aged Dutch tourists, a group of hung-over Liverpudlians in town for a mate's stag weekend, a lone teenager, looking around anxiously to see where her friends had got to and wondering whether this apparent shunning has anything to do with her new boyfriend, and three local businessmen, discussing plans for two of the still-empty shops. A member of a local crime syndicate was with them, listening carefully, working out what percentage of interest they could tolerate, and how easy it would be to use these men to launder some of the drug money his group had squirrelled away around the city, waiting for a legitimate home to wash it clean.

Plus, lost in her thoughts and her still-fresh grief, the widow.

The number swelled further when a striking young woman in a vintage Prince 'symbol' sweatshirt and ripped jeans wandered over from Monsoon and asked the waiter for a flat white. She then selected a seat, making sure she was in the sun, and turned an already bronzed face towards the sky. Several of the Liverpudlians looked over and appraised her, their expressions and the comments they shared under their boozy breath conveying the nature of their lascivious thoughts.

Ten minutes passed. One of the businessmen left to carry out a surprise audit on one of his phone shops (he suspected the manager was stealing from him). More coffees and beers were ordered, keeping the waiter busy but not overworked.

The Liverpudlians started arguing and, in order to placate them, the waiter suggested another round. They agreed. By the time the waiter emerged with the beers, the scene had altered. The Prince symbol girl had gulped her coffee, thrown down some coins and departed. The young man with the thick black hair was about to do the same. He had left his rucksack on a chair. He pointed to it and gestured, asking in sign language if the woman in black would keep an eye on it. She nodded.

The waiter watched him trot over towards the shops. He served the Liverpudlians their fresh pints, suggesting as he did so that they perhaps ought to eat a meal to help soak up the drink, and then looked back at the rucksack. Something about it worried him. He, at least, had stayed awake during the security drills all staff had been made to attend before the Circus opened for business. At that moment a magnesium-bright star flared from the spot where the bag was sitting, and even before the sound reached him, there came a shock wave that drove the waiter back through the bar's window.

The blast had fatally damaged his internal organs anyway, but a triangular shard of glass opened up a vein in his neck and the compressed air sprayed the bar's interior with droplets of blood. One of the tiny spheres of red liquid punched its way into the eye of the barman inside, who was also hurtled backwards, landing spread-eagled in the centre of the shelves of bottles.

The blast wave would later be identified as having an O-dE – an Omnidirectional Effect – meaning it spread equally in all directions, creating casualties in 360 degrees. It was filled with particles travelling at supersonic speed and it killed the Liverpudlians instantly. The blast wind followed, negative pressure that crashed heads together and fused skull to skull as well as tearing off two arms, depositing them dozens of metres away. This hyper-compressed air, as solid as a moving brick wall, slammed into the Dutch tourists, leaving little external damage but emulsifying their insides into a pink sludge.

The lone teenage girl was picked up and flung across the street towards Starbucks, her clothes burnt off her back, her bones snapped, her broken body flailing as if she had been filleted.

Outside the immediate centre of the detonation, eardrums burst as the air pressure stretched them beyond breaking point and airways filled with blood – the so-called 'blast lung'. When the first phase of the detonation had passed, twenty-six people lay dead, with many more injured in some way. Gobbets of flesh began to rain down onto the immediate area, making a wet plopping noise that the shocked and dazed onlookers – at least those whose hearing was still functioning – would never forget. Shoes, handbags, phones, glass, crockery, coins and twisted sections of furniture that had been swept up in the blast also fell to the earth, often striking the living and causing a second wave of injuries.

The motion-sensor systems inside the alarms of nearby cars shook violently as the concussion of over-pressurised air reached them, triggering an uncoordinated display of flashing sidelights and adding a Greek chorus of honks, whines and whoops to the scene. Soon that racket would be joined by the more authoritative sirens of police, ambulance and fire as the first responders arrived.

A rope of black smoke rose from the shattered café, blessedly – albeit temporarily – obscuring the most sickening scenes of carnage. From the gritty miasma of debris at ground level one woman emerged, half-staggering, her dress ruined, her hair standing up as if she had received an electric shock, her skin blackened, a trickle of blood snaking from her nose, but otherwise unharmed. The young widow would never understand why, in the midst of such horror and sorrow, she, already dead inside, had been spared.

FOUR

Riley paused, staring out of the window of the old shoe factory once more, gathering his thoughts before he carried on explaining to Ms Carver that, in fact, Nick never got the chance to pull the trigger of his Sig. He clearly intended to – who wouldn't, given his injuries – but Terry Taliban beat him to it. It was hard to say whether the shot that killed him was deliberate or not. The Taliban had a few Russian sniper rifles left over from a previous war, but most of them had AK-47s, which they used on fully automatic. It was more like spraying with a lethal and particularly lively garden hose than anything resembling accuracy. So it was probably a lucky shot that entered through Nick's right ear and saved him the trouble of committing suicide.

Riley used the word 'lucky' advisedly. When they eventually got to him – after the Taliban had withdrawn, knowing that an airstrike by either A-10 Thunderbolts, remote-operated Reaper drones or Apache gunships would have been ordered up – they discovered that most of Nick's lower half was missing. He couldn't have survived and if he had . . . Well, knowing the kind of guy he was, Riley reckoned he would have gone for the Sig sooner or later anyway.

Nick was also fortunate that, once they had located what was left of his legs, there was a decent, recognisable amount to put in the body bag to take back to Tracey-Jane, his widow. That wasn't always the case with IED victims. Sometimes there was more Afghan dust than person in the coffin.

Riley had to remind himself that Nick wasn't the only casualty that day. One of the soldiers lost an eye, thanks to an unlucky ricochet off one of the Mastiff's steel hulls. And poor Moe, the young terp, caught an AK round in the head. The Taliban got him anyway, despite the scarf around his face.

'So, Sergeant Riley, thank you for your honesty. I know that can't have been easy to share. Now, you do appreciate why you are here?'

'Because of the complaint,' he said, trying to avoid showing his irritation at the whole situation. 'When I got back to my barracks at Loughborough, the CO at the Felix Centre had been speaking to my CO. They decided that I was due either a disciplinary board or should undergo psychological evaluation to see if . . .'

He hesitated. Ms Carver obliged. 'If the anger issues have anything to do with possible PTSD.'

I don't have PTSD, he wanted to repeat. *Just a normal reaction to picking up pieces of your dead mate after you've seen him cut in half by a charge deliberately designed and placed to kill him.*

'I was angry. Angry that this boy . . . sorry, man, was clearly not suitable for the High Threat course.'

'Why don't we start at the beginning? It is my understanding you were invited to . . .' she checked her notes. 'The Felix Centre?'

She had framed it as a question, so he answered. 'It's the main training site for ATOs,' he said. 'Where we learn the skills and drills we'll need in EOD. Bomb disposal. Using both practical exercises and in lectures. I was there to deliver one of the latter.'

She gave a thank you smile for his explanation and looked

down at her notes again. 'Specifically, to present a briefing about conditions on the ground and in particular . . .' She had to check once more. 'TTP acceleration.'

TTP was Tactics, Techniques and Procedures. The 'acceleration' part referred to how insurgent groups learned from each other and shared information, for instance between Iraq and Afghan. It meant that the intervals between new developments of ever-more sophisticated approaches to killing British soldiers became shorter and shorter. Like the rest of society, the world of insurgency seemed to be speeding up.

'Yes.'

'And you rather took against one member of the audience.'

'It wasn't personal. Rather, he kept raising stupid questions.'

'Such as?'

'About our treatment of the Afghans as human beings.'

'And what do you think about that?'

He sighed. 'Of course Afghans are human beings. But some of them were trying to blow my arse up out of the top of my head. You can't afford to . . . humanise them. They are the enemy. You just have to think about what they are trying to achieve on that day, in that place. Not whether they've got clean drinking water at home.'

'Although you agree that is important, Staff Sergeant.'

'Not as important as deciding if the wire you're about to cut is part of a collapsing circuit on the IED.'

The wannabe ATO had also raised the issue of how Britain was treating those who had worked for the army or air force and were now facing reprisals at home. That was politics, Riley had explained. He was bombs, disposal of.

'So how did the complaint make you feel?'

'Seriously?'

'Yes.'

'Pissed off.' Understatement. Thanks to the objection from the trainee, Riley had spent almost a month doing 'admin' at Loughborough – shovelling bullshit into ever-greater heaps of ordure – rather than something useful. Like saving lives. No more Explosive Ordnance Disposal until the trick cyclist finished with him. And then only if she gave him a clean bill of mental health.

'The complainant said you bullied and belittled him. In front of his peers.'

'If I did, I was bullying him into not ending up like Nick.'

'Do you have a problem with authority, Staff Sergeant Riley?'

'No, not at all.' *Not when the authority is earned.*

'Tell me about the anger you directed at him. The trainee.'

He shook his head. 'It was just a momentary thing.'

'I've heard the tape that one of the other audience members made. It wasn't a "moment". It was more like five minutes. A tirade, I would say.'

He shrugged. 'A five-minute tirade that might keep him and the rest of them alive.'

She scribbled some notes. 'You were brought up by your grandparents?'

It took Riley a second to realise she had changed tack. 'Mostly,' he admitted. 'There were spells with my mum, a time in boarding school. But yes, I spent a lot of time with my grandma and grandad.'

'And that was okay, was it?'

Better than being with his mum. His grandfather had loved rugby, horse racing, cricket, angling and fine wines. He was also a first-class shot and gave Riley his first exposure to weapons. Some of the happiest times of Riley's life were spent shooting spinning discs out of the sky with a 'junior' shotgun. Grandad had tried to introduce him to killing living things, but one rabbit had been enough. If the old man was disappointed with his reaction, he didn't show it. He went out and bought the young boy bullseye targets instead. When Riley was old enough, he bought him a junior trail bike to ride through the woods.

Those days were rose-tinted by nostalgia, he knew, the sun always shining, waiting in hides for a tiny firecrest to appear or a kingfisher to swoop over the water – it was his grandad who introduced him to birding, too – fishing in the lake and foraging for mushrooms, wild garlic and dandelion leaves, years before it was fashionable in the City.

He wanted his memories to remain focused on those times, not recall the empty months when his grandfather was away or the days that were filled with gloomy rain tapping windows and a sick mother taken to her bed.

'I enjoyed it,' he said tersely. 'Can we move on?'

'Of course. What about relationships?'

'With?'

'The opposite sex. Or the same sex if appropriate.'

'Opposite is fine.'

'Do you have a relationship at the moment?'

Well, do you?

Nick again, who always seemed to chip in at just the wrong moment. But Riley wasn't going to share that with Ms Carver. 'I hear voices' wasn't going to look good on his psych evaluation. It was up there with 'I see dead people'.

'I'm sure it says in my file that I am divorced.'

'It does. So, no meaningful relationship since?'

Define meaningful. 'No.'

Ms Carver scribbled some more. 'My aim here is not to judge you, Staff Sergeant. PTSD is caused by a trauma. In order to cope with that trauma, we create a coping mechanism. But sometimes the coping mechanism acts like a blockage. Things build up behind it. We have to find ways either to remove that blockage or put a different, less damaging, coping mechanism in place.'

'I don't know about coping mechanisms. I know I made some bad decisions.'

'That doesn't make you a bad person.'

'I feel like that is what I am being accused of here,' he snapped at her.

'Not at all.' Then another change of direction, so fast he almost got whiplash. 'How do you relax, Staff Sergeant?'

'Relax?'

'Yes. How do you take yourself out of the everyday? Sport? Reading?'

'Not much of a reader,' he admitted. Everything he knew about literature he owed to his grandmother who had tried her best to make him appreciate everyone from Dickens to John Dickson Carr. 'I used to fish.'

'No longer?'

'Not for a while. I . . .' He flashed on the ropes and hooks they used to drag bright yellow palm oil containing HME – Home Made Explosive – out of the ground. It was a different kind of angling altogether. The reason for ropes was that HME was unstable and trying to pull out the charge by hand was risky. As an added bonus in the bad-for-your-health stakes, latterly Terry had discovered anti-lift devices – detonators underneath the explosive, designed to deploy if the pressure on them was released. There was a terrible maths to dealing with HME. A five-kilo device meant the victim losing a leg. Ten meant two legs. Any larger and you were red mist. The few times he had tried fishing since Afghan, the lines and hooks had caused sweaty, unwelcome flashbacks.

'Go on,' she prompted.

'I like birds.' He was hesitating because of the response of the average squaddie to such an admission. The ribbing could be unrelenting. And rarely funny. 'Hey, Riley. I just saw a Greater Spotted Arse in the showers.' She showed no reaction, of course, to his revelation. 'I sometimes go birding. It takes me out into the countryside.'

'And you enjoy that?'

'Yes.' Not just the birds; in fact, they acted more as an excuse to get out into the fields and woods, a landscape totally different to that of Afghan. The love of English nature had been there before Helmand, of course, a legacy from his grandfather who taught him to identify not just birds and the telltale signs of fox, deer or badger in an area, but plants such as blackthorn, fleabane, dogwood and figwort. But the smells and sounds of a stroll in the country helped remind him he was no longer in that benighted country and, God or Allah willing, never would be again. Its rugged beauty failed to compensate for the dead and the maimed that populated his image of it.

'It's a very solitary activity. Birding,' said Ms Carver, looking up from her notepad. Her head was tilted to one side and Riley could tell she thought he was an unsuitable candidate for birdwatching.

'Not always. You get something like a Pallas's grasshopper warbler show up on its way to India and there'll be coachloads.' These were hardcore 'twitchers' of course, the sort of birders who chase around the country at the mere whiff of a rare sighting. That wasn't Riley. He just liked walking the footpaths with a pair of binoculars in his pack, just in case. The army gave him enough lists to tick without doing it as a hobby.

'It's a very male pursuit. Or so I understand.'

'What does that mean?'

She made a note without answering. 'And isn't it usually older people who take it up?'

You ought to get out more, he thought. There were millennials with binocs and bivouacs out there these days. 'Not so much now.'

'Can you tell me about your marriage?'

Back into the minefields of his past. 'There's not much to tell. It was just like the song. "Too Much Too Young". Too many months away from home, leaving a wife to get lonely and often scared. Too many fraught reunions, when you drop back into a world where you have to shop and put out the rubbish and worry about schooling and reading the electricity meter. Too many two-week leaves where you have just maybe started to adjust to Civvie Street, at which point you were whisked back to a combat zone. Too many drunken rows. It has a name, apparently. ISS: Intermittent Spouse Syndrome.

'You know what EOD stands for?' he asked.

'I know. It's in your notes. Explosive Ordnance Disposal,' the therapist translated.

'Nope. Every One's Divorced. It's an occupational hazard.'

'But you have a daughter.'

He smiled for the first time, as if on safer ground. 'Yes, I have a daughter.'

'Let's talk about her.'

'There's not much to say. Ruby. Thirteen. She lives with her mother. Lived.'

'Why past tense?'

'She's at boarding school most of the time.'

'You sound like you don't approve.'

'Well, I tried it once. Didn't like it. To be fair, Ruby seems to be getting on with it.'

'And how often do you see her?'

Not often enough was the answer, not since Izzy, her mother, had upped sticks to run an art gallery in Padstow. It wasn't hard to see why Izzy enjoyed school. Thirteen-year-olds might prefer boarding in the Cotswolds to a Cornish tourist trap. 'I'm seeing her tomorrow, as it goes, Ruby. Last day of school. We'll spend a night together.' Along with her mother, unfortunately.

It was at that moment that both his phones rang, work and personal. He could ignore the latter, not the former. Although he was not on the active list, he still received alerts from HQ.

'Excuse me. I have to take this.'

'Of course.' She checked her watch. They were almost done anyway.

He scrolled down the alert. It was what they called a ten-liner, telling him there had been a bomb and detailing where and when. It was the 'where' that brought him up short.

'Fuck,' he said to the phone, then to Ms Carver: 'Sorry.'

'What is it?'

'A bomb.' Not only that, a bomb in a town he knew well. Riley got to his feet, looking for his things.

'Hold on. You're not on duty,' she reminded him.

An ATO is always on duty, he almost said. 'I know the location well, though.' He slipped on his jacket. He was leaving no matter what, but he knew enough not to storm out. Not unless she got difficult. 'They might need me.'

She only hesitated for a heartbeat, then, 'We'll schedule the next session later. Go, if you have to.'

Riley didn't need telling twice.

FIVE

Riley gave thanks that he had signed out a car-pool Audi rather than bringing his own VW. The A3 was nippier and came with superior comms. It also smelled better. Before he had set off, Riley had checked his personal phone, which had rung at the same time as his army one. It had been Ruby. Probably checking he was still coming to the concert tomorrow. Who knew, now the EOD boys had deployed? Rather than ring her back, he had texted that he would call her later. He wasn't entirely certain that would be the case.

Driving north in a manner best described as controlled reck-lessness, Riley managed to get hold of Spike after a half-dozen attempts. Spike was the new *him*. That is, he had the job Riley should be doing rather than unzipping his emotions in some godforsaken office. Graham 'Spike' Denman was still a working ATO, not parked on some shelf. Riley was already a third of the way back to the barracks when the ATO finally picked up.

'All right, mate,' Riley said. 'I got the alert. I know there's a shout on.' Thank God they hadn't taken him off the Intel list when he was moved from active service. 'What's the score?'

Spike knew he would know what the incident entailed, so didn't bother repeating the details. 'We're deployed at the request of East Midlands CTU.' This was the regional Counter Terrorism Unit. 'We're in the truck. We'll be out the gate in five. Fuckers, eh?'

'Yeah. Fuckers.'

The 'we' Spike spoke of was the EOD response team. Spike was the sergeant in charge, and his number two, probably a corporal, was responsible for all the kit, including the explosives, the robots, the electronic jamming gear, the metal detectors, and Kevlar bomb suits. There would be a private or lance-corporal along, too.

'Wait for me,' said Riley. 'I'll jump on board. Give you a hand unloading and setting up the ICP.'

A pause. 'Can't do that, pal,' Spike said flatly. It wasn't unfriendly, just a fact.

'Come on, for fuck's sake, Spike. You need as many hands as you can get.' He could already picture the scene, the devastating aftermath of a bomb in a public space. He had seen it in Afghan, the flattened, blood-soaked market place, police station, polling booth. And now the UK again. *How fucking dare they.*

Stay focused, he told himself.

'I need all the operational hands I can get,' said Spike eventually. 'But you're not operational, mate.'

'Hold on.' Riley floored the pedal on the Audi, flashing his lights as he overtook a string of caravans, which had emerged like mayflies at the first sign of good weather. The lead driver in the caravan convoy leaned on his horn as Riley pulled in just in time to avoid headbutting a Tesco lorry. He gave the caravanner the finger, even though he knew the driver wouldn't see it through the tinted windows of the A3. It made him feel better though. Bloody civilians. They had no fucking idea.

'Who is the duty officer?' Riley asked once he had a clear road in front of him once more.

'Nichols.'

Riley nodded to himself. Captain Nichols. Plum in his mouth and a metal rod up his arse. No, that was unfair. He wasn't a bad Rupert, but he was a typical freshly minted Sandhurst boy, in that he liked to do things by the book. But they rubbed along okay, as much as an NCO and an officer ever did. Nichols would have overall command of the team's deployment. But the ultimate way of dealing with the device, be it robot, human or controlled explosion, that was the ATO's call.

'Dom,' said Spike. 'I gotta go. Got comms coming in re the scene. I'll call you. But don't come. Too many cooks.'

'What do you mean by too many—?'

But he'd gone. Too many cooks indeed. Or, put another way, don't come here telling me how to do my job. He understood that. Nothing worse than a second ATO going: *Oh, I wouldn't cut that wire.* Especially one who had been stood down. Riley turned off the hands-free and the radio kicked back in.

'Reports are coming in of a possible bomb explosion in a suburb of Nottingham . . .'

It was like winding back the clock. Knife and machete attacks, using trucks and cars as weapons; they were the current preferred methods of *jihad*, if that was what this was. Bombs were old school. Bombs were Afghan. Bombs were him.

*

The EOD truck had already left for Nottingham by the time Riley made it to the Loughborough barracks. But Nichols was still there, just putting his gear into an unmarked BMW 5 Series estate. Riley parked the Audi at an angle that wouldn't have been out of place on the streets of Rome and jogged over.

'Sir. Captain Nichols, sir. Wait.'

'Ah, Staff,' Nichols said by way of greeting. Nichols was about the same height as Riley, but bulkier and with a thick neck. His face was fleshy, with a prominent nose that had been broken at some point. His blue eyes were clouded with suspicion. 'What are you doing here?'

'Permission to accompany you, sir?'

'To where?'

'The site of the explosion, sir.'

'We have our ATO, Staff Sergeant Riley,' the captain said stiffly. 'Graham Denman is in charge. But I'm sure you can make yourself useful here.' The words were clipped and stern, designed to brook no argument. 'There'll be Intel to be distributed.'

So he was to be a messenger boy now? Fuck that. He had defused more bombs than they'd collectively had hot dinners. Leaving him behind made no sense at all. He pulled back from giving the officer a piece of his mind. Softly, softly. 'Sir, listen. Spike is a good guy, but he doesn't have my experience. Nobody here does. You know that. I won't get in the way.' He didn't want to sound desperate, even though he was. This was a chance to get back into the thick of it.

'Too many cooks.'

Christ, was that the thought of the bloody day? 'How do you mean, sir?'

'There can only be one ATO, Staff. You have a tendency—'

'I won't,' he blurted. 'Have a tendency. No tendencies. Promise.'

'I'm sorry, Dom, but until you are signed off by the PAS people, my hands are tied.' He didn't sound particularly sorry to Riley.

Riley was aware that one misplaced word would blow his chances. He did have a trump card to play. 'The thing is, sir, it's my hometown.'

'What is?'

'Nottingham.'

Some of the wind went out of Nichols's intractable sails. 'Really?'

'Yes.' Riley nodded to emphasise the point. His memories of Nottingham weren't always fond, but that wouldn't stop him exploiting its misfortune for all it was worth. 'It is. I grew up there. My mum still lives there.' Well, it was a kind of living. 'I know those streets like the back of my hand.'

'You know this Sillitoe Circus?'

'Not exactly. That complex is after my time. But I know the area. What's left of my family are there.'

'And they might well have been caught in the blast, which will put an emotional strain on you—'

That book again. He was quoting chapter and verse. *If there is a personal dimension to any case, stand your man down.*

'That is very unlikely. My mum lives in a care home.' It was a little more complicated than that, but it would do. 'She won't have gone walkabout. Sir, think about it. You are leaving your most experienced EOD guy back at base.'

Nichols grimaced. 'It's my operational decision.'

'I appreciate that.'

'I can't risk you upsetting the chain of command.'

'I understand. But you'll be taking a peashooter and leaving the bazooka behind.'

Shit, had he just called Spike or Nichols or both a peashooter? That wasn't what he had meant.

Despite that blunder, Riley could see doubt spreading across Nichols's face now. The man knew it made sense. He simply didn't like to admit it. 'All right, get in. But you are to be present in an assistance capacity only. Understood? You are assisting me.'

Riley felt an unfamiliar burst of warmth in his chest, a little detonation of pleasure and relief, a welcome change from the corrosive anger that so easily took up residence in there. 'Sir. Thank you, Boss.' He risked the informality, hoping it would better convey his gratitude, and climbed into the passenger seat before the captain could change his mind.

*

Although the BMW was unmarked, it was equipped with blue lights and siren and Nichols turned both on for the drive north up the A60. Most of the traffic in front melted away as the BMW approached. They would catch up with the truck well before Nottingham. Riley was watching a red kite hovering over the edge of the road, when the captain interrupted his thoughts.

'Notts or County?' Nichols asked as they weaved across lanes.

Nichols's radio crackled from its cradle on the dash. It was the command and control centre back at Loughborough base which would be monitoring all the emergency services and would relay the salient points to Nichols. *'Multiple casualties reported in the incident.'*

He blanked the news out. They would only get the real picture once they got to the incident site. 'Sorry, sir?'

'Football. Were you brought up a Notts or County fan?'

'Green and Whites,' said Riley, meaning Nottingham RFC.

Loughborough command and control cut in again. *'Nottingham has triggered its MIP.'*

Every city has a Major Incident Plan, the one its emergency services practise, hoping it'll never be needed.

'Oh, rugby.' Nichols's face brightened in surprise. It was as if only officers were allowed to like games with funny-shaped balls; footie was for NCOs and the like.

'Sir. My grandfather liked rugby, so . . .'

'Did you play?'

He sensed what Nichols was thinking as he glanced over. Riley was nobody's cliched idea of a rugby player. No broken nose, no cauliflower ears or missing teeth. Didn't have more bulk than a Westinghouse fridge and was a shade over average height. But he had broad shoulders, thanks to the weight-lifting regime his grandad had introduced him to and which he continued into the army, albeit in a more desultory fashion. He also had very good ball control and a decent turn of speed. 'Centre,' he said eventually.

'One hundred metre cordon in place around incident site.'

'Ah. Fly-half myself. And your father?'

Riley shrugged. He knew Nichols was just making conversation to avoid brooding too much on what awaited them. 'My dad didn't like sports.' Only the horizontal kind. What was this? A job application? His father hadn't been around to teach him the love of anything, end of story. He certainly wouldn't have shown his face at his grandad's. The latter blamed his father for Riley's mother's mental fragility. His philandering and fecklessness had certainly taken its toll, but Riley had heard from an aunt that his mother had been something of a family rebel with unpredictable mood swings even before her marriage. 'A bit of a maverick' was the phrase she had used and mimed the smoking of a cigarette. Although it wasn't tobacco that she was suggesting his mother liked to inhale.

'Police Incident Commander confirmed as Chief Superintendent Shirley Garcia.'

Of course, Riley had grown to embrace a football team. You had to in the army, or any male institution. It seemed a betrayal of his rugby roots to choose another Notts footie team, though, so he had opted for Arsenal, simply because it was the sort of name an Ammunition Technical Officer should like. He still remembered the friendly rows with Moe the terp, who was a massive Liverpool fan, even though he had no idea where or what the city was. He had nicknamed him Scouse and the lad called Riley Staff Sergeant Gooner.

'Correction. Multiple fatalities. Double figures.'

They both looked at the radio, as if the deaths were its fault. 'Shit,' said Riley glumly. The arrogance and inhumanity of terrorists – *our cause is worth taking innocent lives for* – always made him furious. Right then he wanted to punch the dashboard. Had it been his car, he might have.

'East Midlands CTU attending. ETA twenty-five minutes.' The local Counter Terrorism Unit, which would provide back-up for the city's trained firearms officers.

'There they are,' said Nichols, pulling him back into the moment.

Sure enough, the truck was just ahead of them. Nichols swerved the BMW in front of it, keeping the blues'n'twos going as they scythed their way towards Nottingham and the scene of the crime.

SIX

The door knocker to Dunston Hall's west wing was so large that Kate Muraski almost needed two hands to lift it. The brass was fashioned into the face of a gnarled old big cat, scowling at visitors. Which was appropriate, given that she was about to enter the lion's den, the home of a battle-scarred veteran of the Service. She looked across the front of the building. She could see another wing several hundred metres away, but the whole central core of the house appeared to be missing. Perhaps they ran out of money.

Muraski looked in vain for CCTV cameras on the façade before her. Nothing. Yet there had certainly been conspicuous ones on the main gate and at intervals along the path up to the house. Possibly those had been fakes, deterrents for any would-be burglars.

She heard brisk footsteps crossing the hall and she pulled her jacket straight in anticipation of the sort of once-over old spooks give a younger generation. She was comparatively new to the game. The man she was about to have the effrontery to question had decades of performance at the highest level under his belt. Muraski was under no illusion that she was novice to his master. Unless she was very careful, she would be played with, patronised and dismissed.

However, it wasn't Henry Clifford-Brown who answered the door, but a woman in her seventies, wearing a tweed twin-set and pearls. This would be ... She struggled for a minute, her brain clogged by all the information in the files – both on computer screens and in old-fashioned folders – that she had been reading and memorising for the past forty-eight hours. This would be Barbara. The wife.

'Mrs Clifford-Brown? Kate Muraski.'

'Ah. Hello.' The voice was almost a caricature of RP. Like a radio announcer from the 1950s. Muraski suddenly felt very unpolished in comparison. 'We were expecting you.' She held out a tiny, veined hand and Muraski took it, careful not to squeeze too hard. 'So young.'

'Looks can be deceptive.' Muraski was twenty-eight, but with her cropped hair and relatively make-up-free regime – for work, at least – she could sometimes pass as a teenager. Which occasionally came in handy on surveillance jobs.

'I didn't mean to be rude,' the older woman sighed. 'I was just remembering when I looked something like you. Not as pretty, of course.'

Muraski didn't believe that for a minute. She could see, beneath the lines, that Barbara had been something of a beauty in her day, was a beauty still. And she knew it. Vanity didn't always wither with old age.

'Henry is in his study. Come in.'

She followed Barbara into a hallway that could have been lifted from an old Hammer Horror film set – the movies that her recently ex-boyfriend Toby was convinced were 'masterpieces'. A walnut staircase, almost mirror-polished, rose up in front of her, then divided in two, running up to a barley-twist balustraded landing. All it was lacking was Christopher Lee. There was an acre of wood panelling, cathedral-like quantities of stained glass glowing green and red, and coats of arms on every wall. The air was heavy with polish, coffee and something else she couldn't quite place.

'Good journey?' Barbara asked as they walked over the black and white tiled floor.

'Not bad. A bit sticky out of Grantham.'

Barbara tutted. 'Those blasted roadworks. In here.' She raised her voice before she rapped on the closed door with a bony knuckle. 'Sweetie, it's Kate, the girl from . . . the office.'

Sweetie? From what she had read, Henry Clifford-Brown was anything but sweet.

His voice boomed from beyond the door. 'Come in, come in.'

As soon as she turned the knob and pushed, Muraski identified the mystery smell. Pipe tobacco. Old, stale pipe tobacco at that.

Clifford-Brown was standing with his back to them as they entered, his shoulders hunched over so much that she couldn't see the back of his head clearly. He was looking out over an immaculately manicured lawn about the size of a football pitch that ran down to a pond. No, she corrected, it was a lake. An ornamental lake. It even had a couple of bloody swans on it.

The old man turned. He was wearing a mustard-coloured cable-knit cardigan over a shirt and tie. The latter, as if to make a point, was from the Special Forces Club in Knightsbridge.

'Thank you, darling,' he said to Barbara, a smile on his ruddy face. Her first impression was that, age-derived stoop apart, he looked pretty hale and hearty for a man in his tenth decade on the planet. He was a little more jowly than the last Service photograph she had seen, and his nose was networked with capillaries, but the eyes were bright and alert and he still had a thick head of silvery hair. He held out a hand and she crossed the room, skirted the desk and found her outstretched fingers enveloped by his. He had once been a big chap, six-foot three and prop-forward broad, although he was barely a couple of inches taller than her now. But his hands and feet remained testament to a time when he had been a giant of a man.

'Good to see you. Thanks for coming. I'm afraid I don't get into town much anymore.' *Town* meant London. 'Can't stand the traffic.'

You still *drive*, she thought? Jesus. There had, she recalled, been an elderly but well-kept BMW saloon on the driveway. She might ask for advanced notice of his next visit to London so she could stay off the roads.

'Coffee, sweetie?' Barbara asked. Clifford-Brown nodded. 'And Miss Muraski?'

Not a slip over the foreign-sounding name, unlike many of her generation. 'Please. White, no sugar.'

'And will you stay for lunch?'

'No. Thank you. I have to get back.'

'Of course. Duty never sleeps.' Barbara withdrew, an enigmatic smile on her face.

Clifford-Brown indicated she should sit and he followed suit. It was a very male, clubby room, with more wood panelling and paintings of naval battles hanging from the dado rails. A narrow bookcase was filled with books and novels majoring on naval history: C. S. Forester, Patrick O'Brian and Julian Stockwin. Elsewhere, a couple of stuffed ducks were displayed in glass cases and two glassy-eyed deer heads stared down at her from either side of the picture window. A pair of antique shotguns sat beneath each. Apart from a desk, two chairs and a wooden filing cabinet that might have contained drinks, the only other furniture was a glass-fronted trophy cabinet. It displayed a collection of shields, cups, several small figurines of boxers in full pugilistic mode and a gold-plated pheasant. It suggested Clifford-Brown had been something of a sportsman when younger.

She put her mobile on the desk in front of her in case the office called. She noted a box of Nicorette patches next to a pipe rack, albeit one devoid of pipes. The old boy was probably trying to give up.

'I'm afraid there is no signal in the house,' said Clifford-Brown, nodding at her phone. 'Nothing gets through these walls. So we won't be disturbed. We own this wing. Russian oligarch has the other.'

'Russian? Good grief. That's ironic.' She knew that Clifford-Brown had spent a considerable portion of his career either thwarting or baiting the Russians. And now he had one as a neighbour.

'Isn't it? Hardly here, mind. But yes, it made me chortle when Oleg bought it. Of course, he's anti-Putin so we do have to be watchful when he is in residence. Just in case some FSB or GRU goons come calling.'

She couldn't tell whether he was joking or not.

'Is that an Edinburgh accent I can detect?'

There was nothing wrong with his hearing then, or powers of deduction. Muraski was left with just the softest of burrs after her time down south.

'Yes.'

'And the name? Polish?'

'It is. For a while my family anglicised it to Murray. I decided I'd like the original back.'

'Good for you,' he said, in a way that was barely patronising. 'Polish in Scotland. Not recent arrivals, I suspect, from that accent. During the war? Or after?'

Muraski began to wonder who, exactly, was meant to be asking the questions here. But she indulged the old man. He was probably just demonstrating that he wasn't senile or over the hill yet. 'My uncle flew Spitfires for the RAF in the war. Afterwards, when this country forgot that Polish airmen helped win the Battle of Britain, he drove a taxi in Edinburgh. The rest of the family came over from Poland in the late Forties.'

'While they still could, eh?'

'Indeed,' she said curtly, hoping to draw this episode of *Who Do You Think You Are?* to a close.

'And how are things at Thames House?' he asked. 'Busy, I suspect.'

He had heard the news then. The Home Secretary had announced that morning that the terrorism threat was expected to stay at 'extreme' for at least another three years. And that, so far that year, her outfit, MI5, had thwarted more than a dozen serious attempts to kill and maim UK citizens and its armed forces. Five of them came not from 'Islamists' but from the far right. The latter were an increasing part of MI5's workload, it having rather reluctantly inherited the role of tackling the more extreme right-wing organisations from the police in 2018.

At any one time there were at least four thousand POI – Persons of Interest – under surveillance by the security services. And more, apparently, were on the way, given the jihadist diaspora from Syria. All that and Russia's GRU continuing to come over and cause trouble, although they and their FSB chums had been relatively quiet of late, the odd piece of cyber-meddling notwithstanding. Maybe they knew Kate Muraski was planning on keeping an eye out for them as soon as she could persuade her bosses to move her across from general duties (or floating dogsbody, as she liked to think of it) to more targeted work on the Russia desk. More likely they were simply taking a breather and planning more mischief. Such as another state-sponsored murder or attempt to influence the next election or to sow even more discord between Great Britain and Europe.

Which made her think of Clifford-Brown's neighbour in the east wing of Dunston Hall. Given the house's remote location, she hoped the oligarch had decent security. And wiped the door knob every time he went into the house. Mind you, if he was a proper oligarch, he probably had people to do that for him, like the royal food tasters of old. Then she recalled the CCTV on the driveway to the house. They had, in all probability, been put in to protect the man in the east wing rather than the Clifford-Browns. Not dummies after all.

'Very busy,' she said. 'Which is why I'm here.'

'How can I help?'

From her attaché case she extracted the first of several photographs she had brought along. She placed it on the desk, rotated it and then pushed it under Clifford-Brown's nose. 'We were wondering if you know this man.'

He glanced down at it and then executed a casual double take. When he looked at her any hint of joviality had gone. His face had closed down like a steel trap. In front of her was no longer a retired old duffer with a penchant for fine claret and the novels of Patrick O'Brian, but the man who had once risen to be Director of Production at MI6, in charge of worldwide intelligence gathering and effectively deputy to 'C'.

Clifford-Brown's stare felt like it was boring through her skull, trying to read her thoughts. Her chest constricted. She took a deep breath, waiting for him to speak, but the silence grew thicker.

'Sir?' she prompted.

'I think you had better tell me exactly why you're here, young lady.'

SEVEN

They didn't actually need the satnav to direct them to the site. All they had to do was head for the grey smudge of smoke that sullied the sky. Several cordons had been set up, and they had to show their ID to get past police checkpoints until they reached the inner barrier, as prescribed, one hundred metres from the detonation point.

Riley stepped out of the BMW into a cacophony of shouted instructions, moans and the occasional scream. He and the captain were confronted by a phalanx of ambulances and fire engines, some of the former busy beeping urgently as they reversed out to take their charges to hospital.

The first of many media vans had arrived and were being sent back to the outer cordon with a flea in their ears. A helicopter hovered high above, its rattle not helping the noise level, and a drone circled some distance away, the operator probably afraid of being caught by the invisible net of electronic counter-measures. The air stank of burnt plastic and something else Riley didn't want to think about, because he had smelt it before, out in the desert. As he approached the perimeter and looked beyond the barrier, he felt a jolt of shock and anger. Inside the actual Circus, was a sea of uniforms – police, firefighters, medics and a CSI unit.

'Circus' was the right word. And everything about it was wrong.

Riley approached one of the uniformed coppers who were guarding the entrance point and flashed his ID. 'Where is the Command and Control centre? Why are all those people in there? This area hasn't been declared safe by an EOD team yet. Clear the casualties and then get everyone non-essential out of there.'

The policeman looked unmoved by the demands. 'And you are?'

Riley pulled out his ID again. 'I thought being able to read was a minimum requirement for you guys. Look again. EOD. Bomb disposal. Now, Command and Control?'

Nichols grabbed his arm and spun him round. 'What are you doing, Staff?'

Riley pointed to the shattered shopping centre. 'That is a fucking shambles. What if there's a secondary?'

'I know, and I'll deal with it. You wind your neck in, Staff. Okay? Observe and assist, I said, and you go marching up, throwing your weight around. I am officer on duty. Remember? Now wait right here, I'll call if I need your expertise.' Nichols tossed him the BMW keys. 'Move that if anyone needs the parking space.'

Riley bit his tongue. He hadn't come along for valet parking.

Spike and his corporal came by with the first part of their kit. Spike winked as he passed. The pair would set up the Incident Control Point just beyond the cat's cradle of Do Not Cross tapes. He wanted to shout some advice but thought better of it.

'Step away from the barrier, please, sir.' It was another policeman who had witnessed the exchange with his colleague and with Nichols. He spoke with a wary contempt. 'You're only in the way.'

'You start moving those people out of there now,' said Riley quietly, indicating the Circus once more.

'If you'll step aside. Leave it to the professionals.'

What a knob.

Riley didn't need Nick's chippy voice coming into his head then, stirring things up. He walked away, temper held at a light simmer, aware of a cauldron of pure fury somewhere deep within him. He knew enough to keep that screwed down tight. As he paced the perimeter, his boots crunched over glass. He looked down at the debris at his feet, flung over the roofs of the shops. Not just a thick icing of glass, but twisted chairs, tables, cans of beer, coffee cups and dozens of paper items, carried on the deadly thermals. And a child's shoe. Brand new. He hoped it had been from a store and not . . .

He almost ducked as the drone came buzzing by overhead. The British Army had used them – officially they were UAVs or Unmanned Aerial Vehicles – in Afghan. They could be useful, especially in scanning for any disturbed earth that might suggest a bomb or checking for secondary devices. However, as holiday-makers at Gatwick discovered over Christmas 2018, UAVs could also be a fucking nuisance. And considerably more than that in Afghan, where they would hover over you while you were trying to paint the sand and expose wires. It often made it hard to con-centrate on the job in hand. Which was, simply put, not being blown to kingdom come. Also, it was a good way of pinpointing your location to any watching Taliban mortar teams.

But who would be deploying one here? Maybe the media, but they knew the army or police had instructions to shoot them out of the sky or neutralise the UAV altogether using jamming technology if they crossed the 'restricted airspace' above any incident. Maybe one of the CTUs? They liked their toys, those lads and lasses. .

Riley turned and looked back at the cluster of people by the arched entrance to the Circus, at the corporal unloading the gear from the truck. Nichols and Spike were already inside. He could also see that many of the first responders were being ushered out to safety. Good, he thought.

He took out his personal phone and pressed 'Recent'. He could use this downtime to reassure Ruby that he was okay. She was bound to have seen the news and – not knowing about his suspension – would assume he was involved.

But Riley didn't get a chance to call. He never heard the second explosion as it ripped through the Circus because the blast wave hit him like a giant fist, stole the breath from his body, lifted him off his feet and dropped him into darkness.

EIGHT

Kate Muraski held Clifford-Brown's gaze, refusing to be totally cowed by the old man. The atmosphere in the room was suddenly heavy on her shoulders, the smell of ancient tobacco nauseating. She tapped the photo with an authority she didn't feel she had earned. 'He was your asset, wasn't he? Operation Tornado. An echo of the American's Operation Cyclone.'

Clifford-Brown seemed to relax a little. 'I suppose the Home Secretary has said we security services should co-operate.'

'That's how I got to the Tornado files.'

'You have them there?' He nodded at the attaché case on her lap.

'Afraid not. I had to go into the bowels of VX to read them.' Vauxhall Cross, MI6's less-than-secret HQ on the Thames, was very, very reluctantly letting MI5 – Kate Muraski's outfit – go over reports that had Strap 1 and 2 clearance, that is one and two levels above Top Secret. Strap 3 – the highest security designation – could only be inspected with the blessing of the PM or Foreign Secretary. However, she didn't want Clifford-Brown to know just how much – or little – she had accessed, so she kept quiet about the fact that she had not even been allowed to take notes while reading the Tornado files.

There was a tap at the door and Barbara entered with a tray of coffee and some biscuits. 'Thank you, darling,' said the old duffer version of Clifford-Brown, deftly sliding the photograph off the table and out of sight. There were a few minutes of fussing as cups and saucers were passed out and digestives refused and Barbara withdrew with a final: 'Roast beef sandwiches for lunch, sweetie.'

'Lovely.' He placed the photograph back in play. It showed Clifford-Brown, more youthful and slimmer of face, standing next to a bearded man in traditional Afghan dress. The young man was grinning widely. Clifford-Brown stood awkwardly, as if wishing the earth would swallow him. Spooks don't like having their picture taken. Even when they are pretending to be diplomats.

'You have to remember that when the Russian's 40th Army went into Afghanistan, back in . . . when was it?'

You know perfectly well, you wily old bastard. You were on the next plane to Islamabad. You threw off the desk shackles of DoP and went back into the field, one last time.

'Nineteen seventy-nine,' Muraski prompted.

'Yes. That would be about right. When they went in, we were faced with the prospect of Russia's . . . well, strictly speaking the USSR's borders suddenly expanding to include Iran and a thousand miles of Pakistan.'

Was this the time to get to the nub of the matter? That neither SIS or Clifford-Brown had clean hands when it came to the murky history of covert warfare in Afghanistan? She held her nerve for a little longer. Baby steps.

'And you, SIS I mean, felt you had to do something about that?'

'Well, back then we weren't in the habit of just sitting on our hands.'

She fired her big gun. 'So you backed the insurgency. You supported the Mujahideen.'

He sipped his coffee, apparently unperturbed by her statement. 'Not me personally. The US and France were the main instiga-tors. But we, the British government, did agree to shipping some armaments.'

'Blowpipe anti-aircraft missiles.'

'About six hundred of them. Then some of our people worked with Pakistan's SSG. That's—'

'Special Services Group.'

If he was impressed at her diligence it didn't register. 'Indeed. We set up training camps. We also had a dedicated non-lethal unit. My idea. Train the rebels – or as Mrs Thatcher called them, freedom fighters – how to disrupt electricity supplies, phone lines and the like, without mass casualties.'

Non-lethal bomb-makers? It seemed ridiculously naïve now, she supposed, given the kinds of bombs set off in Kabul and Baghdad. Maybe things looked different then. After all, the IRA tried a campaign against property, not people, on the UK mainland. That didn't always work out, though. 'And this man was . . . what?'

There was a lengthy pause, as if he was deciding whether to answer such an impertinent question from one so junior. 'Oh, he was my eyes and ears. My Pashto was never very good. He could report back on the quality of training. You see we outsourced a lot of the training to private security firms. They had plenty of ex-Special Forces on The Circuit who could do the job. SAS, SBS. Mainly teaching demolition, sabotage.'

Mainly.

'Then you could claim clean hands.'

'Clean-ish. We were footing the bill, after all. Anyway, he was good enough to become an instructor.'

Instructor in what exactly? 'The thing about bombs is it's very easy to switch targets from pylons to people. To mosques and marketplaces.'

The hardness came back into his eyes. 'Miss Muraski, I did my job for a long time—'

'I've read your file.'

This didn't seem to slow him one jot. 'I started in Special Operations Executive. Force 136 out of Ceylon. I'd only just got there when the war ended. Bloody annoying. SOE was disbanded, but luckily SIS picked me up. I was in Berlin for the airlift, Seoul during the Korean War, Hanoi for Dien Bien Phu, Bangkok during the Vietnam War, Paris for the student riots, Washington for Watergate . . .'

'I know all this.'

'Well, I've seen the political landscape shift dozens of times. Moscow is our enemy, Moscow is our friend, no, hold on, it's our enemy again. And don't get me started on South America or the Saudis. So, yes, we did train them—'

Muraski played her trump, hoping she had timed it correctly. 'Here.'

Clifford-Brown put his head to one side. 'I beg your pardon?'

Gotcha. 'You trained people like the man we have tagged Bravo-900. He went by the name Yousaf Ali at this time.' She nodded at his photograph, skipping the fact he was also called 'Bomb Ali' at one point. Nicknames muddied already murky waters.

'Bravo-900 was trained here, in this country,' she continued. 'Yes, you had your privately run camps over there. But a Mujahideen like Bravo-900, a potential guerrilla commander, you would smuggle into this country as a tourist, with three or four others. And then you would train them at secret camps in Scotland. You taught the Mujahideen to make bombs in this country. Bombs that were later used against British forces in Afghanistan.'

'Much later.' He drained his coffee and sniffed. For the first time she thought she caught a flicker of concern in his expression. 'Are you judging me, Miss Muraski?'

'Not at all.'

'It sounds as if you are.'

She wasn't making a judgement about an operation that, in retrospect, might seem foolish or naïve. Five and Six's archives were stuffed full of such undertakings. And hindsight could be a harsh mistress. All she wanted was some straightforward answers.

'I am trying to get the full backstory. It took me a long time to find out about Camp Zero. I believe that was also your idea. And that you implemented it. You brought them back here for training.'

She watched him carefully. Again, his expression gave little away. But she knew he had dreamt up the training scheme. His name and initials were all over the files she had examined. 'It might have been my idea. Although it would have needed C's approval. It was a marriage of convenience.'

Which became very inconvenient when the Mujahideen became the Taliban and started using skills forged in SAS-run training schools to attack US and British troops. In a way, the British and Americans helped kick-start the global jihad. But she kept quiet about that. Clifford-Brown knew what the consequences of Western interference in the Afghan-Russian war had been as well as anyone.

'And, yes, Yousaf later became one of the key bomb-makers for the Taliban. He was an HVT for years. But we never got him.' HVT was High Value Target – on a government-approved kill list. 'Mainly worked his horrible magic in US-controlled areas, so in a way he didn't turn on those who trained him.'

'That's a very fine distinction, given the Americans were our allies.'

'Granted.' He sounded impatient now. He wanted her gone. 'So, why are you bringing pictures of Yousaf to me?'

Time to let the dog see the rabbit. Muraski laid out the next set of photographs. They had been harvested from grainy CCTV footage, taken at dusk. It was possibly, although not definitely, the same man as in the earlier picture, but older, greyer and dressed in tracksuit bottoms, trainers and a stained Gap hoodie rather than traditional Pashtun garb. There was still a beard, but it was neatly trimmed, close to his face.

'These were taken in Caen. As you are doubtless aware, a lot of the people-smugglers have switched to the western routes across the Channel, now Calais and Dunkirk are locked down pretty tight.'

Clifford-Brown grunted. 'When were these taken?'

'Three weeks ago. Although we only received them for facial-recognition scans four days ago.'

'I see.'

'The scans only gave us 60 per cent probability of a match at best. So we need to be certain. We need HUMINT on this.' Human Intelligence. Not machines. 'Is it him?'

'It was a long time ago.'

She said nothing.

After a moment's stonewalling, the old spy leaned forward and sorted through the pictures. Eventually he stopped at one that showed a clear shot of the subject's face.

Clifford-Brown gave a sigh and put the image down. 'I'm sorry. I think you must be mistaken. I'm afraid I really don't know who this man is. It certainly isn't Yousaf Ali.'

Muraski kept her own features impassive, but inside her head, an angry voice was shouting: *If you are lying and if people die because of it, Henry Clifford-Brown, I'll make sure you pay.*

*

Barbara Clifford-Brown walked Muraski out to her Mini with a claw-like hand pressed firmly in the small of the younger woman's back, as if escorting her off the premises. Muraski assumed she was keen to get back to preparing the roast beef sandwiches for 'sweetie'. How much did she know about what he had been up to over the years? For some Service wives, ignorance was, if not bliss, then the preferred option. Others needled every detail out of their spouse, at least once the information was no longer operationally sensitive.

'So how did a nice young lady like you get into this mucky business?' Barbara asked.

'Oh, the usual. University, someone spotted me, interview in London, weekend away in a secret location for silly games . . .'

The real answer was: *actually, my mother was a spy.* Or rather an analyst at GCHQ's Scottish satellite station, initially, before becoming a recruiter of likely talent at universities north of the border. Muraski had known since her teens that her mother was involved in 'important government work'. Which was family code for something anti-Soviet.

Her parents and extended family had never forgiven the USSR for its callous treatment of Poland and its citizens, both during and after the war. Even in the post-Wall honeymoon years, when the new Russia was the West's latest friend, the Muraskis had remained suspicious and cynical. Then came the nobbled US election, Salisbury, the Hague . . . They felt vindicated and, truth be told, a little smug that their instincts had been correct.

Even before the poisonings and penetrations by Russia's security services, by the time she was seventeen, Muraski had known she wanted to be involved in the Defence of the Realm. Her older brother Miles had decided on life as a journalist and writer, like her father, but she wanted to follow the maternal career line. Sadly, Muraski lacked her mother's mathematical brain. To compensate, she was much sportier than her – netball, horse riding, hockey, and, it turned out, a crack shot. Not that she had ever fired a gun in genuine action. In fact, she had only drawn one from the armoury once. It had never left the holster. Still, she did monthly sessions at the range to keep up her Firearm Proficient status.

Her mother had – after feigning reluctance – made enquiries about having Muraski interviewed. Get a degree, they said, so she did – Slavonic Studies at Cambridge, which was when she reverted to the family's original Polish surname – and was then fast-tracked through to MI5. Right from the start she knew it was GRU and its various shadowy tentacles that she wanted to hunt. She saw it as carrying on a family tradition. But getting into the Russian section was not easy, even though she had a decent, if rusty, command of the language. She needed a 'spectacular', a coup that would send her star into the ascendency. Which is why she was bothering to interview these two old lovebirds.

'Doesn't give you much time for boyfriends though, eh?' Barbara said.

'Not really.' They reached the Mini and Muraski pressed the fob to unlock it. 'Thank you for the coffee.'

Muraski opened the door, keen to be on her way now. Not wanting to dwell on the fact the old bat was right. It was only a day or so since she had opened her book of Break-up Clichés 101 with Toby: 'It's not you. It's me.' It was, in fact, the Service's fault. It didn't like nosy partners and Toby had become very interested in her 'office job'. The upshot was one dumped boyfriend and a spy who needed to find somewhere else to live.

She reached in and placed the attaché case on the passenger seat, straightened up and held out her hand. It wasn't taken.

'You know, I'm rather alarmed, Miss Muraski, that Henry seemed a little upset at the end of your meeting . . .'

Her hand went to Muraski's wrist and a jolt of electricity seemed to travel up it to her shoulder. She yelped and snatched her hand away. 'Jesus.'

'The thing is, Miss Muraski, if you dare come here and do anything to make my husband unhappy ever again, I shall break your fucking neck.' For a second Barbara's face was a mask of sheer malice before her features relaxed back into benign civility. 'Have a nice drive back to London.'

Barbara Clifford-Brown turned on her heel and crunched back over the gravel.

Muraski watched the door close and rubbed her wrist. Then she burst out laughing. Had she really just been threatened – and possibly assaulted – by someone with the body weight of a canary? She realised she had underestimated the wife. She, too, must have been in the 'firm' and Muraski had missed it in the files. She cursed herself. She had to do better than that.

As she climbed in behind the wheel a phone buzzed in the case. The office one. She quickly slid the locks and grabbed it. The device was encrypted, but even so, the message from Thames House comms could only be interpreted by someone who knew a swathe of the code words. As she did.

Grenadier.

Terrorist bomb on UK mainland. Casualties.

Then: *Coldstream.*

Her heart gave a little judder in her chest as she mentally decoded the text.

All hands on deck.

NINE

Riley came back to consciousness seconds after he had hit the deck. He had put his arms out to break his fall. The cracked screen on his phone was evidence of that. He rolled onto his side and got to his feet. He took it slow, aware that he could be concussed or worse, and did a quick body check. No major limb loss or even wounds he could find. Angry flies buzzing in his ears, which was normal in the aftermath of a detonation. Blood in his mouth, but his tongue located the tear in his lip where he had bitten through the skin. Christ, even the secondary had packed a punch.

Riley scanned the sky, looking for the drone, wondering if it was hovering like visual carrion, picking images from the carnage. But he couldn't see it and, given the state of his ears and the racket around him, certainly couldn't hear it.

Only then did Riley look over at the Circus, at the fresh plume of dark smoke dispersing over the area, carrying with it the smell of more death. He began to face up to what he was seeing, assessing each fact in turn, so as not to overwhelm himself. There had been a secondary. Spike must be dead. Nichols, most likely dead. Other First Responders, too.

It could have been you, pal.

Nick was right. It could have been him. It still could be. It was

Riley's turn to step up. Suit up, go in, make sure there were no more bombs. What a fucking mess. Secondaries were particularly cowardly, but had they followed protocol . . .

No. It wasn't time for anger or recriminations. People had died.

There was a place inside himself where Spike would dwell. It was where Nick was, when he wasn't floating about in his skull. It also contained every young squaddie he had seen blown to pieces or gut-shot. The detritus of his marriage. The worst moments of his schooldays. Riley could visualise it: that bleak place was funnel-shaped, like a computer rendition of a black hole, and like that anomaly, no light escaped from it. He allowed himself to visit it, now and then. It was a place of crushing despair.

Go on then, go and get into the suit.

Riley did as Nick told him. A bomb or EOD suit consists of layers of Kevlar fabric and flameproof material topped off with a substantial Kevlar armoured plate, backed with soft foam. The Kevlar fabric and plate work together to form an impenetrable barrier that is designed to stop high-velocity fragmentation, or at least that's what the manufacturers spin when they are selling them. The foam is configured to cushion the effect of the blast – helping prevent 'blast lung' in which the organ bleeds even though there is no penetrating damage – and the flameproof material does exactly what its name suggests.

There is a helmet, fitted with a small fan to stop the visor misting up, and there is usually a battery-operated cooling system. The whole lot weighs in excess of eighty pounds. There are no gloves. ATOs need their hands and fingers free to do their work – dexterity is key. Although non-latex forensic gloves were often worn while handling debris from a bomb, to minimise cross contamination. Riley had never worn a suit in Afghan, because they were too hot and bulky. And you couldn't run in one if Terry

Taliban decided to have a pop at you. Now, though, he was about to climb into Spike's bomb suit, which was like walking in a dead man's shoes, only less comfortable.

Riley located the corporal at the rear of the bomb-disposal truck, looking dazed. He was in his early twenties, his thin face still fighting off acne. His eyes were red, either from the dust in the air or crying or both.

'Get me the bomb suit,' Riley said.

'Spike . . .' the corporal began to say.

'Spike's gone,' said Riley. He wasn't being callous. Just practical. He needed to retreat into the physical and emotional bubble that enabled him to work in conditions that should send him running.

'And the captain.'

As he suspected. 'I know. Just get me the suit.'

'But, you're not—'

Riley read the corporal's name tag. He grabbed the man's shoulders, stared into his face, spoke slowly. 'Butcher, listen, I'm all we've got right now. You can't do this. But I can. What if there is a third device? Hear that?'

In truth Riley could mainly hear a buzzing in his traumatised ears, but he knew the air was filled with the cries of the wounded and the dying. 'You want more of that? Get me the suit and give me a hand getting into it. And I need a day sack.'

As Corporal Butcher climbed into the truck, Riley felt his phone buzz in his pocket. The personal one. It was a text message from Nick's widow.

I just heard the news. Are you involved?

You could say that. But he sent back: Yes, I'm here.

Jesus. Is it bad?

Yes, very.

Thank God you're not on duty.

Yes. Thank God.

I need to see you. Please. Can you get away?

I'll come over as soon as I can.

When?

Soon.

He added a kiss in the form of an 'x'. *Look after Trace*, that's what Nick had shouted from the culvert just before the fatal bullet struck him. Look after TJ, as everyone else called Tracey-Jane, his wife.

I didn't mean you should fuck her.

I haven't.

Not yet, pal. Not yet.

Butcher threw the main body of the suit out and it collapsed on the ground like a deflated, headless corpse.

Most EOD suits smell. Stink is closer to the mark. Everyone who puts one on, even in training, sweats like the proverbial pig. It's worse, of course, when an actual bomb is involved. The solution is to spray a whole bottle of Febreze Fabric Refresher in there. He stripped off his jacket and Butcher helped him clamber into the trousers of the suit. It always reminded Riley of being dressed for your funeral.

Butcher gave a little sob.

'Keep it together. Time for that later. You're comms, remember. Usual drill. I want you to record everything I say. Clear?'

Butcher nodded. 'Yes, Staff.'

'Better. And I want the jamming gear set up.'

A nod.

'Come on, Corporal. Don't just nod at me. I want the jamming gear set up. Have you got that?'

'Yes, Staff.'

'Okay. And the robot, just in case.'

'Yes, Staff.'

The robot would normally be deployed first prior to the ATO going forward but Riley had no patience for that. As far as he was concerned, nothing beat the Mk 1 eyeball for investigating a scene. Not yet, anyway.

'And where's the metal detector and day sack?'

'Coming up, Staff.'

'Get a move on.'

Again, Riley wasn't being hard on the lad for the sake of it. You had to cope with these things. It was part of the job. He remembered when they heard that a fellow ATO had gone in Afghanistan. It hit his lads hard. The mood was pensive, bereft. But slowly, the next day or the day after perhaps, the banter would start again. People would dare crack a joke or laugh at one. It wasn't disrespectful to the lost comrade. They would understand. You have to get back on that horse. There's always another bomb. And they all appreciated the next one might be a genuine OCD.

Spike would know all that. And he would appreciate that Riley was determined there would be no more deaths on his watch.

Strapped into the suit, his ears now full of his own breathing, he checked the throat mike. Working. He switched on the visor fan, which squeaked in his ear. It needed a dose of WD40, but he knew his brain would filter the irritating noise out soon enough. Then he pulled the day sack over the helmet so it lay across his chest. He picked up the metal detector, switched it on, watched the light glow red. He ran it over a discarded can on the ground. It gave a reassuring shriek and he felt the warning vibration travel up his forearm. Then, like a clumsy robot from a 1950s sci-fi movie, he turned and started the loneliest walk in the world.

TEN

In the threadbare living room of a detached house in a dreary North London, the bomb-maker laid out the components in front of his son. The boy stared down at the coils of wire and the clips and switches uncomprehendingly. It had been a tense day for the bomb-maker, waiting to see if his 'associates' had succeeded in planting the Nottingham device. That they had was a source of great satisfaction.

The bomb-maker had let his son sleep late. They had said the *dhuhr* prayer together and then had lunch. He was pleased to see the boy mouthing his *du'a* as he fed him. But was that just some muscle memory at work? It was hard to tell. Some days were better than others. They talked about the lad's mother, his wife, and how she would have been disappointed by his version of *ashak* dumplings. There were many things the bomb-maker missed about Benesh but her wonderful food was near the top of the list.

Then he had set up the laptop as instructed and found the live feed from the drone that was hovering just outside the exclusion zone. Chinese-made, it was a remarkable machine, able to zoom in on the moment of detonation and transmit pictures of remarkable clarity. His son had yelped with joy as the explosion momentarily overwhelmed the lens, resulting in an electronic whiteout, before the devastation came into view. Then, as expected, the secondary device had added to the death carnage.

That was when he had spotted him, stumbling through debris, then disappearing from view, masked by a low fog of smoke. Riley was his name. Dominic Riley. ATO. He had texted the drone operator, telling him to find him and follow. The operator had located him, putting on the ridiculous suit that they thought would protect them from Allah's wrath. He was on the screen at that very moment, a clumsy dot moving around the devastation, searching for another device.

Although he didn't know it, Riley was safe. There was no third device. Why hadn't he been caught by the secondary? Whatever the reason for his tardiness, he would live to fight another day. And perhaps he would die on that one.

He had to make the next bomb. There was always a next bomb.

The boy – he still thought of him as a mere boy, although he would be twenty soon – now sat on the sofa, knees drawn up to his chest, while the master bomber got to work. He positioned the coffee table in front of the sofa and ran an extension lead to the nearest wall socket. He plugged in a soldering iron and arranged his wirecutters and crimpers in a neat line. He remembered how he used to enjoy sketching his diagrams, trying to think of new ways to create a trigger mechanism, new disguises that would fool the foreigners. Some little bauble that a curious soldier might bend and pick up, perhaps, or a football, just waiting to be kicked by one of a passing patrol.

He had no diagram before him now. He didn't need a schematic. He would go back to basics, which were all stored in his head. Nottingham had been his calling card. It looked as if it had caused the consternation and anguish he and his new friends – who had planted the devices and operated the drone – had hoped for. The downside would be that the authorities would now be on guard, waiting for the next strike. And, he thought as he pulled on the thin forensic gloves that would prevent contamination of the device, this was it. A change of tactic. Something different. Something more personal.

'Look, my son, this is all we need. This little thing.' He held up the packet containing a glass phial from which two wires protruded. 'It can be bought mail order. Amazon. It is a switch. Used in cars. Think about when a car trunk opens and the light comes on. This makes it work. Very simple, very clever. Do you understand how it functions?'

He looked at the lad, staring into his dark eyes for a response. None came. It was like looking at twin pools of the thickest diesel oil. And about as animated.

'Inside the glass sphere are two contacts, which are a few millimetres apart. This will act as the switch. So, power will come from a battery to this wire. But while the two contacts are separated nothing will flow. From the second wire, we run to a detonator. The detonator, as you know, is the charge that will initiate the larger explosion from that special explosive over there.' He pointed to the carrier bag the woman had delivered that morning.

'All we have to do is find a way of connecting the two terminals in here. Then the circuit is complete. Allah's work is done. Look, inside the sphere. Look at the silver blob.' He handed the switch to the boy. Now there was something in his eyes, something alive as he tipped the transparent unit from side to side and watched the silver sphere roll over the glass, leaving no trace, like a liquidised ball bearing. A smile spread over his face. The bomb-maker was not surprised. The motion of the liquid metal was endlessly fascinating. He himself had spent many minutes watching it split apart and reform, as if it were some living organism.

'Okay, okay.' He gently prised the part from the lad's fingers. The boy frowned and for a second he thought he might cry. 'Here, hold these for me.' He passed a pair of needle-nose pliers across. The lad began to snap the jaws together, as if he was holding a metal crocodile.

The bomb-maker tested a piece of solder on the iron. It sizzled and released a filament of smoke. He breathed in the familiar fumes of tin and copper and felt a little buzz, as if he were inhaling a drug. The act of creation always excited him. 'Come, my son,' he said, 'It is my *fard*, my obligation. Let us build a bomb for Allah. And for you.'

'Bomb,' the lad repeated, then caught the skin of his finger in the jaws of the pliers and began to howl in pain.

SATURDAY

ELEVEN

'You see the blue wire? You can? Yes, don't touch that. Okay? You mess with that, there'll be hell to pay.'

Riley took a sip of the coffee he had picked up at a service station on the M42. He was heading south in his less than pristine VW Passat, towards Ruby's school, Crowley Hall. There was to be a show of some description, a chance to talk informally to tutors and then it was a three-week holiday for Easter. It always baffled him that holidays were longer when you had to pay for the school. Well, he didn't pay. Izzy's parents, the ones who thought she had married beneath her station in life, they footed the extortionate bills. He couldn't really argue: his own grandparents had stumped up for the combined concentration camp and psychiatric hospital known as Royland Hall Middle School that he had once attended.

'What next?' came the voice over the car's primitive comms kit.

'Okay, Alf, listen up. I want you to take the red wire and strip the ends with the pliers.' He waited. 'Done? Okay. Insert that into the brass strip, at the far right. There should be a little screw to hold it down. Clear?'

'Yes. Done.'

'Right,' Riley said to Alf, who was the caretaker/warden of

Silver Lake, his mum's care home. 'You should have a working burglar alarm. Test it and get back to me if you have any problems.'

'Thanks, Dom. I almost fused all of Nottingham this morning.'

'You're welcome. Tell Mum I'll be in to see her as soon as I can.'

Not that she would remember.

'Were you here for that bloody bomb yesterday?' Everyone at the home knew what Riley did for a living. His mother broadcast it far and wide. Strange, she had never been keen to talk about having a son in the army when she had all her marbles. Dementia seemed to have unleashed some latent parental pride.

'Just at the end.'

'Bastards, eh?'

There wasn't much else to say. Nobody had a clear idea who the bastards were yet. The scene had been declared clear of further devices then sealed to all but the forensics, who were still picking over it. His work, for the moment, was done, even if the emotional shockwaves were still reverberating through him, catching him whenever his guard was down. 'Yeah. Give me a bell if you need anything else on the alarm.'

He killed the call.

Silver Lake was costing her elderly parents a fortune. He had offered to help, but army pay was a pittance compared to what Grandpa had in the bank. The least he could do was help the care home with an alarm system. Although at the prices they charged, part of him thought they could get a pro company in, rather than get Alf to fit one from Costco.

Riley finished his coffee, careful not to spill any on his best – and only – Paul Smith suit or the new white shirt. He felt surprisingly well, physically at least. After an unexpectedly good night's sleep, his hearing was almost back to normal. Just a high-pitched whine, as if he had his own personal mosquito stationed on his shoulder. He could live with that. It would fade over time. He knew that one of the risks of being an ATO was NRHL – noise-related hearing loss. All the blowing things up. But it was the same for rock musicians and DJs and probably every kid plugged into his or her phone. Part of modern life.

And what sort of damage were days like yesterday going to do to him beyond his hearing? The images of the dead and injured he had moved among were still etched on his retina – they would grow dim over time, but they had a tendency to return at unexpected moments, stronger than ever, like some false ending to a horror movie. Still, he couldn't worry about the bill for days like that just yet. Nottingham would go into the dark vortex that blemished a corner of his soul, along with Nick Steele and a dozen other traumas. Maybe one day someone like Ms Carver could find it and empty it for him. Like pressing the trash button on a computer. But he wasn't holding his breath for that one.

Riley thought back to the telephone conversation he had had with the therapist before he left earlier that day. She had sounded terse, unhappy. After reviewing his notes, she had said, and in light of the previous day's events, she had recommended his reinstatement to active duty. But *only* if he carried on with more sessions. And she reserved the right to suggest he be stood down once more if she became concerned about his mental state. Great, he said. Thank you.

Don't thank me . . . she had begun.

Which confirmed what he had suspected. She had been leaned on from above. Maybe along the lines of 'if you want to keep your valuable psych eval contract with the MoD, it might be an idea to put Staff Sergeant Dom Riley back into play'. In all likelihood it would have been subtler than that, but the end result would have been the same. He felt some quiet pride in the intervention. He was clearly too valuable to leave on the shelf when bombs were going off.

Not that he had been such a hero at Nottingham. There had been no third device at Sillitoe Circus, which was a mercy. He had worked as quickly as the suit allowed, setting up a cleared path so that the victims could be carried down to ambulances. And later, when backup had finally arrived, he was able to hand over to another team and get out of the torture suit.

He had been in that outfit for more than an hour by then and was suffering the first signs of heat stress. But before he left the scene, he had found something that looked familiar jammed into the tread of his boots. It was in his jacket pocket now, wrapped in plastic. He should have had it bagged and tagged with all the other stuff and sent to the bomb data people, but there was still time for that. He needed it now as a visual prompt for his memory. He still couldn't recall where the hell he had seen the yellow- and purple-striped wire before. But it would come to him.

Riley reached into his jacket pocket and pulled out the bag containing the piece of plastic-coated copper, held it up in front of his field of vision, keeping his eyes on the road, and turned it over between his fingers. *Where have we met before?* he asked it. But the wire stubbornly refused to answer.

His phone buzzed again and the dashboard comms took over. The caller ID came up on the screen. Riley pressed 'accept'.

'Scooby?'

'Yeah. Just wanted to see if you're okay. After yesterday. I suppose you was in the thick of it.'

'You could say that.'

'The second bomb . . . fuck.'

'It's an old favourite.' Just not one used in the UK for a long, long time. 'They should've let it soak,' he said bitterly. The term 'soak' actually meant to do nothing, in case a follow-up, timed device was in place.

'Yeah.' Philip 'Scooby' Roscoe was his oldest friend, another ex-soldier, although they had never served together. They had been mates since school, the state one, not the psycho ward of Royland Hall. Roscoe had been a swotty, unsporty kid, prime bully fodder, but the fact that he was a talented mimic often saved him. One of his favourites was channelling the voice of Scooby Doo seeing a ghost every time they were set homework. And he could also do pretty much every *South Park* and *Simpsons* voice. New boy Riley, too, had been picked on initially and he and Roscoe formed something of a self-protective double act.

'And you saw the shrink?'

'That's my psychotherapist you're talking about.'

'Fuck off with your big words. How'd it go?

'I have no idea,' he said honestly as he joined the A42. 'She wants me to talk about my feelings.'

'You have feelings?' Roscoe asked in Moe the bartender's voice.

'Apparently.'

'Must look out for those.'

'I'll flag it up when I feel one approaching. And I'm in again for another going-over next week. It's like sticking your finger into a bullet wound, rummaging around, seeing what you can dig out.'

'Sounds great. FAP sometime? If you can find your way to London?'

'Fancy a pint'. The army habit of reducing everything to acronyms sometimes spilled over into Civvie Street, which was where Roscoe was now. Technically, at least.

'Sometime. But I'm picking up Ruby at her school.'

'And seeing Izzy?'

'Oh, yes. Seeing Izzy.'

'You told her about TJ?'

Scooby was the only bloke he ever shared details of his personal life with. He had told him about the near-miss with TJ. 'What? No, I haven't. You think I have a death wish?'

'Well, given your jo—'

'Fuck off. It's easier to defuse a bomb than a ticking Izzy.'

'You know, I was reading a piece on why so many people who had lost a partner in 9/11 ended up with someone in the same situation.'

'That's simple. Shared experience that no outsider can understand. End of Second World War, lots of men and women who had been captured by the Japanese ended up marrying each other. Nobody else could appreciate what they had endured.'

'Yeah. But it also said that the bereaved, particularly women, give off this vibe of vulnerability that brings out the white knight in men. They think it might even be a pheromone.'

'In TJ's case it was the booze.'

Which you bought her.

Well, Nick was right there.

I always thought she fancied you.

Really? He doubted that. She was a dark, Italian-looking brunette – Monica Bellucci-ish, he supposed – who could have her pick of men. And he was hardly a like-for-like substitute for Nick, certainly not physically. Nick had stood about six-three, was fair-haired and rake thin. If they ever had a bomb in a tight culvert, they sent for the Pipe Cleaner – Nick – not Riley. He was hardly short, but he felt it next to Nick, who had a handsomeness that brought to mind Michael Caine in his *Zulu* phase. The darker Riley was more akin to one of the better-looking (to his mind, at least) Welsh troopers at Rorke's Drift. Rugged might be the word for it. Yeah, he'd settle for rugged.

Anyway, that boozy lunchtime there had been a fumbled kiss between TJ and Riley that acted more like a bucket of cold water than a stoking of passion. He really hadn't wanted it to go any further and he was pretty sure she felt the same. A momentary rush of blood to the head. And maybe elsewhere.

I would have come back to haunt you if it had gone the distance.

You already have, mate.

'TJ and I are going to have words,' he said. 'And Izzy needn't know anything about it. Besides, it's none of her business.'

'Like that's ever mattered.' Scooby and Izzy had never really bonded.

'True enough.'

Scooby adapted the gravelly tones of a police sergeant from some half-remembered TV series. 'And remember, you be careful out there, soldier.'

'Always, Scooby. Always.'

TWELVE

Kate Muraski hadn't had the best prep for a meeting with her immediate boss. She'd had trouble putting in her eight hours of sleep, given she had been one of the agents selected to help analyse the data and disinformation explosion across the internet in the wake of Nottingham. More like three, all told. And not consecutively. So, her eyes were scratchy and her head full of expanded foam. She felt as if she had just got off a plane from Los Angeles with the worst dose of jet lag ever. Instead of going back to Toby's and run the risk of reopening the argument, she had bedded down for a few hours in one of the 'guest' cells in the basement. It was frowned upon but tolerated. She would have to go back to the flat soon, though, or go shopping. She was running out of emergency knickers.

Before she suffered the meeting with her line manager, she went to the lavatory, splashed water on her face, re-applied her lipstick and took a couple of Pro Plus pills. There was a time when she might have done a cheeky line, back in the days before she joined the Service, after university, during the few months of aimless thrill-seeking that followed. Well, truth be told, for a while after she had been recruited, too, until it dawned on her it wasn't big or clever to be doing coke while Defending the Realm. What she had since discovered about the cocaine trade, and the men who ran it, had only reinforced the wisdom of that decision. Still, sometimes she felt a little echo of the old craving in her stomach.

She looked in the mirror and rubbed at the dark crescents under her eyes, as if they consisted of mascara that could be wet-wiped away. Nope, still there. From her handbag she fetched a travel toothbrush and cleaned her teeth. They still felt as if they were coated with creosote. Too much bad coffee.

Prior to the Nottingham emergency, Muraski's latest assignment had been to track the movements of and assess the potential threat of the so-called jihadi widows, the women who had married ISIS fighters in Syria and whose husbands had been killed in the fighting. A large number had applied officially to return to their country of origin – not that many nations actually wanted them back – but in the wake of Shamima Begum being stripped of her UK citizenship, those who were British had few illusions about going down the official route. So at least twelve of the widows, many with children, had gone missing from Kurdish-controlled camps, with some believed to be heading for the UK, aiming to enter illegally.

It was while scanning CCTV footage of refugees in France that she came across the man whose image she had shown to Henry Clifford-Brown. Bravo-900. A jihadi bomber, trained by British special forces, and heading for, if not already in, the United Kingdom. And then the horror of Nottingham happened, MI5's worst nightmare. Fingers would be pointed. Like every agent, she hoped they didn't find an excuse to point her way.

In one of her fantasy lives, one she barely acknowledged because it was so out there, Kate Muraski solved the Sillitoe Circus bombing and was rewarded with a slot on the Russia desk. This scenario was extremely unlikely given the number of teams across the security services that would be deployed on hunting the bombers. But a girl could dream. Bravo-900 might be her ticket to something other than vetting widows.

Muraski pushed the thoughts away, guilty that she had reduced the unbearable sufferings of Sillitoe Circus to concern about her career. She finished with the damage control on her face, scowled at the dark rings under her eyes, and tried to shake off her tiredness as she headed for the meeting on the fourth floor.

Her line manager at Thames House occupied a relatively spacious office. Although only in his forties, Paul Oakham was old-school Five, Harrow- and Cambridge-educated, who favoured shirts from Turnbull & Asser, suits from Poole or Gieves, shoes from Crockett & Jones. She didn't know where he had his hair cut, but she'd lay a large bet it was Trumper on Jermyn Street. There were hunting scenes on the walls – scarlet jackets, hounds, horses and hedges, the sort of prints that belonged in a naff pub or a Berni Inn, if they still existed. On the face of it, Oakham was a pre-diversity throwback. However, that didn't mean he wasn't good at his job.

When she entered the office, he motioned for her to sit. She placed her notes in a neat pile before her. He had on half-moon glasses and was scanning a paper file in front of him and cross-referencing it with a document on the screen. She looked at his desk. There were three wooden picture frames that she could tell were expensive – the sort of thing Fortnum or Asprey sold on their 'Gentlemen's' floors – but all were orientated away from her. What was held in them? Wife? Kids? Mistress? Gay lover? Margaret Thatcher? That was the sort of icon he would probably go for. Her or Winston Churchill. Eventually Oakham looked up and took off the ridiculous specs, quashing her mindless speculation.

'Well, this is a fucking mess, isn't it?'

Muraski nodded. It didn't really need a reply.

'The CCTV for the entire Circus was down because of teething troubles with the installation.'

'I heard. Anyone claimed responsibility yet?'

'Ansar al-Islam.' Supporters of Islam. 'Which as far as we know has never operated here. But there is always a first time, I suppose. IIE, of course.' Isis In Europe. 'Although they claim responsibility every time someone in government stubs their toe. And someone called the Brigade of Muslim Brothers, about which we know exactly nothing.'

'BOMB?'

'What?'

'The acronym. Brigade of Muslim Brothers. BOMB. Christ, we'll be getting calls from SPECTRE next.'

He looked slightly miffed that he hadn't noticed that the organisation's name was most likely someone's idea of a sick joke. 'Well, yes, as I say Cheltenham says nothing on them, and given the name, it might be a prank. LOL, eh?' He didn't sound entirely comfortable with the acronym.

Oakham flicked a file closed and leaned back into the black mesh of his expensive ergonomic chair. 'You know that we'll be hung out to dry no matter what happens. If it turns out the bomber or bombers were on our radar, then why didn't we stop them? If it turns out we didn't know about them, then why the hell not? COBRA is meeting again in' – he made a show of checking his vintage Omega Railmaster – 'one hour. I think we'll find this COBRA is the spitting kind. No doubt there will be another fucking ISC review.' Parliament's Intelligence and Security Committee had castigated – mildly in public, scathingly in private – the 'compartmentalisation' of intelligence between MI5 and the police in the years prior to the attacks of 2017. In the days before London Bridge and Manchester Arena, the demarcation was clear cut – Five did intelligence gathering, the police made the arrests – but it was now all about share and share alike. Which meant the police were now complaining about being swamped by a slurry of raw data. The ISC had also publicly crucified Five for being too slow in picking up Salman Abedi, a trained bomb-maker, who had detonated the device at the Manchester Arena. The report still made very uncomfortable reading. Thames House had had to offer an *apology*. It was unheard of.

'Any backchat from behind the wire?' Muraski asked.

She was referring to GCHQ. The government's monitoring agency was going back over its intercepts to see if they had missed anything that might have flagged up the Nottingham bomb.

'Not yet. And counter-terrorism says their snitches have drawn a blank. Not a sniff. Usually, hindsight tells you something you missed. Embarrassing, but at least you know the intelligence gathering was working, even if the brains behind it weren't. Nottingham came out of the blue.' He pursed his lips in thought, debating whether she was worth asking the question. 'You think we might have a lone wolf?'

Muraski wasn't sure he really wanted an answer. A lone wolf was a problem, because they only talked to themselves. Nothing for GCHQ to pick up. Groups were easy. They called, they texted, they tweeted, Instagrammed, WhatsApped – they even wrote letters. Deranged individuals operating solo, not so much. 'Anything is possible,' she said. 'My instinct is it is possible that one man—'

'Or woman.'

She sighed. He looked incredibly pleased that she had walked into the gender trap. 'Or woman. Or a person who identifies as a woman,' she said, raising the stakes slightly, 'could be behind this.

Even now, it isn't hard to find a mosque where a lone actor can scoop up some help on an *ad hoc* basis.'

'I think CT might have something to say about that. Most mosques have eyes and ears in place.'

'Counter-terrorism's people didn't see or hear much about Sillitoe, did they?' she countered, as forcefully as she dared.

Oakham sniffed, as if he had caught the whiff of a bad smell in his nostrils. 'Point taken. What's social media say?'

Testing, testing. 'Isn't that Deepika's department?'

'You mean you haven't looked?' he asked frostily.

Of course she had. She wasn't going to be caught out that easily. 'I trawled hashtag Nottingham and several other examples.' Such as hashtag fuck Muslims and hashtag white war. 'As you'd expect. A tsunami of anti-Islam posts, drowning out the moderates.'

'Russian?'

She nodded. 'Ninety per cent SSAs. Just pissing into already murky waters. Sniffers say Moscow this time.' The last big wave of Islamophobic tweets, many of them aimed at the London mayor, claiming he was backing the introduction of Sharia law in certain boroughs, had come from the International Research Agency and another bunch laughingly called World Tolerance, Inc, which had both been traced to St Petersburg. They were unofficially known as SSA – Shit-Stirring Accounts – and were designed to raise blood pressure and promote discontent among the public. They often did the job beautifully.

'So, your Clifford-Brown interview. What have you got?'

She took a deep breath, trying to mask the brain-spin of his abrupt change of subject. 'Bugger all. Says he didn't recognise the man in the recent picture. I'm not sure I believed him. Admitted that he had known Bravo-900 back in the day and had trained him here. Or had had him trained. But said he could not ID the man in Caen as one and the same. So we have no confirmation he is actually here.'

'Yet you are assuming the Sillitoe bomb was his. That's quite a leap.'

'I appreciate that.'

'Not a sniff of Bravo-900. You've tapped every chapter?'

'Of course.' Muraski bristled a little. He shouldn't doubt that she had also checked with GCHQ for any chatter around her quarry's name or his many aliases. Or that she had consulted with the CIA at the US Embassy in Vauxhall, as well as SO15 in London and the six regional CTIUs – Counter Terrorism Intelligence Units – across the country. That was all par for the course. And it had yielded zero intelligence. If Bravo-900 was in the country, he was a ghost.

'Which is hardly proven cause and effect, is it? You claim an active, known actor has entered the country, intent on a bombing campaign. Then, lo and behold, a bomb goes off. But that wouldn't stand up in court.'

'He is most likely in this country,' she said firmly. 'And possibly behind this atrocity.'

'I don't much care for "most likelies". Or, indeed, "possiblies", come to that. Did you really not get anything from Clifford-Brown?'

'Not really. He's as smooth as an eel in a bucket of snot. Sir.'

He chortled at that.

Muraski thought it best not to mention her little exchange with the wife. Her arm still ached, like the afterglow of a particularly bad cramp. 'I think he is being obstructive, given the way he clammed up.'

'Clamming up is probably his default position. He's an old-school Intelligence operative. Old habits and all that.'

'You know they have a Russian living next door. Kutsik?'

'I know of him. He's all over Bellingcat.'

She made a mental note to read the website more often. 'Why?'

'Anti-Putin donor. Always warning about GRU activity, most of which is spurious. It's nothing to do with our business here. To recap, there is no evidence that the two things we are discussing are connected. The bomb in Nottingham and this idea of yours that your bomb-maker is behind it.'

'Occam's razor,' Muraski offered. 'If the timetable we have established is right, he wouldn't have been in the country long enough to set up a network. So, he'd be this lone wolf we were talking about.'

'I think you're using Kate Muraski's Gut Feeling, not Occam's bloody razor. It's not the same thing. Let's stick with the tangibles for now.'

'Such as?'

He raised an eyebrow at her abrupt tone. It was a moment before he replied. Just enough to let her know who was in charge. 'Without treading on CTU's toes, I want you to check about the DNA recovered from the Nottingham site. The Bomb Data Centre has had twenty-four hours. I also want you to make sure they have run it through the FBI biometrics.'

'And Clifford-Brown and his wife?'

Oakham's mouth stretched into a thin slash of a smile. 'They'll keep.'

She was dismissed. She gathered her notes and left the office, head humming from the Pro Plus, unable to shake the feeling that she had just been misdirected.

THIRTEEN

Crowley Hall Academy for Girls was a Victorian red-brick anomaly on the edge of a village of thatch, whitewash and Bath stone. Riley steered the Passat through the open gates of the school and headed for the top end of the car park, well away from the Bentley Bentaygas, Range Rovers and Porsche Panameras and the other vanity marques of the parents. Ruby had made it clear that the VW Passat was so far below the salt it wasn't even in the dining room. No doubt she would have preferred him to have used a car-pool Audi or BMW, but this visit didn't carry even a whiff of official business. It was 'The Heap', as Ruby called it, or nothing. So, he tucked it away in a gravelled bay, shielded by a line of sapling from the pitying gaze of his betters. As he turned it off the dash gave him a warning beep. Low fuel. He would have to fill up on the way to Willow Grange.

The plan was to spend the night in that local country house hotel – separate rooms for him and Izzy/Ruby, obviously – to give them time together and Izzy a break before driving Ruby back down to Padstow. Ruby would no doubt prefer to be driven to Willow Grange in Izzy's Mercedes A Class than The Heap.

Riley wasn't worried about owning a flash car. Given an ATO's peripatetic life he had never felt the need to own any vehicle. The VW, though, had a sentimental connection – it had been Nick's, given to him by TJ to sell. But rather than get involved in the shark pool of *Autotrader* or 'We Buy Any Car' (they'd have probably added 'except that one' on inspecting the Passat), he had paid TJ a few hundred over the odds and kept it. Nick had mainly used it for his fishing trips with mates when on leave, which explained the lingering piscine smell even a deep-clean valet had failed to shift.

It was six weeks since he had seen Ruby – they talked or WhatsApped every few days, but it wasn't the same as actually being in a room with her – and he felt the urge to hold her close after what he had witnessed at Nottingham. All those grieving parents, sons and daughters. It could easily have been Ruby grieving, of course. Better that way round though, if one of them had to go.

As Riley stepped out of The Heap, he felt the air ripple around him and box his ears. He looked up at the black shape in the sky and felt the past reach out and drag him into its clammy embrace.

It was the key sound of modern warfare. The thrum of rotor blades slicing through the air. The otherwise clean *chop-chop* of an Apache came with a multi-layered whine, as if the twin engines were competing with each other, the upper register painful even to the distant observer. The Black Hawk was softer, muffled, as if it was stroking rather than beating the air, and all the more sinister for it. But to Riley it would always be the deep *whup-whup* of the fat blades of a Chinook that brought back the sights, smells and sensations of Afghan.

Sometimes the sound of a Chinook signalled relief – *we are getting out of here* or *there's a MERT on the way for the wounded*. At other times the great beast descending onto the designated Helicopter Landing Site and opening its great maw was a thing of dread.

It's only a hop of a few kilometres, but sometimes Terry Taliban likes to lob a few Stingers or Blowpipes our way. Then it would be a sickeningly twisty flight as the chopper pilot made sure he never flew straight and level for more than a few seconds. Like the scariest theme park ride ever. Every trip in and out of Camp Bastion was like that.

The helicopter he was looking at was not a military model. It was police. What it was doing hovering over the edge of a Cotswold village he had no idea. Looking for Barbour rustlers, perhaps. Or, possibly, watching the back of the ex-PM who lived not too far away. It was when Riley finally looked down to lock the car that he spotted the vet nearby, frozen to the spot, head back, a pair of hedge-clippers held loosely in his right hand.

Some react to loud noises, others to the smell of petrol or a figure in a window that might be a sniper. All vets had their combat Madeleines, memory-triggers that catapulted them back to the front line. With Riley it was smells – blood, dust, sand, even particular brands of cigarettes sometimes. With this guy, it was obviously choppers.

The former soldier was standing close to the hedge he had been trimming. He was slack-jawed and shaking and even a layman like Riley could tell he was having an episode of some description.

Riley walked over and stood next to him, following his gaze into the sky, wondering what he was seeing. It wasn't the cloud-flecked pale blue sky of the Cotswolds, that was for sure.

He examined his new companion from the corner of his eye. Maybe a dozen years older than Riley, although it was hard to say given the sickly pallor of his skin. Plenty of grey in the hair and the beard. He was dressed in green coveralls and wellies. As they touched shoulders, Riley could feel the man was vibrating like a frightened guinea pig.

The helicopter finally had enough, it shifted to nose down

and headed south. The gardener gave a long, ragged sigh. Riley felt him relax.

Then his phone buzzed. He looked at it. Izzy. *Where are you?*

I've hit some turbulence, he replied, then pocketed the device.

'Iraq?' Riley finally asked the vet.

A nod. 'First go-round,' came the reply, uttered in a Brummie accent. 'Tanks.' He closed his eyes for a second, remembering.

Riley knew he couldn't just leave an old soldier. Without someone to talk him down, he might have a full-blown episode. Someone who *knew*. And Ruby would understand. 'You know anywhere we can get a quick brew?' asked Riley. 'I'm parched.'

*

The day after the detonation in Sillitoe Circus, the bomb-maker was in a large DIY warehouse on the outer suburbs of North London. And he was enjoying himself. It was as if God had designed a Paradise for bomb-makers. He stood before a wall – a whole wall – of pliers and crimpers and wire strippers and snips and grippers. Silverline, Irwin, Stanley, MegaValue, Draper. And such an array of colours. He smiled wryly when he thought of the ancient equipment he had once had to use.

Further along there were whole drums of cables and wires of multiple thickness and resistance. In the aisles sat great bins of nuts and bolts. And bay after bay of fixings. He lifted a huge plastic bag of nails and weighed it in his hands. Then he saw the price. Robbery. Worse than the bandits at the Arkahri bazaar. Still, with such pieces of metal – the lethal shower of nuts, bolts, nails and screws known as Kabul Confetti – he could create something truly terrible to behold.

And then there were the components for the switch. What a choice. A switch that would activate the detonator could be made from a lawn sprinkler timer, a movement sensor from a home security kit, a central heating control panel, an egg timer, the many devices for turning room lights off and on. There was even an automatic food dispenser for pets that he could harness. The options were almost overwhelming.

It was true, the place was not so useful when it came to the raw ingredients of the main charge. There was fertiliser, but not of the sort he recognised, not the type he needed. His preferred mixture was ANFO – ammonium nitrate and fuel oil. Neither seemed to be on offer in this vast, shiny emporium. Failing that he would opt for the more unstable triacetone triperoxide, which could certainly be created from chemicals available in such a store as this. Still, he reminded himself, he had no need of such homemade propellants. Not with his new, unexpected source from his new 'associates'. And at $500 a kilo, the price was something of a bargain.

He wondered if his accomplices had actually planted his bomb yet. He would have to switch on the news when he got home. Show the boy what a strike from a soldier of Allah looked like. It was a while since his skills had been tested. The last bomb he had created before this recent one had been at home. A marketplace. Sixty dead, many more injured. He had seen the aftermath, the burnt-out stalls, the twisted skeletons of cars, the sandals, the singed kids' toys, the stubborn bloodstains. It had given him pause. And his wife.

Were those people really our enemy? she had asked. *The Military Commission*, the body that selected the targets, *think so*, he had answered. Now, there was talk of a ceasefire. After all this time? After all this death? Which is why he had decided to shift his attention, to focus on those who had done him harm. Who had ruined his life, his family, his children. Had taken his beloved Benesh from him.

This time, for once, he had a personal stake in the bombs he was building, equity in the people who would die.

Only God would know whether it was the right decision. Should he just let it go? Turn his back on all bombs. But he knew he couldn't do that. Not yet. There was blood to pay for. When he had shared his vision with the local cleric, the man had told one of his baffling tales.

'One very hot day, Nasrudin was relaxing in the shade of a walnut tree. After a while he pondered the huge pumpkins growing on vines nearby and the small walnuts growing on a towering tree.

'"Sometimes I just cannot understand the ways of God," he thought. "Why on earth does he let tiny walnuts grow on such a majestic tree and enormous pumpkins on those delicate vines!" Just then a walnut fell from the tree and smacked Nasrudin square on top of his head. He got up at once and lifted his hands to the heavens in supplication.

'"Oh my God! Forgive me for my questioning ways! You are the one who is all-wise. Where would I be now if pumpkins grew on trees?"'

What does that mean? he had asked the cleric. Like most of them, he spoke in riddles, the truth within the parable harder to pin down than a Schokari sand racer snake.

The cleric took his time answering. *Follow your heart, because that is where God tells you what to do. Do not ask too many questions. And don't sit under walnut trees.*

'Can I help you, sir?'

He turned to see a young man in blue overalls.

'Just looking,' he said.

The boy smiled. 'Let me know if you need anything.'

'I will. Thank you.'

He watched the lad walk off. From his features he reckoned he was Pakistani. Perhaps his ancestral home was not far from where he himself had been born, close to the Pak-Afghan border. A place with no electricity, no mobile phone signal and just one road in and out. He had taken that road one day and hardly ever been back. Weddings. Funerals. Nursing his sick son.

He saw the store assistant glance back at him, as if he had felt his gaze on him. He quickly selected a pair of pliers and went to pay. The girl at the check-out was wearing a hijab. He was impressed. He would return to this place. He paid in cash and hurried home, partly because he was worried about the boy, whom he had left in front of the TV, but also not wanting to miss the next feed from the drone which, he calculated, should be within the hour. He smiled to himself as he thought: *Let's see how good this ATO Riley really is.*

*

Riley followed the former soldier to a wooden pavilion behind the main school building, where he put on a kettle and rinsed a couple of mugs. Milk was found in a small fridge under a table loaded with grubby hockey gear. It was amazing, Riley thought, how the wooden building smelled exactly like every other school pavilion he had ever been in. Rank and damp.

'Sorry about that,' the soldier said, as he handed one of the mugs over. The shakes were still there, but they had settled down to a mere tremor. 'Happens now and then. Brain freeze.'

'I know the feeling. I've been there,' Riley said. It wasn't quite true, but everyone who had been to those wars had ended up in some place they'd rather not return to. He held out a hand. 'Dom Riley.'

The tank man wiped his palm on his coveralls before he accepted it. 'Andy Chambers. What's your story?'

Riley didn't need to ask what he meant. 'Northern Ireland. Afghan. Then Northern Ireland again.' He had missed out a short-term secondment to the Special Boat Service to qualify for over-water parachute drops, essential preparation, so he had been assured, for dealing with IEDs on maritime installations such as oil rigs. Much as he had enjoyed the SBS boys, the actual jumps over rough seas was an experience he'd prefer to forget. He had also omitted it because only tossers talked about their Special Forces deployments.

'You still in?' Chambers asked.

For now, he thought. 'Yeah. ATO.'

His eyes widened slightly. 'The bomb boys.'

'Aye.'

'We always thought you lot were mad.' He coughed a little. It sounded painful. 'Although that's rich coming from me.' He smiled to show neglected teeth in need of a good scale and polish. 'One of the teachers here knows my brother. Got me the grounds-man job. I was homeless before that. Down and very out.'

'What happened?'

'NAPS.'

The Nerve Agent Pre-treatment Set. Riley had never indulged, mainly because chemical and biological weapons weren't the issue in Afghanistan that they had been in Saddam's Iraq. NAPS was meant to help prepare the body for attack by nerve agents. It also gave you the shits, nausea and dizziness. Not ideal for bomb disposal. They had offered Riley anthrax and other jabs when he deployed, but, having heard enough about Gulf War Syndrome to put him off, he passed.

'Then I had the chronic fatigues. Couldn't carry on in the army. Couldn't hold down a job neither. Had a baby. Heart defect. Wife blamed the army, me, NAPS. I smoked too much weed, moved on to stronger stuff . . . lost it.' He supped his tea. 'Thought about topping myself.'

It wasn't exactly a surprising revelation. The army claimed

that suicide rates among vets was no higher than the general population. But until the support packages of 2018, it did not collect stats in a systematic manner, and it was not mandatory to notify the MoD if a suicide had served in the armed forces. More importantly, the data it did collect was from coroners – those dealing with the dead. Nobody kept count of the number of suicide attempts that failed, either among vets or civilians. But Riley had been at a formal dinner where the speaker was from Veterans United Against Suicide and the anecdotal evidence suggested that, among ex-service people, the numbers of both those who tried and those that succeeded in taking their own lives was considerably in excess of the percentage for non-vets.

Riley tried to remember what had happened in the First Gulf War. He could only recall one tank campaign, but he tried it anyway. 'Were you at the Battle of Norfolk?'

Chambers smiled, pleased. 'Didn't think anyone remembered that one.'

'You destroyed three hundred Iraqi tanks, didn't you?'

He winked. 'Not personally, like. Yeah, we did okay.' There was pride in the voice now.

'But you're sorted now?'

He nodded. 'Landed on my feet. Except when those bloody choppers come over.'

Riley's phone vibrated in his pocket again. It felt like it was doing so with a particular impatience, although he knew that was impossible. *Where the fuck are you? It's started.*

'Sorry, I gotta go, Andy.'

'I'll be okay,' Chambers said, 'Thanks for stopping. And … you know.'

'We old soldiers got to stick together, eh? I'll drop by for another brew next time.'

'You got a kid here, then?'

'Yes. Thirteen-year-old.'

Chambers rubbed thumb and forefinger together in the universal sign for stacks of cash. 'You must be doing all right then.'

'That,' Riley said as he stood, 'is a matter of opinion.'

FOURTEEN

Kate Muraski took the call in the office she shared with Lee Robards, Rosanna Chessyre and Deepika Chopra, none of whom ever looked as if they could do with a good night's sleep. She didn't like having to speak out loud on the phone in front of the others. Even when they pretended to be engrossed in their own work, they were earwigging. She would prefer an office of her own, but that would be a long time coming, if at all.

She picked up the secure landline and gave her full name.

'And it is Jamal Malik here. BDC, at your service, Miss Muraski,' came the jokingly formal reply.

'Jamal, how are you?'

He gave a distinctly informal snort of disgust. 'Overworked. And in all weekend.'

'Well, double time tomorrow.'

A rueful laugh came down the line, the various scrambling devices making it sound like an echo. 'I wish. Time-and-a-half if I'm lucky.'

'What have you got for me?'

The Bomb Data Centre was where all the intelligence gathered from every bomb or IED in every conflict was stored. The US had its own equivalent, the Central Explosive Index, and the information was usually shared between the two. It was protocol, though, that the prime distributor of Intel and lead investigator was the country most affected by the incident being investigated. As there was no US dimension to the Nottingham bomb – or, at least, not that they had yet discovered – the BDC was Muraski's point of contact.

'Okay, this bloke you have been badgering me about. The romantically named Bravo-900.'

She almost held her breath. 'Yes.'

'Nothing linking him to Nottingham.'

Shit, shit, shit. 'You sure?' There was near silence on the line, just a low hum and clicks of the machines that made it secure. 'Sorry, of course you are.'

'Of course I am. But I didn't say there was no DNA recovered at the scene.'

'Jamal, I'm really tired. I'm about to go home, kick off my shoes, drink some red wine straight from the bottle, go face down on the sofa and sleep the sleep of the dead.' This was a fiction.

'Sounds good. Apart from the wine.'

'Well, that's the bit I am particularly looking forward to.' Jamal had been in the same year as her at the same university, studying biochemistry, back when she was Kate Murray. They had subsequently met at a seminar on handling bomb data and she recalled him, back when he certainly wasn't averse to a drink or a toke. He claimed not to have recognised her. But the gleam in his eye suggested he was just being polite and choosing to forget her year-two party-girl reputation. 'Now gimme.'

'As you know, we can recover DNA a-plenty if we get the device intact. But once it goes off, most of it is incinerated. One sample, though, survived the blast. And it's really interesting.'

'Why?'

'It's one of ours.'

She sat upright, all thought of sleep and wine banished for the time being. She felt a little fizz of excitement in the pit of her stomach. 'One of ours how? A POI you mean? One we've been tracking?'

'No, one of our boys. You know that we take samples from every serving ATO, so that we can eliminate them during the tests on any devices.'

'I do.'

'So, we have the DNA of a serving British soldier on this bomb.'

'What's his name?'

She heard him draw breath.

'Jamal?'

He exhaled. 'Staff Sergeant Dominic Riley.'

FIFTEEN

Izzy was sitting at the end of a row near the rear of the wood-panelled hall, head turned to watch for him. She frowned when he finally appeared and looked back at the stage, where a confident-looking string quartet of young women were setting up.

'Have I missed the hip-hop?' he whispered as he slipped in next to her.

She shot him a glance that could curdle milk. They both knew there would be no hip-hop. No jazz. No grime or trap or break-beat or any of the many other sub-genres they couldn't actually name. When he was appointed head, Giles Zonack had banned contemporary influences in the arts. Painting would be figurative, literature classic and music symphonic.

'Why are you late? And don't give me some shit about turbulence.'

'You look good.'

'Don't change the subject.'

She did, though, or would do once she stopped frowning. Izzy was from Sheffield and when crossed she had a way of turning her features into something steely enough to have come out of the city's old foundries. The same with her voice, which, when she was angry, was like being smacked with an ingot. But when she wasn't busy eviscerating you – or more specifically, him – she was a petite thirty-something redhead who looked very fine in the sort of navy blue dress with a scoop neck that she was wearing that day.

'And stop looking at my tits,' she hissed.

'I wasn't.'

She reached up and touched his cheek, her fingers dancing over the skin. 'I heard about yesterday.'

'Don't tell me you were worried.'

'Just for Ruby.' But it came with a sly wink.

'How is she?'

'You'll see. Excited to be part of this.'

'Izzy, you know … well … we've had our ups and downs. Right?'

'You need an answer to that?' she said, stopping just short of a bristle.

'I just want to say, you're doing a good job with Ruby. I'm proud of her. Thanks.'

She gave a thin smile. 'I'm not doing it for you, Dom.' But there was no real malice in it.

'Right, ladies and gentlemen.' It was Zonack, the headmaster. He had a gaunt face full of self-denial and long grey hair swept back. He was wearing an old-fashioned master's gown straight from the pages of *The Beano*, which was probably meant to channel Eton or Harrow but to Riley only evoked Hogwarts or the Bash Street Kids. 'The next piece of music is one of my very favourites.'

'I had a strange call from TJ,' Izzy said, clearly not able to keep this news bottled up for a more appropriate time. 'Apologising to me.'

'About what?'

'I thought you would tell me.'

'Borodin's String Quartet number 2.'

They automatically joined in the applause.

Riley put his head back and closed his eyes, tried to listen to the girls playing above the kettle-whistle still ringing in his ears. Bloody TJ. What was she playing at? It was a fleeting lapse of reason, control and common sense. He tried to put her out of his mind and something else took its place.

An image had been fluttering around his cerebral cortex for hours, like a restless bird refusing to settle and be identified. Now, with the soundtrack of surprisingly well-played Borodin to soothe it, the picture had stayed still long enough for him to give it a good once-over.

And now he knew where he had seen the yellow and purple wire before. Northern Ireland. Four years ago.

*

Northern Ireland, summer, he remembered, or so the calendar had said. Nobody had told that godforsaken place. Skies threatened rain, a keening wind promised to drive it along, the thermometer only knew down. They had been deployed to a small copse on the brow of a hill at the edge of a farm, not far from the border with the Republic. When he had pulled up in an unmarked Discovery, Riley had been given the heads-up from the Police Service of Northern Ireland inspector and the RESA, the Royal Engineers Search Advisor. A phone call had suggested there was the body of a 'disappeared' person up a rutted track, among a clump of trees.

Crows had called down at him from the higher branches, as if taunting him. *Come on, if you think you're hard enough.* The birds knew it as bullshit, just as much as he did. When someone was 'disappeared' by the IRA, they tended to stay that way.

It was, of course, a trap. The search team had found the 'grave' and discovered it came with a little surprise. A pressure pad for an IED. The pad had been hidden just in front of the hole containing a crude coffin, exactly where someone might stand to bend down and lift the lid of the box.

Riley had ascended the hill, sweeping the path before him with a metal detector. Using a trowel and brush, he had then carefully cleared around the fake grave until he had exposed the wires. They ran under the wooden lid, where the charge was doubtless located. Along with some other nasty surprises for the unwary, usually. It was standard operational procedure for the IRA. One odd thing had struck him. Both wires were bright yellow and purple, a colour combo he hadn't come across before. Red, blue, green and white striped, brown, grey, yes. But this shade of yellow and purple, no.

It looked simple. Cut one of the wires and the circuit could no longer be made. Bomb safe. But the IRA, be it the Provisional, Real, Continuity or New, rarely did simple. Riley had taken out a flying scalpel and carefully positioned it close to the nearest of the yellow and purple wires.

A flying scalpel was a tube with a pyrotechnic charge at one end that propelled a V-shaped pair of scalpel blades out of the 'barrel'. It was much safer than wondering which wire to cut.

Riley had retreated down the hill, carefully retracing his steps, still probing and sweeping with his metal detector while spooling out the control wire for the scalpel.

His number two had finished connecting up the switch, pressed the twin buttons on the unit with his thumbs and there came a loud crack as the blades deployed and severed the wire. It was two heartbeats before the explosion, which lifted the earth on top of the hill in an enormous shudder, sending branches, leaves and soil skywards, raining it down on them.

That day, in the hall of his daughter's school, Riley also remembered that, as he crouched with his hands over his head, the bomb's debris raining down, little fragments of yellow and purple sheathing had plopped onto the earth around him.

The Nottingham monster had Irish blood in its veins.

*

The applause brought him back to the concert at Crowley Hall and he joined in enthusiastically. As the quartet left the stage, he turned to Izzy. 'When is Ruby on?'

'She's not. She's doing hair and make-up backstage.'

An ungenerous thought entered his brain. *What the fuck am I doing here listening to other people's kids then?* He ushered it away. 'Ah. When she said she had a show, I thought she was *in* it.'

'You are so bloody literal.'

'Look, I've got to make a call. Business.'

'Oh, I'd never argue with your business,' she said, less than sweetly. 'Don't go far. The deputy head wants to see us after this.'

'Why? No, tell me later. I won't be long.'

Riley tiptoed out into the hallway as a piano piece began, closing the door behind him as softly as he could. He walked over the polished parquet flooring to the double-fronted entrance. Through the glass he could see a small clump of fellow parents, taking a cigarette break. He swerved to the left and found a door that opened to the side of the building. That area was empty. Good, because he didn't want to be overheard. The type of conversation he was about to have could freak out the general public. He speed-dialled the National Ordnance Disposal Operation Centre. Bomb Central.

He recognised the duty operator, Intelligence Corporal Carl 'Dobbo' Dobson, and identified himself immediately.

'Hello, Staff. Welcome back.'

'Back where?'

'Back on the active list.'

'Oh, yes.' So, Ms Carver had been as good as her word.

'Thanks. Look, Dobbo, what details have we got on the explosive used yesterday?'

'Semtex.'

'How much?' Riley asked.

'A kilo or so is the estimate for the first bomb, slightly more for the second.'

'Do we know its provenance?'

'Hold on.' Riley heard the tapping of a keyboard. 'No. Nothing. No tags at all.'

'No?' Since the Montreal Convention of 1991, following the Pan Am disaster over Lockerbie in December 1988, all commercially made explosive such as Semtex, which had been used in the destruction of Flight 103 over Scotland, had to have a chemical in them that would release an odour for easier detection. For Semtex, it was usually the highly volatile DMNB, chemically 2,3-dimethyl-2,3-dinitrobutane.

'What do you make of that?' Riley just wanted a sounding board. He was already working through the implications for himself.

'It's a pre-tagged batch. Old shit.'

'Oh, come on,' Riley protested. 'DMNB has been added since '90 or '91. And if it's anywhere near that vintage, it's gash.' The shelf-life of Semtex used to be ten years; it was deliberately reduced to five in the late 1990s to help discourage the terrorist black market. So 'old shit', as Dobbo put it, would no longer work. 'I think we've got a sample that has been cleansed.' There was usually another chemical tag in Semtex, too, although the Czech manufacturer claimed on its website that there was no metallic tagging of batches, but this was misinformation, designed to stop end-users trying to 'wash' the explosive, cleaning out any chance of the authorities knowing where it had originated.

'Or it could be homemade,' Dobbo suggested.

It was possible, although it would take more skill and patience than the average bomb-maker had. Semtex combined two explosives, RDX and PETN. If you could get hold of boron fluoride, acetic anhydride, paraformaldehyde, ammonium nitrate and a few other ingredients you could make both elements. You let the resulting crystals dry completely, then grind each compound to a powder with a rolling pin. Once the two explosives are combined in equal measures, you can dissolve them in petroleum jelly or motor oil to make a paste. It sounded simple but preparing the core ingredients required serious temperature control and a lot of stirring. Plus, anyone making the stuff had to be careful about static electricity, which could cause the batch to detonate. It wasn't really a kitchen-sink job, which is why most bombers preferred to get their big bangs off the shelf or go for simpler compounds.

'It's possible somebody knocked it up in a bucket,' said Riley. 'Can you do me a favour?'

'Sure, Staff.'

'Pull up everything we have on the bomb at McGurk's. It was a shout at a farm in southern Fermanagh that was handled by me.' Riley gave him the incident number. He knew it by heart.

'You think this is *Irish?*' Dobbo's voice was full of disbelief. 'You think it's the Micks having another pop?' There had been incidents linked to Ireland – such as the incendiary letter bombs sent to Heathrow, Waterloo and City Airport – but there had been no 'spectacular' on the mainland for some years.

Riley kept silent as a member of staff came through the door behind him. She looked as if she was about to say something, but Riley just raised his eyebrows in innocent enquiry. *Is there a problem?* Apparently not, for she walked on without speaking.

'You still there?' Dobbo asked.

'Yeah. The Irish? I don't know, pal.' Riley patted his pocket, searching for the yellow and purple lead. Then he remembered he had left it in the car. 'Just get me that info.'

He heard muffled applause leak through the door behind him. It was enthusiastic enough to suggest the concert was over. It was time to go and give his daughter a hug.

SIXTEEN

'That Muraski woman can't be that good at her job,' said Barbara Clifford-Brown to her husband as they enjoyed the post-lunch warmth of the conservatory. Henry was reading his Second World War book but politely kept one ear open when he spoke.

'How do you mean?'

'Well, she hadn't turned up who I was. Who I still am. I must be there in the files. Yet she hadn't made the link between us. She obviously thought I was some old dear to be patronised.'

Henry gave a chuckle at the thought of that. 'Hardly, sweetie.'

Barbara Clifford-Brown, neé Lancaster, was proud of having been more than just a 'service wife'. She had operated as an equal partner to Henry in Tokyo, Singapore and a dozen European cities.

'Anyway, I think we should tell VX to get her to back off. Coming here, creating trouble and upsetting you. Don't you think? Henry?'

There was no answer. He had gone.

Barbara stood, laid the rug across Henry's lap and gently eased the book from his hands. He made a slight snorting noise, but his eyes didn't open. The sun was on his face, unsparing in its high-lighting of the effects of age on his skin. She leaned over and kissed his forehead. Strange how he had such difficulty sleeping though the night, but after lunch and a glass of claret he went out like the proverbial light for an hour or two, awaking with such sprightliness, it was as if he'd sloughed off a decade. She envied him that facility.

After she had cleared the kitchen of debris from lunch and re-stoppered the bottle of wine, Barbara went down to the cellar, carefully locking the heavy door behind her. Force of habit. It was a long time since she had needed to worry about her daughter, Rachel, coming down, wondering what was going on in the vaults beneath the house. Back then it had been a clandestine office, complete with powerful radio transmitter. These days it was a surveillance centre, with a desk, chair and a series of monitors positioned in a gap between the wire cages that once held the finest collection of French wine in the county. Running down now, of course. Some drunk, some given as gifts. Still, depleted though the stocks might be, there were enough bottles to see them both out, no matter how hard they tried.

At the far end of the cellar was the primitive shooting range she used to keep her eye in. At one time she had been able to fire the heaviest of guns, a Colt .45 auto or a Desert Eagle. But her fingers had grown spindly and recently her grip had started weakening. Cups and vases were dropped with increasing frequency. Oh, she could still give a slip of a girl like Kate Muraski a good hard pinch now and then. But her grasping muscles quickly fatigued, thanks, the doctor told her, to a compressed nerve in her neck. Her old bones were letting her down. So, she had moved on to polymer weapons, like the Glocks, and had settled on a Walther CCP sub-compact 9mm that weighed just 22 ounces but still carried an impressive eight rounds in the single-stack mag plus one in the spout. It also had an old-fashioned thumb safety that she liked, even if it meant it was slower to deploy than a Glock, thanks to her often swollen finger joints. But she wasn't likely to be in any quick-draw confrontations at her age.

She had given the heftier weapons to Ben Beaumont, an old colleague from the Service who, like her, had a special dispensation from the Home Office to keep handguns as long as they were stored securely and checked by one of the Met's firearms officers on an annual basis. To people of her generation Ben was known as 'Binkie', after the famous theatrical impresario who dominated the West End from the Thirties to his death in the Seventies. Henry and Barbara had enjoyed many a Noel Coward, John Gielgud and Richard Burton performance under the auspices of the real Binkie Beaumont.

Their version of Binkie, Ben Beaumont, had a basement in Knightsbridge that could give Fort Knox a run for its money. His 'valet' was ex-SAS to boot and the place bristled with alarms and cameras, mainly because Binkie's wife had jewellery that would cause envy among the Royals. The guns were as secure as they could be in the UK.

As usual, she crossed and made sure the weapons safe was locked before sitting down at the desk. Barbara knew she needn't have worried that Henry might have left it open. Henry had always hated using any firearm. No, Henry had been a cerebral operator, one of those who liked to outwit his opponent. She, on the other hand, thought it prudent to pack some firepower, just in case.

Barbara flicked the switch that would pipe Radio 3 into the room. She turned it up. Debussy. 'La Mer'. *Something tuneful for once*, she thought. Didn't have to worry about disturbing Henry; you could set a bomb off in the cellar and nobody above would be any the wiser thanks to the BBC recording-studio quality door that sat close to the top of the stairs that led up to the ground floor. She thought her basement would have made an ideal interrogation room. *At Dunston, nobody can hear you scream.*

Chuckling softly to herself, she switched on the surveillance kit, then pressed the keys on the laptop controller, pecking slowly at them like a bird. Oleg the Oligarch – whose real name was Vasily Kutsik – had installed a sophisticated CCTV system, which he could check from his phone. It had been no bother for the Service to hack into and piggyback on that and put a feed into the west wing, so that the Clifford-Browns could monitor his movements within the house. There were also hidden microphones, which were normally switched off so they wouldn't be detected during routine sweeps. They were, naturally, of Russian manufacture, so if they were found, Oleg would suspect that it was the authorities back home listening in.

Barbara had no need to turn on the listening devices. The screens showed nobody was home. Nobody had been for several days. Her eyes went up to the fixture list pinned on the wall. Kutsik was a keen football fan – it was rumoured he had shares in several Premier League and Championship clubs in London, but nothing close to a controlling interest. He had a box, shared with his expat cronies, at two grounds at least. Kutsik nearly always travelled up to Dunston after a game, throwing a party for his companions and a number of women, who always seemed to be different. Some of the footage they recovered might have made another viewer blush, but Barbara had been in the business too long to be shocked by sex or drugs in any guise. The next fixture Kutsik would be attending, though, wasn't for a few days, so there was little to see now.

Still, like any good operative, she checked every room anyway. It was hardly arduous work, and the stipend that SIS paid them for this surveillance was a welcome top-up to their pensions. Even at their age, they had bills to pay. Dunston Hall was hardly cheap to heat or maintain and it was true that your children were never really independent until the day you weren't there. Rachel was a money pit . . . No, that was unfair. She had Korsakoff's syndrome, a form of dementia triggered mainly by alcohol abuse, although in her case the doctors added drugs and 'we're not really sure'. Never in her wildest days would Rachel have imagined what late middle age had in store for her.

She put her poor daughter out of her mind for the moment and checked the status of each camera. Although it was good to keep her hand in with Kutsik, Barbara did miss the old times, when she felt like a real spy, rather than a voyeur. Missed Moscow, even those bone-shattering winters, the days when she felt like she was making a difference. The dead-letter drops, the cavity in the base of the Harpic bleach container for concealing microfilm, the Minox cameras, the elaborate exfiltration plans. What was she doing now? Making sure that the former Colonel Kutsik – Hero of the Russian Federation, who had fallen foul of a nephew of Vladimir Putin during a business deal in Cyprus – was exactly what he claimed to be. Given that Five estimated that 50 per cent of all Russians in the UK reported back to the Kremlin, there was a good chance he was a bad – or at least, a dubious – actor.

Some might think it was fortuitous that a Russian suspect should move in next to a couple of agents. But it was nothing of the sort. The Service had very good contacts with the handful of top-end estate agents in London that dealt with the rich and ultra-rich. Kutsik had been offered his half of Dunston Hall at what appeared to be a bargain price (the Service always made up any shortfall to the seller). Furthermore, Kutsik had been shown architectural plans drawn up by, it was claimed, no less than Thomas Heatherwick himself, for a spectacular glass atrium that could be built to re-connect the east and west wings. Subject to planning permission. And the vacancy of the west wing. But how long could that old couple go on living in such a place? Surely it wouldn't be long before they were consigned to a care home and Kutsik could swoop in and have the whole estate to himself.

Such was the sales pitch and legend the Service had created to ensnare him. It was work that, strictly speaking, should have been done by Five, given they were on home soil, but Kutsik was in touch with Russian dissidents in Switzerland, the Netherlands and the US, giving it an international dimension that enabled Six to claim him as their own. After all, Thames House wasn't up to snuff these days.

Take that girl, the one that they had sent to try to put the frighteners on Henry. There was nothing there but ancient history best forgotten. The modern generation had trouble grasping that you always did what was best for the national interest *at the time*. Perspectives changed. Both she and Henry had done things that, from this end of the telescope, they regretted. Rory in Finland, the boy in East Berlin. She hadn't, in retrospect, needed to kill him, but at that moment it seemed likely that he would blow her circuit which had infiltrated the Russian army catering corps (you could always tell when troops were about to be deployed from a sudden increase in the order for rations). Nice lad. The sex was good, too. But once she found out his mother and sister were under the thumb of the Stasi, and he could well be compromised, his time was up.

She sighed at the memory, switched off the cameras that showed only deserted rooms and looked at her watch. Henry would be out for another thirty minutes at least. Ah well, she thought, might as well run a magazine through the Walther, then strip and oil it, just to keep them both in ship-shape.

She had just risen from her chair when the telephone rang. She picked it up with a feeling of trepidation. It would be her daughter Rachel, making trouble again. But it wasn't Rachel. It was trouble of a different sort, however, in the form of that Muraski woman.

SEVENTEEN

When the look-how-clever-and-cultured-we-have-made-your-children concert had finished, the parents milled around waiting for their offspring. Riley could hear a few grumblings about the concert being on a Saturday morning, meaning they had missed a whole day of late-season skiing. Others were praising various players, admiring their tone, attack or their precise and rapid technique. 'I mean, she's no Buniatishvili ...' one father kept saying, as if hoping someone would contradict him.

When Ruby appeared from backstage, she wasn't in school uniform, as the performers had been, but in blue elasticated trousers decorated with large, bright orange flowers and a cropped black top. The short T-shirt had a slogan on it: *If Abattoirs Had Windows, We'd All Be Vegetarians*. Riley sensed a new passion in the making. Although he was buggered if he was going to eat nut roast at the hotel that night. She was carrying the holdall she had asked him to buy her for Christmas, stuffed to bursting by the look of it.

Ruby's hair was pulled back into a ponytail and he marvelled once more at how they could have produced such a poised beauty. He felt a phantom elbow in his ribs from his daughter at his crassness. Yes, and smart, too. There was talk of Oxbridge, which made him feel even prouder of his contribution, even if it was mainly in the past.

Riley leaned in and kissed her forehead. He no longer had to stoop to do that. She would overtake him in height soon. Clever, beautiful *and* willowy. A dangerous combo. He wasn't looking forward to the Dating Years. Perhaps Izzy's insistence on an all-female school had been a wise move. He felt a fierce flush of love towards Ruby. Hell, nut roast was a small price to pay for having her in his life. He gave her a hug and felt a little resistance, a stiffness to his embrace. Adolescent embarrassment, he assumed. He unwrapped his arms and stepped away.

'You look smart, Dad,' Ruby said, flicking his tie.

'I reckon I can lose this now.' Riley reached up, loosened the knot at his throat and undid the top button of his shirt. He let out a sigh of relief.

'You all right?' There was concern in her voice, so he assumed she meant after Nottingham, rather than his close encounter with collar and tie. The army had enough occasions where they were required to have to put up with wearing one off duty. But Izzy had insisted on 'smart', not casual for the concert.

'Yeah, fine. No drama.'

'You always say that.'

'Always has,' added Izzy, who had taken a step back to let Riley glory in his daughter. 'It usually means something different.'

Ruby's fingers fluttered up and across his cheek. 'Really?'

'Not this time,' he assured her. He glanced over at Izzy, intending to admonish her for frightening their daughter, but he could tell she had meant nothing by it. Izzy had just been remembering a time when it was her who had to listen to his platitudes. He flashed his ex-wife a smile and got one back, a smile that was over a decade old and put a narrow blade through his heart.

'What did you think of the show?' asked Ruby, dragging him back.

'I thought the hair was the best part. Followed by make-up in close second.'

'Oh, *Dad*. I meant the music. Wasn't Harriet brilliant?'

He had no idea which one Harriet was. The pianist who was no Buniatishvili, perhaps. 'You know I'm more of a Kendrick Lamar guy.'

'You?' she sounded appalled. 'Since when have you heard of Kendrick Lamar?'

Since some of the younger members of his team had started playing him was the answer. Kendrick and someone called Anderson Paak or similar were big in the back of the response vehicles. 'Oh, I've been into him for years now.'

Ruby gave a disbelieving laugh. 'Rubbish. Name a song, then.'

The word 'pimp' popped into his head, but he couldn't recall the context. 'Er . . . "I'm Gonna Slap That Bitch"?'

'Dom!' chided Izzy.

'You liar.' Ruby punched him on the arm to let him know he probably had the wrong sort of rapper. 'Right, I'll just grab my stuff, say goodbye and we'll go hotel.'

'Go *to* the hotel,' Izzy corrected.

'Let's go hotel,' said Riley, and Ruby slipped her arm through his.

They walked outside with Izzy following and had taken a few steps on the gravel when Ruby stopped. 'You didn't bring The Heap, did you?'

'Don't worry, you can lie in the back with a blanket over your head.'

'It's okay,' she said, putting on a brave face. 'We'll see you at the hotel, eh, Mum?'

'I'll be in the spa,' replied Izzy, swerving off towards her Merc. Riley could well believe she wasn't kidding. She had always loved a sauna.

'Bye, Ruby!' another girl shouted, climbing into a giant SUV.

'Bye. Have a good time in St Lucia.' Then, under her breath. 'What a flex. Everyone in the village knows they've bought a villa in St Lucia. It overlooks Marigot Bay. Apparently.'

'Sorry, love, I think our villa got lost in the post. Anyway, you wouldn't like it there. They love country music in St Lucia. It's true. Someone called Kenny Rogers is a god there. Come on.'

They resumed walking and he fished in his jacket pocket for the keys.

Andy the Tank was to his left, weeding part of the car parking area. He looked up and raised a hand. 'Take it easy. Hope it's okay now.'

'Yeah, thanks,' he replied.

Riley's phone buzzed. Probably Dobbo and the Irish details. He raised the key fob and pressed, but the VW, partially obscured by the saplings, didn't wake up.

And then, what in Afghan they used to call the atmospherics changed completely. He sensed a sliver of what felt like ice slide down his back, so real he touched his spine to make sure someone hadn't put icicles down his shirt.

'Hold on.' Riley put Ruby's bag down.

'What?'

'Wait here. I've just got to check something.'

'Can you open the car?'

'No. Stay where you are.'

Riley tabbed back to where Andy was stretching an aching back. 'What did you mean just now?' he asked the groundsman.

'What?'

'You said you hoped it was okay. What was okay?'

'Oh, your motor.' Andy pointed towards the VW. 'I hope the AA or whoever they were fixed it, like.'

Riley spun on his heel to see Ruby walking towards the Passat, bag in one hand, pushing her earbuds into place with the other. 'Ruby!'

She didn't break stride.

'Fuck.' He launched into a run, feet pounding on the gravel, trying to sprint and shout at the same time. 'Ruby! Stop! *Ruby!*'

She didn't.

Ruby was just about level with the rear of the car when he reached her. Or almost reached her. He was still a good few metres short, so he launched himself into the air, grabbing her shoulders as he passed to one side of her, twisting and dragging her down on top of him so he could break her fall.

She screamed loud enough to scare the birds from the trees as he crashed onto the gravel and he felt something pop in his ribs as the air exploded from him. She began to wriggle. 'Get off me.'

A sharp pain flashed up his left side as he filled his lungs. 'God's sake, keep still.'

Riley wrapped his arms around her in a bear hug. Eventually he felt the fight go out of her. He didn't let go, though. He wanted to hold her even tighter, to stay with her forever, to protect her from this fucked-up world. 'Dad, what are you doing? You're scaring me.'

Without shifting his body from where he lay, he turned his head and stared underneath the Passat. 'Jesus.'

'What is it?'

'Ruby, I want you to get up very slowly and move away. Very slowly. As I say, gently does it. Eggshells. Imagine you are walking on eggshells. Back to the school. Find Mum. Use another way out if there is one, don't use the Merc. Go now.'

'What is it?' she repeated, her voice fragile with fright.

He was lost for words. How do you tell your daughter you've just seen a bomb attached to the underside of the car she had been about to get in to?

*

The bomb-maker levered the top off the wooden case that his associate had delivered. 'Handle with great care,' he had warned him. No need. All his adult life the bomb-maker had been handling dangerous components with care. When the Russians came, his job was to plant the bombs rather than build them. Eventually, he became an apprentice to the legendary Abu al-Sayid Umar and quickly progressed to making his own IEDs, ones he took great pride in.

This, he admitted to himself, was different to the kind of bombs that had made his reputation back home. In the box, protected by a nest of polystyrene, were two silver-grey metal cylinders, each blank apart from a red skull and crossbones stencil.

He left them where they were for the moment, moved to the kitchen, made himself some coffee and fetched an apple juice for his son. He sat down next to the boy and gently lifted off the headphones that had been clamped onto his ears. He was listening to a football match from a smartphone, face furrowed in concentration. He slapped at his father's arms as he removed the headphones, spilling some of the juice.

His father spoke softly, without anger. 'Now, now, you can listen. Take this. Leave one ear on. I want to talk to you.'

The boy took the drink in his right hand and pressed one cup to his left ear. The bomb-maker could hear tinny, over-excited voices coming from the other speaker.

'You know not to touch anything unless I say so, yes?'

The lad nodded.

'Especially not that.' He pointed to the wooden box. 'Understand? If you see it, do not go near it.'

'Yes, Father.'

'Good.' He looked up at the clock. 'Well, it should be all set by now. The best that the British Army has, eh? We'll see.'

The boy looked at him blankly. It didn't matter. Talking to the boy was better than a lonely silence. Besides, he had no way of knowing just how much he absorbed.

'It's like a little test, son. If he passes, he lives. If he doesn't . . .' He mimed an explosion with his hands. 'Then he didn't deserve any further attention anyway. Go back to your football,' he said, and slipped the headphones back into place. He took a sip of coffee then switched on the TV, selecting a news channel, but turning the volume down. Then he opened up the laptop and selected the live stream from the drone. Pass or fail, he would no doubt know soon enough.

EIGHTEEN

Jamal called Muraski back as the techs were putting the final touches to the video link from a conference room at Thames House to Nottingham's City Hospital. Thanks to a lot of badgering she was going to remotely sit in on the second interview of Janet Webb, a survivor of the bomb blast at Sillitoe Circus, who might have information on the bombers. She would not be alone in listening in, as analysts of the Counter Terrorist Command and members of the Intelligence and Security Committee would also be eavesdropping. However, they were also remote observers, so she had the meeting room to herself, apart from two technicians who were setting up the monitor and video link.

'Jamal? You got another cracker for me?'

'Maybe. We've recovered part of a circuit board. The ID was intact. It was part of a computer circuit, made in China, sold in Dubai.'

'Dubai?'

'Yup. Halo Trading. Halo is suspected of being an Iranian front company, to beat any embargoes.'

'And Iran supplied and still supplies bomb-making parts to the Taliban.'

'It did. And it does.'

'Which could link us to Bravo-900.'

'It puts us in the vicinity. We're still investigating Halo's trading history.' That meant a bunch of white-hat hackers were probably rummaging through Halo's virtual underwear drawer as they spoke.

'I've been thinking,' she said to Jamal. 'It's not a complete surprise this Riley's DNA was on some components. He was the ATO who went in and checked for a tertiary.'

'They are supposed to wear forensic gloves when handling components,' said Jamal.

'Did he?' she asked.

'I don't know. That's your department, Kate. But it was where we found the DNA that interested me, impregnated on cloth inside the detonator of the primary device. Not an item he personally bagged, according to the labelling.'

'As if it had been used to wipe away fingerprints after assembly. Is that what you're saying?'

She heard Jamal take a sip of tea or coffee. 'Again, that's your job. I'm just telling you the science.'

In other words, *on your head be it*. So far, she had no more than a stray bit of genetic material and the name of a possibly dodgy company in the Middle East. Was that enough to take to Oakham? Probably not. 'Can you get me contact details for Riley? Just to eliminate him?'

'Sure. There'll be an email or a number on the file. I can send it over.'

'Great, thanks.' That would save her from trying to wheedle information out of the army. After all, they invented the concept of closing ranks.

'Listen, Jamal, just changing the subject for a second, you don't know anyone with a spare room going, do you?'

'I thought you were sorted? With whatsisname. Tony.'

'Toby. It's his flat and, as my mother still says, it's gone so pear-shaped you could make Babycham with it.'

'I don't understand that.'

'Neither do I,' she admitted.

There was a pause while Jamal considered whether he could help. 'My brother Bilal is moving out of our place in a few weeks. Going travelling for six months. Be a spare for that long. Maybe longer.'

'That might help. Where is it?'

'Mortlake.'

'Where's that, halfway to Mordor?'

'It's just beyond Kew.'

'I was hoping for London.'

'It is in London, you snobby cow,' he laughed. 'Only about an hour on the train.'

Which meant an hour-and-a-half. People always pretended you could hop, skip and jump into the West End from their postcode.

'When is it free?'

'Two, maybe three weeks. Thing is, it's our parents' flat. No alcohol allowed. And no entertaining the opposite sex. They do spot raids.'

Would suit sober nun, she thought. Would Jamal express those caveats to everyone or just someone he remembered from university who liked a good time? 'I think I need something sooner.'

'Don't you lot have safe houses all over London?'

There were, mainly in big anonymous complexes like the Barbican and Dolphin Square, or in places like Hounslow or Enfield. 'Yeah, but those places are bugged to shit by the Snoops here. I don't want my morning showers to end up on some Christmas compilation tape at their office party.'

Jamal sounded genuinely shocked. 'Does that happen?'

'There's a rumour it did, before our time. Even so, they aren't called Doggs for nothing.'

'Only you call them that.'

'Whatever. Either way, I'd never relax in the shower in case some electronic Norman Bates was eyeing me up.'

'Thanks for that image.'

'Delete it at once if you know what's good for you.'

'All set,' said one of the techies, handing her a pair of Bluetooth headphones and pointing at the screen. 'You can hear them, they can't hear you.'

'Jamal, got to go. Wipe that out of your mind, now. I owe you a drink. A soft drink, I mean.'

'I'm free this evening.'

'Pushy.'

'Just for a couple of hours.'

'I'll think about it. I'll see how the day pans out. Don't forget the number for Riley.'

'On its way. But you have to decide what you are concentrating on.'

'What do you mean?'

'Is it Bravo-900 or an ATO's stray DNA. There's no link between them is there?'

'No. You're right. Headless chicken. Send the number anyway.'

'Will do.'

'Great. And I'll get back to you on the flat.' If she ever found herself living under the arches at Charing Cross maybe.

She turned her attention to the monitor. The screen showed a private room in the hospital. Janet Webb was propped up in bed, looking remarkably unscathed for a woman who had been close to a Semtex bomb. Sitting at the bedside was a female police officer and just out of the range of vision of her camera was another police officer, male. They were taping the interview and identified themselves as DS Susan Chatham and DC Chris Davies.

Chatham began by thanking Webb for her forbearance and apologised that this was likely to be just another in a number of interviews. Muraski drummed her fingers on the table, waiting to get to the meat of the session.

'You see,' Chatham was saying, 'there is sometimes something called temporary retrograde amnesia, often triggered by trauma. So, in the first hours or days after an incident, the memory of what happened just prior to the event is hazy or non-existent. But subsequently small details might come back, things that may be significant.'

'I understand,' said Webb.

Muraski's phone pinged and she glanced down at it. Incoming from Jamal.

'Now, can we take you back to before the explosion, to your arrival at Sillitoe Circus and how you came to be there that day?'

Webb carefully went over the morning of that day, her voice only quivering when she described how she and her late husband used to drink in a pub that had been demolished to make way for the new development. She had a reasonable recollection of the other customers, but really only paid close attention to the waiter, a young 'handsome foreigner'. There was a catch in her voice, when she recalled that he had died.

Muraski leaned in towards the screen as Webb described the man with the rucksack: late twenties or early thirties, she thought, long dark hair, but she had no idea about ethnicity. No, she didn't think he was Middle Eastern. Then she described a woman who arrived and left. Very beautiful, dark-skinned, but Webb wasn't sure if that was a suntan or not.

'Didn't get a suntan in this country,' muttered Muraski. Although she could have been to a tanning booth, she supposed. Neither of those were the man she was after, but that was hardly surprising. Bomb-makers made bombs. Not planted them. A talented creator of IEDs or suicide vests was a very valuable asset whose skills could be harnessed for many years. It didn't make sense to send them for martyrdom.

As for ethnicity, obviously not every Muslim conformed to the Af-Pak stereotype and besides, there were always converts, like Samantha Lewthwaite, Al-Shabah's White Widow, who were sometimes more fanatical than their masters. Germaine Lindsay, the 7/7 bomber who made a widow of Lewthwaite, was actually Jamaican and only converted to Islam in the early 2000s. It was one of the reasons Muraski had been involved in tracing the missing ISIS widows. Not all had seen the error of their caliphate ways. So perhaps Bravo-900 had found willing hands to help him make or plant his bombs. But where from?

On screen, Webb agreed to work with an e-fit artist to try and create images of the man with the rucksack and the mysterious woman. The male was certainly in the frame, as he had arrived with the rucksack that Jamal and others' forensic tests had shown to contain the Semtex. The woman might be an innocent player. But there was also the secondary device to consider – who planted or activated that? The rucksack man or an accomplice?

How did that square with her theory that Bravo-900 was a lone actor? Could it be that he had been brought in by a homegrown group as Bomber-in-Chief? Muraski put that thought to one side. She knew she was falling into an old trap, making the facts support her pet theory.

Janet Webb asked for a cup of tea and the interview was suspended. Muraski took off the headphones and opened the message that contained Staff Sergeant Dominic Riley's contact details on her phone. She typed the number in and heard it ring, thinking she was probably wasting both her and his time.

While she waited, she scrolled down the message Jamal had sent. It was several pages on the military career of Staff Sergeant Riley. Most of it was as expected, but the final paragraph on 'Personal Circumstances' was the one that made her let out a little yelp of surprise.

'Jesus,' she said to herself. She had just found a connection between a British Army ATO and Bravo-900.

NINETEEN

Riley lay on the ground as he watched Ruby run on tiptoes back to the school building, yelling, as he had instructed, for everyone to get indoors. His phone was buzzing in his pocket. He reached in and turned it off. Mobiles and bombs never mix. He could see Andy staring at him, wondering what the hell was going on. He ignored him and turned his head so he could get back to examining the device that some cunt had placed under his car. *His* car. Riley's. The one he transported his daughter in.

He felt a throbbing behind his eyes, a precursor to a burst of fury. But it wasn't the time for that. He kept his breathing steady, tried to stop his heart beating itself to death against his ribcage.

Skills and drills, pal.

At Nick's prompt, he began to recap the correct response to the situation. Car bombs and truck bombs are known as VBIEDs: Vehicle-Borne Improvised Explosive Devices. What Riley was looking at was an Under Vehicle Improvised Explosive Device. These could be set off by remote control – the key fob, for instance, or a radio/mobile signal or by a tilt/vibration switch. The latter used the kind of mechanism found in vending machines to stop them being tipped over or in pinball machines, where they prevent cheating by shutting the whole thing down. Or, like the one under

Riley's car, a simple unit you could buy on the internet from any electrical component supplier. When the vehicle, or part of the vehicle, moves — like the vibration of an old exhaust when the car starts up — the mercury flows within the glass container, bridges the terminals and, mercury being metal, completes the circuit. Current then flows to the detonator. Little boom.

Big Boom.

If not Goodnight Vienna, it was Hello Life-Changing Injuries.

Not only that, but it was entirely possible that there was an anti-handling device in there. Car-bombers often wired a second detonation switch to the interior light. The moment the driver's door opens and current flows to it, the charge goes up.

Riley got to his feet as if he had been dropped into a swimming pool full of treacle. Easy now. The fall hadn't done his ribs or his best Paul Smith suit any good at all, but he shunted that thought away. You don't worry about a muscle pull or your wardrobe when you have an IED up your jacksy.

Nor did you waste time thinking *Who?* Or *Why?* You concentrated on one thing: nobody is going to die here. He hadn't come across a trembler switch of any description in Afghan. Car bombs, yes, where the boot was filled with fertiliser. But they didn't need anything as sophisticated as a tilt switch. The Afghan National Army — through misplaced pride — often tried to defuse any device themselves. They had lost a lot of brave undertrained men that way.

How sensitive was the tilt? Would a door opening set it off? A boot slam? An exhaust vibration? Or would it only do its lethal job when the VW actually moved. He wasn't going to hang around to find out. Nor would he be crawling under the car cutting wires. That was the sort of macho mistake the Afghans made. This was a job for a robot and a controlled explosion to disrupt the whole mechanism – the majority of car bombs viewers see safely deto-nated on the news were actually the result of a smaller charge set by ATOs, rather than the main charge going up. No heroics. No *Hurt Locker* bullshit. When he said to himself nobody was going to die, he included himself.

But here, he was off duty, *with his daughter, for Christ's sake*. This felt personal.

Later, mate. Save it.

Once Riley was at what he considered a safe enough distance, he began to windmill his arms like a madman trying to fly. 'Everybody back inside! Now! Do not get in your cars!'

The small clusters of parents, staff and pupils still in the car park turned to look at him, some in alarm, others with pity in their eyes that he had likely flipped.

'Please! Go back inside, there is the danger of an explosion. Do *not* go near your vehicles.'

He was level with the ex-tank man now. 'Andy, did those AA mechanics go near any other car?'

'I don't think so.' Not good enough. Someone would have to check every vehicle, just to be certain. 'Is there another exit for cars?'

Andy pointed to the left of the house. 'Deliveries and service entrance. What's—?'

It was no time to mince words. 'There's a bomb under my car,' Riley said, cutting him short. 'Help me get everybody inside.'

Andy found a voice that must have come in handy when trying to communicate over the Rolls-Royce diesels of a Challenger tank in the desert. It came deep from his diaphragm and it sounded as if he had swallowed a megaphone. 'Ladies and gentlemen! Your attention, please! This is an emergency! Everybody inside for your own safety! Please move away. Do not—'

Riley turned as he heard the roar of a big engine, a growl followed by a thrum that vibrated the chest. He located the sound, a few rows of cars over. One of the modern five-litre V8 Mustangs. Hugely impractical in the UK, they certainly made a statement: the owner likely had a very small cock.

'Jesus. Hey! Hey! Stop.' Riley began to weave through the parked vehicles. He heard the wheels spin and sharp stones arced into the air. The bright orange Mustang backed out of the space and headed off towards the main gate, fast enough that it was a waste of time Riley trying to follow. He bent down, picked up a large pebble, and threw it ineffectually after the fastback. As it reached the road, the driver engaged launch control and the big Ford took off in a wheel-spinning fishtail.

The air pulsed with the thrum of the big exhaust. Riley felt like he could see it, like ripples in the water, as the wavelets spread out and engulfed his car.

'Oh, shit,' he said under his breath.

The light was brief and bright and stabbed into Riley's retinas. The boom that followed was surprisingly muffled, although Riley felt the heat of the explosion on his face. His VW looked like the donkey from that old Buckaroo game, kicking as it rose into the air, emitting a screech of broken metal, and rolling onto its side, the interior filled with fumes that bled out of the smashed window. A shower of safety glass fell around it like ice particles. Flames began to lick around the interior. *There goes my wire*, he thought. It wasn't worth risking a secondary for that. He stayed where he was.

Pretty sensitive tilt switch then, said Nick.

Whether because it was sideswiped by the blast wave or because the driver panicked, the Mustang lost it on the turn out of the gate. The rear wheels broke away from the asphalt, and it spun, sending the two-thousand-kilo muscle car ploughing backwards across a ditch and into the fence opposite the school gates. It came to a halt with the front wheels off the ground, spinning uselessly in the air.

It was while looking at that, praying the occupants were unhurt, that Riley spotted the hovering drone, and felt the cyclopean gaze of its single lens turn on him. He took out his phone and snapped it for no good reason other than the feeling that two could play at that game. The machine hung in the air for the moment, buzzing like a particularly malevolent bee, before banking away and heading for a line of distant trees.

Riley turned his attention back to the ditched Mustang and the people possibly trapped inside.

TWENTY

Kate Muraski made a call to the Clifford-Browns as soon as the Janet Webb interview had terminated for the day. The poor woman had added very little to the overall picture, but perhaps her memory would improve over the next forty-eight hours or so. They also might get somewhere on the e-fit pictures. Although, in her limited experience, that would be a first.

A head poked in just as she was about to punch in the Clifford-Browns' number. Roger Altrincham, one of the Russian bods. She felt a pang of envy. Altrincham, who had just sailed past fifty without a streak of grey in his cropped dark hair, had started at the very bottom and worked his way up. No fast-track college degree bollocks for him. So, she had to respect him as the real deal: a proper career spook. 'Sorry. We have this booked.' He pointed at the wall clock. 'Ten minutes.'

'That's all I need,' she said, and he disappeared after flashing a tight, humourless smile which suggested it would be best if she didn't overrun.

She tapped in the Clifford-Browns' number and started a silent mantra: *Please let it be Henry, please let it be Henry.*

'Hello?' said Barbara.

Damn it . . .

'Mrs Clifford-Brown. Hello. It's Kate—'

'I know very well who it is,' said Barbara with a frostiness Scott of the Antarctic would have recognised. 'I thought I'd made it clear that I didn't want you bothering my husband again.'

'I know, but—'

'Ever.'

Muraski tried her trump card. '*Eto vopros natsionaljnoj bezopasnosti*,' she said and, although she was well aware she had no need to translate it for the older woman, added: 'It's a matter of national security.'

Barbara actually laughed and her voice softened. 'I know what you're trying to do, Miss Muraski. Play on an old woman's memories. But I do miss the language. I was never very good at it, personally. Henry was more fluent. And it might be a matter of national security, but it is ancient history.'

'Not that ancient. It's about the man Yousaf Ali.' AKA Bravo-900.

'I know nobody of that name.' She was back to steel-trap mode.

'Your husband does. And I have further information now, since my visit. It seems that—'

'It seems that you don't listen, Miss Muraski, which is a very poor attribute in your line of work. You noticed the rather peculiar layout of the hall? Of Dunston Hall?'

That wrong-footed Muraski. 'I suppose so.'

'There is, as you will have seen, a west wing – our part of the house – and an east wing, but no central section. The story is that the original owners, the Crowboroughs, were landed gentry fallen on hard times. But they still had royal connections and every so often Bertie, the Prince of Wales, used to come and stay. He'd put Lillie Langtry in the pub down the road. The Crown. You must have passed it.'

'I think so,' Muraski said impatiently, wondering what this had to do with anything.

'But then Bertie would eat them out of house and home. He'd shoot or ride all day, then come back here expecting a slap-up dinner with fine wines and brandy for himself and his considerable retinue. You can't send the Prince of Wales a bill. And even if you could, he probably wouldn't pay it. Ask his tailors. I think they're still waiting. One shooting season he sent word he was coming up for a weekend. So, the Crowboroughs replied that they had suffered a small fire and they couldn't possibly expect the Prince of Wales to put up with the smell and the smoke damage. Bertie replied that he was sending his architect up straight away to assess the damage and help with repairs. So, the Crowboroughs panicked. There had, of course, been no fire. Well they could do something about that, they thought. They went into the main drawing room and tried to singe the curtains.' She gave a crackly laugh. '*Whoosh.* The entire drapes went up. They tried to put it out, but it took hold. The whole central section of the house burnt down, leaving only the two wings. When the architect arrived from London, he looked at the smouldering ruins and said: "You call that a small fire?"'

Barbara Clifford-Brown gave an indulgent chuckle while Muraski waited.

'Luckily the Robert Adam chapel out the back survived.'

'Your point is?' Muraski asked.

The tone at the other end shifted to belligerent in a smooth change of gear. 'If you light a fire, young lady, you can never control where it goes and what damage it does.'

'Sound advice. Perhaps your husband should have taken it.' *Fuck, fuck, fuck.* She should have played it cooler. 'But, there's another factor in play here—'

'Nothing is in play,' Barbara said firmly. 'I am sure you mean well, but at our time of life we just want some peace and quiet. Goodbye, Miss Muraski. We shall not be speaking again.'

The line went dead. The woman's final sentence had been as much an instruction as a prediction.

There was a rap on the door and Roger Altrincham reappeared. 'Okay?'

'I'm done,' said Muraski rather tetchily.

She gathered her things and walked out past a gaggle of keen-looking youngsters, all clutching yellow and purple-coloured files. New intake. If any of those got the Russia gig before her . . .

She took a breath to calm herself. Every newbie got a talk from a senior manager in each department, to give them an overview of how this machine meshed – or sometimes clashed. Routine.

As she walked down the corridor heading back to her desk, she tried Riley again. No answer. She left a message, giving her name, mentioning that she worked for 'national security', and asking him to call back as soon as he could.

Then she turned on her heels and headed for the domain of Mr Jimmy Fu and his Doggs. Perhaps he could help her firm up the rather tenuous link she had discovered between the staff sergeant and Bravo-900 and probe Mr and Mrs Clifford-Brown, without her ever having to speak to them again.

TWENTY-ONE

The occupants of the Mustang managed to extricate themselves from the car and stagger back into the school, edging past the smoking ruin of the VW as if it might leap up and bite them. There were two of them. The man was in his fifties, wearing age-inappropriate Supreme and Palace gear. The girl was about Ruby's age, although Riley couldn't tell much more because she had her hands over her face and was sobbing. He walked down the drive, hand up to shield himself from the heat of his smoking car, and escorted them back to the school. Most of the parents, teachers and pupils still on the premises had done as he had told them, and gone back inside. He could see faces pressed to the window, mouths wide with a mix of horror, curiosity and shock.

He handed them over to Andy, who said he would take them to Matron. Riley had thought school matrons had gone the way of fagging and six-of-the-best, but apparently not. 'Oh, and Andy,' he said to the tank man as he pointed at the house. 'Get everyone away from the windows, eh? Just in case.' Andy nodded that he understood.

Riley looked around for his daughter but couldn't see her. She would also be somewhere inside. He wanted to find her and hold her again, more gently this time. But he squashed that instinct.

Izzy would be with her. She was safe. Riley had to stay in ATO mode. Two bombs in two days. One of them apparently aimed at him? He had trouble getting his head round that, mainly because one thought dominated all the others ricocheting around his skull.

They could have killed Ruby.

Yes, Nick, and they'll pay for that, whoever they are.

While he waited for the emergency services, Riley checked his messages. A Kate Muraski had called. From 'National Security'. Just the spooks ticking boxes. That could wait. He called Dobbo at the National Ordnance Disposal Operation Centre to dictate a ten-liner, as best he could. This would be sent to the EOD and RESA teams that were on the way. They would check the immediate surroundings and also give the remaining cars a clean bill of health. Or otherwise. Riley had done Izzy's A-Class himself. It was clear. Then he had sent them off, as originally planned, to the Willow Grange hotel, saying he would join them later. That, he could tell Izzy knew, was extremely unlikely. There was work to be done. Izzy knew Riley wouldn't take an attempt on his daughter's life lying down.

'Dobbo?'

'Christ, I just heard. You okay?'

'No drama. I'll give you the run-down. Date today, time . . .' He checked his watch and did a mental calculation as to when he first spotted the device . . . 'Make it an hour ago. Say twelve thirty?'

Line two, the grid reference of the device, which Dobbo said he would look up. Three was the description of the location; four, activity at site prior to find; five, the main PIC on the ground – the police contact (UNKNOWN). Line six, type of ordnance (again, not known yet) and line seven detailed the target/resources threatened, in this case Staff Sergeant Dominic Riley. Ruby, he suspected, would have been classed as 'collateral damage' had she got into the car.

He'd give the bastards collateral damage when he found them. The anger rushed through Riley like a flash fire, hot and fast.

Skills and drills, he reminded himself. Rage certainly had its time and place, but this wasn't it.

Line eight was mission requirement for the Royal Engineers and the Explosive Ordnance Disposal teams. In this case, make sure there was only one bomb – no secondaries on the VW, no other vehicles wired to blow. Nine was protective measure/action, which Riley suggested was evacuating the site of staff, pupils and parents and closing off the road that ran past the school to protect the public. Finally, ten was the priority level: IMMEDIATE, which was one below URGENT, which meant imminent threat to life. He was pretty sure it was a one-shot attempt, but it paid to be cautious.

Once he'd finished up with Dobbo, he turned to see a convoy of police vehicles coming through the Service entrance and heading for the house. There was a helicopter, too, which had crabbed in from over the distant tree line. Of the drone, no sign. He looked around for Andy the Tank, but remembered he was inside. He hoped he was together enough to make sure those stranded by the event kept away from any potentially flying glass. Best place for him, given the chopper.

A Jaguar pulled up outside the main entrance to the school and a senior police officer stepped out of the rear. A tall, lean man with a shaved head, he wrinkled his nose at the stink of burnt plastic and fuel that pervaded the school grounds. Riley was just glad he hadn't had a full tank, otherwise The Heap would still be burning very bright indeed. The policeman straightened his uniform jacket before reaching into the rear of the Jag and fetching a cap, which he put on. By the time he had made himself presentable to the public and camera-ready, Riley was introducing himself with his rank and status.

'Chief Inspector David Blair,' the police officer shot back, his voice carrying the trace of a Caribbean accent. 'I'll be Police Incident Commander for the time being. You need any medical treatment?'

Riley looked down at his suit. 'Maybe a tailor, later. Otherwise I'm fine.'

'You want to bring me up to speed?'

Riley did so, succinct and to the point as always, with zero emotional content when he mentioned Ruby's near-miss. That was busy stoking the furnace burning deep in his gut.

'You think this is personal?' Blair asked.

Does the Queen keep Corgis?

Was Nick right? Was he actually the target? If so, it was a change in MO from the recent carnage, so perhaps this wasn't the same people as Nottingham. There, the bomber or bombers had gone for mass murder and injury. Here, one casualty instead of many. And a different kind of device. But that proved nothing. And trying to demoralise bomb squads by taking out one or more of its members was nothing new. In Iraq, Afghan, Ireland, even Washington DC and New York, it had been used as a tactic. Taking out an ATO was a calling card in the profession of bomb-maker. And the best EOD operatives were not without ego, which meant they could sometimes be lured into situations where they put themselves at risk. Riley had an old army pal, now an EXPO – Explosives Officer – in the Met, who considered robots and remote detonation 'for pussies'. By rights such an attitude should have got Alex Stock killed by now. But he seemed to have as much luck as arrogance.

'I can't be certain.'

Bollocks.

'It seems too much of a coincidence to me. You were at Nottingham?'

'Later stages.'

'And then . . . this.' He pointed to the remains of the Passat.

To be fair, he did need a new motor.

'Oh, be quiet,' he muttered.

'What was that?' Blair asked.

'I said there was a drone. Just over there. I don't know whether it was related to the incident or some local just joyriding his toy.'

'Drones are not exactly uncommon these days,' said Blair as he watched his officers set up the mobile incident room.

'Yes, but there was a drone at Nottingham, too. I saw it. Thought it might be one of yours. Maybe the one here was to film me going up in smoke. There's probably footage of Nottingham, too, waiting to be uploaded to some jihadist atrocity site on the internet.'

'I'll make sure someone is trawling the likely outlets. I am certain they will be. It's a bloody nuisance about the Mustang setting the device off, though. Means it's very unlikely there will be forensics.'

'Better the Mustang than me.' And Ruby, he added to himself.

'Yes. Although you don't seem too bothered.'

'Oh, I'm bothered. In fact, I am completely fucked off. But I am also used to it. It's my game. For the last year in Afghan they were after the ATOs. There was a price on our heads. Actually, it felt like there was a price on our legs. And they knew us all by name. I found an IED once with a message scratched into the wood of the pressure pad: *Hello Riley, hope you have better luck than the last ATO.*'

'That's pretty sick.'

'The thing is, while they carry on trying to blow me up, I can handle it. Snipers, though. No thanks. Always hated being shot at. Snipers, they give me the willies. Better a bomb any time. No drama.' He wasn't joking, although most people always assumed he was, when he explained that explosive ordnance held little terror for him compared to unseen assassins.

'No drama?' Blair shook his head as he spoke. 'You lot really are a breed apart, aren't you?' Riley couldn't detect any admiration in the words, just bafflement.

'So they say.' He had given talks about how with, say, a sniper, the man with the rifle was in control of the situation too many times for them to repeat it. With an IED, Riley had the upper hand. If he died, it was his fault, his mistake. You couldn't say that when a telescopic sight or a laser dot was trained on you. That was just bad luck. Being proactive, the one who decided your own fate – that was the important thing to Riley. 'But what really, really pisses me off is that they put my daughter at very real risk.' He let his rage bleed through a little. 'I'll have them for that,' he growled.

'*We'll* have them, Staff Sergeant. It's a team effort.' Blair lifted his cap with his right hand and ran the left over his shaven head. He let out a great sigh, as if he had sifted the evidence and come to a monumental decision.

'Of course, CTIU will want to hear all this again when they get here.'

'I'm aware of that.'

His debrief would be the next stage, alongside the collection of evidence by the forensics team from the VW and its immediate area. He was sure he would have told the story half-a-dozen times before that day was out. Counter Terrorism Intelligence Unit would just be the first in the queue. And they would, as was their wont, go back to his days in the womb, just to be certain he didn't make enemies while he was in there.

'And, Staff Sergeant Riley, once your CTIU interview has been completed, I think we should confine you to quarters.'

It took a moment for that to sink in. 'What? You have no authority over me.' He pointed at his chest. 'Army, remember.'

'I don't need reminding. But I expect CTIU will speak to your CO.'

'Will they fuck,' he said, fighting and failing to keep the indignity from his voice. Putting him in lock-down meant he would be off the investigation altogether and that he would be unable to see Ruby. Neither was acceptable. 'Why would you confine me to quarters?'

'For your own safety. And other people's. If a rogue bomber really is targeting you, we can't let you wander the streets, at risk of being blown to bits. And therefore of injuring innocent bystanders. Like your child. You need a ... what do you call it? A biff chit?'

A biff chit was a note excusing a soldier from a specific activity for a set period of time. Riley, who had never had a biff chit in his life, thumped the side of his leg with his fist.

'That's not an option. My job is to be out there dealing with IEDs.'

'And what if by being out there you are *causing* the bombs?'

Riley thought for a second then nodded, knowing argument was useless. He needed to take a different tack. 'Fair one. All right. I'll do whatever CTU recommends.' He pointed over his shoulder. 'Is anyone coming to put that out?'

Blair checked his watch. 'Fire brigade are about two minutes out.'

'Do you mind if I go and check on my family? My daughter nearly got caught up in that. She'll be very shaken.'

'They're still here?'

'Inside,' Riley lied.

Blair consulted his watch. 'Don't be too long. EOD and CTU will be here within ten.'

'Roger that.' Riley tabbed off purposefully, as if he really was going to find Izzy and Ruby.

Confined to barracks, my arse.

*

The aerial footage showed the scorched car, the savagely cropped and singed shrubbery next to it and the shallow crater that the blast had excavated in the car park surface. The Volkswagen now lay on its side, steaming like a champion racehorse in the paddock. Most of the retardant foam that had once covered it had collapsed, leaving what looked like patches of snow on the bodywork and exposed chassis. The camera pulled back to show the surroundings, including the apparently undamaged gates and the garish American car marooned on its rear tyres. The media was clustered at one end of the B-road that led to the school, some pressed against the barriers, others up step-ladders. The TV image switched to a police officer approaching the media scrum. The bomb-maker turned the sound up.

The policeman was in his early forties, bald, well turned out, wearing a crisp white shirt that looked fresh out of the box. He spoke with an accent the bomb-maker couldn't place. He was filmed from the waist up, standing at a length of Do Not Cross tape. The occasional outstretched microphone or mobile came into view as he read from a prepared statement, concluding: 'I am not going to speculate on any motive at this point. A full investigation is already underway, being carried out by local counter-terrorism officers with assistance from the Metropolitan

Police. At this stage I will only confirm what we know happened. An improvised explosive device has been detonated at a school in the Cotswolds. Counter Terrorism Units and bomb squads were instantly notified of the incident. Some elements of the bomb-disposal teams were already in the vicinity and secured the area. At the same time, officers from the regular force, accompanied by trained firearms officers, were sent to help with the clearing of the school grounds and houses in the immediate vicinity, which was, thanks to the co-operation of the public and the school staff, achieved smoothly. The grounds were then searched by qualified technicians and no other explosive devices were discovered. There were no casualties of any kind within the school or its grounds.'

He paused here, catching his breath as questions began from the unseen journalists, but raised his hand and his voice to silence them. 'I would like to stress two things. One, it is not helpful to speculate whether this incident is connected to any other recent events. The various agencies will establish that in due course. Secondly, if anyone has any information about today's events, they are urged to call the number now being shown on screen.'

'At this stage does the incident seem to be over?' asked a male voice off camera.

'As I said, I am not prepared to speculate. This area will remain sealed off for the foreseeable future while experts continue to sift for evidence. It is our priority to keep the public safe. Ladies and gentlemen, I am going to thank you very much for your time here and we will update you as and when fresh information is available.'

'Was this a terrorist event?' a woman shouted, but the policeman had already turned his back and was walking off.

Another voice, German-sounding, barked over the sudden

hubbub of scrupulously ignored queries. 'How could someone plant a bomb in broad daylight?'

The TV switched to the helicopter shots again. The bomb-maker turned the sound down once more. He leaned back on the sofa, snaked his arm around the lad and pulled him close. He kissed the top of his head, inhaled the scent of the shampoo he had used on his son's hair that morning. The bomb-maker nodded at the screen and said with some pride: 'We did that.'

'Dead. Goner.'

'No, not dead. Not this time. But soon, my son. Very soon.'

TWENTY-TWO

Kate Muraski had decided she would meet Jamal after all. Always good to keep him sweet. He could be a very useful contact. Plus, she wanted to see if the fact that she had persuaded Jimmy Fu and his team to come on board by taking a look at the Clifford-Browns would impress him.

She chose *Ognisko Polskie*, the Polish Hearth Club, on Exhibition Road in South Kensington for the meet. She sat in the elegant, high-ceilinged dining room which had recently been repainted in crisp white – the rather stern portraits of old soldiers who had founded the club now exiled to the bar – and ordered a plate of blinis and a vodka. She was starving, having failed to eat anything other than a packet of Quavers all day. She'd wait and see if Jamal would eat before ordering properly but she also wanted to get a hit of vodka before he got all finger-waggy or lip-pursey.

She eyed the menu with a little dismay. Quite a lot of pork was on there in one form or another, which Jamal wouldn't like. She hadn't thought this through. Ah well, he was a nice enough guy not to kick up a fuss.

She looked at her phone. Nothing from Riley. It was beginning to piss her off. She sent a text to him, stressing it was urgent.

'Aren't you overdoing the Polish schtick, coming here?' said Jamal as he sat down opposite. He had filled out since university days, with cherubic cheeks poking out over a rather magnificent black beard. His eyes twinkled as he added: 'You've only visited the country once.'

'Twice,' she said. 'And this place has several things going for it, apart from the food, which is delicious. One, they put the tables a decent distance apart. Two, there's fabric in the room, so it doesn't echo like St Paul's bloody Cathedral and you can hear yourself speak, and three, there are no hipsters this far west. Nobody tries to give you small sharing plates.'

'Fair enough.'

'Drink?'

'Coke.' He glanced at his watch. 'I'm sorry, but I won't be able to stay long. I'm on till ten tonight.'

'This was your idea.'

'That was before there was a car bomb in the Cotswolds. More bags of shit arriving for analysis as we speak.'

'What kind of bomb?' she asked.

'Not sure yet.'

'Any link to Nottingham?'

Jamal shook his head. 'Early days. I'll know more tonight, maybe.'

'And you'll call me?'

'I wouldn't dare not.'

'I'm not an ogre, Jamal.'

'Not yet.'

Before she could answer, her smoked salmon blinis and vodka turned up and, after she had ordered the Coke, she necked the clear liquid in one and pushed the plate of buckwheat pancakes towards Jamal. 'Just a starter snack. This is on me. And try the goose leg or the chicken livers. Best in the city.'

'Isn't that a line from *The Godfather*?'

'Never seen it,' she said. Before he could translate the surprise on his face to words, she moved on to the meat of the meeting. She outlined her recent call with Barbara Clifford-Brown and the subsequent dressing-down from Oakham. She kept her big revelation back, however, for the time being.

'Oh dear,' he said. 'That'll be brought up at your assessment.'

'Bollocks to assessments. They play favourites no matter what your assessment says. You know when I handed my stuff over to Deepika, she had a Russian-language page open on her computer. She doesn't even speak Russian.'

'Maybe she's learning.'

'My thoughts exactly. I'll fuckin' kill her if she goes over before me.'

Jamal put the menu down. 'Can I give you a word of advice?'

'As long as you don't quote the Koran at me.'

'Have another vodka. It suits you.'

She flinched at the rebuke. 'Sorry.' She ran a hand through her hair. It didn't feel any cleaner than the last time she did it. She needed a shower. 'Just a little stressed.'

'I think you're trying too hard. Rather than enjoying the job in hand, you're always looking one step ahead. You also arrived at the office with a sense of entitlement.'

'How do you mean?'

Jamal put on a spoilt, whiny voice. 'My mummy was a spy, I speak Russian, why can't I be Head of Station?'

Muraski was taken aback. 'How do you know my mother was a spy?' she hissed.

'You told me at that conference on data handling. At the bar.'

'I don't think so,' she said, less than convincingly.

'You did. I'm saying that gives you a sense of entitlement, as if it's a family right that you'll move up the ranks.'

'Like I sit back and wait for the fast-track promotion train to stop outside the office because of my *mum*?'

'I'm not saying you don't put the effort in. Look, working for your lot is like a cross between *Spooks* and Marks & Spencer.' Before she could ask how, he went on: 'You have all the Defence of the Realm stuff, even if most of it is dull, dull, dull, but you also have management bollocks all over the place. Assessments, targets, strategic staircases, blue-sky thinking. Personal Development Plans. You have those?' She nodded. 'Yes, us too. Utter crap. But you have to play the game. Or give them a good reason why you shouldn't conform and just wait your turn.'

Sensing an opening, she jumped in. 'Which brings me to—'

'Can I order first?' Jamal said quickly. 'Like I said, I haven't got much time.'

Muraski chose the chicken livers, Jamal the beef, and she resisted the urge to drink more alcohol, opting for sparkling water.

'You know on the way here, someone shouted, "Go home, Paki." Haven't had that for a while.' It was said with an undertone of sadness rather than the anger she expected.

Muraski felt a surge of fury on his behalf. 'Fuck's sake. What did you do?'

'I said I don't get off till ten, then I've got to get the District Line, so it'd be a while before I'm home.'

She gave a small laugh. Then, 'I hear there's been some defacing of mosques in Bristol and Luton.'

'And Newham and Whitechapel. Par for the course in the aftermath of any terrorist incident.'

She saw her opening and jumped in feet first.

'Right. And in the aftermath of a terrorist atrocity, your lot can order up a TAP, can't you?' A Threat Assessment Protocol meant that the harsh glare of full surveillance was turned on an individual or group of individuals who may or may not have been involved in an attack.

'And you could go through the proper channels at Thames House.'

'But if you do that, everything just gets swallowed by the machine. If it is a solid lead it gets kicked upstairs. Nobody ever remembers where it came from originally. They take it off you, every time, with a little pat on the head.'

Jamal gave his head a little shake. 'Tell me, what's more important, catching the bombers or Kate Muraski's career?'

'. . . I'll get back to you on that.'

'Oh, for crying out loud. When? Before or after I've lost my job?'

'You aren't going to lose your job. You're using your initiative.'

Jamal was quiet for a moment, then said, 'What do you want?'

She held up her phone. 'This guy Riley is avoiding me.'

'He might be busy. Bombs'n'shit. Maybe they've sent him to the Cotswolds incident.'

'I'm Five. Nobody's supposed to be too busy to talk to us.'

'Yeah, right. Entitlement, remember?'

She laughed at that. 'Anyway, I want you to put a TAP on our man Staff Sergeant Dom Riley.'

'Just because he won't return your calls?'

She pushed a piece of paper over to him. It was a print-out of the details he had sent her about Riley. 'Look at that.'

'What am I looking at?'

'Next of kin.'

'Wow.' Jamal puffed out his substantial cheeks even further. 'You know, I really could do with a drink right now.'

TWENTY-THREE

Strictly speaking, Riley hadn't gone AWOL. He hadn't disobeyed an order from a superior officer, as Blair had no authority over him. And it hadn't been an order, but a prediction. True, he had left the scene of a crime, but then, he felt like it was his crime scene to leave.

He was driving north in a Citroen Nemo van that actually belonged to the school. Andy the Tank had turned over the keys without hesitation. Riley promised he would say he helped himself and also said he would let Andy know where to pick it up. He had then driven out through the deliveries entrance, just in time to avoid the EOD truck. He would waste hours entangled in red tape if he stayed. Meanwhile, those fucking bastards who had wired his VW to blow would be plotting some other little wheeze.

No, he had a lead, thanks to the strangely coloured wire he had retrieved from Nottingham, and he was going to follow it.

His first call was to Ruby. He knew the enormity of what had happened – or nearly happened – at the school would hit her hard, once it had time to sink in. The number was busy. He considered phoning Izzy, but thought he would wait on that one. He wasn't sure how she would react once she realised that he had put their daughter in danger. He wasn't in the mood for a shouting match. He phoned Scooby instead.

'Christ, Dom, don't you feel like the Typhoid Mary of explosions?' he asked when Riley had given him edited highlights of the day so far.

'How is Ruby?'

'Not sure. She's my next call.'

'She'll have nightmares, you know.'

Riley was aware that Scooby had suffered from night terrors for months after the explosion that took his eye. He wanted to get him off the subject of Ruby for the moment. Riley didn't want to dwell on the mental fallout of the bomb just yet. 'So will I. And I'm fine, thanks for asking, Scoob.'

'Yeah. That was my next question. How can I help?'

'I think I've been dicked.'

'Been or being?'

'I don't know.' He glanced in the rear-view mirror. 'Nothing untoward that I can see. I didn't notice anything when I drove to Ruby's school. But they located me somehow.' A sudden chill of anxiety about the near-miss made him shudder once more. 'I was lucky, Scoob. *We* were lucky.'

'Well, you always were a lucky cunt,' interrupted Scooby. 'I repeat: what can I do to help?'

'I want to hire you.'

He put on another of his voices. 'You can't afford me.'

Jack Nicholson, *A Few Good Men*, at a guess. 'Don't you do interest-free?'

Scooby laughed. 'I do easy terms. Tell me what you need. You can have the F&F discount. Friends and fuck-ups.'

'Which am I?'

'Both. One thing I'm wondering. Are you being targeted because you're you or just because you're an ATO?'

'Scooby, you read my fuckin' mind, pal. I've been wondering

that myself.' Although 'wondering' was an understatement. The idea that this might be a vendetta against him – and possibly his family – had been barging other thoughts aside for some time now.

'And what have you decided?'

'I think some fucker is after me.'

*

Even as she made the tea, Barbara Clifford-Brown was thinking of the martinis she would create within the hour. It started as something of a ritual, beginning on Saturday nights, but it slowly spread across the calendar, elbowing out the weekday gin and tonics like some invasive species. It began when she stumbled across the classic martini glasses that their daughter Rachel had given them for Christmas, back when she still did such things as gifts. And Christmas.

She had discovered the glasses six months previously and had found the martini recipe that came with them. At first, she wasn't impressed, but their old friend Ben Beaumont had recommended the 'duke's method' as he called it. This entailed keeping a bottle of vodka and a bottle of gin, along with the glasses, in the freezer, for a sustained icy kick. She hadn't asked which particular duke had introduced this innovation but, like the Earl of Sandwich, they owed him a vote of thanks.

She carried the tray of Earl Grey plus some shortbread biscuits through to the drawing room, where Henry sat in one of the high-backed padded damask chairs that she had inherited from her parents. In fact, every item in the room, from the fussy carriage clock on the marble fireplace to the enormous Georgian bow-fronted sideboard and the silverware inside it, had come down through one side of the family or the other. Everything except the 4K TV, although even that sat on an Epstein art deco coffee table from the 1930s. It saddened her to think the whole lot would probably go to auction to pay for Rachel's care when they were both gone.

She set the tray on the table next to him and he looked up over his glasses. 'Thank you, sweetie. Can you fetch me a new nicotine patch?'

'Fancying a pipe again?'

'I always do when I'm concentrating.' He had on his lap a large yellow pad, the page covered with his still-neat, tiny writing. He was revising and censoring his memoirs. They had originally been intended for publication, but the very mention had brought a civil servant from the Foreign Office out of the woodwork. As oily as Sir Humphrey off that old television comedy about politics, he had taken Henry out to lunch and, without saying as much, left Henry with the distinct impression that their pensions would be under threat if he went ahead. A highly bowdlerised version would be allowed, subject to the usual vetting, for family and close friends only. And it must stop at 1989, the year the Wall came down.

Henry agreed to these terms, carried on for Rachel's sake, and continued even when her Korsakoff's dementia set in. Barbara's theory was that the psychosis was a violent reaction to the knowledge that she was slowly losing her mind. Why the symptoms should have begun in her mid-fifties, when they, her parents, both still had their marbles, the doctors had no idea. Henry thought it was the drugs she had taken well into her forties. Barbara wasn't so sure. She just hoped Rachel's son wouldn't inherit the trait.

'I'll fetch a patch in a moment,' Barbara said as she poured the tea. She hadn't yet told Henry that the private clinic-cum-home had announced that its fees would be going up by 10 per cent. There were very few institutions that dealt with Korsakoff's patients, so they had them over a financial barrel. She had to admit to herself that she had been eyeing up the provenance of the furniture out of more than mere nostalgia. Sadly, daytime and early-evening television shows suggested the market for their kind of antiques was rather depressed.

'What was the name of the girl in Berlin?' Henry suddenly asked.

She passed him his tea in a cup and saucer from the second-best china. Alfred Meakin. Was fine bone china worth anything in these days of mugs with funny slogans on the side? Possibly not.

'Which girl?'

'The one who ran the brothels. Delius.' This was an operation to entrap Russian officers through pillow talk.

'Christina?'

'Christina! Yes, thank you, darling.'

The mention of Delius prompted her to put on some music. Something low and soft so as not to disturb Henry. Debussy, perhaps. They had a gramophone – a stereogram as her father had called it – with a Thorens deck hidden in a mock-antique cabinet that he had bought from Heal's sometime in the 1960s. It still worked fine, although when she cared about such things Rachel would mock them for not adapting to the CD age. Now she had heard on Radio 4 that long-playing records were fashionable again. What goes around, as they used to say.

She had just laid aside her cup and saucer and risen from her chair when she heard the weighty thud of the door knocker. The two old spies looked at each other and then at the mantelpiece clock. Barbara sighed.

'If it is that young woman from Thames House again, I swear I'll shoot her in the face.'

*

'You at the hotel yet?' Riley asked Ruby when he finally got through to her.

'Yes. Mum's just checking in. There's a spa.'

'I know. Try and get her out of there every now and then.'

'Can I get a pedicure?'

'Of course. You feeling all right? After this afternoon?'

The brightness in her voice faded a little and a more sombre tone crept in. 'I think so. I was a bit shaky on the way over. That's gone. What about you?'

'Nothing a pedicure won't sort.'

'Oh, Dad. I've seen your feet. You need major surgery, not a pedicure.'

It was good to hear the brilliance return.

'Where are you?' she asked.

'Almost at my barracks. About half an hour to run.' And still driving with one wary eye on the rear-view mirror, he neglected to add. 'I've been calling you for the best part of an hour.'

'I had to check everyone was okay. My friends from school, I mean.'

And no doubt tell her story of the near-miss. He couldn't blame her. He had told enough war stories in his time. 'I think they should be calling you.'

'Some of them did. To check up on me.'

'Good. And are you okay?'

'I think you've asked me that.'

'You know I love you.'

'Of course.'

'I'm so sorry you got caught up in it.'

'Do you know who put it there yet?' Ruby asked. 'The bomb?'

'Stop it.'

'Stop what?'

'Being so bloody calm,' he said. 'You're allowed to shout and scream and call me names.'

'Would it help?'

Riley laughed at that. 'Probably not. But this is my job, Ruby. I'm used to it. If you have any trouble, any strange feelings or worries, bad dreams, whatever, you tell Mum. It's nothing to be ashamed of. And no, we don't know who did it yet. But we'll find out.'

'And then?'

Good question, he thought. A very good question.

*

It wasn't that nuisance woman from Thames House at the door, but Hector the Handler as they called him. Hector DeMontfort Clarke was their liaison for the data gleaned from the monitoring equipment in the cellar and also their de facto case officer. Like every CO, part of his job was keeping his assets happy.

Hector was a most unlikely spy. He was short, about five-five she estimated, had a cherubic face topped with a mop of curls that he never left alone, seemed unable to sit still for more than five minutes and dressed in a lot of corduroy.

'Henry, it's Hector. A delightful surprise visit.' The stress on the third word of the last sentence was almost subliminal. But not quite.

'I would have called ahead, but it seemed important to get here before evening turned to night. Apologies.'

'We're just having tea. Would you care for a cup? Or a martini perhaps?'

'Good lord, no, I'm driving. Tea would be fine.'

'Earl Grey?'

'Perfect.'

When she returned with the tea, Henry and Hector were still catching up with VX gossip.

'You know that Jim Boodle has retired?' said Hector.

Henry nodded. One of the last of his contemporaries still on the SIS payroll.

'Where's he gone?'

'Bermuda, I believe.'

'Really?' laughed Henry. 'I can't see him in those shorts.'

'I don't think they're compulsory, Henry. His wife is Bermudian, if that's what you say.'

'Really? I never knew.'

Barbara gave a loud sniff as she lowered the tray holding a fresh pot onto an occasional table. 'Made a pass at me once, Jim Boodle.'

'Did he?' asked Henry, alarmed. 'When was this?'

'Some drunken party. Helsinki, I think. Tongue down mouth, hand up top.' She turned to Hector. 'Do you think I should make an official complaint?'

Hector's jaw worked up and down, but no words came. Eventually a squeak emerged.

Barbara laughed. 'Only joshing, Hector. It was a different time. Different standards. I bit his tongue and told him to fuck off.'

'You didn't mention this to me,' said Henry.

'If I told you every proposition I received back then, you wouldn't be on speaking terms with half the office. You forget, Henry, we were all viewed as fair game back then.'

'Especially the pretty ones, sweetie.'

Hector quickly raised the cup of tea, as if embarrassed by their intimacy.

Barbara thought she had made him uncomfortable enough to proceed. 'You are here about the girl. Miss Muraski?'

'Well, here to apologise that you were bothered by her.'

'It was no bother,' said Henry. 'Just surprising. I mean, that was all a long time ago. She showed me photographs . . .'

'I know,' said Hector, putting a hand through his already tousled hair. 'And we have told our friends at Thames House that they had no business—'

'I suspect the fault lies closer to home,' said Barbara sternly. 'Those photographs were in files in VX archives, were they not?'

'Yes. And before you ask, she did access them legitimately.'

'Sometimes,' said Henry, 'I think this transparency and cooperation between the services has gone too far.'

'I think we preferred the days of opaqueness and not-so-friendly rivalry,' added Barbara as she sipped her tea. 'Hot enough for you?' she asked Hector. 'The tea?'

'Yes, lovely, thank you.' He took a quick gulp and smiled.

'What do you propose we do?' asked Henry.

'The files are being purged of the evidence she had located. She has handed over her files to another Five junior officer. Those, too, will disappear . . .'

'Is he really in the country?' asked Henry. 'Is Yousaf Ali here?'

'We don't know.'

'More to the point,' Henry went on, 'was he behind the Nottingham atrocity?'

'We doubt that. Our friends in Thames House doubt that. It's likely a coincidence.'

'We don't like coincidences,' sniffed Barbara.

'That doesn't mean they don't happen,' retorted Hector, the steel she had always suspected lay somewhere within that diminutive frame suddenly showing. 'I have one important question. Does anyone know his real identity?'

'We do,' said Henry.

'Apart from you. Did this Miss Muraski mention anything that might lead you to believe she knew who Yousaf Ali really was?'

Barbara and Henry exchanged glances. 'No,' said Henry, firmly. 'I denied recognising him. Felt like the safer option.'

'Good.' He seemed relieved. 'And the name of the operation?'

Hector had the old Service superstition that even knowing the name of an operation was a massive breach of security. Especially when it didn't take an ease with *The Times* crossword to figure out what the operation involved.

'No,' said Henry. 'She didn't mention it by name. I assumed it was redacted.'

'Well let's hope so.'

Barbara examined him for a second before she spoke again. 'And if we said "yes"? What then?'

'I'm sorry?' Hector asked, baffled by her sudden change of direction.

'If we had said "yes" and told the pretty Miss Muraski we did know who Yousaf Ali really was. What then?'

Hector gave an elaborate above-my-pay-grade shrug. 'Ah. Those sorts of decisions . . .'

'Are you here to kill us, Hector?' Barbara asked.

Henry looked at his wife with benign interest, as if she had asked Hector if he wanted a top-up.

'Good grief, what gave you that idea?'

'You might be doing some house clearing? Do you still call it that?'

Hector began to laugh so hard he slopped the remainder of the tea into the saucer. 'You think I'm some sort of . . . hit man?'

'Nothing so melodramatic, Hector. But we could be considered loose ends,' said Barbara.

'You've kept this secret for . . . decades. You are consummate

professionals. Why should VX think you'd break cover now?'
Hector put down the cup and saucer on the side table. 'Let me
assure you, Barbara and Henry, you are in no danger whatsoever
from me or any of my colleagues.'

'Oh, that's a pity,' said Barbara.

'What do you mean?' asked Hector, confusion written
across his face.

'Well, I wouldn't have bothered drugging your tea if I'd
known that.'

TWENTY-FOUR

The bomb-maker had to leave the boy alone. This next task was not something that could be carried out in the house. He needed plenty of space. Luckily, he had performed most of the preliminary work already. All he had to do was check the systems were operational, that once circuit one fired, it also initiated the back-up circuit and a second set of explosives. A double bang.

He placed the boy on the sofa, propped up so he could see the television. He laid a blanket over his legs and tucked it under him. On a tray next to him he laid out a drinking cup full of orange juice and a paper plate of brides' fingers and *payra* fudge. He loved sweet things. It was probably not healthy, especially as it was hard to get him to brush his teeth. They were showing signs of black decay. Perhaps, once this was all over, he should get him to a dentist. The bomb-maker chuckled to himself. He doubted they had – or needed – dentists in Paradise.

He put a DVD into the player and turned it on. He could hear Benesh, his late wife, scolding him. *The boy watches too much television.* Yes, my love, but there are so few pleasures left to him. Look. Look at his face.

The lad's eyes widened as he recognised the opening credits of *Mr Bean*. The annoying programme was one of his favourites, along with *Pingu* the penguin, which was in a nonsense language, and *Tom & Jerry* dubbed into Pashto. 'Bean!' he shouted and wriggled with pleasure. The only other thing he liked to watch was football, especially if Liverpool was playing, but there seemed to be precious little of that on television, unless one paid a small fortune or went to a pub, which they would never do. He could not understand how a nation crazy about soccer could allow this to happen, that only the rich could enjoy the game created by the people. But he had long given up trying to understand the British and their ungodly ways. He had no real idea why they had come to his country and sacrificed their young men so readily. For what?

'Yes, Mr Bean,' he said. 'I'm going out for some time. I won't be long, I promise.'

The lad looked panicked. 'Out.'

He knelt down and spoke to the boy, cupping his face in his hands. 'Yes, I am going out now. I shall be no longer than one hour or two. You will be fine. I will lock the door. Do not answer the bell, eh? I know you won't. Watch TV, eat, and, as I said, I'll be back very soon.'

The boy said something. He took a guess at what he had asked.

'Where am I going? To work. They call it the Munroe Effect. The British and Americans, I mean. We call it the *Kiss of Allah*. I am going to build a wonderful *Kiss of Allah*.'

'Allah,' the boy said warmly, as if he knew very well that he would be seeing him soon. The bomb-maker thought of number 56 from the sacred text.

AL-WAQI'AH: THAT WHICH IS COMING.

And those on the right hand; what of those on the right hand?
Among thornless lote-trees
And clustered plantains,
And spreading shade,
And water gushing,
And fruit in plenty
Neither out of reach nor yet forbidden,
And raised couches;
Lo! We have created them a (new) creation
And made them virgins,
Lovers, friends,

For those on the right hand.

This, he was certain, was what awaited him and his son, God willing.

And those on the left hand: What of those on the left hand?
In scorching wind and scalding water
And shadow of black smoke,
Neither cool nor refreshing.
And thereon ye will drink of boiling water,
Drinking even as the camel drinketh.
This will be their welcome on the Day of Judgment.
We mete out death among you, and We are not to be outrun.

He buttoned up a thick coat over his *khet* and left the house to deal with some of those on the left hand, those accomplices who had nothing but boiling water and scorching winds to look forward to during the endless days to come. Those like Dominic Riley.

*

Riley was well aware that he couldn't waste much time if he was to avoid being locked down. He had to get off base, in case what Blair had suggested was actioned and the police and his CO decided that he was at too much risk to be allowed out. *Confined to quarters?* That was hardly his style. In Afghan a special kind of contempt was reserved for those who never left the relative comfort and safety of Camp Bastion or the Forward Operating Bases. They had a very different war from the soldiers who went out on patrol every day from the FOBs, to see and be seen, even though they knew they were putting their arms, legs, knackers and life on the line.

No, just like in Afghan he was going out there into the wider world to find out what the fuck was going on. And if that exposed him to danger, so be it. He was used to it.

They could have killed Ruby.

I know that. I fucking know that!

Steady, pal.

The problem was, the moment he thought on what could have happened to his daughter, all logic and reason went out of the window. He wanted to punch someone or something. To grab throats, knock heads, kick shins. To scream at the top of his lungs. It didn't help. He had to try and find an inner stillness for the moment. He focused on the task in hand.

In his spartan room, Riley laid out everything on the bed. He needed one change of clothes. Pack light for this one. Very light – he was going to feel naked without a weapon but trying to extract one from the armoury was beyond his skills. Alarm bells would ring if he so much as attempted it. Even a little target practice was supervised these days. He wished he had done what several others in his unit had and brought a 'souvenir' back from Afghan. But it was done now.

He looked at the two phones lying next to each other. The work one would be able to track him as a matter of routine. So that had to go. He took the battery out and then, after a moment's reflection, put it back. Just in case someone was checking up on him at that moment. A blip going off screen might cause someone to take an interest in him. Of course, he could just be being paranoid. Probably was. But being suspicious and paranoid had kept him alive when he was dealing with IEDs out in Afghan. And someone had placed a bomb under his car. He hadn't imagined that. So he clipped the battery cover back on and placed the phone on the bed, where it would remain.

He had checked his messages on the other mobile – Kate Muraski had called that too and was still very keen to talk to him, but there was no way he was getting involved with her lot just yet. He doubted very much that MI5 would approve of what he had in mind. He took the SIM out of the personal one and made sure it was turned off. The battery was sealed in that one. The only way to get at it was to crack the case open. He would take this one with him, although he hoped he wouldn't have to use it again.

He sat down at his desk and used his laptop to make a money transfer to a corporal on base. He was now the proud owner of a Yamaha YBR125. He didn't want to risk the school's Citroen that Andy the Tank had loaned him. They would be on to that by now, the licence plate logged into computers with vehicle recognition technology.

He could have signed out a pool car, but they were all fitted with trackers too. The Yamaha was hardly the bike he would have chosen – one of the big Honda STs or a Triumph would be his preferred option, given that he had mainly A-road and motorway riding ahead of him – but it was the only one for sale on the barracks' notice board that he could take immediately. That sealed the deal. Plus, the corporal had thrown in a helmet. So, he was good to go.

Riley had five hundred pounds in cash hidden behind the mirror which he extracted and threw in the bag. He stripped, showered and then carefully selected which clothes he would put on. T-shirt, shirt, dark chinos, Converse leather hi-tops, Carhartt jacket. Like the Yamaha, nothing to stand out. He put underwear, socks and similarly dark clothes in the black zip-up holdall he was using.

He picked up his wallet, went through the cards, discarding most of them. He went through his unopened mail and found the one that had arrived a week previously. It was a credit card that had yet to be activated. If someone was tagging him through money withdrawals or card spends, it would take a while before a newly activated card showed up on any watcher's radar. Or so he had heard. He went through the rest, mostly junk mail, until he had located the envelope with the activation code inside and pocketed it.

When he was sure he was ready, he grabbed the bag and left the room, leaving a side lamp on just in case anyone should come to watch his digs from outside. He had one more port of call before he could collect the bike keys and hit the road. Just a little dodging of CCTVs on base. Nothing too challenging. Then he would be away and on his own. Just as an ATO should be.

TWENTY-FIVE

Following the events in Nottingham there had been incidents – ranging from yelled abuse, through to graffiti, up to bricks being thrown – at almost a third of Leicester's seventy-three mosques and half of its twenty-eight Muslim community and cultural centres. It was hardly surprising, therefore, thought Eric Coates as he drove by in the anonymous van, that there were two armed policemen bracketing the doorway of the Islamic Community Centre on Cutler Street. Two was one more than most had. There simply weren't enough weapons-trained officers to cover every place of worship and gathering. Not with synagogues being targeted too. Cutler Street got the brace of firearms officers because there was a community meeting, attended by the deputy mayor and the police commissioner, going on in the building. Its aim was to discuss the threat of anti-Islamic sentiments in this part of the city and tactics for defusing the situation. With people milling outside unable to get in, it appeared to be well attended, even though it was called late in the day. Which was good, Coates thought. Bit of civic pride, misplaced though it was.

Coates took the Transit van past the entrance to the centre at a steady speed, gaining hardly a glance from either of the officers with their Heckler & Kochs. He drove around the block – reaching out to catch the crash helmet on the passenger seat that nearly rolled into the footwell as he took one of the corners – and, as he had been instructed, parked up in the bay marked 'Loading Only'.

From there he could see the car wash that backed on to the Islamic Centre. The main building of the drive-through was cocooned behind heavy roller shutters, but the U-shaped court-yard around it was free of any gates or barriers. You could drive to the rear of the car wash and be out of sight.

Coates waited five minutes and was rewarded with a glimpse of one of the armed officers strolling around the back of the Islamic Centre. They did this every half-hour or so. Otherwise they relied on monitored CCTV located high on the rear wall of the community centre. The cameras he had been assured were no longer functioning due to petty vandalism. Recent, deliberate petty vandalism.

He had to admire this new team. He had been part of many radical outfits over the years – the English Defence League, British Action Group and England Waffen. This lot, the Real Albion Front, were better organised and better funded than any of the others. No stupid rallies, no drunken brawls, no cult of personal-ity as with Tommy Robinson and the like. Just genuine strategy and clear goals. The main one being simple and biblical: an eye for an eye.

Coates thought of his father, now in his eighties. He mainly talked about the days when you didn't see a brown face in Leicester. And how when Idi Amin kicked out the Asians, the city council took out ads telling the immigrants to stay away. Leicester didn't want them. Still they came. And now? He'd read that British whites made up 43 per cent of the population. Less than half. They were outnumbered, a minority in their own country. It was the same in Luton. And Slough. Of course, not all the other 57 per cent were Asians. There were the Poles, Bulgarians, Romanians, Albanians. But that lot didn't set off bombs in Nottingham. And the RAF would deal with them later. In the meantime, he was going to gouge out an eye in retaliation for the Sillitoe Circus bomb.

When Coates was sure the policeman had turned the corner, he started the engine again and crawled onto the forecourt of the car wash in second gear and then, foot light on the accelerator, took the van around to the rear. There was a wooden fence, topped with razor wire, separating the community centre and the car wash. He had been told a splash of yellow paint on one of the wooden staves would mark the spot where he was to park the Transit, nearside headlamp level with the mark.

He eased it into position, overshot, hit reverse, backed up six inches, and killed the engine. As it ticked and cooled he let out a relieved sigh. That was probably the worst part over. For him, at least. The evening was going to get a lot hairier for plenty of other people. And they deserved it. The people who had killed and maimed with impunity – or implicitly supported those who did – would now get a taste of their own medicine. He glanced over his shoulder at the wooden partition that separated him from the cargo compartment of the van. He had been briefed on what was in there.

The Munroe Effect, it was called. It was a way of turning a sheet of metal into a projectile. A hollow created in a lump of explosive which was then lined with metal had the effect of channelling the resulting blast in one direction. Hence the term 'shaped charge'. It had been developed in Iraq to penetrate the armour of the US Army's Hummers, where they were used to punch a hole into the side and release a stream of molten metal into the interior of a vehicle, cooking those inside.

It had been refined into something even more brutal, the device known as an Explosively Formed Projectile, EFP, aka the *Kiss of Allah*. The explosion would deform and fold a metal plate – usually, but not always, copper – into a crude rocket projectile or slug, travelling fast enough to pierce the best protective armour. Once inside a personnel carrier, the red-hot metal would ricochet around the interior, causing massive injury and death.

All this had been carefully explained to him by the RAF people. And that now it was not a kiss from Allah but a smacker from the white man's deity. *Jesus's Love Bite,* he chuckled to himself. Now all he had to do was arm the device and get out of there. He had a ten-minute window once he pushed the red button taped to the console. Part of the wooden fence had been cut through, the cuts hidden with sawdust and glue, and would offer no resistance to the lethal round that would be fired from the rear of the van. Of course, the van walls would have offered serious obstruction, which is why, just before the device deployed, the sliding door would automatically roll back, giving the shaped charge an easy passage to its target.

Coates's finger hovered over the button, but he snatched it away when he heard the sound of a motorbike. He looked through his side window, watching the black-clad figure stop the bike just next to one of the metal shutters of the car wash. The rider raised a fist. This was his getaway. He touched the crash helmet on the passenger seat. He showed the palm of his hand in a return greeting and turned his attention back to the button.

He felt a sudden squirming sensation in his stomach. He had never done anything like this before. Coates was forty-five and had spent thirty of those years mouthing slogans about Pakis and ragheads. About deportation and white jihad. He had spent several weeks talking about this night with the RAF, but only now was the reality hitting him. They had warned him it might happen. They had instructed him on what to do, should his resolve waver.

Think of Nottingham. London Bridge. Manchester. Houses of Parliament. Madrid. Paris. Nice. Strasbourg. Think of those gangs of men grooming and raping our children in places like Rotherham and Bradford. Think: revenge.

Eric Coates waited until the familiar white-hot anger set his insides aflame again and he pushed the button. Immediately he heard the whine of an electric motor. The door was sliding open already. Yet he was told he had ten minutes to get clear. Malfunction. Someone might see the device and evacuate the building.

He looked with some alarm at the motorcyclist. But the rider had turned the bike to leave. As he reached for the door handle the automatic lock deployed and the catches went down with a snick like a rifle bolt.

'Hey! Wait!' Coates yelled, panic making his heart judder in his chest. He banged the glass with his fist. 'Stop! Come back! *Cunt!*'

The realisation dawned that they were going to put him in the frame for this. They were going to leave him trapped in a van that had just been part of a terrorist attack on an Islamic target. A patsy. He leaned back and brought his elbow against the window with all the force he could muster, succeeding only in nearly dislocating it.

Coates screamed in pain, grabbed the crash helmet and began hammering at the windscreen with it, watching the world before him crack and star. That vision blurred as the *Kiss of Allah* deployed, far sooner than he had been told, destroying most of the rear compartment and buckling panels as it did so, causing the van to tip onto two wheels. His head whiplashed and smashed into the side glass, knocking him unconscious. Which was a blessing from whichever god was watching over him.

The sheet metal that had been placed in front of the shaped charge deformed exactly as predicted, burst through the wooden fence without a backward glance and punched a hole through the bricks of the cultural centre's rear wall, showering those inside with sharp-edged flints of flying masonry. With the apparent accuracy of a top ten-pin bowler – actually more by luck than any judgement – it neatly decapitated the speaker at the lectern and continued on into the audience, fracturing skulls, cheeks and jaws, singeing hair and blistering skin and killing one further person before it thudded into a tiled section of the far wall and came to rest, leaving an acrid cloud of dust and smoke and the wails and screams of the injured in its wake.

Meanwhile, in the van, the deployment of the device had scorched, blackened and twisted the inside of the vehicle and ignited the petrol tank, turning the cab into an inferno that consumed Eric Coates within seconds.

TWENTY-SIX

Barbara Clifford-Brown took the two martini glasses and the alcohol out of the freezer. She uncapped the ice-cold vermouth and poured a few millimetres in each of the glasses. Then she swirled the liquid with a practised hand until it coated the inside of the cone. Any excess she tipped down the sink. Now she poured in the viscous gin nearly to the rim. Henry liked an olive, but she preferred a twist of lemon peel. Once those small details had been taken care of, she smeared the rims with lemon and placed the glasses on the tray, added a small bowl of mixed nuts, and went through to the drawing room.

Henry was sitting in front of the TV, feet on a small stool. The sound was down. He was waiting for the news to start. She placed the tray on the side table, lifted her martini and sat in the second armchair.

'You are wicked, you know, sweetie.'

'It's just the one,' she said.

'You know I don't mean about the martini. Poor Hector. I thought he was going to spit the Earl Grey all over the carpet when you told him it was drugged.' He chortled at the memory, shoulders shaking. 'Even I believed you for a moment.'

'Well, I just wanted to warn him he wasn't dealing with some senile old fools. That we still have claws.'

'I am sure he appreciates that, my love. Especially you. Still the wildcat.' He lifted his own glass. 'Cheers.'

'Cheers.' She sipped, relishing the icy hit of alcohol. *This must be what the rush of cocaine is like*, she thought. She had never tried it. She had succumbed to an invitation to sample opium in the Far East once, but it had made her sick as a dog. No, a martini was as about as racy as she expected to get in her dotage. She had friends who had been forced to give up drinking for various medical reasons. She pitied them. She wanted to sail into the sunset of life with a stiff drink in her hand. A stiff something else would be nice, too, she joked silently to herself, although Henry was little help in that department these days.

'I hate it when history comes back to bite you,' said Henry solemnly.

'My advice is to bite back. You did nothing wrong. We did nothing wrong. It's not your fault. These days people are all too willing—'

She realised Henry wasn't listening. He was fumbling with the TV remote. He managed to accidentally change channels before he got the news back on and increased the volume.

They watched in silence as the screen showed images of the ruined wreckage of a van, and the shattered wall of a community centre. A reporter, standing in the forecourt of a car wash, gave a summary of what had happened. A rocket attack of some description on an Islamic Centre. Two confirmed dead. Many casualties. Some seriously injured. No responsibility claimed. But local religious leaders say it is an attack on all Muslims. Condemnation from the PM.

'This is how it starts,' said Henry, his face hangdog.

'What does?'

'Civil war.'

Barbara gave a chuckle that had little mirth in it. 'Sweetie—'

'I know. It sounds melodramatic. But we have had civil war in this country before.'

'In the seventeenth century.'

'In the twentieth. Northern Ireland. A civil war in all but name. If the Muslims retaliate and then the far-right do the same . . .'

'A cycle of violence begins,' she said, now serious. 'I'm sure they are on it. I hope Five has better people than that Muraski girl.'

'I'm certain. She was an office junior, darling. Cobb is a decent cove.' Cobb was DAT, Director of Anti-Terrorism, at MI5. 'And the Met have some decent chaps.'

'And women,' prompted Barbara. 'There's that Olsen woman. Seems quite competent.'

'Oh, yes. Still, I fear the worst. I'm glad we won't be around to see what this country will become.'

'Oh, I suspect we'll be around long enough to see yet more changes we don't approve of.'

The images on the television showed the interior of the community centre. The dark splashes on its walls looked an awful lot like blood.

Henry stared across at Barbara, the gin now sour in her mouth. He pointed at the screen. 'I can't help wondering, though. Is this all our fault?'

Barbara's response was loud enough to mask the soft tinkle of glass breaking in the conservatory.

TWENTY-SEVEN

Riley had arranged to meet Scooby in a bar in King's Cross, not far from the spruced-up Granary Square. He had booked into a nearby Premier Inn which had a secure storage area for the bike. He would have to buy a decent lock if he was going to keep using the Yamaha – it was the sort of bike that Herberts intent on petty crime liked to half-inch.

Riley positioned himself in a corner booth of the bar, which was mostly filled with tipsy, glassy-eyed millennials slugging back lurid cocktails. Their volume was substantial enough, but it was laid over the top with an ear-bleedingly loud soundtrack of R&B, majoring on Slowthai and Childish Gambino. He imagined it was clever marketing, because if you couldn't actually hold a conversation the only alternative was to drink. Or maybe he was just getting old.

Scooby turned some heads when he entered, spotted Riley and crossed over to the booth. It wasn't just the height – he was around six-four – or the fact that he was handsome in a chiselled, posh-boy way (even though he went to a comp in Nottingham). It was the eye patch. Scooby still had an eye under there. It just didn't work. It was also prone to infection, which is why he wore the patch.

He slid in next to Riley and they bumped fists. 'Christ, this your idea of a quiet spot?'

Riley smiled. 'If you can't hear me, then neither can anyone else.'

'I wish I'd brought a Fisherman's Friend. I'm going to have no voice left after this. Your car is all over the news. Or what's left of it. That's some serious shit you're in, Dom.'

'Tell me about it. That's why I need your help.'

'Okay, let me get a drink. Another one?' Scooby asked, nodding at Riley's empty beer bottle.

'Sure.'

Riley watched Scooby use his height to jump the crush at the bar. He had been one of those soldiers who could have had a cushy war, safe behind the blast walls of Bastion. He was with the Royal Logistic Corps, making sure supplies – food, ammo, clothes, medicine – reached the troops at the forward bases. Frustrated at living a sedentary life and bristling at being thought of as a REMF (Rear Echelon Motherfucker), he had volunteered to go out with some of the convoys, despite knowing how hazardous road trips could be. He simply didn't want to be labelled a REMF. On his third sortie his truck hit an IED and a splinter of metal, dislodged from the interior of the Ridgeback he was riding in, penetrated the eye and severed the optic nerve.

Now, he did the same sort of job for the Met, a civilian employee responsible for, as he put it 'ordering the right number of truncheons', even though they no longer called them that. It was a misleading description of his real role, which included assessing and recommending equipment new to the law enforcement market. The reason the Met had recently been given improved stab vests was down to Scooby, who had found some superb Brazilian ones and argued down concerns about cost. Scooby was part-owner of ProTek, a private security firm, specialising in close protection. Bodyguards, to the layman. He was a handy man to know.

Scooby came back with four beers and placed them on the table. 'We'll only be going back up again soon,' he said, sliding back into the booth. 'Might as well stock up. You know, I look at some of those girls and wonder how their parents can let them go out like that.'

That was a dad speaking. 'How is Evie?' Riley asked.

This was his daughter, fourteen, almost as tall as her father and head-spinningly beautiful. Scooby had been fighting off model scouts for about six months now. 'She's good. Decided to settle down to school work. Still have to tell her off about going out in her underwear, though. How's Ruby? Did you get through to her?'

'Eventually. She's fine. For the moment. As you said, it usually takes a while.'

'So what about you? You AWOL?'

'Technically. But I'm fucked if I'm letting them lock me down.'

'But if you're the target ...?'

'Then I should be out there drawing fire.'

Scooby shook his head. 'This isn't Afghan.'

'No, it's fucking not,' Riley snapped back, pointing with the neck of the beer bottle. 'Not yet. And we've got to stop it becoming like bloody Afghan.'

'You all right, Dom?' Scooby asked, the concern heavy in his voice.

Riley realised he had been shouting. The booze had gone straight to his head. He needed to eat something. 'Yeah. Sorry. It's the thought of Ruby, you know, having to deal with this shit. And me not being there for her.'

'You ever think of trying to give it another go? With Izzy?'

'For Ruby's sake?'

'Yeah. It's rough. Not having a dad.'

'Tell me about it.'

Scooby grimaced. 'Sorry. But you had your grandfather, eh?'

'And Ruby's got me.'

When Scooby didn't answer, Riley prompted him. 'What?'

'I don't know,' his friend said. 'Just, given your job. It won't give a girl a sense of security, will it? Not when people go putting bombs under your car.'

'Which is why,' Riley said through gritted teeth, ' I am trying to find the fuckers.'

'And then? You'll give up with the bombs? No, I didn't think so.'

'To answer your original question, no. I don't think it would work with Izzy. It's too late.'

To Riley's relief, Scooby let it drop. 'Where are you staying?'

'In a hotel, locally.'

'Not ideal.'

'I paid cash in advance.'

'That helps. But you're still on a database. You want me to get some security over?'

'Not for me, no. The fewer eyes on me the better as far as I'm concerned. I'll move.'

'Where?'

'Don't worry, somewhere I'll be safe.'

Scooby reached into his pocket and slid a phone over the table to him. 'Let me know, eh? Number is on the back. Pay as you go. I topped the credit up. And put my number in. You need to set up the thumbprint security.'

'Thanks.'

'And don't use any other handsets, eh? Five'll get you ten that's how you were dicked. Unless there's a team tagging you.'

'I don't think so. But I can't be certain.' He pushed a piece of paper across the table. 'This is where Izzy and Ruby are staying. Willow Grange. It's a country house hotel. Can you get some of your guys down there?'

'I can get some of my gals down there, which might be even better.'

Riley nodded. A brace of female CPOs would be preferable. 'Great. The second address is my grandparents. Can they all go there tomorrow? Then I can scoop them up once I know it's safe.'

'Will do.'

'And bill me.'

'Oh, don't worry, my girls don't come cheap.' He was channelling Groucho Marx now.

'Glad to hear it.'

'Give me a minute.'

Scooby left to find a spot where he could hear enough to make a call. Riley used the time to set up the new phone and activate the credit card.

When Scooby came back he said: 'Done. Two of my best. Lisa Baxter and Jackie Dawson will be on their way within thirty. Top-flight female PPOs.' Personal Protection Officers was what bodyguards liked to be known as, just in case someone confused them with bull-necked bouncers.

Riley felt a little of the tension leave his body. 'Thanks.'

Scooby held up his phone to show the BBC news feed. 'I'm guessing you haven't heard about the Islamic Centre, then?'

Riley had a good idea what was coming, but he said: 'No. Go ahead.'

Scooby gave him the edited highlights of the attack on the community meeting in Leicester, and the latest theory about the modus operandi used in the incident.

Riley banged the table with the flat of his hand. 'Christ almighty. Who claimed it?'

'Real Albion Front. RAF. New kids on the execution block,' said Scooby.

'The far right don't use bloody projectile charges,' said Riley. 'Do they?'

'There was that soldier convicted of stockpiling weapons for the coming race war. One of those neo-Nazi nutters. National Action, was it? Remember? He and his mates had an arsenal that included some crude mortars and a couple of home-made RPGs.'

'True.'

'They also copied their encrypted communication from ISIS. These people don't just learn from their allies. You know that.'

'I do. I was just hoping they didn't imitate shaped charges. What's the fallout?'

'Usual. Call for calm by the more moderate imams. Call for infidel blood by a few of the others. Not good. There's a solidarity march planned for Leicester town centre tomorrow.'

'And a candle-lit vigil tonight?'

'Don't be cynical.'

'It's hard not to be,' said Riley. 'It's like there is a post-atrocity script everyone follows.'

'And you suggest?'

'I think someone is stirring the pot. Trying to get a reaction. Maybe trying to get the whole country up in arms. There's plenty of people of all stripes who would like that.' Riley clinked his beer bottles together. 'I suggest we find the bombers on both sides and string them up by their bollocks,' he said with feeling.

'At least you know that one wasn't aimed at you.'

'There's that,' he admitted. Perhaps he would have to re-think that big bullseye that he felt was painted on his back. Not just yet, though.

'Let's stick with your bombs for the minute. You said you had a yellow and purple wire? Where is it now?'

'It was in the VW,' said Riley. 'So it's gone. Which is a bloody nuisance.' Then he remembered a detail he should have mentioned to Scooby earlier. 'There was a drone too.'

'What kind of drone?'

'I don't know. The hovering kind. I took a photo of it. Which is on my old phone.' Scooby seemed to have found something more interesting over Riley's shoulder. He resisted the urge to turn and follow his one-eyed gaze. 'Scoob,' he prompted.

His friend blinked and turned his concentration back to Riley. 'Yes, photo. Pass it over.'

Scooby took the mobile and pocketed it. 'I'll take a look.'

'There was a drone at Nottingham too.'

'Same type?'

'I dunno. They all look the same to me.'

They both moved on to their second bottles. 'I think you've pulled,' said Scooby. 'The girl at the bar.'

Riley craned his neck and the woman gave a small flash of a smile and turned away.

'Friend of yours?'

'I think she's looking at you,' Riley said.

Scooby held up his left hand and wriggled his ring finger. 'Kryptonite.'

'I've got Kryptonite written through me like a stick of rock,' said Riley. He emptied his beer bottle. 'I need another favour. But I'll get another couple in first,' said Riley, standing.

'Just the one each,' said Scooby. 'Then I really must be going.'

Riley shouldered his way to the bar. The girl who had smiled at him was nowhere to be seen. He didn't like women smiling at him for no reason. Not today. He looked around, but nobody was taking any particular notice of him.

Sometimes women just smile. It doesn't mean anything.

Right now, he thought, everything meant something. When he finally got through the crush and managed to yell his order, he bought four beers, just in case, and then threaded his way back through a swaying, gesticulating crowd. He thanked his lucky stars he had bottles, not pints, because they would have been half-empty by the time he got back, given the amount of shoving and stumbling going on.

'I said one.'

'Maths was never my strong point,' said Riley. 'Cheers.'

'What else do you need? And is it legal?'

'Yes, of course it is. All I need is an address.' And once he had it, then legality might take a holiday, but he decided not to mention that. A second slip of paper went across. Scooby looked at it, frowning. 'Is that . . .?'

'Melton Mowbray, yes.' It was a would-be terrorist atrocity from the 1980s that had been thwarted.

'Fuckin' hell, Dom. George O'Donnell? A Big Daddy? Do you know what you're doing?'

'Just a house call. Can you get me it?'

'I know how to get the address. He'll be on a watch list. But—'

'Scooby. Don't ask. It's safer that way.'

They chatted for another ten minutes, then Scooby took his leave, promising to get the address to Riley first thing the next day. He left Riley with two more bottles to finish. He could already feel his head swimming slightly. He needed to eat.

He was just debating whether to abandon the undrunk beer, when a flash of sequins moved in opposite him. It was the girl from the bar. Short blonde hair, slightly turned-up nose, lips that might or might not have fillers in them, but certainly plump. 'Hello.' It was followed by a lopsided grin.

You're a little bit pissed, he thought. Or doing a pretty good impression of it. 'Hello,' he said, although there was no real greeting in there. Just suspicious.

'Sorry,' she said. 'This must seem weird. I know you saw me looking over, and I thought I should explain. I think you're the father of one of my children.'

Riley blinked a few times, making sure he had her face in focus. He didn't recognise her at all. But there had been a few nights . . . fuck, was he a dad twice over? 'I don't think so,' he said, with a confidence that was, in reality, completely lacking.

'Max, right?'

'No, my name's Dom,' he said with some relief.

'No, your son. Max. He's in my English class. The one I teach.' Her forehead wrinkled as she frowned. 'I thought you were his dad. No?'

Riley burst out laughing. 'No! Jesus. For an English teacher . . . you've got to learn how to phrase your questions more carefully. I don't have a son.'

She considered this for a moment, rewound the conversation and put a hand to her mouth. 'Oh, I'm sorry. I see.' She giggled. 'No, no. I didn't mean . . . that we had a son together. I was worried that you'd seen Max's teacher out getting on it with her mates and would, y'know, be disapproving. Christ. Must have—'

'Given me a moment, yeah.' He held out his hand. 'Dom Riley.'

She took it, a good, firm grip, and made an exaggerated shake. 'Charlotte Keech. Charlie.'

He pushed one of the spare bottles across to her. 'Fancy a beer, Charlie?'

*

Jamal stood outside the Tesco Express, finishing up the call with Muraski. 'So Halo is a dead end,' he said. 'Unless you want to go to Damascus any time soon and knock on their door.'

'I'll pass on that,' said Muraski in his ear. 'But it could still be a front for the Iranians?'

'Well, the Iranians supported Assad from day one. And they're always looking for sneaky ways to trade. Halo could be a sanction-busting ruse. But it could also just be a business that sells components and asks no questions. There's a few of those.'

'I guess.' He heard a stifled yawn at the other end.

'You all right, Kate?'

'Just tired.'

'Where are you staying tonight?'

'The delightful CitizenM. It's not far and I need a good night's sleep. Briefing about the Leicester bomb tomorrow first thing. I guess some of that will be heading your way?'

'No doubt we'll have a shufty. Look, I did as you asked and requested a TAP on Riley.'

'And?'

'There's already one in place.'

'What? Why?'

'The car bomb in the Cotswolds? That was him.'

'I knew it!'

'Hold on,' warned Jamal. 'It was his car, I mean. He was the target.'

'Oh.'

'And he's on the run.'

'From what?'

'At a guess? The people who are trying to blow him up.'

'Christ.'

'We'll speak tomorrow. I've got to go. Goodnight. Get some sleep, girl.'

'Girl? I will, *boy*. Night.'

Jamal switched off the phone and let out a disappointed sigh. He always got it wrong with Kate. Just couldn't get the tone right. It veered from too crude (the shower joke) to too prim (his attitude to drinking). And the DNA cock-up. There was very likely no significance to Dom Riley's DNA being on the bomb. He had just wanted to phone her, play the big man. But she had run with it. He'd tried to tell her at the Polish place it was probably nothing, but she didn't want to hear.

Despite pretending otherwise, he did remember her from uni. She was a bit of a wild thing for a while, running with a mostly female group that did ketamine and shit like that and seemed to never need any sleep. There were 'hook ups' but no real steady boyfriends. The liaisons in the group – known initially as The Beeches, after the hall that most of them lived in, which of course soon mutated to The Bitches – seemed pretty fluid.

There was a rumour of a second-year burn-out with Kate. The Bitches seemed to disband during year three and, although you could hardly accuse the former members of embracing sobriety, a new work ethic surfaced.

The truth was, he had always fancied Kate, he just didn't know how to get around the obstacle course she had set up around her. He'd been a little in love even back when she was the kind of girl his parents thought would suffer eternal punishment. He didn't share his parents' views on such things. Didn't share much at all with them. Including what he did for a living. They knew he did something in security, but had no idea what. But they would surely be proud that, sometimes, he was chasing down the Muslims who gave Islam such a toxic name in the aftermath of events such as Manchester and Nottingham. Muslims who enabled the Leicester bombers to come out of their wormy hiding places and claim justifiable retribution when they blew the Islamic Centre apart. White trash.

He stepped into the Tesco and strolled the aisles, unsure of what to buy for dinner. He shouldn't have another ready meal. He was eating too many calories late in the day, and he was putting on weight. He really didn't want to be the size of his father by the time he was forty. He selected a salad, then put it back and went for pizza. It was quick, after all. *Not as quick as emptying salad into a bowl*, a voice murmured in his head. Tastier, though. He would walk to a station further down the line the next day to work it off. He added a couple of bottles of alcohol-free lager to his basket and went to pay.

Jamal turned right out of the Tesco and was just level with the estate agent, heading for the tube, when he noticed the group shadowing him on the left, walking in the road while he stuck to the pavement. Five of them. Hoods up, hands in pockets. He slowed. They slowed.

'Got the time, mate?' one asked.

'Sorry, don't have a watch.'

He quickened his pace but so did his new companions, three of them managing to curve around so they were in front of him. One of them turned and walked backwards. 'No, but you got a phone, eh?'

They had been watching him make the call outside Tesco. He stopped. The five regrouped in front of him. He could make out something of their faces in the light from a baker's window. Two white, two black, one Asian. A Benetton ad's-worth of muggers.

'The phone's no good to you,' he said truthfully. It had a double-code system as well as voice recognition.

One of the white lads stepped forward. There was something familiar about him. 'Let's have a look.' He held out his hand and clicked his fingers. Jamal looked around for help. How could a street be so deserted on a Saturday night? Fight or flight? With the extra weight he was carrying, flight probably wasn't an option. These lads could probably run like whippets. And fight? Over a poxy mobile he could replace within hours?

Jamal pulled out the phone and handed it over. The young man pressed the on button. The screen lit up. 'Code?'

'Nine-seven-six-three.'

The young man entered it. The screen glowed brighter and Jamal could see his spotty, ferret-like face more clearly. The kid looked delighted, but he had about two minutes before the next layer of security kicked in and the phone died for good. Oh, and before it did so, sent out an alert. 'Safe. Credit cards?'

Jamal nodded at the phone. 'Apple Pay.'

'You hipster. Password?'

'Deadmaus@5.'

'Ha. Cool.'

Cool? What was cool about being robbed by a bunch of feral rats? As they turned to go, Jamal felt a flash of rage at this 'taxing'. He glared at the Asian lad and said: 'How can you run with this low-life scum, bruv?'

For once the word didn't sound false on his lips. Then the lad slipped back the hood and he could see it wasn't a *bruv* at all. It was a *sis*. A girl, no more than fourteen or fifteen.

'What did you call us?' the chief mugger demanded, pointing a finger into Jamal's face. Jamal had him. This was the kid who had called him a 'Paki' the other night and told him to go home. Something snapped inside him at the realisation and Jamal punched the boy as hard as he could. A bone in his hand broke, but he was compensated by the bloody rose that bloomed over his opponent's features.

The others stepped in and Jamal dropped the Tesco bag onto the pavement. There was the crack and fizz of a bottle breaking. Jamal clenched his fists – the right one already painful – ready to take whatever beating they would offer, prepared to inflict damage as best he could. As he let out a howl of anger to stoke his aggression, he felt a sting of pain, like a sudden stitch, and looked down, surprised to discover the Asian girl had stabbed him.

SUNDAY

TWENTY-EIGHT

Barbara was in a deep sleep when, reluctantly, she felt herself rising into consciousness. She listened for the rustle of the duvet as Henry tried to scratch at his troublesome limbs. But all was quiet, apart from the soft snuffle from the nearby bed. Henry was fully occupied in the land of nod. Something had woken her, but it wasn't a noise as such. A feeling. A disturbance in the atmosphere. It was that hour just before dawn, when the terrors of darkness gripped the heart. Soon the rising sun would lighten the sky and the monsters – guilt, regret, fear of the death that must be imminent for both of them – would creep back into the shadows. But at that precise moment, dread of night was still abroad.

She slid out of bed, back into the chill air, sacrificing some hard-won heat – the bedrooms of Dunston Hall could never be described as *warm* – padded across the carpet to the window, swished one side of the curtains back and looked out towards the lake. Its surface was silvered by moonlight, highlighting a series of small, concentric circles. Fish rising, she assumed. She heard an owl hoot and scanned the woods and the grounds closer to the house. Nothing on land appeared to move, apart from the dark shapes of rabbits on the lawn. The owl again. The rabbits, spooked by that sound or a movement, flicked their heads up, twitched and scattered. She shivered and felt a soft breath on her neck, as if someone had walked up behind and embraced her with phantom arms.

As she turned away from the window, she saw a dark silhouette, this one by the door. It was the draught from its opening which she had felt on her neck. She cursed Henry and his cans of WD-40. A few weeks ago, those hinges would have shrieked in alarm, but he had put them on his DIY to-do list. A beam of dazzling light shot out from the figure and played over her face. She instinctively looked away and closed her eyes to preserve her night vision. 'Hello?'

'Forgive me,' said a soft voice. 'Do not be frightened. I am not here to hurt you. Please do not do anything foolish.' The torch was clicked off.

Foolish? Chance would be a fine thing. Barbara had often thought of having a lightweight pistol in the bedroom, as they had done in Moscow, but it had always seemed melodramatic in England, where shooting intruders was considered bad form. Now she regretted the decision. Especially as, if she could interpret the shadows correctly, the intruder was holding a gun on her.

'Barbara? Sweetie?' Henry stirred. 'Is that you?'

'Put the bedside lamp on, Henry. I think we have a visitor.'

He did so as he sat up, blinking like a mole rudely plucked out of the ground. 'What's going on?' Then, finally taking in the situation, a burst of anger erupted from him: 'Who the devil are you?'

Henry reached for the telephone on his bedside table and put it to his ear. He listened for a dial tone, then replaced the receiver. Must be dead, she thought. The mobile next to her side, of course, was worse than useless. Perhaps they should have installed that ludicrously expensive alarm and camera system a security company had offered them, with a guaranteed response – meaning humans would arrive – within twenty minutes. Or up to thirty, in their case, as Dunston was relatively remote. But, Barbara thought, perhaps it would have been a waste of money. A lot can happen in half an hour.

Aware that she only had a nightdress on, she crossed her arms over her breasts. With the extra light from the lamp, she was able to examine the intruder. The visitor was not a young man. By her quick estimate he was well into his fifties. Old for a burglar, she thought. The oldies tended to concentrate on safety deposit boxes and the like, didn't they? He had short, greying hair, newly cut by the look of it, and was clean shaven. The pallor of his lower face suggested that the shave had been recent. He had thick, caterpillar eyebrows above chocolate-brown eyes and a strong, square jaw-line. He was, she decided, quite handsome. For a thief in the night.

Henry reached for the glasses he hated to wear and put them on his nose. He gave a sharp intake of breath. 'For fuck's sake,' he said, as he focused on the trespasser holding a gun on his wife. 'What the bloody hell are you doing here?'

'Hello, Henry,' said the interloper casually, as if greeting her husband on the street or in the bank.

There was pause of four or five heartbeats as Henry composed himself before he spoke again. 'Hello, Yousaf.'

TWENTY-NINE

Riley sat in the window of Charlie Keech's flat, knees pulled up to his chest, watching the early morning light grow stronger, chasing the darkness and shadows from the street. He had been there since dawn was just a rosy promise on the clouds. Behind him, in bed, was Charlie, snoring softly.

When she had gone to the toilet at the bar, without her bag, he had unchivalrously checked the contents. She did appear to be exactly who she said she was. A school teacher. The driving licence checked out. She was twenty-nine and lived on the Caledonian Road, in the studio flat he was currently in. When she returned, she came bearing tequila shots. It was surprisingly easy to dispose of a thimble-full of clear fluid while he still had her eyes screwed shut from the liquor burn and the acidity of the lime.

It also wasn't difficult to persuade her that they should share an Uber, nor that he should come in for one last drink. She probably thought they were going to have sex. The sort where, the next morning, you not only asked: *How was it for you?* but threw in *And how was it for me?* for good measure as well.

Well, you could've done it as a bonus ball.

Yeah, thanks Nick. When I want moral guidance from the dead, I'll ask for it.

He wasn't after sex. He was after somewhere to spend the night that was off the grid. He had held her shoulders while she vomited in the bath, helped clean her teeth and rinse her mouth, had put her to bed, fully clothed, cleaned up the mess, and got in a couple of hours of semi-slumber in an armchair. He had made sure he had her mobile in his pocket, just in case he was wrong, and it was a honeytrap.

His new phone rang, startling him. He answered the call. Only one guy had the number. 'Scooby? Shouldn't you be asleep?'

His friend ignored that. 'Where are you?'

A heartfelt groan came from the bed. 'At a friend's place. Keeping a low profile.'

'Okay. All good?'

'Peachy.'

He watched as Charlie Keech surfaced into the land of the living and then wished she hadn't. He smiled at her. He got a grimace in return.

'I've got that address. I'll text it.'

'Thanks, Scooby. That's brilliant news.' Now he could move forward and at least start eliminating some of the possibilities regarding who would put a bomb under his car. First up, a certain George O'Donnell. A man who might be able to join the dots from Nottingham to the piece of wire he lost in the conflagration.

'It'll be on your itemised bill. All well with Izzy and Ruby. No dramas. Lisa and Jackie are in the room next door. They'll make themselves known this morning and escort them to your folks'.'

*Grand*folks', he mentally corrected, but just said: 'Great, thanks.'

'And I might have something on the drone. I'm just looking through the footage from Nottingham, to see if I can see the one there. Then I'll fill you in.'

'Good. Send the address. I'll get that over with first.'

'You sure you know—'

'Catch you later, Scoob.' He rang off. 'Mornin',' he said to the figure struggling to sit up in bed.

'Fuck.' She squinted at him, trying to focus. 'Can you pull the curtains closed? Too much light.'

He did so, went to the kitchen area, filled a glass with water and took it to her. 'I think you're going to need this.'

Charlie took the glass in both hands and gulped down the contents, spilling a good proportion of it on the sheet she had pulled up to her neck. When she had finished, she looked at him with suspicion and fear.

'Did you put something in my drink?'

'Whoa. No. Absolutely not.' He raised his hands in a gesture of surrender. 'Nothing happened. You passed out. I slept in the chair.' And spent a couple of hours at the window, making sure he wasn't being dicked.

'Christ.' He could see the full morning-after effect in her face: guilt, patchy memory, head like a jackhammer.

'I know. It could have been a lot worse. Luckily I'm not a psychopath.' A thought occurred to him. 'But I am wanted by the police.'

'What?' He hadn't thought she could go any paler, but he was wrong.

'The Military Police. It's a long story. I'm going to have a shower. And then I need you to do me a favour.'

She shook her head and regretted it. 'Fuck. I'm never drinking again.'

*

The Saturday-night meeting had been declared for senior management and case officers only, so Muraski could safely skip it. She made sure she was in good and early for the 10am one, though, which would be for officers of her pay grade and below. Not that there were many levels below her.

As she entered the building, she saw Oakham hovering at the front desk, speaking to Cobb, the Director of Counter Terrorism. She instinctively smoothed down her skirt and checked the collar of her blouse, aware that her hasty packing and unpacking had left her looking less than crisp.

As she passed through the security pods, Cobb slipped away. Oakham gave one of his hard-to-read smiles. 'Kate. Can I have a word? In my office.'

Fuck, what now?

They rode the lift in silence and as they walked the corridor to his office, he politely asked how the search for a new place was going. She kept the answer short, as he clearly didn't give a shit. There was a tension in the building, she could feel it, a hum like a giant tuning fork. As if the very bricks were vibrating with some negative energy from the attack on the Islamic Centre, which suggested a possible outbreak of tit-for-tat outrages. She wondered what had happened at the meetings the previous night and the inevitable conference calls with senior government fig-ures, including, in all likelihood, the PM. Whatever transpired, it had probably left the top floor peevish, which of course cascaded down the levels of more junior staff, the sour mood amplifying at each stage.

Or perhaps Oakham had discovered that she had asked Jimmy Fu and his Doggs to put surveillance in place on the Clifford-Browns, without clearing it with him first. That was worth a bollocking.

Once Oakham was behind his desk, he gestured for her to sit down. When she had done so, he leaned forward intently. There was no smile on his lips or in his eyes. 'Kate. Jamal Malik.'

Fuck, fuck, fuck. It was about the TAP. You need Home Office clearance to go tapping/tracing phones and demanding call records from the mobile companies, unless you had a Cat One exemption on grounds of expediency or time. Had Jamal made sure he cited Cat One? No, hold on. There had already been a TAP in place. Jamal would have retreated as quickly as possible.

'Works at Bomb Data. I know him from uni.'

'I'm afraid I have some bad news.' She could see him struggling to find the right words and braced herself. 'He was attacked and killed last night.'

When she spoke, her voice was croaky, as if she had smoked too many cigarettes. 'What? No. Last night? No, that can't be right. Killed?'

'Murdered,' he corrected.

'Fucksake. That can't be right. How? Who?'

'He was stabbed. By a gang of youths. Or one of them. He died in hospital. The blade had pierced his heart. There was nothing they could do.'

She felt all the heat drain from her body, apart from the warm tears that coursed down her cheeks. 'Was it . . . was it racial? Or work? What? Why Jamal? He wouldn't hurt a fly.'

Oakham folded his hands on the desk and squeezed his fingers until they went white. 'Police think it was a random robbery. There is CCTV footage. Some witnesses, apparently. Arrests will be made, Kate and—'

'Shit!' she banged the desk and a photo frame flopped face down. 'I mean, shit. They always say that. The CCTV will be dark and grainy and the witnesses too frightened to identify anyone.' She gulped some air and regained a little calm. 'You're sure? Sure it's Jamil?'

A solemn nod. 'There's no doubt, Kate.'

'I only spoke to him last night—'

'We know,' Oakham said. 'It's why we are having this conversation. You were the last person to talk to him.'

'Oh, Jesus.' Why did that make her feel complicit in his death? As if she could have done something to stop it. It was illogical. But the hurt was real enough. 'He was running down something on a company called Halo. It was going to be in my next report.' She hated herself for even thinking about covering her back, but it had to be done. 'But we were friends, too. From uni.'

'You said.'

Grief was scrambling her brain. 'Oh, yeah. Do his parents know?'

'I think there'll have been a DN delivered by now.' Death Notice, one of the many tasks she really didn't envy the police. 'And they'll have had to formally identify him.'

'Shit. Can I have contact details? I've never met them and I'd like to . . .' She took a deep breath, not wanting to sob in front of him. Emotional vulnerability was not a prized trait in Five. 'I'd like to send my condolences.'

'Of course. I'll get the investigating officer's details over to you. She can give you what you need.'

'Thank you.'

Oakham re-arranged his face into what he probably considered was a 'caring' mode. It was slightly scary, like he was an oncologist with bad news. 'Kate, I think you can skip this morning's briefing.'

'No, no,' she protested. 'I'll be fine.' She wasn't sure, though, how true that was. Not yet.

Oakham unclasped his hands and righted the fallen photo frame.

'Take some time, Kate. Deepika or one of the others will debrief you later. This is a shock. Takes time to sink in.'

'Sir.'

'Go and get a coffee. Something to eat. You looked pretty rough before I told you the news. You look even worse now.'

'Thanks for your honesty, sir.' She couldn't keep the sarcasm from her voice.

'Kate—'

'Sorry. Not thinking straight.'

He waved her transgression away. 'Quite. Get out of this cesspit and get some air. And when you get back, go and see Jimmy Fu, he wants to see you.'

'What for?'

'Your watch request on Dunston Hall.'

'I was going to—'

'Mention it but it slipped your mind,' he said, with an indulgent smile. 'I think you might as well run with it. If you feel up to it, all things considered.

'I do. I'll be fine.'

'Go and get that coffee.'

'Sir.'

She stood.

'And Kate?'

'Yes?'

The smile had faded. 'Never, ever do that again. I'm cutting you some slack here, you understand? Jimmy isn't there for your sole benefit. There are protocols for a reason.'

'Won't happen again.'

'Make sure it doesn't. Coffee. Now.'

She left, feet leaden, as if the sorrow of Jamal's death was a physical weight, pressing down on her shoulders, and aware she had to shrug it off if she was to do her job properly. Oakham wasn't in the habit of cutting anybody some slack more than once.

THIRTY

Riley sat in the house and waited for George O'Donnell to return. The man clearly felt more secure than he ought to, given his history. It had been ridiculously easy to break in through the rotten kitchen window. After picking up his stuff from the hotel, Riley had driven to the address Scooby had texted him, a two-up two-down in Bedford. O'Donnell was the man behind, among many other incidents, the Melton Mowbray bomb.

That IED never got much publicity. Why should it have? It was rightly overshadowed by the two bombs which detonated on the same day as its intended deployment – 20 July 1982. The first device was concealed in the boot of a Morris Marina parked on South Carriage Drive in Hyde Park. It consisted of eleven kilos of gelignite with a further fourteen kilos of nails wrapped around the explosive core. It was almost certainly radio-controlled – although no forensic evidence was left to confirm this – as it detonated just when a troop of the Household Cavalry was passing. The Blues & Royals are immaculate time-keepers, and the Changing of the Guard that the troop was part of ran like clockwork, but not so precise that you could pre-set a bomb to explode for the exact moment that they rode by a set point. No, thought Riley as he jemmied open the rotten window of the old kitchen extension, that one was triggered by human hand, possibly a radio signal, although it was before the days of mobile phone activation, personal handsets being some way from escaping the realms of sci-fi.

Three members of the Blues & Royals died instantly, a fourth succumbed to his injuries three days' later. Seven horses were either killed by the blast and a steely rain of hot metal or were so severely injured they had to be put down.

At 12.55pm a second device exploded in Regent's Park. This one was on a timer, the exact moment of detonation being less crucial, as it simply had to deploy during the lunchtime concert by the Royal Green Jackets. The bomb was secreted under the bandstand. It did not contain any nails or shrapnel. Six of the thirty bandsmen were killed outright. A seventh died of his injuries. Eight civilian spectators were injured, but there were no fatalities among bystanders. Investigators concluded the devices were probably the work of two separate bomb-makers.

Melton Mowbray was a mixture of the methods used in the two devices. It contained nails, nuts and bolts, but it was on a timer. It was another car bomb, this time a Ford Cortina Mark III. It was parked outside Remount Depot, the Royal Army Veterinary Corps' HQ in Melton Mowbray, where animals – horses and dogs – are selected and trained. The blast radius included some of the stable block and the exercise yard, both of which were busy at the intended hour of the explosion.

The bomb was designed to go off at 12.40pm, an hour after Hyde Park, around fifteen minutes before the bandstand atrocity. Fortunately, when news came through of Hyde Park, the CO decided that his horses might also be a target. He ordered all animals and personnel away from perimeter fences and a sweep of all vehicles parked in close proximity to the barracks.

The Cortina was tagged as suspicious and an SAS bomb-disposal team was helicoptered in. The car had been fitted with some crude anti-handling traps which were quickly disposed of. The bomb was in the boot, as expected, and the detonator was destroyed using a disrupter water jet, rendering the device safe. There was one big difference to Hyde and Regent's Parks: the explosive used was Semtex, not gelignite. One other difference: the wiring featured a very distinctive yellow and purple loom. Just like probably Nottingham had, before the blast fragmented it, leaving just stray lengths like the one Riley picked up in his boot.

Although they had an intact bomb at Melton Mowbray, forensics were simply not up to modern standards back then, and it was human intelligence that led investigators, some six months later, to George O'Donnell, who was charged with 'intending to cause an explosion likely to endanger life'. Although he was released for lack of evidence, he continued to be under suspicion, but any hope of a future conviction was thwarted when he was sent a letter in the aftermath of the Good Friday Agreement, stating – in error – that he was not at risk of prosecution. The letter was enough to give him immunity in perpetuity from the law for Melton Mowbray and any of the many other bombs he was suspected of building or planting.

Riley pondered all this as he set up his own bomb in the gloomy living room, careful to keep the two wires that would complete the circuit well apart, even though they were heavily taped. It might seem extreme, but he was dealing with a murderer. And one with a direct link to the bomb in Nottingham and, therefore, possibly to the one that could so easily have killed his daughter. He was in no mood to fuck about.

Satisfied with his work, Riley sat in the armchair that faced the TV, the house's Airedale dog a few feet away, eyeing him warily.

Riley placed the knife he had also liberated from the kitchen at his barracks on the greasy arm next to him.

Then he leaned back and waited.

*

George O'Donnell didn't look particularly alarmed when confronted with an intruder in his home. Perhaps he was a man who had grown used to the idea of strangers turning up unbidden at any time of day or night. Even after church on Sunday. As a young man he had lived with the ever-present threat of a visit from the Nutting Squad aka The Sweenies, the internal enforcement boys.

O'Donnell stood in the doorway and took in the scene, examined the homemade suicide vest, the man holding the two wires, the ends bare, one in each hand, the threat implicit. *Do anything stupid and I'll touch these together and . . .*

'Who the fuck are youse?' he asked. 'The Grim Reaper? If you are, I think I preferred the big scythe, you know.'

'Sit down, George. I just have a few questions.'

'Mr O'Donnell to you.'

Riley could see the old man was running his professional eye over the circuitry. 'It'll work all right, George. I know what I'm doing.'

O'Donnell sat, raising a cloud of dust from another grubby armchair. He also took in the fact that his dog had his collar and lead on. The lead was looped under the leg of the armchair. Which was why Astral hadn't come to greet him at the door. 'Do you now? You know who I am, then? What friends I have?'

Riley nodded. 'I know your reputation. I know that was a while ago now. Look, I'd make us some tea, but . . . you know. One false move. *Boom.*'

'You're a cheeky fucker.' It was the first real flash of anger since he had arrived. But Riley was aware it would be in there, boiling away, building. He had something very similar cooking inside himself.

'As I say, answer me a few questions, George, and I'll put the old tape back on the wires and be gone.'

'You'd better go far away, m'lad. Because I'll be after you.'

Riley looked at him. He was in his seventies, liver-spotted, sparse of hair, eyes rheumy. He had heard him place a stick in the holder in the hall when he arrived. He wasn't running after anyone any time soon. But, as he said, he might have people who would do that for him. Too late to stop now. You build and strap on a suicide vest, there's not really any turning back.

'Melton Mowbray,' said Riley.

'The pies?' O'Donnell asked, all faux innocence.

'The bomb.'

'Ah.'

'And McGurk's farm. Fermanagh.'

He shook his head. 'I had nothing to do with any of that shite.'

'Your file says otherwise.' Riley moved the wires closer. 'I had a drink last night. Few beers. More than I intended, in fact. Still feel a bit rough. DTs. Touch of the shakes on the hands.'

O'Donnell watched the gap between the wires reduce. They were indeed dancing a little too much for his comfort. 'What do you want, son? I'm an old man. Made my peace with God this morning. You don't frighten me. Say your bit and fuck off.'

'My name doesn't matter. All you need to know is I'm an ATO. And what I want to know is: are any of your old friends after me or my mates?'

He shook his head and sighed in exasperation. 'How would I know that?'

'Oh, come on. I bet you keep your ear to the ground. If there was a shout out to take down an ATO, you'd know. And we EOD boys were never that popular with your lot.'

'I've heard nothing.'

'No? Because I reckon someone has my name on a list. I reckon Nottingham was to draw me out.' If Riley hadn't been suspended, it would have been him, not Spike, who caught the full blast of the secondary. 'Then someone wired my car. Now that's personal. Especially as my daughter was with me.' The last came out as a growl. He had to keep calm. Any histrionics on his part and O'Donnell would see that as weakness and clam up. Riley might be seething inside, but he had to use that anger sparingly with George, showing just enough to convince the Irishman that he might be someone who really would touch the wires together.

'As far as I know there is no action on the mainland linked to what you call "my lot". Is that it? Can you fuck off now?'

Riley shook his head. 'Not just yet. I want to know one more thing. Where the kit you used for Melton Mowbray and McGurk's came from. The yellow and purple wires. Remember them?'

The Irishman kept quiet, his eyes on the glinting twists of copper in Riley's hands. The dog gave a whimper, as if she knew what was being threatened. 'It's okay, Astral,' O'Donnell said as soothingly as he could manage, 'He'll be going soon.'

'It's not much,' said Riley, indicating the dog and the make-shift vest he'd created for it using the items he had taken from the stores at the barracks before leaving on his Yamaha. 'Just a little sausage of explosive on his belly. Just the right amount to . . . *ping* . . . open Astral up. He might not die immediately, but it'll take a supervet to save him. Got one of those round here, have you?'

'You cunt.'

'Don't come over all Paul O'Grady on me, George. Melton

Mowbray would have killed some horses, maybe dogs. And your pals did murder and maim innocent horses at Hyde Park.'

'They were *war* horses,' he hissed. 'Legitimate targets. This is a companion, a pet.'

'Soon to be an ex-pet if you're not careful. I'm not sure you were responsible for McGurk. It might have been after your time. Maybe a protégé. But I think Melton was yours. You know the man who took the bomb out of the Cortina? He taught me. Colonel Ross, as he became, was something of a mentor. Talked us through your bomb, the Pizza Bomber's, the one at Harvey's Resort, the American bombs in Hong Kong, the British in Berlin . . . you're one of the famous examples he used on the High Threat course. Should be proud, in a sick kind of way. C'mon, George, let's get a move on. After I turn Astral here inside out, I'll start with the knife on you.' Riley nodded to the blade, just in case O'Donnell hadn't really clocked it, his attention distracted by his dog being wired to a suicide vest. 'And I've got more explosive to make sure I cover my tracks. I'll burn this whole place to such a crisp Gary Lineker'll start advertising it.'

'Very funny.'

'Yeah. Sadly, I'm not here all week. Time is pressing.'

O'Donnell narrowed his eyes and Riley could tell he was struggling to get a handle on him. The shifts in tone were disorienting the Irishman. His cockiness was fading. Which is exactly what Riley intended.

'Who the fuck are you?' the old man asked, more subdued this time.

'That's where you came in, George. I don't want to go round in circles. I want to know where the purple and yellow wiring came from. It was there at Melton Mowbray. Before my time, but it's in the reports. The first occasion I came across it in person was in

Fermanagh. The second time, Nottingham. It's not a coincidence, is it, George?' Annoyingly, his one sample of the Nottingham batch had gone up in The Heap, so he had no visual aid to dangle before O'Donnell.

Riley brought the wires so close, it was as if a keen spark could leap the gap between them.

O'Donnell looked at his dog again and smiled to try to reassure her. It was more a rictus grin. If he was a dog swathed in explosives, Riley wouldn't have been placated by that at all. Eventually, the Irishman's shoulders dropped and the tension left his body. Whatever he knew, Riley figured, it wasn't worth losing Astral for. He licked his lips and spoke quietly, as if even loud words could trigger the device wrapped around his dog. 'Libya. All that stuff came from Libya. Yellow and purple used to be the colour for the live in the south of the country, before everything got standardised. After that, there were drums of the stuff sitting in warehouses.'

'And they sent them to you?'

'Yeah. But not just wire. You got a kit. Just like IKEA, you know? Build your own bomb. Everything you needed for a variety of types, switches, wire, batteries, blasting caps, det cord, all except the Semtex or gelignite. The main charge had to be sourced separately.'

'So you had off-the-shelf flatpacks?'

'Aye. Or something you would have got at that store that's gone now. What was it? Maplin. A DIY bomb kit. Dozens of them. You got some with timers, some with tilt switches, others with radio-control dets. It meant any fuckin' eejit could put one together. Came with circuit diagrams, the lot. Of course, they were pretty basic.' His Adam's apple bobbed in his scrawny neck as he swallowed. 'Okay, now move those wires apart a touch, you're makin' me sweat here, and me in my best suit.'

Riley's arms were growing tired. He moved them to rest his elbows on the chair. 'There's a link here somewhere, old man, between your IKEA kits and Nottingham. The same distinctive wire. And if you don't make the connection for me, I'm going to sit here till I get bored and blow up your dog just for the fun of it.' He allowed just a little hint of the hatred he felt for the man to creep into his tone.

'I've met some mad people in my life, son. Fuckin' nutters. You can imagine, can't you? The Provos had their fair share of psychos, I can tell you. You don't strike me as one of them.'

'It's the quiet ones you want to watch out for,' Riley said. 'I'm going to tell you what I used to do for a living.' He gave a run-down of an average day in Afghan, at the height of the plague of IEDs. Bomb, after bomb, after bomb in temperatures that could boil the blood. Then go back and do it all again the next day. With not so much as a beer in between.

'I take it back,' said O'Donnell when Riley had finished. 'You are feckin' mad.'

'You don't know the half of it.'

'Okay, look. I'd fuckin' strangle you with my bare hands if I could. And I reserve the right to do so, should our paths ever cross again. But, Jesus forgive me, I know how the yellow and purple wire got to Nottingham. Although I didn't know what they would use it for.'

Perhaps he thought 'they' had a big re-wiring job on for Barratt Homes, thought Riley, but he didn't want to puncture the mood of confession. But the old man said no more. 'Yes?' Riley prompted, impatient.

'I think I should move back to Ireland. I'm only here for m'boys, and how often do they come and see their old da? No, I think it's time to go home. England's a shitehole. What do you think?'

There was a fizzing in Riley's brain, like acid on alkali. He went for the wires once more, so furious that he knew, this time, he would call the old terrorist's bluff. And fuck the dog.

'Hold up, hold up. Only kiddin',' said O'Donnell in alarm. 'Jesus, you're a hot one. I believe you now. Tape up the ends of the wire and I'll tell you. God's honest truth. You've still got your little pocket knife there if I make any trouble. I don't want you blowing up Astral by mistake.'

Riley waited while order was restored inside his head. He took a deep breath, willing himself to calm down. It took a few minutes. O'Donnell clasped his hands in front of him, as if he was about to kneel and pray. How can a man with his history make any kind of peace with any kind of god? Riley wondered. Still, he had just come close to some sort of edge himself. *Breathe*.

'Why Astral?' Riley asked eventually.

'*Astral Weeks*. Van Morrison. I know he's a Prod an' all that, but the man's a genius.'

Riley carefully laid down the wires several inches apart on one of the arms of the chair and picked up the roll of black insulating tape from the cushion next to him. Riley sensed O'Donnell holding his breath as he unpeeled a decent length, bit it off with his teeth and entombed the bare copper of one of the wires. That was enough to be going on with.

'There, safe as houses.' Riley let his fingers settle on the handle of the knife. 'Now, George. Yellow and purple wires. From Libya to Nottingham. Do tell.'

O'Donnell looked at his dog and nodded, as if to reassure her that the danger had passed for the minute, laid back in the chair and began to talk.

THIRTY-ONE

After she left Thames House and emerged from the shrouding of scaffolding currently covering it, Kate Muraski walked across Lambeth Bridge. She desperately needed a black coffee or three, but there was fuck-all available on a Sunday morning in the immediate vicinity. Even the restaurants at the base of the Millbank Tower didn't open till midday.

She eventually found herself across the river in Lambeth Gardens, sitting on a bench, head between her knees, wondering if she was going to throw up. The façade she had put on for Oakham had crumbled, and she could feel waves of nausea and weariness breaking over her, with the pain of Jamal's death not far behind.

The number of Jamal's parents appeared on her screen, sent from the investigating officer. Oakham had been as good as his word.

She sat staring at the digits, hoping they would go away. She didn't feel strong enough to call. What would she say? She wasn't even sure her voice still worked, given the tightness in her throat.

Still, eventually she steeled herself and pressed the screen. Bilal – the brother – answered. Muraski found herself garbling that she was 'a work colleague, university friend'. He knew who she was, he interrupted. Bilal explained in a voice shot through with torment that his parents were too distraught to come to the phone. They wanted some time to take it all in. Perhaps tomorrow would be better? She asked if he could let her know about funeral arrangements, knowing that, as a Muslim, he would be buried as quickly as possible, although that might be delayed by a post-mortem she supposed. Of course, said the brother, we will keep you informed. Then Bilal said it.

He talked about you all the time, Kate. I had to tell him to shut up about you. He really liked you.

She thanked him, rang off and then cried so hard that a middle-aged woman came and sat next to her. Muraski let the woman put an arm round her while her body shook. Eventually the sobbing subsided. She accepted a tissue and assured the woman she would be all right. She just needed to compose herself.

She had no idea how long she sat there watching the pigeons and wondering about how unfair life was. You join MI5 or MI6 and you assume that someone, somewhere would get killed on your watch. Some unfortunate 'asset' in North Korea or the Ukraine, an undercover officer infiltrating gangs, perhaps. You'd log it and move on. But it seemed to her that these days walking the streets late at night in London was as risky as being a spy. If Jamal had died as a result of an operation – not that he was any kind of field agent – that would be one thing, but to be murdered as the result of a chance encounter, that was just so unfair. The randomness of it put ice in her veins.

He talked about you all the time.

The phrase echoed around Kate Muraski's mind, stuck on a seemingly endless loop, like a piece of bloody Philip Glass music.

She checked the time on her phone. She had been out of Thames House for hours, it seemed. She was tired and hungry and thirsty. But before she could address any of those issues, her phone pinged.

It was a message from Jimmy Fu, head of surveillance, asking if she was coming. He had footage she ought to see. She had forgotten that Oakham had told her he wanted to see her. She shook her head vigorously, as if it could somehow throw off her grief. It didn't, but she had to put it to one side for now. She stood and retraced her steps to the office. It was time to get back on the horse.

*

The Fus were a wealthy family from Asia, with branches in Singapore, Hong Kong and Macau, dealing in hotels, restaurants, fashion and gambling. Jimmy was only a second cousin of the patriarch of the business. Nevertheless, the rumour was Jimmy didn't have to work, thanks to his shareholdings in the Fu conglomerate. One thing was certain, he was the best-dressed man in Thames House, probably to Oakham's chagrin. He was probably like those rappers who ditch sneakers after one wear, because everything about Fu looked box fresh.

His fiefdom, the 'Surveillance Suite', occupied three large interconnected spaces on the third floor. They looked much like the newsroom of a large newspaper or the trading floor of an investment bank – clusters of men and women peering into computers, occasionally grabbing the phone to report or check something. Fu had an office just off one of the rooms, which was glass-walled and actually had no door, as if he didn't want to block the flow of information from his Doggs. The suite was actually a satellite of GCHQ, and the raw data was always shared with the bigger brother in 'The Doughnut' at Cheltenham. It was, on paper, a duplication of work, but every so often having teams with different perspectives analysing the same material paid dividends.

Muraski sat at Fu's desk while he brought up a file on his laptop. She had tried to fix her face as best she could before the meeting, but she knew she looked rough as a pineapple's arse. She needed sleep. Fu obviously thought so too.

'I won't keep you long. I know . . . well, I heard about Jamal. I'm sorry. We had dealings. Good guy. Fucking disgrace.'

'Yes. It is.'

Fu had inevitably been called Fu Manchu when he arrived at Thames House in less racially sensitive days, something he got wind of quickly and squashed. Two of his Doggs who had exchanged jocular emails – which required a fair degree of stupidity, given what their section did – were moved to less exciting jobs in the quartermaster's stores. Fu was as far away from Sax Rohmer's Yellow Peril character as possible, smooth of skin, lightly perfumed, with a floppy fringe of dark-black hair. Age difficult to pin down, but, by all accounts, very clean living, which made it even trickier. He had a genetic aversion to alcohol which caused him to flush if he had even one glass of wine, so he didn't drink. He did do triathlons, which Kate always thought was a cry for help, but he seemed to thrive on it.

'Okay,' he said, satisfied he was ready to roll the footage he had been preparing. 'As your request was to monitor the CCTV installed on the grounds of Dunston Hall . . .'

'Yes.'

'. . . we hacked in to the cameras – piss easy – and installed a second motion-sensor alarm system to indicate to us when something happened. To save us trawling through hours of flowers coming into bloom. We actually had very little activity, if you discount some fox that kept triggering the lights at night. Then, this morning, this.'

He swivelled the laptop around so she could see the screen and pressed play. She was looking at the driveway of Dunston Hall, with the Clifford-Browns' BMW parked on the gravel.

She watched as the door with the giant lion knocker opened and Henry Clifford-Brown stepped out into the chill early morning air, wearing an overcoat, gloves and a hat. She could see his breath steaming and he adjusted the scarf around his neck. Behind him, another figure she didn't recognise, dressed in black. Younger than Clifford-Brown. It was hard to make out his features, but the position of his body suggested one thing to Kate.

'Christ. Has he got a gun on the old man? Can you zoom in?'

'Not without it pixilating so badly you won't see anything. But I agree, that could be. I can run it through some software. It won't be like *CSI* though,' he said with a grin.

'It never is.'

They climbed into the BMW, with Clifford-Brown behind the wheel, the other in the passenger seat, and it drove off at a stately pace.

'No Mrs Clifford-Brown?' she asked.

'No. And whoever that man is, he didn't come in the front door.'

'How do you mean?'

'We've checked all the CCTV footage for the past few days. No sign of his calling.'

There was also no evidence of him or anyone else other than the Clifford-Browns being in the house when she had visited. 'You think he broke in?'

'It's possible.'

'Are there cameras at the rear?' Muraski asked.

Fu shook his head. 'Not on the west wing, just the place next door. The Russian's place.' She nodded to indicate she knew all about Kutsik. 'Obviously we recorded the licence plate number of the BMW. It is registered to Clifford-Brown. Then put in an urgent request for road monitoring to track it.'

'And?'

'Drawn a blank. Hasn't appeared on anything, no motorway or A-roads covered by cameras in the vicinity.'

'Which means what?' she asked.

'At a guess? They switched cars down the road. I've got local police checking the immediate vicinity.'

'Good. Christ, he is a slippery one,' said Kate.

'Clifford-Brown? Well, that's as may be, but if what we think we saw is right, and it is a gun, then he isn't calling the shots. Is he?'

'No. And I'm concerned about Mrs Clifford-Brown's absence, too.' Kate was pretty sure Barbara could take care of herself in most situations. But she was also certain that she wouldn't willingly let her husband out of her sight. 'My guess is that they're pretty inseparable.'

'Now look at this.'

Onscreen a car pulled into the driveway. A 7-series BMW. A woman – slight, blonde, dressed in black – got out and did a 360 before she approached the door of Dunston Hall.

'Pro?' Muraski asked.

'Well, she's on her toes about something. Look, she gets no answer. Alarm bells ring in her head. She runs back to the car. It leaves in a hurry.'

'You checked the car plates?'

'Of course,' said Fu. 'Registered to a Lisa Baxter. She's on The Circuit.'

'Bodyguard?' she asked.

'Yes. What do you make of that?'

'I don't know. Can we see who else was in the car?'

'Windows too heavily tinted.'

'Okay, thanks. I have a feeling none of this is going to make any sense till we find Dominic Riley.'

'That rings a bell.'

'There's a TAP on him.'

'Who is he again?'

'Well, he's many things. One of them is the Clifford-Browns' grandson.'

THIRTY-TWO

The smell told the bomb-maker that the boy had soiled himself again. The second time in three hours. He put down the drawing he had been studying and looked over. His son was watching television again, apparently unaware of what had transpired. He would have to buy the boy some diapers or whatever they were called in this country.

He walked over, turned the TV off – it was another programme about the Islamic Centre bombing – and pulled the boy to his feet. Together they made the ponderous journey to the bathroom. He had insisted they get him a house with a downstairs bath or shower and a room where the boy could sleep on the ground floor. He could manage stairs, but it was easier if everything was on one level. The house they had selected was at the end of a row of terraces, detached from the main run, apparently constructed by the builder of the surrounding streets for his own family. So it came with a large garden, hedges, trees, a driveway and, most importantly, a great sense of privacy.

Once in the bathroom, he turned on the shower and stripped off his son's clothes, setting the clean sweatshirt aside but putting the underwear and trousers into a basket. Luckily, he stayed compliant. Sometimes his son railed against being manhandled and when he did, he showed a frightening strength. The bomb-maker thought the damaged young man's muscles should have atrophied by now, but there was still steel in those sinews. He had hurt his father once or twice, bruised his face. He hadn't punished him. It wasn't his son's fault that he was like this. It was the British Army's.

He checked the temperature of the water from the shower head, rolled up his sleeves and helped the lad in. He sponged him down with a flannel, cleaning down his legs as well as his buttocks, and handed him a towel. He could manage to dry himself, mostly.

While he did that, he went to the laundry room – another luxury the house had – and put on the washing machine. Perhaps he should buy some more clothes, even though they were approaching the end of days. He had seen some shops close to a B&Q that sold cheap, anonymous jeans, tracksuit bottoms, sweat-shirts and hoodies. That was all the boy needed. And diapers, he reminded himself.

He returned, finished drying off the boy and re-dressed him in clean clothes. He guided him back to the living room and sat him on the sofa once more, switching the TV back on. The news was reporting that there were marches in several cities against the far right who had dared target innocent, peace-loving Muslims. He wondered how the marchers would feel if they knew that one of their own had created the bomb and that, rather than white extremists, a foreign power was ultimately behind the atrocity.

And how did he feel about being responsible for the death of Muslims? Well, if they were righteous, they would be in Paradise. If not, and they were suffering the first tortures of eternal pain, they only had themselves to blame. He used the same logic when he was making the bombs that would destroy marketplaces and police stations back home. Besides, his associates' logic for targeting the Islamic Centre had been irrefutable: it would cause chaos and social unrest in the UK. He had no problem with that, just as long as, at some point, he got his own revenge. It was a symbiotic relationship with his partners: they both needed each other. And they would both achieve what they wanted by the time the bombing campaign was over.

The bomb-maker returned to his work, laid out on the dining table, but kept glancing at what was left of his son. He was getting worse, no doubt about it. He had begun wetting the bed. Soon, he would need full-time medical care, because his son's needs would become a two-person job. He looked down at the schematic he had sketched and put a pencil line through it. Then he picked up the handset of the landline and dialled the number he had memorised. The man who called himself Rick answered, although the bomb-maker assumed that was not his real name.

'Hello?'

'It's me.'

'Yes?'

'I have the cylinders,' the bomb-maker said. 'You have the list of other components?'

'Yes. Nothing that will cause us any problems.'

'Good. Bring them in the van. Change of plan. I will build what you want here, inside the van.'

Now he sounded surprised. 'Not in the workshop?'

'No. I want to stay close to my son. You can prefabricate the panels for me.' It wasn't a question. The man was not without technical abilities.

'I can. Enough for both units. You are sure about this?'

'I am. It won't affect delivery. We are still on target.' There was more to his plan than simply constructing devices. He had a particular scenario for this end game in mind. However, that was none of his associate's business. He looked at the wall clock. He needed a post office, but it was Sunday. Perhaps he could find a shipping agent – DHL, UPS – to deliver his parcel overnight. 'Do as I ask and the Vipers will be ready to deploy.'

It was obviously the first time the man had heard the term. The bomb-maker's instruction had been simply to build a 'spectacular'. This was what he had come up with. 'What's a Viper?'

The bomb-maker chuckled. 'The most fiendish IED ever devised. And impossible to defuse. Even for an ATO like Staff Sergeant Dominic Riley.'

*

It was just as he was leaving the Irishman that Riley snapped. Whatever toxic waste had been building up inside him burst out into his bloodstream and a roaring filled his head that drowned out all rational thoughts. If O'Donnell hadn't said anything, he would have left him and his dog alone. But he had to have the last word.

'It's just a shame we didn't get any of you at the farm. I was proud of that coffin-bomb.' The combination of the smug tone and the smirk on his face made Riley flip. He grabbed O'Donnell by the collar of his suit and pulled his arm back, ready to drive his fist into the old man's face.

Not now, eh, pal?

Riley ignored it. Nick was hardly qualified to be the voice of reason here.

Give the old cunt a break, eh? It was a long time ago.

Almost against his will, Riley lowered his arm a little.

Dom! How you going to protect your family when you're in the dock for GBH?

He dropped his clenched fist away altogether. He shook the dog off his leg, although the insistent yapping continued. The swirling in his head diminished, as if all his anger was flushing down a neural plughole. O'Donnell pushed himself away from the wall and grabbed the rear of the armchair for support. 'I was right. You are . . . a fecking . . . nut job,' he croaked.

Talk to his shrink, said Nick. *She knows. PT—*

'Shut up,' Riley growled. He was growing tired of his late pal. Didn't the dead ever sleep?

Riley raised a finger and stabbed it at O'Donnell. The man flinched. Good. Job done. Even if it wasn't premeditated, he had put the Fear into him. 'You just remember that before you go talking to any of your old pals, eh?'

He reached down and gave the dog's neck hair a quick ruffle. 'I'm sorry you got caught up in all this.'

As he left, he heard the sound of the old man's courage returning. 'Just piss off. I see youse again, I'll kill you.'

He was still sitting outside O'Donnell's, legs astride the Yamaha, pondering his next move, when the call from Scooby came in.

'We have a situation, mate.'

'What?'

'Lisa and Jackie took Izzy and Ruby to your grandparents. There was no answer and they got out of there, just in case. SOP.' Standard Operating Procedure.

'Shit, I forgot to phone Barbara and Henry to warn them they were coming. Idiot. What did they do?'

'They're fine. They've taken them off for lunch. Izzy is kicking up a storm, apparently. Wants your number so she can give you an ear bashing.'

'Yeah, hold off on that for now, will you. I know where there is a key to Dunston. I'm on my way now. I'll call you.'

Riley tried the Dunston Hall main line but there was no reply.

Nor from either of his grandparents' mobiles, which he knew, given the atrocious reception in the area, only worked if they were away from the hall.

'Please leave a message for Henry Clifford-Brown,' said the voice in his ear. At least there was an answer service on the cellphone.

'Grandad, it's Dom,' he said. 'Can one of you get back to me? I need your help. Nothing serious.' He started the Yamaha and set off. *Nothing serious?* Who was he trying to kid?

THIRTY-THREE

On the final stretch of the switchbacked road to Dunston Hall, Riley reviewed what he had learned from the Irishman, the methods he had used to gain that knowledge. He felt a sharp pang of guilt thinking about Astral. That poor dog. What sort of crackpot wires up a *dog*? Of course, he wouldn't have eviscerated it. The bomb wasn't set up to explode. Had he touched the wires, the Airedale would have received a mild electric shock, enough to make her yelp and scare the bejesus out of George O'Donnell.

Riley hadn't known there would be a dog, it was just a spur-of-the-moment idea. The vest was originally intended for George. And in the original scheme of things it would have been a fully operational one. At least he wouldn't be on PETA's blacklist for that. But Astral worked. Riley was fairly sure O'Donnell would have held out under any threats to harm his person. Menace the dog, though, and he bleated like a flock of sheep.

Sometimes he worried he had inherited something from his mother that wasn't altogether rational.

I think you should stick to blowing up inanimate objects.

You could be right there, Nick.

His old pal kept quiet as he hammered the Yamaha down the motorway to Dunston Hall. By the time he finally pulled up in front of the façade of his grandparents' wing of the house, the over-worked engine was making an odd whining noise of protest. As Riley dismounted, he felt a twinge in his back and an ache in his kidneys. He also couldn't feel his arse cheeks. The bone-shaking bike wasn't designed for such urgent dashes. Neither was he. He took a few seconds to stretch, took off his helmet and stowed it in the top box, then walked over the gravel to the front door. It took a second to realise something was missing. The BMW. Had they just gone out?

Riley reached the front door and lifted the heavy lion's head knocker and let it drop. He listened to the noise boom around the interior of the hall. But that was all. No sound of footsteps. Yet he knew it was pretty unusual for both of them to be out these days. He waited a couple of minutes – they were not the speediest pair – then knocked again. The same response. Zilch.

Riley went to the third plant pot from the left, the one with the bay tree, and sunk his fingers deep into the soil. He came out with a plastic bag containing two keys, one for the Yale, the other for a Chubb mortice lock. He wasn't sure that leaving buried keys was a particularly clever move for a pair of spooks but they always shrugged his concerns off, saying Dunston was 'neutral territory' in their war. Not for burglars, he used to say. Maybe the hidden package reminded them of the dead-letter drops in Moscow in their youth. When he tried the Chubb, the latter hadn't been thrown. Which was odd, as his grandparents always double-locked.

He slotted the key into the Yale, turned it and stepped inside, closing the door behind him. 'Grandad? Grandma?'

Nothing.

'Henry? Barbara?'

Riley shrugged his backpack onto the polished floor and

listened to the house but the only noise it gave back to him was the grave tick of a grandfather clock. He looked at his phone. No signal. As usual. He did a quick recce of the ground floor, pausing to look out over the lawn and lake to the woods where he had spent what seemed like the majority of his childhood, whenever his mother Rachel was 'indisposed'.

He was so consumed with worries about his grandparents that he almost missed it. In the conservatory, the broken pane of glass that had been repaired. The Sellotape used to fix the shards in place looked new. There were specks of glass glinting on the floor. The window had been broken recently and the repair didn't look like one that Henry would approve of. Riley opened the door and stepped onto the patio, examining the ground near the glass. There was something that might be a footprint, but nothing clear and definitive.

With renewed vigilance he went in and swept each room for clues, but they were unyielding. Out in the hallway he stood beneath the stairs and stared at the door that, he knew, led down to the cellar. *The forbidden catacomb*, his mum used to say. Or *the Gateway to Hell*. He never knew what was down there, apart from the shotguns his grandad stored in a locked cabinet. Henry used to make up scary tales of what was beyond that door. He realised later in life they were to stop him being curious. Even now, when he knew a little about his grandparents' extraordinary story and the sort of work they did, he had still never been down there. But he knew where the key was kept.

Except it wasn't where it should be. He felt under the console table, where it usually rested, held secure by a magnetic pad. The pad was still there, but not the key. His sense of unease increased and he tried not to give in to a full-blown panic attack. But something wasn't right.

Riley went back to the door, examined the lock. He could probably kick it in, but old doors like that never yielded the way they did in the movies. Feet and knees often gave out first. He decided to come back to it.

A search of upstairs confirmed that something was amiss. The bed in the master bedroom was unmade – not like his grandmother at all – and there were clothes on the floor. Pyjamas and a nightgown. One of the two wardrobes was open and several hangers on the left were unoccupied. Again, Grandma would not have liked the lack of symmetry.

He forced himself to breathe easy, not to jump to conclusions. Perhaps there had been a medical emergency and they had driven to hospital. At their age such events were increasingly likely. A fall, a stroke, a heart attack.

Riley quickly gave the other bedrooms a once-over, found nothing, and returned downstairs. He examined the entrance to the cellar carefully. The lock was heftier than he had first thought. The door didn't have so much as a rattle in it. The key actually threw what felt like steel bolts. You really would break a leg trying to kick it down. He doubted you could even shoot it out, even if he had a gun. It was possible the entire door was a steel-plate sandwich, so it was no use trying to batter it down with an axe or some such.

It was while examining the frame that he found the splodge of blood on the woodwork. He wiped at it with a finger. It was recent enough to smear. Someone in the house had been injured. Okay. Time to take that fucking door out.

From his backpack Riley fetched a length of the det cord he had taken from the barracks' stores and ran it down the door jamb where the lock mated with the frame. He then taped an electric detonator to the end of the det cord and ran a length of twin-flex firing cable to a safe distance around the corner before completing the circuit.

The sharp crack bounced around the hall and the familiar stench of a detonation hit him. When he walked back around, the door was open. He looked at the shattered lock. It had been a substantial piece of kit. It was the wood around it that had mostly given way. He peered into the cellar. The stair lights were on. Someone was at home.

There were heavy stone steps down to the space below, but there was a landing after he had taken a dozen of them and the kind of padded door you found in recording studios blocked his way. Above it was a bare red light bulb, unlit, clearly designed to warn when entry would be inadvisable. Luckily, this door was unlocked and it opened with the tiny gasp of rubber seals parting.

He stepped gingerly down the stairs. 'Grandma?'

At any other time, he would have marvelled at the cages of wine and the various electronic equipment that had been installed – none of which was on – but he was transfixed by the sight of his grandmother.

She was slumped in the chair under a bare bulb that made her features look yellow and waxy. Her head, disfigured by a gash and bruise at her temple, was on her shoulder, her eyes were closed, and a thin trickle of red had spilled from the corner of her mouth.

'Oh, no, no, no. Fuck, no.'

A wave of pain hit him. Riley's cry of anguish battered the brick walls of the cellar as he fell to his knees next to her, put his head on her lap and sobbed.

*

The bomb-maker pushed up the roller shutter on the rear of the Transit 'Luton' van and peered inside. Tied to the side walls, covered in felt blankets, were the main panels of the bombs he would create. Six crates contained the rest of the components. He could start assembling now. He had given the lad a sedative so he would sleep for a few hours. He would check him every half-hour or so, just to be sure. Sometimes, if he slept and then woke during the day, the boy would scream at the top of his lungs. The last thing he needed at this crucial juncture was a neighbour calling the authorities, saying they thought someone was being abused. Police might be called. Such things happened in this country.

The van was parked to the left side of the house. 'Rick' had backed it in. Nobody overlooked the driveway, apart from one house at the rear, and he had never seen any movement or lights on in that particular dwelling. He was as private as he could be in the suburbs of this city.

He climbed inside, pulled the shutter back down and switched on the internal lights. He began untying the panels from the wooden slats that lined the van.

When they had taught him to build the Viper at the bomb-making school in Kandahar, they had called it a Harvey. He had no idea why. He had asked the Iranian who ran the course where the name had come from. He said something about a giant rabbit in a movie, but the bomb-maker thought he was lying. Anyway, when they first deployed it against the Americans, he had re-named it, using the term the Americans had used for their mission against Taliban sites in the Daychopan district of Zabul province. That action was called Operation Mountain Viper. He had shortened it to *Maar*. Viper. After the device had been used in attacks in Kabul and Herat and the Americans had listened to the chatter about the bomb and translated the name, the Viper became something for the unbelievers to fear across Afghanistan.

In the back of the Transit van, the bomb-maker uncovered and laid out the panels. The man had done well. Each sheet of shiny metal was a composite. They had been expertly cut and glued together like a sandwich. A layer of metal, then a thin rubber filling, and another layer of metal. This would be the casing for the bombs. The inner and outer tinplate would be made live, with only the insulating layer between them preventing a circuit being completed.

One classic way to render a bomb harmless was to flood it with water. Which meant drilling a hole through the side or top to insert a hose. If anyone tried such a procedure on this bomb, the metal drill would pierce the rubber and act as a bridge between the two layers of metal. A current would flow. It would cause the main charge to explode.

It was just one of many little tricks he would incorporate. The Viper had many, many ways to bite.

*

As he knelt next to his grandmother, head on her arm, Riley reflected on how much he owed Henry and Barbara. His grandparents had always done their best to look after him. They had sent him to boarding school, which he had hated – he had eventually persuaded them that he belonged at a comprehensive – although in retrospect it might have been the best option for him in the long run. His father didn't want him, and it was increasingly clear that his mother, despite her protestations, was incapable of prolonged caring. So, he had shuttled between his grandparents and, when she had been consumed by guilt and remorse at her mothering skills, Rachel. She didn't have the breakdown until after he joined the army – in some moments of lucidity she blamed his decision to enlist for her mental fragility. He didn't buy it. She got to her final destination all on her own.

Helped along by a river of booze and God knows what else. And through it all, his grandparents had been the only safe haven he could rely on.

Riley started as he felt the hand on his head. 'Dominic? Is that you?'

He leapt back and to his feet. She was stirring, coming back from the dead. Her eyes were fully open now. 'What are you doing here?'

'Me? What the hell are you doing locked down here? I thought you were dead! Is that blood? Are you hurt?'

He pulled a handkerchief from his pocket – a habit Barbara had drilled into him as a young man, as she despised paper tissues – and dabbed at the red streak at the corner of her mouth.

'Blood? No, I don't think so. That's wine.' She pointed to the wound on her temple. 'This is real. I foolishly tried to fight back and ended up bashing myself on the frame upstairs.'

'Here.' He handed her the handkerchief and she pressed it against the gash. It came away with old blood only.

'That's not too bad. Stopped bleeding. Probably leave a mark. I'll claim it was a sabre gash I picked up in Mongolia.' She gave a little chuckle.

'I'll get you to hospital. It needs a steri-strip.'

'Oh, don't fuss, Dominic. It'll be fine. I thought while I was down here, I might as well try a bottle of the Château Martet.' She pointed to an empty glass next to the monitor. Beside it, Riley noted with some alarm, was a compact Walther pistol.

'No wonder the bang didn't wake you.'

'Bang?'

'It would have woken the dead. I had to blow the door to get in. Some damage to the woodwork, I'm afraid.'

'Tsk, don't worry about that. And you could set off a nuclear device and the sound wouldn't get past that door on the stairs. The BBC installed that. Back when the BBC had men in brown coats to do such things. Did you find Henry?'

Riley shook his head. 'No. No sign. And the car has gone. Your BMW.'

She frowned. 'I thought so.'

'What's happened?'

'All in good time. Let's get upstairs. I need coffee.'

'Grandma!'

She struggled to her feet and caught her breath before speaking. There was an uncharacteristic quiver in her voice. 'I fear Henry has been kidnapped.'

THIRTY-FOUR

Despite having made a sizeable dent in the bottle of Bordeaux, Barbara was only marginally more unsteady on her feet than usual, so it was relatively easy to get her upstairs and on to an armchair. Riley made a pot of strong coffee and two cheese sandwiches. He polished off one in double-quick time, realising he still hadn't eaten much in the past forty-eight hours. Hardly anything since breakfast with Charlie, before he had gone to the hotel to pick up his gear.

As he wolfed down the sandwich, Riley wondered how Ruby and Izzy were getting on. Scooby had told him they had been to the hall, but when there was no answer, the minders had decided to pull out and re-group. Perhaps they would come back. The two bodyguards probably had other ideas. No matter, Scooby had assured him the two women were top PPOs, so he could relax on that score. He would make sure he intersected with them once he had sorted out the situation with his grandfather.

What was worrying was what O'Donnell had told him, the pair who had turned up at his place, offering inducements for him to go back into the bomb-making business. The Irishman had refused their blandishments, or so he claimed. Actually, he believed O'Donnell. He had never been motivated by money. But now, months later, the recruiters had obviously found someone who would take their cash and who knew their acetone from their ethyl azide. And that someone had wired his car with explosives.

And, lest you forget, almost killed your daughter.

I haven't forgotten.

Riley pulled himself back into the moment and the job at hand. While Barbara finished her coffee and pecked, bird-like, at her sandwich, he went back downstairs and fetched the pistol he had spotted next to the empty wine glass. It might come in handy. It felt both flimsy yet solid, the lightness giving it the feel of a toy, but the action was reassuringly positive. It had also been fired recently – he could still smell the faint residue of a discharge – and subsequently cleaned and oiled. Given its probable muzzle velocity he could see why she hadn't tried to use it to shoot the lock off the door – she would be in serious danger of being hit by a ricochet off the steel casing of the lock.

Back in the drawing room, he poured himself a second cup of coffee, sat opposite her and asked: 'Okay, feeling better?'

'Much, thank you.'

He took a deep breath. Time to start over. 'What the hell happened here? Who has Grandpa? Is he at risk?

'The answer to the last pair of questions is – I really don't know,' said Barbara, her hand shaking just a little as she brought the cup to her lips. 'At least, not very much. He must have broken in at some point during the evening or night.'

'The conservatory,' Riley said. 'There's a broken pane. It's been repaired. I suspect so you wouldn't notice it on your evening rounds.'

'Henry's evening rounds. He has always locked up. And he always said we needed a sturdier lock on those French doors. But that means he was here all night. It was the early hours when he came into our bedroom.'

'Who is this "he"? Did you know him?'

'I knew who he was. Henry had actually met him before. Years ago.'

He waited for her to continue, but she simply took more coffee. Blood from a stone, he thought. 'Maybe you'd best start from the beginning.'

'Of course. Not much to tell.' She went through the man telling her to get dressed, then locking her in the cellar while he and Henry 'had a discussion'.

'What about?'

She gave a thin smile.

'Grandma, I have signed the Official Secrets Act, you know.'

'Oh, Barbara, please. I thought we got over Grandma years ago.' Riley nodded, knowing he couldn't make the change to informality. 'I don't know what they talked about. But I do happen to be au fait with the bare outlines of the background.'

'And?'

'I think it is too dangerous for you to know.'

Riley laughed at that. 'You do remember what I do for a living?'

'Don't be impertinent,' she said, a coolness in her voice. 'We had a visitor the other day . . . yesterday was it? Yes. Hector, I had the feeling he was checking how secure we are. By which I mean, trustworthy.'

'Now that's impertinent,' said Riley.

'Indeed.'

'But look, I can handle myself. It's important I know the background if we are to find him.'

'Can you fetch me some water? I feel a little parched. Wine and coffee, you know. The cheese was a little dry, too.'

Riley went to the kitchen and returned with a pitcher of iced water and two glasses. 'Tell me,' he asked, pointing to the pistol he had left on the sidetable. 'Why the gun?'

'Well, if any harm came to Henry and that chap returned to let me out as he promised, I would kill him. If, on the other hand, I was left down there to rot, I would have drunk a lot more wine – there's two bottles of Petrus left, you know, and a half-case of Grange – and killed myself.'

So matter-of-fact, thought Riley, as if she were choosing between two different brands of tea.

He sat down and watched her drink some of the water. A little colour returned to her cheeks. 'Ready?' he asked.

'Yes. I find this very difficult to talk about. Years of conditioning, you know.'

'I can imagine.' His grandparents had only revealed they had been spies after he had completed his ATO course. Even then, it was all broad-brush strokes. It had explained a lot, though, filled in many of the gaps in his childhood where they had disappeared and left him in the chaotic clutches of his mother. He had resented that. But, in their world, Queen and Country always came first, he supposed. They always tried their best to make it up to him afterwards.

'Even the name of the operation is secret. Very ill-advised name in my opinion. Bloody stupid, in fact. Not Henry's doing. No wonder they are so nervous about people knowing it, even now.'

'What was it?'

She took a deep breath, as if steeling herself to jump from a great height. 'Operation Homegrown.'

Riley felt a stab of irritation. Obfuscation had been this woman's stock in trade. She was having trouble giving him clarity, not helped by all the claret she had consumed.

'You're not really telling me who or what the guy who has taken Henry is.'

'As I said, I had never actually met him before. Heard of him. Oh,

I know *what* he was,' she said airily. 'And who. Henry knew him as Yousaf. Yousaf Ali. Although I do believe his real name is Joseph.'

Riley was about to ask for more detail when he heard glass crack and shatter and the thump of something heavy landing on the carpet behind his grandmother. He just had time to yell at her to close her eyes, when a supernova bloomed in the room with the noise of a thousand galaxies exploding at once.

*

They stopped for breakfast once the sun was well up. They were in an anonymous blue Renault, the BMW having been ditched in favour of the French car. The man he had known as Yousaf had promised him no harm would come to himself or his wife, and Henry actually believed him. Or, at the very least, believed that he thought that. But the visitor – who had not only shaved off his beard but was also dressed in Western clothes now – was one of many worms in a can that certain sections of his old firm would rather never wriggled into daylight.

'Are you going to tell me exactly what's going on?' he asked once more.

'I told you, all in good time.'

'At my age, you don't have much time left. Good or bad, Yousaf. You owe me an explanation.'

'And you'll get one.' He looked at Henry, his tone impatient. 'Can you stop asking questions now. I have to see if we are being followed. I will tell you everything when we are in place.'

Henry's fieldcraft skills were a little rusty, but even so, he was fairly certain nobody was following them. Not physically, anyway. But the CCTV cameras on motorways and main thoroughfares would be searching the screens for a BMW, if they were looking for him at all. His car had been swapped for the

239

Renault in a clearing off the B-road some three miles from Dunston Hall, which Henry knew for a fact was not covered by any surveillance systems.

Maybe his lot hadn't managed to tag Yousaf and had no idea where he was. But what about Five? That Muraski woman had been digging pretty hard, and she might well have his abductor on her radar. In which case, they might attempt a rescue. He hoped not. The man had a very serviceable Glock and rescue attempts could go either way for the 'hostage'. Which, he supposed, was what he was. That or the 'abductee' in this whole strange and sorry mess.

Yousaf was a lot younger and stronger than him. He moved with a sinewy grace and his muscles had been hardened by the life he had chosen for himself. Trying to wrestle him or outrun him was out of the question. But another kind of opportunity would come along and Henry would take it.

He normally lacked Barbara's ruthlessness, but the man's treatment of his wife – even if her colliding with the doorframe was more by accident than design – meant he would have no compunction about tackling Yousaf if he got the chance. Even though the cellar room was furnished with food, drink and lavatory facilities, she must be feeling very trapped by now and the thought crushed his chest with both anxiety and anger. He only hoped that, when the time came, his aim was as good as Barbara's. The thought of his imprisoned wife made his mind turn to thoughts of escape, of overpowering Yousaf.

Henry Clifford-Brown had boxed in his youth. Light heavyweight. Before he had bulked out. His most useful features were his long reach and the size of his hands. Although lacking in the combination of grace and danger that defined the best fighters he had come across, Henry was more than capable of catching a technically superior opponent off guard and flooring him. But he knew he had to pick his moment.

He told Yousaf he was hungry and Yousaf, obviously in need of food too, turned off the M1 and stopped at a bright red café, emblazoned with the words *Rita's Truck Stop*, next to a petrol station. Henry reckoned Yousaf had chosen Rita's place because, unlike any service station, it would not have CCTV connected to the police or highways authority. The Formica forest inside was filled by lorry drivers, of both sexes, locals and company reps. Henry ordered a disappointing full English breakfast that acted as fuel and little else. The sausages, in particular, were egregious, gritty and greasy. But he ate them anyway. He knew he needed to keep his strength up. He turned his attention to the tea. Yousaf had settled on black coffee and a pastry. He finished both with indecent haste and was clearly impatient to be on his way.

'Are you going to tell me where we are going?' Henry asked.

'Not yet. All in good time.' His English was accented with traces of Pashto.

'Why am I here?' he asked, not for the first time.

Yousaf thought for a while. 'Very well. Because you know our destination. At least, you know how to get there. I have no idea.'

'Ah.' Now he had more than an inkling of where they were heading. Why, that was another matter, to be drawn out of Yousaf during what was going to be a long, tiring drive. 'I could simply sketch you a map, perhaps.'

Yousaf laughed, something of a cackle. 'No, you need to be there, Henry. You are part of the plan.'

Henry didn't like the sound of that. He was too old to be part of anybody's plans. He finished his tea and nodded over to the door marked *Truckin' Men*. 'I shall have to use the facilities before

241

we go. When you reach my age, you'll understand the needs of an old man's bladder.'

Yousaf fixed him with a doleful gaze. 'That's one thing I won't have to worry about, Henry,' he said.

'Why not?'

'Because I have no intention of reaching your age. Come on, let's be going.'

*

Riley was hooded for the entire journey. He had only really started to re-connect with the world once he was in the van, or whatever was transporting him to parts unknown. They must have hooded him while his senses were scrambled. There was still a residual hum in his ears and his retinas were feeding him a light show worthy of New Year's Eve. He didn't actually recall being taken out of the house. Didn't even know how many flash-bang grenades they had used. It was normally more than one, with a maximum of three in that sort of space. He could smell the acrid smoke they produced, taste it at the back of his throat. Nausea was trying to get a foothold, but he did his best to keep it at bay. Throwing up in a hood wasn't a good idea.

A quick survey of his body told him his wrists were bound with what felt like a plastic tie, then secured to a belt of some description so although he could sit more comfortably than if he had his hands behind his back, he couldn't lift them to take off the hood. Straps around his forehead and neck secured him to the headrest of the seat, so he couldn't bend down either. Someone had thought this through. All in all, it seemed rather OTT for a simple AWOL.

If it was the army who had him, of course. It didn't fit with its MO, the flash-bangs and the yelling. Not for someone who had gone over the wall. It smacked more of special forces or anti-terrorism police. They always liked to go in mob-handed. He stopped speculating. It was only adding to the kernel of anxiety he felt in his chest. He would find out soon enough.

He only hoped they hadn't done the same to his grand-mother. Surely they wouldn't treat an old woman like this? One who had served her country so brilliantly? Well, he supposed, that depended on which organisation had taken them. And if O'Donnell was telling the truth, they might well have been snatched by what used to be known as a foreign power.

As the turbine whine in his ear finally wound down, he tried to judge if he was alone in the van. But his hearing hadn't recovered enough to be sensitive to the sound of breathing or the squeak of a seat as someone moved. He tried a cruder method.

'Hello? Anybody there?' The words sounded like they were spoken underwater. 'Grandma? Are you here? Are you safe?' Anyone?'

Whatever it was that jabbed under his ribs felt like hard steel, but it could easily have been the rigid fingers of someone who knew what they were doing. His breath exploded out of his mouth, hot and wet against the fabric of the hood. "kinell,' was all he could gasp. Unable to bend double to offer even slight relief, the whole of his solar plexus was aflame. Now there was a good chance he was going to toss the cheese sandwich he had wolfed down at Dunston Hall.

Eventually the fire dimmed and he was able to stop panting. He became aware of someone at his shoulder, breath warm on his ear. He spoke so softly, Riley could barely hear him. Luckily, he enunciated carefully and slowly, in one-word sentences. 'Shut. The. Fuck. Up.'

Riley decided he should take his advice and shut the fuck up.

*

The journey took more than an hour, less than two. Riley couldn't be more precise than that because of having to rely on what was left of his senses when the trip was underway. He felt the van or truck slow, a slight grinding of the gears, and then a tipping sensation as it went down a ramp or slope. The noise of electronic gates or shutters operating just about penetrated the steel wall behind him.

Then, the engine was killed. Doors slammed. Voices.

A rush of chill wind entered as the doors at the rear of the transport were opened, along with a smell of diesel, petrol and oil. The temperature and the stink suggested somewhere underground.

Hands began to work at the various straps securing him to the seat. Once freed, he was hauled – although not roughly – by the arms and on to his feet. 'Step down here, mate. Two of them. One, two. Turn left. Walk forward. One step up. Now.' This voice was firm but reasonable. He reckoned he had been handed over to someone who hadn't told him to shut the fuck up.

He heard swing doors pushed back, the beep of electronics and he was manoeuvred through a barrier of some description, deliberately brushing the side to try and ascertain its size and shape. It felt like the ones found on the Tube.

It was warmer now, although the air felt artificial, processed. They were some way below the surface, he surmised.

He was guided by his two minders through a series of doglegs, before one of them told him to stop. A key turned in a lock and a hand in the small of his back pushed him through it. The hood was finally yanked off.

The strip lighting hurt Riley's eyes and he blinked away tears. He turned to face the two men. They were almost identical: stocky, heads shaven, necks a distant memory. Dumb and Dumber (the latter the slightly taller one) were dressed in black army-style sweaters and dark trousers with heavy-soled and probably steel-capped boots. No weapons were in evidence, apart from a short baton and a Taser, clipped on to their belts. No badges, either. These were not military, or at least not any branch of the military he had ever seen. Nor, he suspected, were they the police. Private security? Possibly. One positive. He was pretty sure they were British. Those unfriendly faces were homegrown.

'Where am—?' he began.

Dumb cut him short, stepping into his face, breathing what smelled like wet cardboard on him. 'Oi. Do us a favour. Don't ask where you are. Or who we are. Or what's going on, eh? It'll be a waste of time and energy. All right?'

British, all right. In fact, he could narrow it down to somewhere along the Thames estuary.

Riley nodded. He was sure the man was telling the truth. The second of his minders used the snips on a multi-tool to cut the plastic ties on his wrists and he rubbed at them. Riley had one question it was worth trying.

'What happens next?'

A long-suffering sigh escaped from the taller man. 'You wait here.'

'You're not going to take my shoe laces or belt?'

The shorter one laughed at that. 'You want to top yourself? Be our guest.'

With that they withdrew, locking the door behind them.

Riley finished massaging the life back into his wrists. Then examined the room. Windowless, of course. Painted an institutional green, naturally. A cot bed, a side table, a chemical toilet. And that was it. Not even any graffiti scratched into the walls to pass the time. Christ, surely they wouldn't take Barbara to somewhere as bleak as this? She was an old woman. A tough old bird, certainly, but this would be tantamount to torture for her. Imprisonment without a good bottle of claret? Inhuman.

Riley walked over to the door and, although he knew it was

useless, tested the handle. No give at all. He slammed it with the side of his fist. If anything happened to his grandmother, he'd eviscerate Dumb'n'Dumber in a heartbeat.

He sat on the cot bed. A foam pillow the thickness of a pizza. Scratchy wool blankets. A slight smell of damp rising from the sheets. The Ritz it wasn't. Nevertheless, he lay back, put his hands behind his head and swung his feet on the bed. He was exhausted. And angry. That anger was directed as much at himself as anyone else. After the Cotswolds, he had gone into some sort of funk, running on animal instinct, rather than logic, blinded with fury generated by Ruby's brush with a bomb. Most decisions he had made since then had been flawed. Drinking too much with Scooby. Not calling in the information he got from George O'Donnell straightaway. Sitting around with his grandmother and allowing himself to be snatched by . . . whom, exactly?

Good guys or bad guys? Bomb-hunters or bomb-makers?

He lay there, trying to put together the puzzle of what, exactly, was going on with the bombs and bombers, but too many pieces were missing. How did the abduction of Henry Clifford-Brown fit in with the bombings? Or did it? If only he had been more skilful at drawing information out of his grandmother. He wondered if someone was doing that now and he felt another pulse of hot fury. How dare they use flash-bangs in a room containing an old woman? The shock might well have killed her. In which case . . .

In which case what? You'll turn into Sylvester Stallone? Robocop? Deadpool? You're fucked, Riley.

There was that unexpected visitor in his cranium again. Nick, poor dead Nick, offering an opinion from beyond the grave. Still, his old pal was right. He was fucked, powerless, trapped. Riley did the only sensible thing he could in that situation. He fell asleep.

THIRTY-FIVE

They were still a hundred miles from their destination by Henry's reckoning and it was getting dark. He traced his finger along the road atlas – the Renault was a basic model, without sat nav – and double-checked with the phone that Yousaf had propped up on the centre console. They were on the M90, heading for Perth, with Yousaf driving – fortunately not like an Afghan cabbie in a hurry. Normally Henry would have revelled in the countryside they had crossed, but he was too irritated to relax and soak up the sight of the hills and dales or tick off the birds he could see wheeling in the skies above them.

'I'm tired,' he said eventually. 'I missed my afternoon nap. We always have one at home.' At least, he did. Barbara liked to 'get on' while he was snoozing. The thought of his wife set off pangs of guilt and longing in his gut. But he couldn't afford to worry about her right now. He made a mental apology to her, secure in the knowledge she would understand. And that if there was any way she could make the best of the situation, she would. 'And I would love a cigarette.' The nicotine patch was obviously overwhelmed by events. He needed a stronger hit than it could supply. Ideally, he would like a pipe filled with Peterson Limited Edition.

'I can't help you there.'

'We could stop.'

'Not far now, you said,' Yousaf protested.

'Two hours at least. It'll be dark. What do we do then? There's a dearth of streetlamps up there.'

Yousaf had no answer.

'And I'm hungry.'

'We'll stop then,' Yousaf said huffily. 'But we aren't staying the night. We'll get near to our destination and you can put the seat back and have a snooze.'

'Don't you need to sleep?' Henry asked.

'No. I haven't got any time to waste on sleep. We'll begin at first light.'

'What if it is occupied? The house?'

'Why would it be? I thought Homegrown was dead?'

'For years now. But that doesn't mean it hasn't been replaced with some other . . . scheme.'

Yousaf waved that concern away. 'We'll worry about that when we get there.'

'If there is anyone in residence, they'll probably be armed.'

Yousaf turned to him and gave a crooked grin. 'Good. I look forward to it. See if you can find a pub near Perth on the phone. Now you mention it, I could do with something to eat.'

Henry closed the Here navigation app, selected Google and did as Yousaf suggested. 'Pitcairn Inn,' he announced. 'Close to Almondbank. Pub of the Year 2018, it says.'

'Let's hope it hasn't gone downhill since then.'

They found it without difficulty, to the north-west of the city. The bar was busy, but they elicited barely a glance as they sat down at one of the small number of tables in the rear. A waitress took their order. Henry opted for a whisky, Yousaf for Coca-Cola. Then, steak-and-ale pie for the older man, halloumi burger for the younger. Chips with both.

As they waited, Henry stretched out some of the cramp from being cooped up for hours and asked the question that had been on his lips all day. 'Was Nottingham yours?'

Yousaf used his napkin to wipe perfectly clean cutlery, then laid the white square over his lap. He looked Henry in the eye. The older man stared back, noting that there was nothing to read in there, as if the humanity had been sucked out, like a faulty lens. 'Why would you think that?'

'Because you are a bomb— because it is your line of work. What you have done for years. Since we brought you here.'

'Not any longer. That's why I am here. To renounce such things.'

Henry remembered only too well how difficult it was to get a straight answer to a question once you crossed into the tribal lands. 'Is that a "no"? That the Nottingham incident was not your doing?'

'Correct. Not mine.'

'And the Cotswolds? The car?'

'No.' A firm shake of the head. 'You are not listening. I am done with such foolishness.'

'Then who?'

'I do not know.'

'You are telling me that there are two ... people with your skills in the country?'

'Very likely more, thanks to you.'

Henry did not wish to be reminded of this fact. He kept quiet as the drinks arrived, apart from asking for a small jug of water. When it arrived, he poured a splash in to release the aromas of the whisky and breathed deeply. 'You don't know what you're missing,' he said.

'Ah, but I do. I had my fill.' Yousaf sipped his Coke. 'Before I saw the error of my ways. Before you found me. God is great.'

Henry was relieved he had stuck to English. These days people's ears tended to prick up when they heard *allāhu akbar*. 'So you have no idea who did Nottingham? Or the others?'

'None. We don't have a bombers' WhatsApp group, you know. Or any sort of social club, like old spies do, I believe.'

Two bomb-makers, he thought. When that Muraski woman had shown him the photograph of Yousaf he had convinced himself – as she clearly had – that the chickens had come home to roost. But he was mistaken. 'You still haven't explained why you are here. In this country. If not to make . . . things like that.'

Yousaf waved a hand. 'You wouldn't understand. You never did know Afghanistan. You visited the country, yes. Like a tourist. You never found the soul of the people there, you never truly understood.' He looked a little crestfallen.

'I am not sure I do even now,' Henry said with genuine regret. 'They are beautiful people, it is a wonderful religion, corrupted by outsiders. Like you.'

A shadow passed between them and the waitress slid a plate before each of them. A large bowl of chips was placed in the middle. 'Ah, lovely,' said Henry, with genuine anticipation. 'Nice and quick. Can I have some mustard? English? Thank you.'

When the waitress had left, Yousaf gave a chuckle. 'I had forgotten how ridiculous it is. Being English. So many rules. So many pleases, thank yous, would you minds.'

They were in Scotland, but Henry let it pass. 'Not like that freewheeling Islam, eh?' retorted Henry, laughing at his own joke.

Yousaf's face clouded. 'We all know why those rules are there. It isn't just politeness or embarrassment speaking. It is a map for living a good life. It is laid down in the Koran.'

Henry hated being lectured to. He particularly hated having his own words echoed back to him. There was a time when he was telling Yousaf he had to live by the good book. 'Eat your burger. I don't want to hear about all that right now. Don't spoil my meal.'

'You can do anything to an Englishman, but never come between him and his pint, his tea or his pie.'

Henry decided not to rise to any more bait. 'Or his pipe. That's not a bad code to live by. And in this case, it's a very good pie. Excellent chips, too. Thank you.' The waitress had swished by, depositing the mustard on the table. He unscrewed the top, peered in and began excavating the contents with his knife.

'Before I retired, I made one last bomb,' said Yousaf, leaning in and speaking so quietly, the words barely travelled the space between them. 'The final sign-off. One last job. You know that convention? In the movies. Yes, we did watch films. Jihadists love Hollywood. Know thine enemy. Anyway, "We do one last job," says the master criminal. Normally it goes wrong. Not this time.' Henry waited, knowing the man would say what he meant eventually. 'London was my one last job.'

Henry put down the knife with the blob of yellow mustard balanced on its tip and let it rest on his plate. Had he missed something? Was he getting even more forgetful than usual in his dotage? 'London? There hasn't been one in London. Not recently.'

Yousaf took a bite of his burger and chewed it well, swallowed, and helped himself to a couple of chips, which followed the halloumi into his mouth. He made appreciative noises before he leaned back in his chair and spoke again, this time at normal volume. 'Not yet.'

*

Riley awoke with his ears still ringing, an almost permanent situation over the past few days. His brain, however, felt less foggy than before. He swung his legs off the cot bed and looked around

251

the windowless cell. As before, there was little chance that he could execute an escape. The only vulnerable place was the door. Given the right gear he could blow it off its hinges. Wouldn't take much. But he didn't have the gear. The question he had asked himself before he went to sleep remained stubbornly unanswered: who had taken him? White hats or black hats?

He stepped back as the door clanged opened. Dumb and Dumber were standing in the entrance, the latter with a telescopic baton held loosely at his side.

'Come with us, please, sir,' said Dumb. The civility was certainly an improvement, even if it didn't sound particularly heartfelt.

Riley stood and stretched his arms above his head.

'What time is it?' he asked.

'If you'll follow us, sir.'

It seemed silly to refuse. They led him down a corridor – Dumb in front, Dumber behind – that looked like something from the bowels of a ship, all shiny gloss paint, exposed pipes, harsh bare bulbs and steel flooring. After a hundred metres or so, they turned a corner and it was like being taken above deck – carpets, paintwork that wouldn't cause convulsions at Farrow & Ball and softer lighting. They passed a series of anonymous wooden doors, each with a letter and number on it. Dumb halted at 4c, turned the handle and nodded at the interior as he opened the door. 'If you just make yourself comfortable in here, sir, someone will be along to see you shortly.'

It sounded like he was being asked to wait for a medical inspection. He hoped not. He didn't exactly have clean underwear on.

Making himself comfortable wasn't going to be easy. There was a metal desk and three chairs plus a waste-paper bin. One wall was what appeared to be a mirror but was most likely an observation panel for the watchers whom he reckoned were – or were going to be – next door.

He sat on the single chair, assuming his interrogators would take the pair opposite him, placed his hands on the table and closed his eyes, concentrating on his breathing, blocking out all useless speculation. It will be what it will be.

A well-dressed man entered within five minutes, trailing behind him the faint whiff of expensive cologne. Pink shirt, grey suit, highly polished Grenson brogues. He took one of the chairs and put a folder on the desk.

'What the hell am I doing here?'

'My name is Paul Oakham, Mr Riley.' Public school tone, clipped, confident. 'I am a senior officer here at MI5.'

Well, at least that was one question cleared up. It could be worse. However, spooks, even UK ones, weren't necessarily the nice guys. He was careful to show no surprise at the revelation. His training was to give no quarter. 'It's Staff Sergeant Riley. And I repeat. What the hell am I doing here?'

'Well, it remains to be seen whether you retain your rank, doesn't it? Given your behaviour over the past twenty-four hours.'

'Am I under arrest?'

'You were cautioned at . . .' He opened the folder and consulted some notes. 'Dunston Hall. And placed under arrest for offences under the Explosive Substances Act. You have not, however, been charged.'

He was referring to the contents of his backpack, the material he had 'borrowed' from the explosives safe at the barracks. 'Listen, pal. A caution is only legal if you are compos mentis,' he said. 'That is, awake to hear it. Some tossers had just thrown flash-bangs into a room. I think my hearing might have been impaired.'

'That is academic. You're not being detained here against your will. You are free to go. But the moment you walk out of the building it will be a toss-up right now who arrests you first, the Met or the Military Police.'

'Perhaps they could arm-wrestle for me.'

Oakham looked as if he had just smelt a fart. 'I wouldn't make light of your situation, Mr Riley. You have been a very foolish man. However, we do think you have information that might be of assistance to us, which might shine a more, um, favourable light on your activities. Am I right?'

Riley knew the best way to thwart an interrogator was to stick to a list of not entirely unreasonable demands. It helped put you in the driving seat. 'I want a phone. I want to know how my grandmother is, and I want some action on tracing my grandfather.'

'All in due course.'

'Mrs Clifford-Brown. How is she?'

'She is being well looked after.' Riley sensed evasiveness.

'Where? Here? In a cell like the one you put me in? She's an old woman. And a bloody national hero. Your pet thugs subjected her to noise and light which could induce, at the very least, a heart attack or stroke. How the fuck is she?' He shouted the last sentence.

Oakham drummed his fingers on the table. Riley could just glimpse an Omega watch beneath the pink cuff of his shirt. It was after seven. It had been a very long day. And he couldn't bank on it being over yet, not by what his grandfather always called a long chalk. 'Can you explain how your DNA came to be on a component of the first device used in the Nottingham bombing? One apparently you did not handle.'

Really? Riley was careful not to react. It would give Oakham the upper hand. Maybe the lab had fucked up and cross-contaminated. Perhaps it was a component from Afghan. Was that possible? Riley decided he could interrogate the possibilities later. He adopted an I-speak-your-weight tone. 'A phone and an update on my grandmother. Action on my grandfather, who has been abducted.'

'Or perhaps you can explain why you left the scene of a crime? A car bomb.'

'I want a phone and an update on my grandmother. And a brew.' A pause grew into silence. Riley couldn't help but fill it. 'And why would I plant a bomb in my own car?'

'You remember that American actor who faked his own racial abuse and assault? To generate some sense of victimhood? Might not an ATO do something similar to make himself a hero?'

A little piece of the black vortex within broke away and spun up into his consciousness. Riley found himself on his feet, stabbing a finger at Oakham. His short fuse had just burnt out. 'I lost friends at Nottingham. I could have lost my daughter at that school. You think I fuckin' planted those bombs? MI5? You're the best we have? Jesus, no wonder the country is in such shit.' The door opened a few inches and Dumber's face appeared in the crack. Oakham raised a hand to reassure him.

'Sit down, Riley.'

He leaned over the desk instead. 'I want a phone and an update on my grandmother. Action on my grandfather. Or you won't get what I know.'

'Which is?'

'I can tell you who is planting the bombs.'

'We know who is planting the bombs.'

'Is that so? A second ago you were convinced it was me. I want a phone—'

'Sit down.'

The voice was hard and inflexible. Riley sat.

'I know this will come as a surprise to you, Riley, but I do have other pressing matters to attend to. I shall send in a Mobile Surveillance Officer who has taken some interest in your case. She will listen to what you have to say. If we like it, then perhaps you'll get your phone call.'

'And a brew.'

Oakham stared at him for a second, letting contempt and irritation show on his face. *'Perhaps.'*

THIRTY-SIX

As they walked along the asphalt path that led from the side entrance of the Pitcairn Inn to the car park, Henry felt his resolve strengthening. Maybe this was the moment for action, he thought, as they escaped from the shadow of the building and began crossing the deserted gravelled car park to its far corner where Yousaf had left the car. Yes, he decided, now – he suspected few others would present themselves before they reached their destination. So he stepped back and, channelling the young boxer he once was, swung his right fist at Yousaf's ear. It connected nicely and Yousaf let out a gasp of pain and staggered to one side. Sadly, time seemed to have drained Henry's strength and speed. In his prime that blow would have sent a man to the ground. And he would have been fast enough to move in for a follow-up, rendering his opponent helpless. Neither of these two things happened.

But Yousaf recovered quickly and spun around, snarling like a wounded beast, and launched a furious counter-attack. There were no Queensbury Rules obeyed in the response. Henry would only remember a blur of fists, the percussive sound as the blows made contact and the loci of pain exploding all over his body. Yousaf used all four limbs, driving Henry back, the old man yelping helplessly with each strike, until he fell to his knees and vomited up most of the pie he had eaten onto the gravel.

Yousaf stood over him, panting hard, but his voice was firm. 'I wondered when you would try something like that. You're lucky I didn't break your skull. No more, eh?' He jabbed the old man in the side of the head. 'Eh?'

'No more,' Henry managed to utter between shallow breaths.

'You all right over there?'

A woman's voice from the darkness. What had she witnessed? He turned. He could just make her out in the light from the pub's window. Out for a smoke on the rear verandah?

Henry made an effort to speak, perhaps to yell for help, but Yousaf grabbed his arm and squeezed hard. 'Stay quiet.' He took a gamble that the woman had come late to the party and seen nothing. 'I think the meal was a bit rich for him. At his age.'

'Aye, I thought I heard someone spewin' their guts.'

'He'll be okay now. Thanks. Come along, old chap. Let's get you in the car. Good night.'

'Good night,' came the reply. 'And good luck.' A light flared and was replaced by a glowing red spot. His supposition had been correct. A smoker.

Yousaf pulled Henry to his feet and half-carried, half-dragged him to the Renault. He opened the door and managed to fold the old man's long and rubbery limbs into the passenger seat. Henry put his head back against the rest and opened his mouth. Small groans escaped from it with each exhalation.

'You'll be fine. I never got out of second gear.'

'Very . . . very . . . considerate of you.'

Yousaf slid behind the wheel. 'You want some water?'

'In a moment, perhaps.' He could smell the smoke from the cigarette, triggering his craving again.

'Get us close to the lodge and we will rest up, perhaps.'

'Why? Why did you do it?'

Yousaf turned the key in the ignition, gave a little blip on the throttle. 'You started it, remember? You punched first.'

'No. London,' Henry protested with some effort to his ribs. 'Why build another bomb? Why would you kill innocent men and women? To what end?'

Headlamps on, Yousaf reversed the Renault out of its space, the wheels spinning on the gravel. 'Why? It was what I was trained to do.'

'You were trained to kill Russians.'

'Times change, Henry. Priorities change.' Yousaf bumped the car out onto the road and headed north again. He put his phone on the dash and called up the Here app. 'Wars change.'

'But London?'

'At the next junction, make a left,' said the robotic voice of the sat nav.

Yousaf saw the signpost to Pitlochry and took the turning, accelerating now he was certain he was on the right road.

'London is a statement. But I'll tell you something. Part of the reason you are here with me. Perhaps all of the reason you are with me.'

'What's that?' Henry asked.

'You can stop it happening, Henry. You can save all those men, women and children. It's in your hands.'

*

The new arrival opened the folder she had placed on the desk. Riley looked her up and down. Like policemen, it seemed spooks were getting younger. She had an attractive enough face, he thought, but it was drawn and pale. The smudges under her eyes suggested she had been crying or was sleep-deprived. Maybe both. But he found it hard to imagine MI5 operatives weeping.

'My name is Kate Muraski,' she announced in a voice somewhat deeper than her small frame suggested. 'I am a Mobile SO and an Intelligence Officer with MI5. I left multiple messages for you.'

He folded his arms. 'I told your pal. You'll get nothing from me till you get me a phone, tell me about Barbara Clifford-Brown and try and find my grandfather, who is missing with a very dangerous man . . .'

'Which very dangerous man?'

'I asked about my grandmother. '

Muraski appeared to gather her thoughts before answering. 'Your grandmother is in good hands. The incident left her some-what confused. She is under observation. Not here. We don't have those sort of facilities. She is in Guy's Hospital. She has a female armed police officer from SO19 guarding her round the clock.'

'Prove it.'

'Prove what?'

'That my grandmother is where you say she is.'

'Why would I lie?'

Riley laughed. 'Let me think. Is it because you're in MI5? I want to talk to her.'

'I told you, she is not really . . . up or alert at the moment.'

'Then you can go and whistle. I'm saying nothing.'

Muraski muttered something obscene under her breath, plucked a phone from her bag, tapped the screen and held it up so that Riley could see it. The image showed Barbara in bed, asleep, with a plain-clothes policewoman – or so he assumed – next to her. 'Look at the time,' Muraski instructed. 'Ten minutes ago. I captured it from the CCTV to reassure you she is in good hands.'

'It could be faked.'

Muraski sighed. 'And we could be wasting valuable time. I want to talk about why you left the scene of the car bomb.'

'Simple. I didn't want this to happen.'

'What?'

He waved around the room '*This*. Interrogation. Debriefing. I needed to find out who had put a bomb under my car.'

'And did you?'

'I want a phone.' He pointed to hers. 'That one will do.'

'A lawyer can't help you here.'

'I want to talk to my *daughter*.' He put heavy, angry emphasis on the last word.

'You said something to my colleague about knowing who is planting the bombs.'

'Planting, yes. Making, no. They are always two different sets of people.'

He could almost hear the workings of her brain. Eventually, she pushed the phone over. He picked it up and dialled Izzy.

'Izzy? It's Dom.'

'Christ, Dom. What the hell is going on? Are you okay? Ruby's scared silly.'

'Let me talk to her.'

'She's asleep.'

'Where are you?'

'Heading for Padstow. We're in two cars. The blonde one is driving my Merc. Lisa. We're all in the BMW with Jackie.' Riley knew the BMW was probably a High Security model, effectively bullet- and bomb-proof, which was why they would insist on the clients riding in that. 'They're going to stay with us, so they say. This must be costing a fortune.' She lowered her voice, and he could hear the fright in the next sentence, probably more for Ruby than herself. 'Are we in danger?'

'I doubt that.'

His ex-wife did not sound reassured. 'It's possible, though?'

'I'm working on it. Right now. Give my love to Ruby. I'll call when I can.'

He rang off and handed the phone back. 'Thanks. My grandfather has also been kidnapped.'

'We'll come to that. You have something to share about the bombs?'

Riley hesitated, wondering if he had anything else useful to extract from Muraski before he handed her his treasure. 'After I left my daughter's school, I went back to my barracks and then to see George O'Donnell.' She looked blankly at him. 'Before your time. George was one of the Big Daddies, as they called them. The elite bomb-makers for the IRA.'

'The IRA?'

'Yes.' He could see from her expression that she was slightly rattled by the new player on the table. The Irish had not been on her radar. Riley carefully explained how a yellow and purple wire had led to George O'Donnell.

'You got him to talk. How?'

'I asked nicely.'

'Really? I find that hard to believe.'

'And I threatened to blow up his dog in front of him.'

'Jesus.'

The look of distaste on her face angered him. 'Yes, Jesus. Look, that man was responsible for scores of deaths and maimings. We can live with that. But hey, threaten a poor innocent animal and suddenly I'm a monster.'

'You won't be invited to Crufts, that's for sure.'

'Yeah, well. No animals were harmed during the making of this threat. I wasn't going to do it,' Riley said firmly. 'But he had to believe I would.' He thought it best not to mention that he had nearly choked the old bugger out. That hadn't been him. He wasn't sure *what* that had been.

'So, what did you get from him?'

Riley knew this was the crux of the matter. 'I'd like a brew. Those flash-bangs leave you very thirsty.'

'As soon as you tell me what he said.'

When Riley didn't answer, Muraski unsheathed her claws a little. 'There is still the matter of your DNA on the Nottingham bomb. You know how long we can keep you here based on that alone.'

'Bullshit. That had to have been some sort of cock-up in storage or collection. It'd never stand up in court.'

Muraski arched one eyebrow. 'Who said anything about a court?'

Riley sighed. 'Okay. About a year ago, two people turned up asking if George's services were for hire. His skill at making bombs.'

'Who were they?'

'A man and a woman. His descriptions were vague. Young-ish, thirties maybe.'

'Nationality?'

'Not initially obvious from their appearance or accents. European, possibly Mediterranean.'

'What did he say?'

'He said no. That his bomb-making days were over. And he only did it for a cause he believed in. Not money.'

'How very principled. And that was that?'

'No. He also sold them a bomb cache,' said Riley.

Her eyebrows shot up in surprise. 'What? What kind of bomb cache?'

'Timers, detonators, det cord, circuits, the usual. There are still IRA ammunition dumps in this country. You know that, right? Well, he had a stash of Libyan bomb kits that had been buried around the time of the attacks on the City of London. He sold the kits to these people, which is how that yellow and purple wire ended up in Nottingham.'

'And he also sold them the explosive?'

'No, the Semtex he had stashed was u/s. Well past its sell-by date. They would have had to get their own supplies.'

'But no further clue who they were? You said their nationalities were not obvious *initially* earlier.'

'Right. Just the one clue. Once, the old man's dog gave the man a not-so-friendly nip. The man responded by swearing. George remembered it. Che-or-tova Su-ka.'

What little colour there was in Muraski's face drained away completely. '*Chyorta suka*?'

'Yes. You know what it means? I Googled it. *Fucking bitch.*'

'Yes,' said Muraski thoughtfully. 'Fucking bitch. In Russian.'

*

Muraski left the room and came back with a mug of tea for Riley, as requested. In contrast to her earlier pallor she now looked flushed.

'My guess is that the Russian pair wanted a bomb-maker and when George refused them, they went elsewhere. But why would the Russians be behind a bombing campaign?'

'Because they like to fuck us up,' said Muraski. 'It's why they liked Brexit. Threw all our security arrangements and NATO into doubt. What if they were behind both the Nottingham bomb and the mosque attack? Divide and rule? Christ, did you see the clashes in Bradford last night?'

'You're forgetting,' he said, with only the merest sprinkle of vitriol. 'I've been banged up in a cell the last few hours.'

'Of course. It was a virtual riot. Casualties on all sides.'

'What about the car bomb aimed at me? Where does that fit in?

I don't think the FSB or GRU have any beef with me. O'Donnell said it wasn't the Irish heavies and I believed him.' He took a drink of tea. 'But then maybe this isn't linear.'

'How do you mean?'

'In Afghan we used to think "A" plants bomb just to kill soldiers. That wasn't always the case. There was such an intricate network of family and tribal affiliations, sometimes "A" planted a bomb to show "B" who was boss or to get the reward for an ATO, even though they didn't actually support the Taliban. Then there were the ones who planted for money. They filmed themselves hiding an IED, then the result of it detonating, and took the evidence to a local Taliban commander, who paid a fee, according to how much damage they did. It was an easy way to generate cash. Others just did it for fun. If it was a slow night in Kandahar—'

Muraski didn't let him finish. 'Stick to the point. I really don't need your war memoirs right now,' she said brusquely. Now she knew the Russians were involved, she seemed keen to get to the end of his story. 'So, after O'Donnell told you about the Russian man and the woman . . .'

'I went to Dunston Hall to see my grandparents, who happen to know a thing or two about Russians. I was going to let them press the alarm button, because they'd be taken seriously. Much more than me. I found out that Grandpa had been taken and Grandma locked away. I was just about to get to the bottom of it when some cowboys started lobbing grenades about.'

'Perhaps they over-reacted,' Muraski admitted. 'They came in heavy because you had a weapon.'

'It was my grandmother's gun.'

'It was apparently next to you. So, the incident commander decided to play it safe.'

'Well I'd hate to meet him when he is feeling reckless. What has my grandma said?' Riley asked.

'Nothing yet. She is still sedated. Did she say anything useful about the man who had taken her husband?'

'That she had never seen him before. But that she knew *what* he was and who he was,' said Riley. 'I'd like to see her. My grandmother. In person.'

She nodded impatiently, not wanting to lose the thread. 'And?'

Riley took more of the tea. 'And that's just when the heavy mob came in.'

'Ah. Bad timing.'

'You're not kidding.' He put the mug down and ran through all that his grandmother had told him before they were so rudely interrupted. 'There was one thing she remembered about the intruder. My grandpa called him by his name.'

'What was that?'

'Yousaf Ali.'

Muraski jerked as if she had been plugged into the mains. She reached down into the tote bag and extracted a thin file. She placed it on the desk in front of Riley and invited him to open it. There was a series of photographs, including one of his grandfather as a much younger man.

'What am I looking at?'

'That is Yousaf Ali. "Bomb" Ali, as he was known.'

'Yeah, I've heard of him. He was a study on the High Threat course.'

'I think he is behind the bombs here.'

Riley shook his head. 'I don't think so. One, Bomb Ali only ever operated in US territory. It was the Americans he hated. And more than them? The Russians. From what I know, he wouldn't put in his lot with anyone from the former Soviet Union. Ever.'

'Then . . .'

The sentence died before it had even got going. He could see her struggling to compute. Riley had had plenty of time to think this through. He reckoned he had a working theory of how it all fitted together: the Russians, the bomb-maker and Yousaf Ali. He was careful not to sound patronising.

'I have an idea how it all fits together. Let me lay it out for you.'

*

Inverstone Lodge is not marked on any Ordnance Survey map produced after 1914. It does not have a postal code. It is not on any commercial satellite maps. The entrance is down a small, unmarked track off a B-road, hard to find during the day, virtually impossible at night. So, as Yousaf intended, they pulled over to settle down and wait for dawn.

They found a place to do so just past the memorial to the Commandos, most of whom had trained in the area during the Second World War. Out in the darkness beyond his window, Henry knew only too well, was lovely scenery – lochs, mountains and forests – that hid the inhospitable wind-blasted hillsides and bleak moorland where men were made to do forced marches or turned loose with minimum rations and asked to fend for themselves for four or five days then make their way to a pre-arranged rendezvous. And then, in the midst of it, was Inverstone Lodge, in many ways the most secret of all the covert establishments dotted across the Highlands.

It was known for a while as The Cooler and later as Camp Zero. It was officially Number 7 Special Workshop School. But few of the people who were sent there underwent any training in a workshop. Some volunteered to make equipment for Company Linge, part of the Norwegian Resistance, which was sent over via the boats known as the 'Shetland Bus'. Most, however, simply cooled their heels. Hence the nickname.

Inverstone's function back in the Second World War was as a holding camp for those secret agents of Special Operations Executive (SOE) who had failed the rigorous training in sabotage and subversion – for being unreliable, inept, violent, drunk or too loose-lipped around the opposite sex – and needed to be sequestered.

In another country they might have simply been shot to prevent them imparting information about SOE – back then a name that was never even spoken – to the enemy. Some were incarcerated there ('retired' in SOE speak) for as long as four years. Several were rumoured to have gone mad. But there was no chance of escape, as they were guarded by tough members of the Highland regiments and a dozen dogs that were almost as fierce as the men in kilts. The guards were given permission to use lethal force if necessary, to prevent any absconders making it to the local railway station, the only realistic option to flee the region.

After the war most of SOE's assets were absorbed by MI6, which had long considered SOE a bunch of dangerous amateurs, and the agency disbanded. Inverstone, however, was taken over by MI5, where it was used for training and debriefing, although its distance from London, an advantage in wartime, became an inconvenience in peace and it was mothballed. Until, that is, Six came asking if there was a suitable venue for something called Operation Homegrown.

When they had picked a spot off the road and parked up, Yousaf fetched a blanket from the boot of the Renault and tucked it around Henry. 'It'll get cold. Are you okay?'

Henry actually felt like he had been hit by an express train, but he just nodded. Yousaf switched on the interior light and looked at him. 'You sure?'

'I'll live,' he said glumly, wondering where this sudden concern had come from. 'Why do you care?'

Yousaf laughed. 'I don't want you pegging out before we get there. You have a role to play yet.'

'So you keep saying,' he said irritably. He was done with this man's games and riddles. 'What role? And why? How can I stop whatever you are planning?'

The bomber rolled up the left sleeve of his coat and then his shirt and displayed his forearm. It was covered in rows of what looked like black tear drops. 'You know what this represents?'

'All the people you killed?' guessed Henry.

Yousaf gave a bitter laugh. 'Oh, no. Each one of these is a bomb I made that went off and killed someone. But usually many more than one. I couldn't fit the number of dead on my arms if I was an octopus. I have a similar number of tears on my right. With space for just one more.'

'Why?'

'Going out with a bang,' Yousaf said, turning off the light.

'I don't understand,' said Henry.

'No. You wouldn't. All will become clear in the morning. Try and get some sleep.'

'But what did you mean when you said that I could stop it?' Henry demanded again.

Yousaf sighed. The words came reluctantly, as if they had to be dragged out, one by one. 'I mean, Henry, that there is a way you could find out where the bomb is and have it rendered safe.'

'And how's that?'

Henry could sense rather than see the sardonic smile on Yousaf's face. 'It's very simple. I have the location on me. But you'll have to kill me to get at it. Get some rest, Henry. Big day tomorrow. It'll be just like old times.'

THIRTY-SEVEN

Paul Oakham scanned Kate Muraski's hastily scribbled notes from Riley's stream of suppositions and guesses. 'Riley might be right about the DNA. Poor Jamal might have led us up the garden path.'

She grunted her agreement.

'But two bomb-makers?' he asked, unable to hide his disbelief. 'They're not like London buses, you know.'

'But it explains a lot. Yousaf is here, but his focus is Clifford-Brown, for some reason. The Russians, on the other hand, have their own tame bomb-maker, who has a side interest in Riley. Remember the car bomb at his daughter's school?'

Oakham nodded. 'So isn't it possible that someone is also trying to get to Riley by taking his grandfather?'

'Possible,' she admitted. 'I still think we're looking at two sets of actors here.'

'So who did what? Three bombs – Nottingham, the Islamic Centre and Riley's at the school. Are they the work of both? Or just one for all three?'

'I don't know yet.'

He shook his head, still not convinced. 'I'm not sure I buy all this. Where is Riley now? Still in the interview room?'

'No, I've told him to get some more sleep.'

'Do you trust him?'

'Riley? I think I do,' Muraski said. 'I'm not certain he has all the answers. But I don't think he is the loose cannon we thought.'

'You thought,' he corrected. 'Riley is sure that Barbara Clifford-Brown has it right that her husband called this man Yousaf?'

'Absolutely certain. Think about it. It means that one of the bombers has kidnapped Henry Clifford-Brown and taken him to some unknown destination. Possibly to set off another device.' She tried hard to keep the sense of vindication from her voice. She had been right about Yousaf Ali all along. True, she hadn't figured in the Russians but, for the moment at least, that was an unexpected bonus.

'Perhaps,' said Oakham, 'your man Riley has been busy spinning us a Jackanory. IRA? Russians? Is there anyone who isn't planting bombs in our country according to him? The radical wing of the Wombles perhaps?'

Muraski didn't know who the Wombles were, so she let it pass. 'Look, sir, if Riley is right and it was the Russians who bought up the IRA bomb kits, wouldn't it make sense for them to front the bombs with a Taliban terrorist? He would act as a cut-out. It makes us look in the wrong place. It's a classic distraction and diversion technique. That's what the bomb at the Islamic Centre does. Has us chasing our tails when far-right dipsticks jump onto the bandwagon and claim responsibility. The country tears itself apart while GRU or FSB get on with their real agenda.'

'Bearing in mind that you love to see Reds everywhere . . .'

'That's not fair.'

'Let me finish. Even taking that into account, there is some plausibility in it. By some I mean this much.' Oakham held his thumb and forefinger an inch apart. His phone rang. He picked it up. 'Yes?' he snapped impatiently. He listened for a few seconds, lips pursed in displeasure. 'Very well. Keep me posted.' He stared into space for a second, digesting the information he had just received, and then spoke to Muraski.

'You know, if there is a Russian dimension to all this, I should call Roger in.' Roger Altrincham of the Russia desk.

They'll take it away from you.

'Well, that link is only so much speculation and the word of a murderer, this George O'Donnell, who might have his own reason for leading us on a merry dance.'

'That's the fastest U-turn since I last watched something with Jeremy Clarkson in it.'

She laughed, not at the joke, but because he was right. She did not want Roger Altrincham waltzing in, patting her on the head and telling her to run along, that he'd look after it from now on. 'I think the priority right now is to find Yousaf and Clifford-Brown. We can worry about who is pulling the strings later. No sign of them, I assume?'

'The BMW was abandoned not far from Dunston Hall,' he said. 'We have no idea what vehicle they are travelling in. And the amount of CCTV footage to analyse ... there's just not the manpower.'

'Barbara Clifford-Brown might have an inkling about where he would take her husband. We should talk to her as soon as the doctors allow.'

'She might well know something,' admitted Oakham. 'But that phone call I just took? It was to tell me that Barbara Clifford-Brown has gone missing. Given her escort the slip while going to lavatory and disappeared into the night.'

'Bloody hell.' Her mind quickly scrolled through the possibilities. Could the Clifford-Browns be playing some extended game? Was she being befuddled by old hands from Six who might just possibly have been turned? She felt like she was staring into an abyss and her head span for a second. She needed some sleep too. 'Look at page three of my notes. Another thing she mentioned to Riley before the grenades went in. Operation Homegrown.'

Oakham frowned, but out of puzzlement or annoyance she couldn't tell. 'Homegrown? Where did he get that?'

'You know it?'

'Only since you started digging around ... Fuck.' He slapped a palm against his forehead, admonishing himself for some unknown transgression or stupidity.

'What is it?' Muraski asked.

'Shush. Let me think.' Oakham picked up one of his pencils and began to drum a little tattoo on the desktop. 'I don't know why we didn't think of it before. I think I know where they are.'

'Who?'

'Clifford-Brown and his pet bomber.' He picked up the phone. 'Go and grab a coffee and get ready for a trip, this might take some time.'

'What are you doing?'

'Whistling up some back-up. Be ready to leave here ...' He looked at his watch. 'Sometime in the next few hours.'

'Are we going after Yousaf then?'

'Yes.'

'In which case we need to bring Riley along.'

'Why?'

'Yousaf Ali is a bomb-maker. A specialist in booby traps, no doubt. It might be a good idea to have our own tame bomb disposal man, don't you?'

Oakham paused mid-dial. 'Brief him, will you?' *On what?* she was about to ask, but the next sentence made her heart flutter a little. 'And you'd best draw a weapon.'

MONDAY

THIRTY-EIGHT

Dawn brought a countryside mostly shrouded by a wet, low mist. A few distant peaks, still snow-capped, were visible, but the loch and the woods were completely blanketed. Henry unfolded himself from the car as if he were made of seasoned wood rather than flexible flesh and bone. Every joint seemed to creak as he stood and he staggered a little as one knee gave way. There was no sign of Yousaf. The driver's seat was empty and he wasn't within the hundred yards or so he could see in each direction. Call of nature, perhaps. His own bladder was uncomfortably stretched.

'Hello?' he shouted.

Nothing, just the noisy chatter of an invisible flock of crossbills. It was, he remembered, a great place for birding, not just the startling red crossbills, but lapwings, choughs, grouse, of course, and, on the coast, the memorable sight of the rare and majestic sea eagle lording it over the lochs. He would have brought Dominic up, had it been practicable.

He walked over to the edge of the gravelled area and relieved himself. As he zipped himself up, Yousaf loomed out of the mist, carrying what looked like two coffees.

'You were snoring, so I thought I'd get some breakfast.'

'Don't tell me they've opened a Starbucks up here.'

'No, there's a café about a mile that way. I noticed it last night. Breakfast from 6.30.'

'Weren't you frightened I would run away?' asked Henry.

Yousaf just raised his eyebrows. It wasn't as if he hadn't thought about it. It was just that he wouldn't get far. And after his pathetic attempt to out-box the man, maybe he would decide it was easier just to kill him. 'No, perhaps not.'

From his jacket pocket Yousaf produced a small, wrapped parcel. 'Bacon roll. You need some food. Go on, I've had one.'

'You've had bacon?' Henry asked in surprise.

'Egg.'

'You still believe?'

'Oh, yes. Strange, isn't it? When you brought me up here, hooded, in a van with no windows, I was Joseph Shaftab Khalid, the confused young Muslim and petty criminal. By the time I left, I was Yousaf the bomb-maker, the freedom fighter, ready to take on the Russian army on behalf of my brothers. I had the passion of the convert. Some of it still burns, Henry.' He looked Clifford-Brown up and down, like a butcher might examine an animal ready for the slaughter. 'Do you believe in anything?'

'Not any longer. As the end grows near, you'll find that it all seems more and more like desperate fairy stories we tell each other.'

'We'll see soon enough, Henry.' There was anger in his voice.

Henry didn't like the sound of that, nor the slightly crazed smile that came with it. He was in no hurry to test the veracity of the fairy tales. He realised the nice, polite, breakfast-buying Yousaf was just a veneer. Underneath was still the monster they had created years before. A monster very capable of killing him and leaving his body on a cold Scottish mountainside.

He placed his coffee on the roof of the Renault, leaned against the rear door and tucked into his hot and salty snack. He felt a little life coming back to his stiff, cold limbs. How was Barbara faring, he wondered, stuck in that cellar, wondering what was happening to him? His gut feeling was that all this would be over soon and he could get back to her. At least, he hoped so. The alternatives were unbearable. He finished the roll in three large bites and started work on the drink. *Unbearable*.

'That bad?' asked Yousaf.

Aware that he must have spoken aloud, Henry became flustered. 'No, no ... not the food. It's good. I was ... I was hoping Barbara is well.'

'She has something to eat, drink, heating. Everything except communication. She'll be fine.'

'I know that. Barbara will be fine. I just wish you hadn't had to ...'

'There's a lot of things I wish I hadn't had to do. Hit you, for example.' He held up his arm, pointing to the tattoos. 'I even regret some of these. But I am not the final judge in such matters.'

'I'd throw myself on the mercy of the court if I were you.'

The younger man snarled at him. He had transitioned from benign to belligerent in a heartbeat. 'Do not mock me, Henry. I don't need you that much.'

Yousaf's head flicked to one side in alarm when he heard the engine of an approaching vehicle. He waited for it to appear from the thinning mist, but it drove on past the turning for their stopover. Gears whined as the driver changed down for the climb up the hill. A delivery van or truck of some description.

'Come on,' said Yousaf, sullen and impatient now. 'Let's do this.'

'Do what?'

'Get it over with,' came the hardly illuminating reply. 'Get a move on, old man.'

Henry drained his coffee and put his cup and the food wrapper into an almost overflowing Keep Scotland Tidy bin. Then he climbed in next to Yousaf and settled back for the final leg of their journey, trying to ignore the olfactory spectre of pipe smoke that was haunting him. And the feeling that he was in the company of a madman.

The turning was as hard to find as he recalled, more or less at the apex of a bend, which meant both entering and leaving could be hazardous. However, Henry remembered and recognised the strange conifer with a profile like an old-school drawing of a witch, complete with pointed hat and hooked nose, and warned Yousaf to slow and prepare to make a left.

The track was once wide enough for a decent-sized truck, but the hedgerows on either side were overgrown, and branches scraped along the side of the Renault as he drove the half-mile to the turning circle in front of the gates.

Inverstone's entrance was hung with signs all conveying the same message: *Keep out, you're not wanted here*. There was also a symbol of a vicious dog, although Henry doubted there had been any of those around for a while. The gates were tall and, like the wall running either side of them, were topped with razor wire. There were CCTV cameras, but they were covered in cobwebs and ivy. The main obstacle to gaining entrance was the thick chain and padlock holding the two sections of the gate closed.

'What now?' Henry asked.

'Ideally, I'd blow them open. But I'm a bit short on explosive.'

Yousaf got out, walked to the rear of the car and returned with a hand-held, battery-operated grinding wheel and a pair of goggles. 'This is what every bicycle and moped thief uses.'

He set to work on a link of the chain which, after a long spark-filled five minutes, finally yielded and pinged apart. Yousaf pushed the right side of the metal gate back with some difficulty. He carried on until he had created an entrance wide enough for him to fit the Renault through.

Inverstone was a flat-fronted, grey granite Edwardian shooting lodge, with an array of stone-built annexes and some drab twentieth-century additions. There was an ornamental pond in the front, green with scum, its fountain dry. Yousaf steered the Renault around the back of the house and parked up. They got out. A weak sun had dispelled the mist and they had an uninterrupted view over the extensive grounds, all the way to the line of the double-wire fence, the evergreen woods beyond and, in the far distance, the long, steely-grey finger of the unlikely named Loch Lochy and the rugged mountains.

'Still beautiful,' said Yousaf.

'Yes,' agreed Henry. 'Now will you finally tell me what this is about?'

'I will. First, let us go and find my grave.'

'What?'

Yousaf gave a mischievous smile. It didn't pacify Henry's fears one iota. 'You'll see.'

They walked over the once-manicured, now distinctly ragged lawn, crossed the overgrown ha-ha and made their way through what could have been a fashionable wild-flower meadow, but was actually a tangle of weeds. Yousaf was heading for a small copse of deciduous trees in the right-hand corner of the grounds, about a thousand yards away, and Henry found the going tough, stumbling several times.

'I remember when this grass was short enough to practise burying IEDs. Do you, Henry?'

He said nothing. He didn't wish to be reminded of the terrible skills they had taught in this forsaken place.

Yousaf pointed to the trees. 'Just there. That's where I am buried.'

'What are you raving about, man?' panted Henry, his patience shot, the energising effect of the bacon and coffee now forgotten.

'Joseph Shaftab Khalid. Laid to rest here in . . . 1982, wasn't it?'

They reached the treeline and Henry peered in. The thin sunlight was illuminating a carpet of brown leaf-litter that had clusters of shiny-capped mushrooms poking through.

'I buried everything here. Passport, clothes, my driving licence . . . all of me.'

'You were meant to burn it,' said Henry crossly, as if addressing an aberrant schoolboy.

'I know. But here lies poor Joseph, long live Yousaf Ali. Freedom fighter, scourge of the Russians, hero of the Taliban. Bomb-maker extraordinaire.'

Henry was taking the weight off his feet by leaning against a tree and Yousaf turned to face him.

'I'm dying, Henry.' It was so matter-of-fact that it hit Henry like an unexpected slap.

'What do you mean?'

Now there was a slight break in Yousaf's voice. Was it self-pity he could hear? 'Cancer of the pancreas. It's very quick. They looked inside.' He unbuttoned his shirt and Henry glimpsed a livid scar. 'It's all over the place. Riddled, that's the word they use, isn't it. Such a cruel, heartless phrase. Riddled with cancer.'

'You've come home to die.'

The repressed fury came back into his voice. 'Do you know how many of us are left? The men and boys you radicalised to create Mujahideen in there?' Yousaf asked, pointing back at the house.

'I don't know.'

'What, you didn't keep track of your protégés? How many were there altogether?'

'Thirty? Forty? I don't know. I didn't run it.'

'But it was your idea, wasn't it? Concocted when you were out in Pakistan? Why bother flying Afghans to the UK, where they stood out like a sore thumb. Take some hotheads from the mosques in the UK, British Af-Paks, and tell them their duty was to go and fight the infidel invaders. Bring in scholars and imams to convince them. How many are left, Henry?'

Henry's voice was thin and reedy. 'Just you, I believe.'

'Just me. The others?'

'There's a lot of ways to die out there.'

'That's true.' Yousaf took his pistol from his waistband and pointed it at Henry.

'You know, we didn't think far enough ahead. It's a common failing in the West. Look at Iraq.'

Henry was speaking very quietly, as if he was frightened of being overheard, and Yousaf took a step closer. It wasn't often that Six admitted its mistakes..

'In Afghanistan we should have thought: what happens when the Russians go? We have trained all these so-called freedom fighters . . . what do they do then? Well, you turned on Kabul for a civil war and eventually you turned on us. I see now we only have ourselves to blame. We are the monsters. We are the Dr Frankensteins.'

'Yes,' Yousaf agreed, 'you created some of the people who ended up killing your own soldiers with your own techniques and weapons. Homegrown terrorists.'

For the first time, Henry could see the madness and sickness in Yousaf's eyes. He flashed on his wife again, confronting the possibility of eternal separation, and thought he might throw up. Even though he didn't believe, Henry wasn't afraid of dying. That was pointless. Just of dying many miles away from her.

Henry tried to be calm and persuasive, as if he were a lawyer addressing a jury, presenting the facts. 'What can I say? I'm sorry. Killing me won't help, though. Won't bring back all the people who died in your explosions over the years. Won't bring Joseph Khalid back.'

'No. You're right. Joseph has been dead a long time. But you are wrong about one thing. I'm not going to kill you.' Yousaf turned the pistol round and offered it, butt first. 'You're going to kill me.'

THIRTY-NINE

Henry took the pistol, gripped the butt and slotted his finger through the trigger guard. He looked at it like it was an alien presence. He had been right. The man was insane. He should kill him, but he was reluctant to start this late in life. 'I've never shot anyone before. Why am I doing it now?'

'It is a sin to commit suicide. Unless one is to become a *shahid*.'

'For a man like you, martyrdom is always an option.'

'But I don't want to take any more people with me. Not even infidels. God will deal with them. I have enough tattoos,' he said, holding out both arms before him. 'I found out about the cancer and I thought: *God must be telling me to stop. It is time, Yousaf. Enough.*'

'Or you could just have been unlucky. There is no *reason* behind cancer.'

Yousaf ignored that. He had a prepared script and he wasn't going to deviate from it. 'If you shoot me, my old friend and now my foe, I die in warfare. That will be enough.' He dropped down to his knees.

'Wait,' said Henry. 'You said something about being able to stop the bomb.'

Yousaf nodded. 'Where the bomb is, you will find it in here.' He put a hand on his solar plexus.

Henry began to suspect some metaphysical trap or religious obfuscation. 'In your heart?'

Yousaf laughed. 'In my heart and on my liver. The last time they opened me up, I asked the doctor to use a cauterising pen. To write on my liver. You know some doctors sign their name? With a pen.'

'I've heard of it. I do believe it is illegal.'

'In this country, perhaps. Where I come from, if you ask, they will do.'

'And so . . .'

'The bomb's location is written on my liver.'

Henry swore under his breath in disbelief. The cancer must have metastasised to his brain. 'How?'

'A postcode. You must kill me and cut me open to find it. Then bury me, quickly. A proper *Janazah* is all I ask. With the correct *salah* and the grave pointing towards the Qibla. Can you do this for me?'

It wasn't much of a request. Whether the authorities would allow it was another matter. 'I'll try.'

'Then kill me now.'

Henry raised the gun, his hand shaking. 'This is madness.'

Spittle flecked his lips as Yousaf almost shouted his reply. 'Everything that has happened in Afghanistan and Iraq, that's the real madness. Sending young men to be murdered and maimed in a country where they had no business, that was madness. Training people like me, that was an act of insanity.'

'Perhaps it was,' said Henry. 'But that's no excuse for what you've done. What you are doing. How do I know you are telling the truth about this writing? You could be feeding me a load of clap-trap.'

Yousaf blinked hard and Henry wondered if he was in pain. His words became more measured. 'Because I am a coward. Yes,

I am. The doctors told me I have weeks and that death will be . . . unpleasant. This way you help me avoid that and die at the hands of an old enemy. And I am giving you a chance to save many lives by taking one.'

Henry found the pistol was growing heavier. He let his fatigued arm drop a little. 'I said I had never shot anyone. Have never killed a man before, either,' he admitted.

Yousaf tutted his disbelief. 'In your line of work? I find that hard to believe.'

'Oh, I've been responsible for people dying. I have just never had to do it myself.' Barbara had, of course. The boy in East Germany, the Greek traitor, Rory Little, the mole. But she was made of tougher stuff than he was when it came to such things.

Henry watched something change in the man. A skin sloughed, perhaps. When he spoke, all traces of the terrorist who had kidnapped him had gone. He spoke like a doctor giving a patient bad news, much as some medic must have talked to him not that many months ago.

'Henry, this is a fast-spreading cancer. There is a good chance it will kill me before you make up your mind whether to pull that trigger. There is a phone next to the spare wheel in the car. You can call for help once we are done here. Just do it, Henry. Choose life for the many.'

The gunshot echoed mournfully between the close-packed trees. Henry's world then became engulfed in a terrible, roaring maelstrom of sound and fury and he fell to the ground, hands covering his ears in a futile attempt to drown out the bedlam.

*

The dawn chorus had just fallen silent by the time the bomb-maker had finished. He stepped back and admired his handiwork.

287

The structure he had created certainly looked convincing. He eased the steel panel over the rows of switches, peeled off his gloves and took off his mask. He pulled up the shutter and gave a start when he saw the figure standing there.

'You said you would be ready at dawn,' the Russian who called himself Rick said.

'I did say that.' He extended a hand and helped Rick up into the rear of the van, pulling the roller back down. Rick examined the wheeled trolley in silence, stroking his chin. The bomb-maker wondered how long he had been in the country. He still had an accent, but that was no longer unusual, especially in the capital. Most people would assume he was Polish. A good-looking Pole, he admitted to himself. He wore expensive-looking dark jeans and a leather blouson jacket that was a cut above the sort you found on market stalls. 'Very good,' he said eventually. 'You have worked hard.'

'And now I must go and check on my son.'

'Oh, yes. How is he?' It actually sounded like he cared.

The bomb-maker shook his head mournfully. 'Not well. He needs taking care of. I shall have to do it.'

'I'm sorry to hear that,' Rick said. 'I have a son myself.'

This was a surprise. The Russian never revealed personal details. 'With you here?'

Rick laughed at that. 'No. He lives with his mother. We are not together. I see him once, maybe twice a year.'

'That is not enough. A boy needs a father.'

'He has one. A good man.' He gave a little shake of his head. 'We all make sacrifices for our cause, eh?'

The bomb-maker knew what his own ideology was, what he hoped to achieve. He wasn't sure what ideology drove Rick. 'What cause is that?' he ventured.

'To make my country great again. Afghanistan humiliated us. Then the West helped chop us into pieces. But we will rise once more. It has already begun. But most in the West are blind to it.' It was said matter-of-factly, devoid of the heat of fanaticism. Then, with a little more passion, Rick asked: 'But this thing is ready? I can take it now?'

Thing? he thought. These people still had no idea about the relationship between bomber and bomb. This was no thing, it was another child, one that would function perfectly, unlike the boy. 'Once I have secured it to the side to stop it rolling around.' He pointed to several coils of rope. 'It is very stable, but just in case. You don't want to damage the casing. A dent risks tearing the rubber insulating layer. If you do that . . .'

'I'll be careful, old man. What about arming it?'

The bomb-maker removed the cover panel from the upper part of the device again and showed the rows of toggle switches. 'You simply flip this red one up. It arms the bomb.'

'And to disarm you flip one of them back up? But only you know which one does the job, right?'

'What do you mean?'

'You flip one of the switches to disarm? Obviously not the red one.'

The bomb-maker feigned surprise. 'I told you. This is a Viper. No ordinary bomb. And now, no ordinary Viper.'

Rick nodded. 'And I am sure you have done a very good job. Just wondering how it works.'

'The thing about a Viper, my friend, is that once armed, those switches become useless. One of them arms it, but it does not disarm it. One of the others does, but there is no way of telling which.'

'Really? What is the point of that?'

'To give the bomb-disposal people something else to fret about. If they find this device, they will spend a lot of time worrying about the switches until they realise they are of no consequence. You have the rest of my money?'

'I do. I have left it at the rear of the house. Everything we agreed.'

He was certain that would be so. The pair had been very good at keeping to their word so far. Besides, they had no way of knowing if he could set off the device prematurely, should they try and cheat him. He had warned them of that possibility when he had been recruited. Never short change the bomb-maker, or face the consequences. Not that the money was for him or his son. Later that day he would use a *hawaladar* or money broker to make sure the money got back home. It would enable his mother to live out her days as one of the wealthiest women in the village. The thought made him happy. That and the knowledge that it was almost over now. The end was in sight, for him and his poor son. The bomb-maker's heartbeat quickened a little at the thought of the release to come.

'Make no mistake, Rick,' he said, using the name for the first time. 'Once this bomb is armed and the timer begins its countdown, nothing can stop it. Nobody can neutralise it.'

'Except you.'

The bomb-maker shook his head. 'No. Not even me.'

'Wow,' said Rick, with admiration in his voice. 'And the secondary device we asked for?'

'Almost done. It will take me half an hour more to assemble. I am more familiar with the material in that one. This ...' he pointed at the silver machine, 'was new to me.'

'But it will work?'

'They will both work,' he said, offended once more.

'Then you have done well,' said the Russian.

The bomb-maker gave a rare smile. 'I know.'

*

There was a combination of words that Riley was particularly averse to: the close proximity of 'helicopter' and 'fog' to each other in a single sentence. Choppers were never his favourite form of transport, being too reliant on complex mechanics for his liking, and choppers and fog usually came with an accompanying newspaper article about flying into hillsides or buildings. And although the flashbacks such headlines generated weren't as strong as those of Andy the Tan, helicopters still equalled Afghan for Riley.

So, he was relieved when the pilot entered the waiting room at the London heliport and announced there was a delay because of adverse weather en route. They didn't take off until close to five in the morning, destination unknown. To Riley, at least.

The helicopter, though, was something of an upgrade from the Chinooks and Sea Kings he had been used to in Afghan. Plush was the word that came to mind. It was a long-range AgustaWestland, fitted out as if Five had borrowed it from the Sultan of Brunei. For all he knew, they had, because Paul Oakham shut him down when he asked who actually owned (and more importantly to his mind, serviced) the machine.

The original AgustaWestland could seat fifteen in comfort. This had been re-configured to take ten in luxury. They weren't so much seats as flying sofas. It was remarkably quiet, too. Noise-cancelling headphones were provided as ear defenders, but you didn't actually need them. It seemed the corporate world valued its clients' hearing more than the army did its soldiers.'

There were six of them on board: Riley, Oakham and Kate Muraski plus three fully kitted and armed counter-terrorist officers. Police or MI5's very own, he couldn't tell from their outfits. Why was Oakham packing his own firepower on the chopper? No matter where they were going, there would be local CTUs available that could be ready and waiting. Unless he was keen not to involve an outside agency, one that was open to more scrutiny than Riley supposed Five was. Still, the Three Musketeers they had with them looked tasty enough and all had nodded to him, even though nobody had bothered with any introductions and Riley was in civvies. You just *knew* when the other person had some shared history.

Immediately after a stomach-dropping take-off over a twink-ling London, Kate Muraski had given him a tight smile and closed her eyes. A few seconds later she had clearly transitioned into a deep sleep, head propped on one of the pull-out headrests. Oakham was busy reading papers; the three heavies also seemed to be dozing, listening to their phones or both in the absence of any in-flight entertainment – there were screens, but they remained stubbornly blank – or reading.

Riley wondered if they really trusted him. He was along for the ride because he could tell one end of a suicide vest from another. For the time being, MI5 had their very own bomb-disposal man. In the early hours Oakham had created documents claiming that Riley had been working for MI5 'in a covert nature' for some time and that his erratic behaviour was all part of a masterplan. It requested he be seconded to Five 'for the foreseeable future'.

The army would not like this one bit. Spooks with their own ATO? But it just might keep the Military Police off Riley's back and avoid one of their size eleven boots finding its way up his backside. Oakham would just have to say the words 'national security' and wave the letter he had requested from the Home Secretary con-firming Riley's recruitment to send them packing.

He still felt as though he was on probation, though. But he

would worry about that later. If they survived the helicopter ride. Riley closed his own eyes and tried to sleep. He didn't have to try very hard.

He woke with a jerk as the engine note of the helicopter changed and penetrated through to his idling brain. It took him a second to remember where he was. Muraski was still out, probably not as attuned to the risks of a plummeting chopper as he was. The black ops blokes were also apparently in the land of nod.

'Refuelling,' Oakham said when he noticed Riley was back in the cabin.

'Where are we?'

'Edinburgh. It won't take long. Captain was worried about the margin of error if we didn't top up.' It sounded like he was going to add 'the pussy' to the end of the sentence. Riley had no problem with getting more squirt in the tanks. He was all in favour of big margins of error, the bigger the better.

'And then?' Riley asked Oakham.

'Go back to sleep.'

But he couldn't. While the fuel tanks were being replenished, he wondered if Muraski or Oakham had his phone. He would have liked to have texted Izzy and Ruby, to check they were hunkered down safe. 'Do you have my mobile?' he asked Oakham. 'It was taken off me by your blokes.'

'Not me,' Oakham said. 'Kate might. But let her sleep.'

'Sure.'

The co-pilot came back on board with black coffees for all, and Riley drank the snoozing Muraski's too. He figured his poor grandfather, if he was still alive, would need him to be bright-eyed and bushy-tailed for what was to come.

Whatever the fuck that might be.

*

Henry watched the leaves around him twitch and rise up as the wind roared into the forest. Above him birds took the wing in screeching alarm. He turned his head, looking beyond the gun in his hand and across to the slumped figure of Yousaf, the side of his head now a splodge of gore. The gale subsided, the leaves see-sawed back to earth and now he could hear the churn of the helicopter's rotors as it turned away from the woods.

'Are you all right, sweetie?'

Ah, thought Henry, *I have it. I am either dead or I am seriously wounded, lying on an operating table, pumped full of morphine.* How else to explain the hallucination of Barbara that he could see from his prone position, striding up to the trees, dressed in, of all things, a mink coat.

'Yes,' he said softly, unsure whether he was addressing a phantom of his own making. 'It's bloody good to see you. How are you, my love?'

'Oh, you know. Didn't think my knees were up to a sprint. Hell to pay later. But I'm more worried about Binkie.'

He looked behind her to where his old friend Ben Beaumont was struggling to cross the overgrown meadow. He had on a Crombie coat, brogues and was holding on to a trilby-style hat. 'Hello, Binkie,' he shouted.

'Hello, Henry. Sorry, didn't have time to change for the country.'

This dream was just as insane as Yousaf had been. Very realistic, though. What did they call it? Lucid dreaming?

'None of us did, darling,' said Barbara as she reached Henry's side, and held out her hand. 'Up you come.'

As Henry struggled to his feet and touched Barbara, he realised this wasn't any sort of dream. It was still insane, though.

'Barbara, what are you doing here? I don't understand.'

'It's a long story.'

He threw his arms around her and pulled her close, his eyes stinging. 'I thought I might never see you again.'

She pushed him away slightly. 'Don't be silly, Henry. You don't get rid of me that easily.'

Then she looked down at Yousaf and stepped away from Henry's embrace. 'That was a lucky shot. Thought my Deadeye Dick days were over. Especially with this monster.' She raised her hand. She was holding a rather large Desert Eagle pistol. 'You remember I gave this to Ben for safe keeping? Never thought I'd use it again. But after those fools had blown my hearing out and put me in a damn hospital, I thought, *I bet I know where he has taken my Henry. I'm going to go up there and shoot the bastard.*'

'And you did, sweetie.'

She looked at the dead man. 'Yes, I did, didn't I?' She gave a little giggle.

'Well, thank you. I hate to sound . . . ungrateful. But it was me who had the gun on him, not the other way round.'

'Oh, I know that. But I don't think you would have pulled the trigger, would you, sweetie? Not quite your style. So, whatever was going on, I thought it better to take one player off the board. Did I do wrong?'

He hesitated. 'No, my love. Perfect timing.'

She beamed at him.

'Long time since I pulled an all-nighter,' gasped Beaumont as he finally reached them.

'Ah, poor Binkie. I not only made him open his gun safe, I borrowed one of Angela's coats and then I made him drive here through the night.'

'Devil to find,' said Beaumont with a shake of his jowls.

'I think that was the idea,' said Barbara. 'Who are those people?' She pointed at the helicopter that had landed on the far side of the field, well clear of any trees.

'I don't really know,' said Henry.

'Give Ben the gun, sweetie. Just in case.'

Henry did as she suggested and the three of them stepped out of the shadows of the wood and waited as six people emerged from the helicopter, ducked beneath the slowly turning rotors, and headed straight for them.

'I hope one of them has a scalpel about their person,' said Henry softly. 'Or a pipe.'

*

'On his liver?'

'Yes, young lady,' Henry said patiently. 'He told me the location of the bomb was written on his liver.'

'Get the fuck out of here,' Muraski said.

'And you believed him?' Oakham asked.

They were standing on the edge of the copse. Yousaf Ali was still on the floor, attracting the interest of the more opportunistic flies and insects of the Highlands. The three armed officers had been sent off to 'secure the grounds' and 'guard the helicopter'. In truth, it was Oakham's way of getting rid of them. Secrets and lies, not blood, were about to be spilled and it was better if they were elsewhere.

While Henry was talking to Oakham, Riley was giving his grandmother a hug and thanking Ben Beaumont, who, along with his wife Angela, had been a frequent visitor to Dunston Hall when Riley was a teenager.

'There was a case,' said Muraski, trawling deep into her memory. 'A doctor used ... an argon beam I think it was. They are usually used to seal the bleeding after a liver transplant. He used it to sign his initials.'

'What was he charged with?' asked Oakham. 'Unlawful autographing?'

'Unlawful force to a patient whilst anaesthetised,' she corrected. 'He was struck off, I believe.'

'Well this chap is hardly anaesthetised,' said Henry. 'Shouldn't we just open him up?'

Oakham shook his head. 'We do this properly. We need someone who knows his way around the insides of a corpse. First, though, we need a coroner.'

'There are no coroners in Scotland,' said Henry. 'We had one of the staff here die. Accident. Had to contact the Procurator Fiscal, who in turn authorises a post-mortem. And informs the police.'

Oakham took out his phone. No signal. 'Damn. It sounds like it might be a long-winded process.'

'Did he say where the bomb was?' asked Riley, who had left his grandmother and moved over to stand next to Muraski.

'London,' replied Henry. 'It's the postcode that is on his liver.'

Oakham gave a snort of disbelief. 'And was he responsible for Nottingham?'

'He says not,' said Henry.

'I told you,' said Riley. 'There is another bomber. This one' – he indicated Yousaf – 'was a spent force. Apart from, if he is to be believed, one last bomb in London.'

'You don't believe him?' Oakham asked, looking for an ally.

'Only one way to find out. Cut him open.'

'We can drive down the road and get a signal,' said Muraski. 'There's at least two cars here now we have the one Barbara came in. We use the chopper to fly the body of Yousaf to, I don't know, Fort William. It must deal with a lot of climbing accidents and fatalities, so I bet it's set up for post-mortems. But in the meantime, we send Henry here back to London for a full debrief.'

Oakham nodded. 'Agreed.'

'And Riley as well,' added Muraski.

'Why?' asked Oakham.

'Because,' explained Riley, 'if the bomb is in London, that's where I need to be.'

'Exactly,' agreed Muraski.

Maybe they do trust you after all, pal.

TUESDAY

FORTY

When Kate Muraski had finally located and given Riley his phone back it was full of messages from a concerned Scooby, giving him updates on Izzy and Ruby. His daughter, too, had sent a sit rep, assuring him that they were safe and in good hands and wondering if she should be a bodyguard when she grew up. By then it had gone midnight – he and his grandparents had flown back on a commercial flight from Inverness (Ben Beaumont had opted to drive his Jaguar back south, with, he insisted, at least one nice comfortable stopover this time). Riley had then accompanied his grandparents, with an MI5 driver/bodyguard, to Dunston Hall and made sure they felt safe and secure. The officer from Five had turned a blind eye to Barbara's trip to the cellar to fetch a pistol – she had not been foolish enough to try to get a Desert Eagle on a plane, so Binkie had been entrusted with it for the return trip. The Bersa Thunder she had taken from the gunsafe would be under her pillow that night. The bodyguard, despite his protests, was told that his services would not be required.

After returning to London, Riley was put up by the duty manager of Thames House at a hotel on Bankside, near the Tate Modern – which also managed to launder his clothes overnight – and left a message for Scooby to meet him outside the gallery at mid-morning to plan what should happen next for Izzy and Ruby for the foreseeable future. He then slept like he had been coshed until almost nine o'clock.

Scooby was on time and together they rode up the escalator and then took the stairs to the café on the sixth floor of the Natalie Bell building. It was pretty empty, so they sat on adjacent stools overlooking the river and the Millennium Bridge across to St Paul's. It was quite a stirring sight, that dome, Riley thought. He didn't go in for cheap patriotism, but a sight like that made you think London, despite its vicissitudes and its glaring inequalities, was a city worth protecting.

After they had ordered coffees, Riley gave Scooby a brief run-down of the previous day. In fact, it wasn't so much brief as skeletal. He didn't mention his grandparents or Inverstone Lodge. He did mention the security services, but only in that they had asked for his help dealing with a rogue bomber.

Scooby hardly touched his coffee as he listened. 'On his liver?'

Riley was going to have to get used to disbelief whenever he told the story. 'Yes.'

'And?'

'It was a code. En, oh, bee. Then on another lobe of the liver, oh, em, bee.'

'Where was it? The device?'

'Nowhere. It spells No Bomb, with unfortunate spacing after the third letter, not the second.' It had, apparently, caused some consternation until Oakham had realised what the message was trying to spell out.

'Shit. So . . .'

'He just wanted to die in some sort of battle. He needed someone to kill him, an enemy, so he could pass Go and collect his virgins.'

'At least he didn't go down the suicide-vest route.'

'There's that,' admitted Riley. 'Maybe that's old hat in Jihadist circles. So, what about Izzy and Ruby?'

Now Scooby took a sip of his coffee and grimaced. It had gone cold. He went to stand. 'I'll just get . . .'

Riley gripped his wrist. 'I haven't got much time.' Kate Muraski was at a funeral, Oakham had told him to 'stand down but stand by'. He couldn't shake the feeling that disaster was imminent. The atmospherics felt way off. Yousaf may have gone to Paradise, but if he really wasn't responsible for the other devices, a bomber was still active. A bomber who had made one attempt on Riley's life already. Riley gave him the essential details of the trip to Scotland and its implications.

Scooby sat back down. 'Thuckerin' thunder—' he began.

'No voices,' snapped Riley.

'Just the facts, ma'am?'

'That'll do.'

'You know Joe Friday never said that in the original series—'

'Scooby, knock it off, eh?'

His old friend took a breath. 'Women might like the mean and moody act, Dom. It's not great as a pal.'

'I'm suffering from PIT.'

'PIT?'

'Post Impressions Tension.'

'That's more like it,' said Scooby with a grin. 'I've put them up in a place called the Red House in Padstow. Much more secure than Izzy's flat. It stands on a rise, overlooking the Camel Estuary. You can see who is coming, who is going. Lisa and Jackie are still on the case.'

'Sounds good. Let me know if you need an interim payment.'

'We'll worry about that when it's all over. There's something else.'

'Hold that thought. I'm going to call Ruby. I'll get right back to you.'

'Okay. I'll get more coffee.'

Riley stood and walked way, to gain some privacy. Ruby answered on the first ring. There was disappointment in her voice. 'Dad?'

'You could sound more enthusiastic,' he chided gently.

'Sorry, Dad. I'm expecting Becky to call me back.'

'Did you check it was okay to call people? With Lisa and Jackie.'

'With Lisa. Jackie is a bit scary. Lisa's cool. She said to keep it short and not say where we are.' There was excitement in there at the subterfuge.

'Mum okay?'

'Kind of.'

'Kind of how?'

'We had a sort of argument. When I said I wanted to be a body-guard like Lisa. She said it was enough you had a . . .'

'A what?'

The answer came out in a rush. 'A fuckin' stupid job. That's what she said.'

'I'm sure. Well, maybe she's right. Like the army, bodyguarding is mainly waiting around. Ninety-five per cent inaction, five per cent adrenaline.'

'Where are you?'

'No locations, remember?' he said with mock severity.

'Oh, yeah. Sorry.'

'I'm teasing. London. I'll be down to see you as soon as I can.'

'Is the man who put the bomb under the car still out there?'

'For now. We're getting closer.'

'Dad, be careful. Please.'

He felt himself well up a little at the concern in her words.

Must be even more tired than he thought. 'Always, darling. Always. I'll see you soon. You take care.'

'And you take double-double care. Love you.'

She clicked off before he could reply in kind. Riley waited a few minutes before he went back and sat down with Scooby again. There were fresh coffees on the table and he took a sip of one. 'Sorry. I'm all yours. What was it?'

'The drone. I looked at your photograph of the one at the school. Good job you're an ATO, because you'd starve as a snapper. But there was better incidental footage of the one at Nottingham. They were the same make and model, best I could tell. I was involved in buying six similar drones for the London Fire Brigade. The Met are interested too. They are JCKs, commonly called Jacks. Israeli-made. They are very robust, totally battle-hardened, with four-hour endurance and a range of well over a hundred miles. Brilliant but fuckin' expensive.'

'And they used a Jack? The bombers?'

'No. I looked at the footage very closely. The Chinese, of course, make a copy. JAX, they call them. Almost indistinguishable, and not quite as good in operation, but a third of the price. I looked into getting one of those when I was sourcing the LFB Jacks. But . . .'

'But.'

'With the LFB and especially the Met you have to be sure of what you are buying. That they are fit for purpose – remember Boris's bargain water cannons? – and that the company you buy from is above board. The fake Jacks are marketed through a company in Dubai. Halo Trading.'

'Owned by . . .?' Riley asked.

'At first glance, a UEA conglomerate. But a major investor is a company called Mozart. It's involved in post-war exploitation of assets as well as distributing military hardware in Syria.'

'Syria?'

'There's also a Wagner operating there. A Beethoven and a Handel. They're all Russian in one way or another. I'm just surprised there isn't a Tchaikovsky or a Shostakovich.'

Riley let this sink in. This fitted in with the half-formed theory that he and Muraski had about Jihadists as the front men of the apocalypse for Russian mischief-makers.

'It might do. Does Halo have a distributor here?'

'I called them. One man in a unit in Stevenage, it sounds like. Worth checking out, but I don't think he's Goldfinger. *Do you expect me to talk? No, Mr Bond—*'

'Scooby.'

'Sorry.'

Riley's phone vibrated in his pocket and he answered it while Scooby went off for more sugar. 'Yes?'

'It's Muraski.'

'You okay? I thought you were at a funeral.'

'I am. I've sneaked out.'

'What's up?'

'I just got a call on something. To do with you. Can you be at my office in an hour or so?'

'What is it?' he asked.

'I think I know how your DNA got into that bomb.'

*

The item was delivered by a forensic technician and laid out on a rubber mat on the table in Boardroom D. Oakham, Riley and Muraski stood and stared at the plastic-encased cloth for a good few minutes before Riley finally spoke.

'It's mine,' he said.

'How come it was sent to you?' asked Oakham. Five's TAP on

Riley had included interception of suspicious mail. The black and white square of material before them had been sent by courier to his barracks. It had been intercepted en route from a depot in North London. There was no return address.

'I have no idea.'

'And the blood?' asked Muraski, pointing to the dark patches that disrupted the pattern. 'Also yours?'

He shook his head. 'No. If I'm right, the blood isn't mine. The scarf is. It's from Afghan. The bomber must have sent this to me.'

'Why would he do that now?' asked Oakham.

But Riley had left the room. He was back inside Nick's head, watching the lead-up to the command wire detonating the IED that blew his legs off.

It was hard to tell how young Moe was, because like all interpreters in Afghan, his face was almost permanently covered by a scarf, so he couldn't be recognised by any Taliban scanning us through binoculars or sniper scope. Recognition would mean certain death for him and his family. That very morning the Boss had given the lad his own shemagh *scarf, just to make certain he was properly masked up. Now only his dark, sad eyes were visible.*

'Riley?' Oakham's insistent voice cut through the memory.

Riley struggled to keep his voice steady. 'I had a friend, Nick, another ATO. He was killed trying to defuse an IED in Afghan. I remember everything about that day. Including that I gave *this* scarf to a terp, an interpreter we called Moe. All the terps covered their faces when out in the field. It helped protect them from being identified by the Taliban. For some reason, his had become too small, ripped, shrunk in the wash, I don't remember. So, I gave him mine.'

'What happened?' asked Muraski.

'After Nick triggered the IED we came under fire. A stray bullet bounced off a hull and went through Moe's head.'

'It killed him?' asked Oakham.

'Yes. Well . . .' Riley's words stalled into silence.

'What?' Muraski prompted.

'Well, I always assumed so. We never saw him again. AK round through the head, you just assume . . .' Riley felt the two cups of milky coffee he had drunk with Scooby congeal in his stomach. 'I was so fucked up about Nick, I didn't even . . . We had a whip round and sent money to the family. Asked how he was. We never heard anything. Assumed they were grief-stricken and angry and that he must be dead. But after that, we had a new terp and . . . you move on. You don't look back.' He was sounding defensive and he knew it. But people who hadn't been there would never understand what Ms Carver would doubtless call coping mechanisms. You had to ask people like Battle of Britain pilots or Bomber Command crews how to cope when you lost colleagues day in, day out. They knew what a toll it took.

'It seems someone has been looking back,' said Oakham.

'It doesn't mean Moe isn't dead,' said Riley. 'It could be family out for revenge, blaming the British Army.'

'But it might be why your DNA was on one of the bomb circuits in Nottingham. Deliberately. Look.' Muraski pointed to a clean corner where a small square had been clipped off.

'It's been about me this whole time?' Riley asked, trying not to feel the weight of responsibility for the dead and maimed of Sillitoe Circus.

'Not necessarily,' said Muraski. 'But weren't the interpreters allowed to settle here? Once the war was over.'

Over? Try telling that to the Afghans, Riley thought. The war never ended, it just changed direction.

It was Oakham who answered. 'Yes.'

'Some,' corrected Riley. 'Not all. You had to have served

twelve months with ISAF and be considered to be in danger if you remained over there. Originally, they got five-year visas for themselves and close relatives. I think they extended that. Gave them the right to remain indefinitely.'

'And allowed an extra four hundred in,' Oakham said. 'Which was a security headache for us.' He was silent for a moment. 'Why send this to you now?'

'A warning?' suggested Muraski.

Oakham huffed his disagreement. 'I think Nottingham and the car bomb were sufficient warning.' He scratched the side of his face, worrying at a small crop of bristles he had missed while shaving that morning. 'The Home Office insisted on DNA testing for all the Afghan nationals when they resettled here. Remember? It was deemed illegal a while back. An infringement of their human rights.' The slight sneer in the final sentence was almost undetectable.

Riley saw where he was going. 'Would the Home Office still have the samples?'

'Possibly. In the way of all bureaucracies, either they destroyed the samples with indecent haste, or the wheels are still grinding and they are languishing in some storage facility somewhere.'

'Can we check?' asked Riley, aware that he had just said 'we'. Was he thinking like a spook now?

'I'll get Deepika on it,' said Muraski with some relish. 'But if he has sent us this, which must be awash with the forensics ... You know what that means?'

'Yes,' said Riley. 'Our man wants to be found.'

*

The bomb-maker fed his son a spoonful of the thick soup. The boy slurped at it, a good third of it splashing down his front onto the towel that had been arranged around his neck. 'There. Good?'

The boy managed a smile. He said something that sounded like the word for soup. 'I made it myself. Your mother's recipe. I never thought I would be cook and carer. I miss her, you know. Do you?'

The boy let out a small mewl of pain. He knew, he understood.

The bomb-maker felt tears sting his eyes. 'They couldn't have saved her, you know. One thing I can't blame the British for. It is wicked, cancer. Almost as wicked as what happened to you, my son.' He fed him some more soup. Most of it went into his mouth this time. 'I do blame them for that, though.'

'Dead.'

'Yes, they'll be dead. The ones responsible for this. They'll be coming for us soon.'

'Nooo.'

'Yes, they will. Do not worry, it won't be too bad. Not compared to this.'

He spooned more soup in then sipped his dark, bitter coffee. He knew the British weren't entirely to blame for Mohammed's injuries. He had used his son. Used him as a spy, to report back every day on where the soldiers went, what they did. He would then design the appropriate bomb, to be placed by Mohammed or, more often, one of his friends. He was always one step ahead of the British because of the interpreter they called Moe. And a freak accident took his son from him. It was a Taliban bullet, that much was true. But if the British and the Americans and the others had stayed away, had never come to his country, it would never have happened.

Because of his son's condition, it wasn't difficult to get settlement papers for Great Britain for the family – a young man and his parents. But even here, they could do nothing for his brain.

And then his mother got cancer, caused by the suffering of her son, he was sure. This so-called great country couldn't save either of them.

Eventually, in his grief, the Russians came, offering him a chance for revenge. They had their own agenda too. But one that he could fit around. They told him they could supply everything he needed to make a bomb, including Semtex and gas, if needed. The offer was too good to refuse. With his wife gone and his son slipping away, what else did he have to live for?

'Come on, two more mouthfuls.'

The lad shook his head. The bomb-maker tried to slide the food into his mouth, but his lips had clamped shut. 'Just one more then.' The lad shook his head and the spoonful tipped down his front.

'Bad, bad,' the lad shouted.

'No, not bad.' He had learned to supress the anger and frustration he felt at such times. It was not the boy's fault. 'We'll have some more soup later. Yes?'

He looked at his phone. Soon, he supposed, the British would come for him. He would be ready, of course, and so would Mohammed.

'Shall I tell you about what the Viper will do?' he asked the boy. 'And then we will watch some television.'

The lad made a sound in his throat he just about caught. He reached over and ruffled his hair.

'Yes, I'll try and find you some football.'

*

Riley and Muraski went for a coffee while the files were checked for the contact details of Mohammed Safi, Moe the terp's full name. They found a Costa Coffee and sat towards the rear.

311

Muraski insisted on facing the door. Riley fetched a pair of macchiatos and sat, careful not to block her line of sight.

Spies, eh?

'Staff Sergeant Riley, I owe you an apology,' she said.

'How's that?'

'It was Jamal who flagged up the DNA on the bomb. Later, he tried to persuade me that it might have been contamination after all. I didn't listen. I convinced myself that, you know . . .'

'I was a mad bomber?'

She smiled. 'Something like that.'

'You were right though, weren't you?'

'What, you *are* a mad bomber?'

'No, my DNA being there was significant. Just in a way you couldn't have guessed. It was the bomber's first calling card, the first clue that he was after me. Or, at least, that I was on the agenda.'

'As I said, that was Jamal . . .' There was a catch in her voice. 'It was his funeral I went to. Jamal picked up on it.' She began to cry, despite every effort to stop the flow of tears. A few other customers shot them furtive glances. He checked his pockets, but he was all out of handkerchiefs. He fetched a fistful of paper napkins from the counter and passed them over. She gave a Dumbo-sized blow of her nose and wiped her eyes.

'Sorry. I didn't even cry at the funeral. Sorry.'

'Stop saying that. Surely being a spy means never having to say you're sorry.'

She gave a half-choked laugh and blew her nose again. 'If only. Oh, God, what a mess. Are your family okay?' she said, seemingly to try and change the subject.

'They are.' He gave a quick run-down of what Scooby had told him.

'And the Clifford-Browns? You seem very close.'

To his surprise, Riley gave her chapter and verse on what they would probably now call his 'blended' upbringing. For some reason he couldn't quite grasp, she was easy to talk to. Perhaps she should have been a therapist rather than a spy. Or maybe that's what made her a decent spook.

'That's quite a story. You must love them very much.'

'I do. They think I don't know that neither my mother nor father wanted me when they split up. They've kept it from me all these years. But a boy at school took great delight in telling me that he had heard it from his parents.'

'What a little shit.'

'Kids are. Or can be.'

Just then her phone beeped and she looked at the message. She started hurriedly gathering her things. 'They've got an address for the terp and his family.'

*

Barbara Clifford-Brown was worried about her husband. Since the ordeal with Yousaf he had seemed distant and detached, as if his mind was permanently elsewhere. There was a haunted look in his eyes. She had seen it once before, in Beirut, when he became convinced that a Bulgarian assassin had targeted her. It had annoyed her at the time. Worrying about his new wife had taken the edge off his ability to do his job. His fieldcraft, as she forthrightly told him, was shot to shit.

In the end, she had sought out and killed the Bulgarian, if only to put Henry's mind at rest.

The BMW had been picked up from the spot where Yousaf had dumped it and delivered back to Dunston by the local garage. So they were at least mobile again. Barbara thought she might take

Henry out to The Stag, his favourite local pub, that evening, see if that cheered him any. But first, Barbara made a light lunch from what was left in the fridge and ordered an online delivery from Waitrose. After they had eaten, she left Henry reading a book by James Holland on the Normandy campaign in 1944, the sort of thing he loved. She had given him another nicotine patch, so he wouldn't bang on about having a pipe again. Then she went back to business as usual.

Yousaf had disabled the whole of the cellar computer/camera complex by taking out a fuse from the box in the hallway. It had been rather conspicuously labelled, she supposed. She replaced the fuse and pulled open the door Dominic had blown. She would have to get a locksmith in. There was a time when she could have trusted Henry to do it – he had been remarkably dextrous, considering the size of his hands – but he could no longer be relied on. It would involve a lot of fuss, preparation, tool-buying, procrastination, cursing and then she would still have to call in a locksmith.

As she made her way gingerly down the stone steps and past the acoustic door – which she dutifully locked behind her – she mused on how pleasant it had been to spend time with Dominic, despite the circumstances. He, too, had changed from the sad-eyed boy they looked after during Rachel's 'episodes'. The word covered a multitude of sins – a new lover, a new drug or a dark spiral into depression when one or the other let her down.

It had been difficult giving the boy all their attention, given their other commitments. It was easier when they decided that Barbara should not accompany Henry on all his trips. Barbara thought, quite rightly, that she might prove a distraction. Certainly, a weakness a canny opponent could exploit.

She wondered how much Dominic really knew about his parents. When they divorced there was a custody battle, of sorts.

However, rather than the conventional argument that they deserved the child, each party argued that the other person should be responsible for his upbringing. How must it feel to know that neither parent really wanted you? That you would be an encumbrance on their chosen lifestyles. Young and in the way. She hoped, especially now, that he never discovered the truth.

After putting on Mahler's Symphony No. 3, Barbara fired up the screens and rebooted the computer. She checked for alerts that the motion-sensors had been triggered. She watched the footage of Yousaf taking Henry, the arrival of the bodyguards with, presumably, Izzy and Ruby in the rear and, finally, Dominic himself. All the activity had been at their east wing. The house next door had been and remained empty, which wasn't unusual for a rich Russian with homes across the globe.

Dominic had hinted at Russian involvement in the recent bombing campaign. Of course, he should have done no such thing. But he was new to operating in their world, hadn't yet discovered that you never drop hints. Still, his supposition didn't surprise her. The Russians were acting with brass-balled impunity. They needed taking down a peg or two. And, as Dominic had said, they probably hadn't seen the back of them yet.

Satisfied everything was running as it should, Barbara made her way back upstairs and through to the sitting room. To her surprise she had been down there even longer than the Mahler lasted, close to two hours. 'Tea, darling?' she asked.

Henry was in his armchair. The Normandy book was on the floor next to him, its pages splayed open. His head was back, mouth open.

She walked over, knelt down and took his still-warm hand. She shook him gently, hoping he might have merely dozed off, but knowing in her heart he had done no such thing. Her training pushed her to search for a pulse in her husband's sinewy wrist but she could find none. Barbara briefly placed her husband's fingers against her forehead and then rested her cheek on his thigh, the wool soft against her skin. She gave his knee one final squeeze, as if reassuring him. 'Oh, sweetie.'

FORTY-ONE

The property that was registered to former army interpreter Mohammed Safi and his father Aalem was located in Enfield, North London. MI5 notified the Counter Terrorism Command of the Metropolitan Police of a possible bomb factory on its turf. Using thermal imaging it was confirmed that two persons were in the house. Over the course of the evening, nearby houses were quietly evacuated and an ICP set up inside an unmarked van in a side road almost opposite the target address.

MI5 handed control over to CTC but went to the scene with its own anonymous command truck, parked even further down the road. It was equipped as a mobile surveillance unit, and was pretty cramped for Oakham, Riley, Muraski and two MI5 officers. On the screens was a Google Earth map of the location, plus live feeds from the CTC cameras trained on the house. Armed police were in position in adjacent and facing gardens.

'They know we want them alive?' asked Muraski. 'For the Russian connection.' Riley had explained about Halo and the drones. Muraski had heard of the company, apparently. The man in Stevenage was going to get a little visit. He doubted he'd be anything other than an innocent dupe, but Muraski said it was another piece of evidence that pointed to – albeit obliquely – Russian involvement in the bombings.

'Chief Inspector Mercer doesn't need to be told that,' said Oakham. They knew he was going to try to make contact with the bomb-maker, having got his phone numbers from the Department of Work and Pensions, which paid a carer's allowance to Safi for looking after his disabled son. Riley was well aware there was no rulebook for negotiating with suicide bombers, if that was what Safi had become. Hostage negotiation was a well-practised art, and often succeeded because the motivations of the hostage takers were complex. And they usually wanted to get out alive. Suicide bombers, not so much.

CTC were making contact with the Safis on a landline. They heard a phone ringing. The receiver was picked up. 'Hello?'

'Mr Safi. I believe you speak English.'

'I do.'

'Good. I'd like to discuss the situation we find ourselves in.'

'Who is this please?' *Butter wouldn't melt*, thought Riley.

'This is Chief Inspector Mark Mercer of the Metropolitan Police's Counter Terrorism Command.'

'And what can I do for you?'

Now there's a stupid question, thought Riley.

'We have reason to believe your premises have been used for the manufacture of explosives.'

Silence.

'There are armed police officers outside. We don't want anyone else to get hurt. Not you. Not your son.'

There was a bitter laugh at the other end. 'A little late for that, Chief Inspector.'

'Mr Safi, we would like you to leave the house now. Come to the front door, with your hands up, and we can continue this discussion elsewhere.'

'The house is wired to blow, Chief Inspector. Mines, grenades, what you call IEDs. Booby traps. You know what a Bouncing Betty is?'

Muraski looked enquiringly at Riley.

'Spring-powered booby trap,' he whispered, even though there was no way the men on the telephone could hear him. 'It sends a shrapnel bomb up into the air before it explodes at chest or head height,' he added. 'Or sometimes groin height.'

She grimaced.

'This isn't helping,' said Mercer to the bomb-maker. 'Come outside, Mr Safi. We have people who can dismantle whatever you have set up.'

'I doubt that. You will lose many men if you approach.'

'If we can't come in, then it means you can't leave. Every exit is covered.'

'So be it.'

'You have a son who is not well. What can we get him?'

'Nothing,' he said sharply. 'He has everything he needs here. But you can bring us one thing, Chief Inspector.'

'What is that?'

'Staff Sergeant Dominic Riley.'

FORTY-TWO

Normally it would be a member of CTC's bomb squad who would climb into the suit. But the bomb-maker had said he would only negotiate with Riley, and not by telephone. Aalem wanted him to approach the house, so Riley could see his son, see what he had become, or so he said. Shielded from view by the CTC vehicle, Riley donned the cumbersome suit as Kate Muraski and Alex Stock, the Met's EXPO, watched.

'Surely they could just storm the place?' said Muraski. 'Stun grenades like they used on you.'

'They don't work quite so well if you're expecting them,' said Riley. 'In all likelihood all he has to do is pull a wire or press or release a button and *boom*, the house goes up along with anyone nearby. And before you suggest it, one, there's not a lot of these to go around, and two, you can't storm anything in them.'

Riley worked his arms into the jacket as he continued to explain his thinking. 'And even these suits don't always help. Not with a full-on blast. Of course, he could be bluffing. He might have booby-trapped the place. He might not. Bouncing Betties are a good way to scare anyone. So, I don't think they want to take the chance he is telling the truth. I know I wouldn't.'

'But you're still going up there?'

'It's in his job description,' said Stock. 'You comfortable?'

'Yes.'

'I'll do comms,' said Stock.

'Appreciate it, Alex.'

The EXPO nodded and went into the truck to set up his end of the communication link. There was a Beep at work in there, putting out electronic interference. The Met were also using SkyFence, which disrupted communication to a drone, and Aerospot, which could pinpoint both the machine and its operator. Nobody wanted another Cotswolds or, indeed, Gatwick.

'You be careful, Riley,' Muraski said.

'Always am,' he said, slightly taken aback by the concern in her voice.

'He's obviously a tricky character. Safi, I mean. Not Stock.'

'Well, you wouldn't be far wrong with Alex. But, yes. Safi will be tricky.'

'And disturbed,' she added.

'Whereas I'm obviously completely sane doing this.'

'You know what I mean,' she said.

'Staff Sergeant Riley.' It was Mercer. He was tall and thin like a force-grown sapling, but for the prominent hooked nose that seemed to protrude further than the peak of his cap. He reminded Riley of an eagle in need of a good feed-up.

'Sir.'

'Your skipper just briefed me.'

Oakham was no such thing, but he let it pass. 'Sir.'

'You have history with this man.'

'The son.'

'Safi blames you for the condition of the boy.'

'I think I'm standing in for the whole British Army, sir.'

'There will be trained marksmen on the house. If your life is in danger in any way, they will act accordingly.'

'Sir,' said Muraski. 'We'd like them alive if possible. The bomber and the boy.'

Mercer turned and stared down his nose at her. He looked like he might peck her eyes out with it. 'And I'd quite like Staff Sergeant Riley here to make it back in one piece.'

'So would I. Sir,' said Muraski.

'Me, too,' said Riley. 'So it's pretty unanimous. I'm touched by both of your concerns. But you two can argue about this among yourselves. I need to put the helmet on and test radio comms with Alex.'

First, though, he phoned Izzy. Ruby was asleep, all was well. Izzy either heard some background noise or knew from something in his voice that he was on an op.

'You're on a call.' Not a question.

'Yes. I'm putting this thing to bed.'

'Oh God, I always hated this feeling. Why did you call? Just to wind me up?'

'No, of course not. Tell Ruby I love her. I've got to go.'

'Dom? Dom?'

'Yeah?'

There was a silence on the other end, as if she was struggling to find the right words. 'Nothing. Be safe.'

The line went dead.

*

Fifteen minutes later he began the walk across the street, aware of dozens of pairs of eyes and probably some crosshairs on him. Any civilian doing that journey might be terrified or nervous – probably both – but once Riley began, he was simply impatient to get down to it. His heartbeat was slow, sweating at a minimum for the moment, saliva plentiful. He was simply going to work.

The main building was hidden behind a hedge, apart from a break for the doors to a driveway to his left and an ornamental metal gate straight ahead of him. Beyond the gate he could see the front door, which had two stained glass panels in it, showing peacocks. As he got closer, he could see the nameplate on the gate echoed that representation: the place was called The Peacocks.

'There's movement in the house,' came through his headphones. It was Alex Stock.

'What kind of movement?' he asked.

'Not clear. They're talking, softly. Not English.' There were listening devices trained on the house as well as snipers. 'Hold on.'

'You want me to stop walking?'

'No. Keep going.'

He was in the centre of the deserted road now and he began sweating despite the cool of the night. He adjusted his man bag. If he was going to step into the house, he was going to deploy all the tricks to look for devices – mine detector, tripwire probe, the bright light attached to his helmet.

'They are moving upstairs,' said the tech.

'Okay, thanks.'

'Helmet camera on?'

Riley reached up and flicked the switch that would give Stock eyes.

'Got it.'

Riley continued on and stepped onto the pavement outside the house, one heavy foot at a time. Three steps to the gate. That was where the danger zone began. Even pushing the gate open might snap an invisible cord.

'Front bedroom. Moving towards the window.'

With difficulty Riley looked up to see the curtains on the bay window whisked back and the shape of the bomb-maker and his son behind the glass. 'Tell whoever is in charge of the marksmen to hold their fire,' Riley said.

'Roger that.'

'Tell them twice, Alex.'

'Will do.'

The top sash of the window slid down about halfway. The bomb-maker said something. But Riley couldn't hear. He reached up and began to undo the helmet.

'What you are doing, Dom?'

'I need to hear.'

'I'll lose visual,' Stock protested.

'I'll put it back on if I'm going in. Don't worry. I know what I'm doing.' Riley was lying. He was improvising and for the first time he felt a little stab of the jitters. He took a deep breath, steadied himself.

He pulled off the bulky helmet and carefully laid it on the ground beside him. With freer head movement he studied the façade of the building and down the path, looking for any sign of devices. Nothing stood out. He turned his attention back to the bomb-maker and Moe the terp.

'Hello, Scouse,' he said to the boy. 'Long time no see. Liverpool doing well, eh?'

'He can't understand you,' said Safi.

'Klopp,' said the lad with a lopsided grin.

'I admire his passion,' said Riley. 'You know they say he wanted to come to Arsenal, but Wenger wasn't ready to go. You got lucky.'

'Arse! Gonner!' the boy yelled.

Riley felt a lump in his throat, remembering the casual banter between them. He addressed the next sentence to the father.

'Seems to understand fine to me. Why don't you let him go? Come on, we can get him looked after. Better than you can.' *From a prison cell.*

'You did this,' said Safi. 'To my son. What happened to him, it killed my wife.'

'Dead,' said the boy. 'Kill.'

Riley shook his head. 'Look, it was a fuckin' stupid war. On both sides. But you have to know, it was a Taliban bullet that did that.'

'You know that Mohammed here was working for us all along. Spotting your every move. He told me where to place my bombs. He was one of us. A soldier. *Riley, hope you have better luck than the last ATO.* Remember that? We did it.'

It felt like a slap across the face. It had the ring of truth. There had been rumours of terps, coerced by blackmail or bullying or simple fatherly dominance into acting as eyes and ears for Terry. But he had thought they were just that – paranoid rumours. But maybe Moe had been a mole? Right then wasn't the moment for such analysis, however. That was a scab to be picked at later.

'Even if that were true, it doesn't matter now. It's water under the bridge. Let the boy go and we'll talk.'

'Die,' said the lad. 'Wiped.'

'Nobody has to die, Moe.'

'Gonner. Arse!' Moe became agitated and the father put his hand over the boy's mouth.

'You are upsetting him.'

Me? he almost yelled. But he kept calm. 'Look, play your cards right, we can all walk away from this place. Choose life. If not for you, then for your son.'

'You,' said Safi, the words carried along on a wave of fury. 'You might walk away. It is possible. But you will feel my pain if you do.

325

Misery will be waiting for you. The two of us, my son and I, our fates are bound together.'

'You do what you want. But leave your boy out of it. Or are you scared to die alone, just in case everything you've been promised on the other side is a big, shiny lie?'

Safi's face folded like a clenched fist into a mask of hatred.

'Give me Moe.'

Safi pushed the top sash further down, although Riley didn't have a clear view of them because of the reflection in the glass. He could hear the speaker in the discarded helmet rasping something. He leaned to one side and could just make out Stock's urgently shouted words. *'Can you hear me? Put the fuckin' helmet back on. He's got a sheet of some sort wrapped around both him and the boy. Get out of there. Riley, I think it's a giant suicide vest. Get out of there!'*

Riley looked up, just as Safi raised the detonation switch and showed it out of the window, the thumb hovering over the plunger.

He yelled at the top of his voice. 'No, don't be—'

'This life you think you live is nothing but the illusion and the rapture of delusion. *Allāhu akbar!'*

At that feared exclamation, Riley turned to run, scooping up the helmet as he went, struggling to get it over his head. His limbs would not move fast enough, the weight of the suit making him slow and bovine. Ahead he could see people taking cover, although Mercer was out of the truck waving him on and yelling encouragement.

He heard the crack of a marksman's rifle, trying to take out Safi. Whether he succeeded, they would never know. He could easily have rigged a dead-man's switch that activated when pressure was taken off. It could have been the last wilful act of a bitter, dying man.

Riley had just cleared the pavement when the front of the bay window blew out, spewing glass, wood and bits of human into the hedge and over it, spilling across the asphalt. The blast of that was somewhat attenuated by the shield of shrubbery, but still knocked him sideways, causing him to stagger. Then came a bigger one, blowing the front door off its hinges and hurling it down the path, spinning as it went. Moments later the second detonation wave hit him, carrying with it a large chunk of debris that smashed into his protective suit's Kevlar plates, pitching him off his feet and sending him sprawling across the road.

WEDNESDAY

FORTY-THREE

It was Ben Beaumont who found Barbara, still kneeling next to Henry, who was by then quite cold. Beaumont had broken his journey from Scotland by stopping over in Perth and then at an inn in Yorkshire. Feeling fully recovered from the rather frantic drive with Barbara, he decided to call in on the Clifford-Browns on the way back to London to see how they were faring. Having received no reply from banging the door knocker several times, he had walked around to the back of the property. He found the kitchen door unlocked and entered. With his heart beating loudly in his ears, he began calling their names. He still had the two guns from the woods at Inverstone Lodge – it was one reason why he had decided to drive back rather than fly – although they were in the car. Besides, unlike Barbara, he was too old for brandishing weapons in anger.

In the living room, Henry was slumped back in his chair, with Barbara at his feet, her face tear-stained, her make-up streaked. She looked up, unsurprised by Binkie's unexpected appearance. A spark had gone from her eyes. For the first time he could ever remember, Barbara Clifford-Brown looked lost and confused. 'He's gone, Ben.'

'I know. Oh, Barbara, I'm so sorry. But best leave the rest to me.'

Beaumont helped Barbara into a chair. She didn't resist as he gently wiped her face with a handkerchief.

He had carried a torch for her for years. Many of them had in the Service. She had not only been a great beauty, she had a pragmatic and ruthless streak that many of the men envied. Never prone to sentimentality, she was a formidable player. *Gunfighter eyes*, they sometimes said behind her back, among other more dubious utterances that wouldn't be tolerated in the modern age. Barbara rose above it or gave as good as she got, depending on her mood. And, distressingly, she was stubbornly faithful to Henry, apart from a few honey-trap operations in the early days of her career. Lucky Henry. Till now, of course. He switched his attention to the final needs of his old friend.

'I won't be a second,' Beaumont said. 'I'll make some calls.' She would know the drill. MI5 and MI6 had their own undertaking service. There would also be an autopsy, routine when a senior officer died, no matter how old they were. He went out into the hall to use the house's landline but swerved into the kitchen and poured two large brandies. Then, from his wallet, he extracted the piece of paper with the contacts he had written down in the aftermath of Inverstone Lodge. He sipped his brandy, went out to the hallway and dialled the number he had for the Clifford-Browns' grandson.

There was no answer.

*

'Just because the bomber is dead doesn't mean there are no bombs,' said Kate Muraski. 'Riley told me the bomb-makers are usually separate from the bomb-planters. The skill of a good bomb-maker is too hard won to sacrifice needlessly.'

They were in Oakham's office, waiting to update the top floor on the events of the previous night. The explosion and its after-math had run on all the news channels. So far it had been blamed on a gas leak, but there was a good chance someone had managed to film something on their mobile phone that would puncture that particular balloon.

'You think the Russians might still have a trick up their sleeve?' Oakham asked. She wondered how he managed to still look fresh and fragrant, whereas she felt like she'd had an argument with a hedge and lost.

She rubbed at her left eye as it started twitching. 'At least one. Who knows how many bombs that bastard made before the one that got Dom?'

'You know, when we go upstairs, I'd rather you didn't adopt an alarmist tone. Or too much of an emotional one. What happened to Riley was . . . regrettable.'

'Regrettable?'

'Perhaps not the best choice of words. Is there an update?'

'I spoke to them half an hour ago. The doctor said he should have a shattered spine, given the force that the metal hit him. All he's got is a chipped vertebra. The Kevlar took the brunt of the force. They're still worried about concussion.'

Her phone rang. 'Speak of the devil. Riley? How are you?'

'On my way out of hospital.'

'What? I thought they were keeping you in.'

'They tried. I've promised not to drive. Had to sign something in my own blood.'

'Drive where?'

'Dunston. I got a message from Ben Beaumont.' There was a small, unexpected break in his voice. 'My grandfather is dead.'

Another punch to the stomach. Henry Clifford-Brown, after all he had been through. She thought to ask how it happened but realised it would just waste time. 'I'm on my way. I'll give you a lift.'

*

'There used to be nightingales in those woods,' said Riley, pointing to the trees across the lake. 'They think the muntjacs did for them.'

'Muntjacs?' asked Muraski. They were sitting on stone steps outside the drawing room where the body of his grandfather had been found. It was gone now, whisked off by the tame undertakers. A man from Six, one Hector DeMontfort Clarke, was drinking tea in the kitchen with Ben Beaumont, who was half-cut on brandy. Barbara Clifford-Brown was upstairs, trying, and probably failing, to get some rest.

'Small deer,' said Riley. 'The RSPB think they eat the same vegetation as nightingales and are more efficient. They leave just some tough old shoots for the birds, which starve. Muntjac escaped from captivity at Woburn and have spread up here, driving out the nightingales. My grandfather used to go down at dusk to listen to them. It's the male that sings, you know. Not the females as everyone thinks.'

Muraski put a hand on his shoulder. 'You okay?'

'There's a whistling in my left ear. And a bruise that looks like a map of the world on my back.'

'That's not what I meant.'

'I know. Numb,' he said.

'I think that's normal.'

'I suppose,' he sighed. He thought about Ruby, how she would take the news. The first death in the family. He decided he would break the news personally, rather than over the phone. She wasn't close to Henry, but she knew her father was.

'Or it could be the concussion,' said Muraski, breaking into his thoughts.

'I haven't—' he began, before he realised she wasn't serious.

'It must have been quick and . . .' She tailed off, clearly unsure of where to go with the sentence.

'He'd had a good innings?'

Muraski shook her head, annoyed that she had been about to spout platitudes. 'Something like that.'

'I guess it's more tragic with someone like Jamal, a young man.'

'That's not what I meant.'

'It's true though. But like I said, he was like a father to me for much of my childhood. Maybe this is what Safi meant? About me feeling his pain.'

'Safi didn't do this. Old age did.' She paused. 'But what's left of Safi's house is being pulled apart as we speak, although it could take weeks to sift everything. That might yield some clue as to what was on his mind when he said that.'

'I doubt it.' After the butane explosion a good portion of the downstairs had been gutted. It had taken the fire brigade close to two hours to get it under control. Meanwhile, a considerable chunk of the upstairs had been blown out into the street, along with the remains of Safi and Moe.

'Why do you say that?'

'You won't find any of the devices he made for the Russians in there, will you? They'll be long gone. Your lot don't have anything on them yet? The Russians?'

Muraski shook her head. 'We are trawling back to see if any likely GRU agents, a man and a woman, entered the country. Like we did with the Salisbury agents. Nothing. Those Novichok clowns made themselves bloody obvious though, as if it was deliberate. This lot? They might have been here years, of course.'

'Sleepers?' he asked.

'Deep cover, certainly,' she said. 'Of course, they might just be hired hands.'

'Who swear in Russian when a dog bites them?' He pointed across the missing central section to the empty east wing. 'You looked at the oligarch next door?'

'Kutsik? We did, of course.'

There was a ripple of irritation in her words. Maybe he was teaching his grandmother to suck eggs.

The phrase reminded him once again that he had lost such an important man. The man who had spent hours out in the fresh air, teaching him to fish and shoot, had turned a shy, bullied boy into someone with the confidence to join the army and become an ATO. He wiped a tear away with his sleeve and fished in his pocket for a handkerchief. No word from Nick, who normally butted in to call him a pussy or some such when he showed any emotion. But Nick's not real, he reminded himself. He'll be down there in that black cavern where his grandad would dwell. And, real or not, Nick could just shut the fuck up. He'd mourn if he wanted to. No, more than that. He *needed* to mourn.

'Kutsik hasn't even been in the country during most of this,' Muraski continued. 'Putin put Kutsik's son in prison for fraud. Seized a good chunk of his assets. Kutsik is no fan of the regime. So I doubt he's a player in this. We're also trawling all the CCTV near George O'Donnell's house, although given the timescale since his new chums came calling, a lot of it has been lost. Counter-terrorism has pulled him in. He's given them, and they've passed to us, the approximate dates of the visits by his possible Russian buyers, so we can narrow down the search. Who knows? That might throw something up. Of course, he claimed he sold them nothing. And we don't have any proof at the moment.'

'Just my word.'

'I'm not sure any testimony extracted via exploding dog is valid in court.'

'Fair one. Meanwhile we just wait?' Riley asked.

'No, there are stones being turned everywhere. But, in the end, it's their move, Dom.'

'That's what I am afraid of.' He loathed waiting for the other side to make their play.

'Dominic?' It was his grandmother, looking frail and shaky as she stepped down from the kitchen. 'Walk with me, please?'

'Off you go,' said Muraski, getting to her feet. 'I might join Mr Beaumont in a brandy. Mrs Clifford-Brown, I'm sorry . . . about Henry. I misjudged him when we first met.'

'You were just doing your job.' She gave a glacial smile. 'I was like you once.'

Riley could see the tension beneath Muraski's thinly returned smile. He suspected that his grandmother would have eaten ten Kate Muraskis for breakfast without a second thought – and that Muraski knew it.

*

Riley and his grandmother strolled towards the nightingale wood, taking the path that skirted the lake. He couldn't believe his grandfather would never walk over this lawn again or across those fields and through the trees that made up the wood. He slid his arm through his grandmother's and pulled her close. 'How are you, Gran?'

'Hurting, to be frank.'

'We all are.'

'I knew it would come one day. This moment. Still hit me like a train. Isn't that silly?'

Riley put his arm around her shoulders and pulled her close, as if he could absorb some of the pain she was feeling. 'No, Gran. He was a fine man. One of a kind. Like you. I'll miss him.'

'I can't stay here now. In the house. He's in every brick of it. I can't bear it. I'll have to sell it. Would you mind terribly? I always thought it might be yours one day.'

'What would I do with a country pile? You do what you have to do. Where will you go?'

'Well, for the moment, Ben has a place in town.' London. 'A little *pied à terre*. Just while I sort myself out. There'll be a funeral of course, but a memorial at St Paul's would be nice.'

They reached the edge of the wood. The bluebells were out, a splash of vivid colour in the sun-dappled shade of the canopy. A dove was cooing and a woodpecker was knocking himself silly. Riley took a breath and it choked him on the way out. His grandmother ruffled his hair, as she had when he was a teenager. 'It's cruel, but it's nature's way.'

He sniffed back more tears. 'I'm supposed to be comforting you.'

'Oh, I don't need any of that,' she snapped, a flash of her usual self. 'But I do need a favour.'

'Anything.'

'Go and see your mother. Tell her about Henry. I can't face her just now. I know that's ghastly, but there we are. You can take the BMW if you don't want Miss Muraski to come along. Can you do that for me?'

He kissed her on the cheek. 'Of course, Gran. It's the least I can do.'

FORTY-FOUR

'Have you come to take me home?'

It was the usual greeting from his mother. It always came with a beaming smile of relief, a face raised in hope.

Rachel Clifford-Brown – she had reverted to her maiden name – was sitting in The Snug. It was one of several day rooms at Silver Lake, the secure care home that Barbara and Henry had settled on. Or rather, had settled on them. UK care homes in general did not like 'customers' who had Rachel's profile of problems, so the choices were surprisingly limited. Riley didn't know how much it cost per year, but his grandfather's bushy eyebrows had always conveyed that it was a lot.

Riley had always been able to see why. It was decorated more like a hotel than the usual care home cliché of floral patterns and swirly carpets. Rooms were spacious enough, there were plenty of staff and the public areas looked over an expanse of water on the edge of the university. The Snug had leather chesterfield-style sofas, deep armchairs that might have been lifted from a St James's club and triple-glazed French windows that gave the impression that any of the inhabitants could throw them back and wander freely in the grounds. But it was an illusion. The doors did not open and to reach the grounds you had to go through three locked doors in the presence of a 'companion', as members of the care staff were known.

On the face of it the place seemed like paradise at the end of life, at least compared to some establishments. But under the perfumed air there was always an undertone of piss, and the room known as The Retreat was full of those who had withdrawn from life and were waiting for death to show up. Skeletal, befuddled, soiled and in pain, collectively they spoke eloquently of everyone's final destination, even if you had the money for Silver Lake.

'Shall I get my things?'

'Not now, Mum,' Riley said softly, reminding himself that she was stuck in a loop. It was all too easy to get irritated, as if she had any choice in the matter. He walked over to the fireplace where a rather convincing fake, and therefore safe, fire burned in the grate and turned down the radio on the mantelpiece a notch. The Snug did not have a television, the focal point of daily life in many homes. There was one in The Lounge, but his mother preferred to sit and listen to the Radio 3 or Classic FM broadcasts that were the norm for The Snug.

They had the room to themselves. The only other occupant, a woman in a towelling dressing gown, looking as if she was waiting for a spa treatment, had tutted when Riley entered and left, taking her copy of *Country Life* with her. Rachel was dressed in a two-piece black trouser suit, smart enough for an evening cocktail party. A five-diamond Elsa Peretti Tiffany necklace was at her throat. She still looked glamorous, her hair cut short and spiky, her cheekbones sharp; just the backs of her hands, veined like a river delta, and a slight sagging of the neck hinted that she was a good decade older than she might appear at first glance. The elegance was offset somewhat by a pair of 'bunny' slippers and a bandage on her right wrist peeking out from under the jacket.

'How are you, Mum?'

'Oh, I'm fine,' she said airily. She poured a few inches of water from a plastic jug into a glass, took a sip and replaced it on her side table. 'Right. Shall we go?'

Her body had held up well, but her mind had begun to slip when she was in her early fifties. Drink and drugs, said the doctors. After a concerted and exhausting campaign of interventions, her parents had got both out of the picture. But once they had been stripped away, it revealed that the damage was both irreversible and ongoing.

'Are we off?'

'Hold your horses, Mum.' He caught himself once more. Time had told him that impatience with Rachel was unfair and counter-productive. 'In a bit, maybe.'

'How long's a bit?' She looked at her watch, a Cartier that had been pawned more than once. Henry had always retrieved it amid empty promises that the heirloom – it had been his mother's, a present on her 'coming out' at a debutante's ball – would never leave her wrist again. 'We'll miss the next bus,' she said with a tremor of anxiety.

'There'll be another,' he said calmly. There was a bus stop on the premises of the care home for buses that never came. Some of the inhabitants insisted they wanted to leave, and they would be taken to the bus shelter by their companion. After a while they would lose interest or forget why they were sitting in the shelter and ask to go back to watch a favourite TV show or have tea. It had seemed a cruel deception to Riley when he first heard about it. Now, he wasn't so sure.

'What happened to your wrist?' he asked.

She looked at the bandage as if it were newly applied 'Oh. I don't know.'

KIM HUGHES

'Did you fall again?' Whatever had eaten away at her mental faculties had also sideswiped her balance mechanisms.

'No, no. Nothing like that. Just a . . .' She couldn't seem to make her mind up what it was.

Riley made a mental note to ask at the desk about the dressing and what lay beneath.

'How is Ruby?' Rachel asked, apparently keen to change the subject.

'Ruby?' He couldn't keep the surprise from his voice. On his last visit she couldn't remember him being married, let alone having a daughter. 'Tall, bright, creative.' And probably a little bit scared right now. 'Both lovely and a bit of a handful.'

'How old is she now?'

'Thirteen.'

'A difficult age.'

'Apparently.' Riley didn't want to go into the fact that he was sitting out of most of the storms of adolescence. 'Look, Mum, I have some bad news.'

'Rachel! You want to do the sweepstake?'

The man who had entered The Snug was so bent over he appeared to be looking at the floor. All Riley could see of him was the mop of silver-white hair on top of his head. He was dressed in a high-tech blue anorak and Rohan-style outdoor trousers. On his feet were sturdy hiking boots. He looked as if he had popped in from a stroll along Scafell Pike.

'What sweepstake?' Rachel asked. 'Bill, this is my son . . .' Just a moment's pause punctuated the introduction. 'Dominic.'

'Pleased to meet you, Dominic. Match tonight,' Bill held up a hard-backed notebook. 'Guess the score. You in, Rachel?'

'I'll do it,' said Riley, reaching for his wallet. 'How much?'

The man laughed. 'We're not allowed to gamble for money. Winners get to choose a film on film night.'

'Oh, okay. Who's playing?'

'Arsenal versus Liverpool.'

'Two—one to Arsenal,' said Riley, against the current form of the sides. In a different world, many years ago, it would have been him and Moe the terp betting on the result and first to score.

'Yes, two—one,' said Rachel. 'And I'll have *A Star Is Born*. The Streisand one.'

Jesus, she had gone mad.

Bill wrote it down in his book. 'Only if you win.'

'Oh. Yes.'

'And you did choose it last time.'

'Did we watch it?'

'Yes. But never mind. Most of us don't remember what was on the news five minutes ago.' Bill left, laughing softly to himself, having still not made eye contact with either of them. Riley had rarely seen such a bad curvature of the spine. He wondered when the poor guy had last seen the sky.

After a pause, Rachel asked, 'How old is Ruby now?'

For fuck's sake, he thought. Then, calmly: 'Thirteen.'

'Difficult age.'

'Yes. Mum—'

'Are we going home now?'

'Look, I have some bad news. Barbara and Henry. Your mother and father.'

'I know that,' she snapped. 'I'm not doolally yet.'

'I'm afraid Grandad, your dad, has died.' He stumbled for a moment, the reality hitting home once more. 'I . . . it was a heart attack. It was very quick, Mum.'

Her face collapsed into a terrible mask of grief and he stood to try and give her a hug, but she pushed him away. Her face quickly regained its composure. 'How? How did he die?'

'Natural causes. Heart attack,' he repeated.

'Can we go home now?'

'No, Mum.'

'But surely it's mine now.'

'What is?'

'Dunston Hall?'

'No, Mum. Your mother is still around. It is your dad who's gone.'

'When is the funeral?' Rachel asked.

'I don't know yet. I'm waiting to hear from the undertaker.'

'I'll need a new outfit.'

'We'll sort all that.'

'How old is Ruby now?'

'A hundred and three.'

Alarm flashed across Rachel's face. 'What?'

He felt a stab of guilt at his flippancy. It wasn't his mother's fault. None of it was. He shouldn't take his frustration out on her. 'She's thirteen.'

'A difficult age.'

'Look, are you going to be all right? After hearing about Dad? I'll tell one of the companions to come and sit with you, eh?'

'That would be nice. Or Bill, when he's done his . . .' Her brow furrowed in thought, the memory just out of reach. He wondered how long the news would manage to cling on to the cliff face of sentience before falling away into the abyss.

'Football sweep,' he said eventually.

'Yes. That was it. A sweep. Who was playing again?'

When he didn't answer she looked into his face. 'Are you all right? You've gone quite pale.'

Riley's mouth was suddenly Sahara dry. He reached over and took a sip of her water before he replied. 'I'm okay. I've got to go.'

'Why?'

Because I know where the bomb is.

'Lots to sort out, Mum. I'll be back soon, promise.'

And I know when it's going to go off.

*

'Have you gone mad, Dom?' said Alex, the Met's EXPO.

'There's a precedent.'

Riley was hammering back down the M1 in his grandparents' BMW, ignoring the pain in his spine. He doubted the old, but immaculately maintained, crate had hit such speeds in its lifetime. It didn't seem to mind. The engine was humming sweetly.

'What precedent?'

'Manchester United's game against Bournemouth. Last day of the 2015–2016 season. Game called off.'

'That was some dork who left a packet in the bog after a training exercise,' said Stock.

'They didn't know that when they abandoned the game.'

'You know they'll probably sue the Met for lost revenue if you're wrong.'

'I'm not.' There was a silence at the other end for a full minute. 'Alex?'

'I can't do it. I haven't got the authority.' Riley knew that. This was going to go past the commissioner all the way to the mayor.

'You can back me up.' He pressed on the horn and flashed his lights to get a cruising Range Rover out of the fast lane. 'Look, SO15 will have filmed the scene at the house when Moe died. Play it back. Listen carefully to what Moe says.'

'Are you sure this isn't wishful thinking?'

Possibly, he thought, but this was a time for certainty, not vacillation. But he said: 'I'm going to call my contact at Five.'

'Get you. Who's got the big swinging bollocks now?' Alex sighed, a difficult decision made. 'I'll make the calls. You better be right.'

'Thank you.' Riley punched the dashboard and then dialled Muraski. He didn't waste time with pleasantries. 'The bomb is at the Emirates stadium. It's due to go off sometime after kick-off I would guess. That's 8pm tonight.'

'Christ, Riley. You sure?'

'No, but if I'm right . . . I think it seats sixty thousand or more.'

'How do you know?'

'It might be seventy,' he corrected.

Muraski snapped back at him. 'Not that, you idiot. About the bomb.'

'Moe. He wasn't saying *gonner*. He was saying *Gooner* or Gunner. Think about it. Moe was trying to tell us there is a bomb at the match. It's why Safi put his hand over the kid's mouth. I said it wasn't personal, but I was wrong. Safi would know we used to josh about Arsenal and Liverpool. What better target?'

'That's pretty thin stuff, Riley. It's a bit of a WAG?'

'WAG?'

'Yeah, the army doesn't have a monopoly on acronyms, you know. What we in Five call a Wild-Arsed Guess.' He knew she was rehearsing in her head how this would play with her bosses. 'And the cost . . .'

'Jesus, does everyone think about the money first?' *Bloody capitalists*, he thought. 'Hold on.'

'What?'

'Just hold on. Think. This was a you-scratch-my-back, I'll-scratch-yours op, wasn't it? WAG or not, just listen. A marriage of convenience – I'll make the bombs, you do some targets of mine, then I'll hit one for you. This one does both parties.'

'I thought you said it was personal.'

'The teams are. Me and Moe. But who else likes football these days? Like to own the odd club or two? Take their mates along to an executive box and show off their investment?'

'Rich cunts?' she offered.

'Rich Russian cunts, maybe?' he countered.

'Fuck. Is Arsenal Russian-owned?'

'I haven't a clue,' he lied. It was mostly in American hands, but he had her attention now. 'That doesn't matter – they don't have to own the whole shooting match, having a swanky box at one of the big clubs is enough of a status symbol for most oligarchs. I suggest you get Counter Terrorism and your bods to start checking what Russian nationals have season tickets and get that ground cleared. Because I reckon there is a bomb under one or more of their seats.' He looked at the dash clock. 'And you've got about two hours till it starts ticking.'

*

'This is Billy Reeves with Radio London traffic. There is chaos in North London following the postponement of tonight's fixture between Arsenal and Liverpool due to an unspecified security incident. Highbury & Islington tube and mainline are currently closed and trains are not stopping at Arsenal and Holloway Road tubes because of overcrowding. Roads around Drayton Park are closed as is normal on match days. As you'd expect, traffic is very heavy on the Holloway Road between the Highbury & Islington roundabout and the Nag's Head in both directions. Police are advising ticket holders not to travel but to contact the club regarding refunds or replacements. Elsewhere, the North Circular is heavy at the Hangar Lane gyratory system in all directions due to roadworks. There is a restricted service on the Waterloo & City line and there is only one Woolwich Ferry running this evening. More in an hour.'

'You're listening to the Robert Elms show on Radio London . . .'

FORTY-FIVE

Riley looked through the glass curtain wall and out over the brightly lit stadium. Although there were no fans, the various stands were full of activity as police, trained ground staff, Royal Engineers and accompanying sniffer dogs examined each tier. It was 7.10, fifty minutes to kick-off. Riley was standing with Alex Stock and Liz McCracken, the events and security manager for the stadium. McCracken was a no-nonsense former policewoman in her early forties, bottle-blonde hair cut into a bob, dressed in a dark grey trouser suit and flat heels. They were in one of the glassed-in hospitality areas, coffees and plans of the stadium laid out on the table before them.

'You know, I hope you are wrong about this,' said Liz McCracken. 'It's a terrible waste of a good match ... bookies are up in arms. Fans have wrecked a couple of pubs. Players are pissed off, of course.'

Tell them to go buy another Porsche, cheer themselves up.

Nick would never have made a diplomat.

Riley reached out and took his coffee. He had been forced to abandon the BMW at Archway and, ignoring his aching back, he had sprinted down the Holloway Road. He still hadn't quite caught his breath. His confidence in his prediction had wavered with every metre of his run. Maybe he had just cost everyone a lot of time, effort and cash for nothing. A wild goose chase. *Better safe than very sorry indeed.*

That might be true, but few people would think that if they came up empty-handed. And he knew this one was on him and nobody else.

'I'm not wrong,' he said with as much confidence as he could muster.

Liz and Stock exchanged glances and a not very professional look went between them. Maybe they knew each other. EXPOs often did tours of PTs – Potential Targets – such as football grounds to offer advice. Perhaps they got friendly then. Maybe they were just confirming what the rest of the world was probably thinking: Riley has really lost it this time.

McCracken's radio let out a beep. 'Liz McCracken.'

'Is Riley with you?' It was Kate Muraski. She was in the main Arsenal office with the admin people. He knew she thought she should be out kicking arses at the Met, pushing them to find out who shanked her pal. If he was wrong about this, she'd probably carve Riley up herself for wasting her time.

'Yes.'

'Tell him we have a ten-seater VIP box on the Club Level bought in the name of Vasily Kutsik. The man who owns the house next to his grandparents.'

'I got that,' said Riley. 'That can't be a fucking coincidence.'

'Which box?' Liz asked.

'Wembley '98,' replied Muraski.

'Yeah, I know it,' said Liz. 'One floor below us.'

'Thanks, Kate. Can you access any CCTV footage of that area?' asked Riley.

'Not from here.'

'I can sort that,' Liz offered.

'Thanks. And tell everyone else to clear that floor.' He turned to Stock. 'I think we're up.'

*

The Wembley '98 box celebrated the FA Cup win of Arsenal over Newcastle United at the original Wembley Stadium. Inside, it was decorated with giant blow-ups of members of that victorious team, including goal scorers Marc Overmars and Nicolas Anelka, as well as images of the iconic twin towers of Wembley, which had been demolished in 2003.

Stock and Riley could see none of this. They were looking at an anonymous set of wooden double doors with the name of the box on the left-hand one. Stock's equipment was laid out on the floor around them. His number two, a police warrant officer called Chris Hilton, was checking the robot over, just in case it was needed.

'You sure you want to do this?' Stock asked Riley.

'Of course I don't,' he said, with some certainty. Right then he wanted to get into that abandoned BMW, drive to Cornwall and be with Ruby, talking about his grandfather. He knew, though, that this had to be his shout. 'But this is aimed at me. So, I'm more likely to spot any message Safi left me from the grave.'

'Yeah, mate, and I'm worried about you popping over to collect it personally. You going to suit up?'

'No.'

'It saved your life last time,' Stock reminded him.

'This isn't the same environment, is it? Would you wear it?' Riley asked.

Stock hesitated, apparently not wanting to admit Riley was making a decent judgement call. 'No, I suppose not.'

As in Afghan, it wasn't worth the encumbrance, albeit for different reasons. If a bomb went off in what was effectively a concrete box, no suit on earth would protect you. And wearing one would just make the process of trying to render any device safe much more difficult.

Riley checked his phone. Several missed calls from earlier, but he ignored them. There was no signal inside the Emirates anyway. It meant the Electronic Counter Measures operator didn't have to worry about activation by mobile phone, but Hilton had put the gamut of counter-measures in place anyway, over the full bandwith available.

Riley handed his phone over to Stock and took a radio and headset in return. He put the headphones on and turned on the microphone and camera. Hilton would tape the feed from the camera, so they had a record of what Riley had seen and done. 'Ok, I'll start with the door. You and Chris fuck off, eh?'

The ICP had been set up in one of the VIP dining rooms, a safe distance from any explosion, unless it was a real monster.

'Break a leg,' said Stock.

'At the very least,' said Riley.

When he was alone, he stared at the door for a few seconds. It was now 7.25. Maybe the timer had started. Maybe it was designed to initiate at 8pm, kick-off. One thing was for sure: whatever was beyond that door wouldn't have a large red digital clock clicking down to detonation.

He examined the frame for anything unusual – a thin piece of wire stretched across it, an electric eye sending out a beam that would cause the device to blow when broken. But he doubted the bomb-planters had had time to set up anything so complicated or liable to accidental deployment by a staff member. The idea was to get the victims inside the box, not stop them entering. Still, he didn't skimp on his visual inspection, switching his full attention to the silver handle, shining a torch beam over it, looking for tell-tale scratches.

Then Riley walked up and opened the door next to Wembley '98, crossed the hospitality area of the box, slid back the glass and stepped into the open air, where the seats for viewing the match were located. The hand search was still underway, but he ignored it. He leaned over the low glass partition that acted as a dividing wall between the VIP areas and, using a monocular, examined the interior of Wembley '98 as best he could.

Riley took a second to compose himself. Normally he could slip into ATO mode, the hyper-vigilant, focused state you needed to stay alive. He was having trouble erasing the clamour in his brain from the past few days, though. Nottingham, Spike, the near-miss with Ruby, the bomber in Scotland, the grim deaths of Moe and Safi, losing his grandfather. The images and sounds refused to leave him, like reluctant party guests in the early hours. And of course, Nick would think it was high time he made an appearance.

Come on, Dom. One last push. What did you always say? It isn't the bomb that kills you, it's complacency.

I'm not complacent.

You're not focused, either. Store the grief. You won't lose it. You need to be in the moment and nowhere else.

Riley took a deep breath and felt the cacophony in his skull diminish. A familiar stillness flooded through him. Time to go to work.

He eased himself over the divider and examined the concrete floor for any signs of wire or a mat or carpet that might hide a pressure pad. Nothing. Using his torch, monocular and fingers, he examined every inch of the sliding partition that would give him access to the indoor hospitality area, but there was nothing. He gently pushed one of the panes back, knelt down and probed at the carpet with a knife. No nasty surprises waited there. He stood and stepped inside. Again, he took his time to take in every surface, interrogating the room, demanding it give up its secrets. It was now nearly 7.45. He was beginning to think the room had no secrets to give up.

He turned on the radio. 'Alex?'

'Here.'

'Drawing a blank here. Nothing untoward.'

'Good,' said Stock.

'Any other thoughts?'

'Not yet. Nothing from the other search teams either.' There was a pause. 'Fifteen minutes to kick-off. The most likely deployment time if there is a bomb.'

'Roger that.'

Riley imagined what would happen if the device detonated at eight on the dot. The shock wave would kill him instantly, probably blasting what was left of him through the glass. The velocity would be such that pieces of him would probably be scattered on to the pitch. He knew Arsenal fans who would give their left nut to be scattered on . . .

Unless it's an EFP. Thought of that? Like someone used in Leicester. Maybe the same people, playing both ends against the middle. You being the piggy.

Riley imagined Nick sitting on a rock in the desert, one leg outstretched, boot off, wriggling his toes, the SA80 within easy reach. Maybe risking lifting his helmet off to wipe away the sweat. A shake of his head, releasing a cloud of dust. That wide grin, showing the incisor he chipped opening a beer bottle with his teeth.

You aren't thinking outside this particular box, pal.

Outside the box. Riley looked at the ceiling. What if you used an Explosively Formed Projectile to make sure the full force of the blast came downwards? Inside the concrete shell it would be like sitting in an erupting volcano: limbs would fly, flesh would melt. But when? If you were the bomb-maker, when would you set this monster to deploy? With the first kick of the ball? Eight o'clock on the nose, perhaps. It was as good a time as any to choose.

'Alex. Ask Kate or Liz to check who owns the box above this one.'

'Above?'

'Yes. Directly above.'

'Shit. You thinking ...?'

'Just ask her.'

'Twelve minutes to kick-off. Just saying.'

'Can you ask her?'

The answer came in just over a minute. 'Christ, that put a rocket up Kate's arse. She says it's a corporate box.'

'In the name of?'

'Something called Halo Trading.'

FORTY-SIX

Stock lit his cigarette and offered Riley the pack. He shook his head. 'Those things'll kill you.'

Stock half-laughed and half-coughed. With the clock ticking and two ATOs being better than one, Stock had come to join him at the Halo Trading area to check the exterior for traps. They were standing in the outside, open-air portion of the box. They had gone over the door and the sliding partition, but in truth they knew immediately where the bomb was. It didn't so much speak to them as bellow at the top of its voice. It was a steel trolley, of the sort used everywhere to deliver hot food in hotels, hospitals. This one was designed to deliver something else altogether. Next to it was a coil of thick hose, although it wasn't clear if that was part of the set-up or not.

They had both examined the device through the glass using monoculars. As far as they could tell, the two metal cubes that made up the device were completely sealed. There was no orifice for them to put in a flexi-camera scope and check out the interiors. They'd have to drill a hole for that. And even with a ceramic drill, there was no guarantee that a stray curl of metal couldn't complete the circuit. The upper cube did have some sort of lid on it, which looked as if it could be removed. But the procedure was never to blithely remove anything, just because it was inviting you to. Riley knew he would have to approach that very carefully indeed.

Stock looked at his watch. 'Best get to it. You still want to take point?'

'More than ever.'

It was fully dark now, the whole stadium spookily empty and lit by floodlights. They had called off the fingertip search of the stalls for now. They had no idea how powerful the trolley-bomb was. Best that nobody was in the line of fire.

'You sure we shouldn't X-ray it?' asked Stock.

'No time.' It wasn't easy to interpret the sort of X-rays you got from complex IEDs. 'The FBI had about 33 hours to study their version of this, remember, and still got it wrong. We have about ten minutes' left. Maybe a bit longer. But not days, pal.'

Stock nodded, threw his half-smoked cigarette down and ground it out with his boot. 'I'll be listening in.' He hesitated. 'You know most US bomb squads have a rule about married men not doing this shit. And I'm single.'

'I'm separated.'

'Or fathers.'

Well, he was still that. For the moment. He tried, and failed, to keep an image of Ruby out of his mind. It didn't help with the concentration, wondering how your daughter would get on without a father. He forced himself to focus on the task in hand. 'God bless America. But we're not so squeamish,' Riley said. 'Go back to the ICP, Alex. I'll give you a full report before I try anything.'

'Sure?'

'Promise.'

Riley adjusted the headset he was wearing and turned on the radio and the camera. He walked up to the glass partition and peered in, as if expecting the device to have moved. But there it stood, with its odd-looking rectangular box where the tea urn normally was and that coil of hose.

He pulled the mouthpiece close to his lips. 'Hilton?'

'Yes, Skip?'

He slid back the panel. 'I'm going in.'

As he crossed the carpet to the silver contraption on the far side of the hospitality area, he felt himself detach from his physical form. For a fleeting second he was floating up near the ceiling, looking down on himself, staring at the steel trolley. No, it wasn't Riley down there. It was Nick. He looked up and spoke to Riley.

Fuck me, Boss. You know what this is? It's the Rolls-Royce of IEDs.

*

Riley ran his hands over the outer casing, as gentle as the most considerate lover. His fingertips were searching for hotspots or vibration, something that might give a clue to the inner life to this object.

'That's four minutes, Skip.' Hilton again, the speaking clock.

'I know.'

He moved round to the side, examined the hose. It didn't seem to be part of the rig. He put it to one side. Careful not to jar the device, he lay down and examined the underneath. He could see soldered joints, but no screws or nuts. Of course, one couldn't just randomly undo a screw or a nut. They were very easy to turn into lethal traps.

'Two minutes.'

Riley got to his feet and examined the switches once more and the panel behind it, looking for scratches or smudges left by human contact. But it had been buffed clean. The single red switch stared at him, defying him to touch it.

'Speak to me,' Riley commanded.

'Ninety seconds.'

'I was talking to the bomb,' he said to Hilton.

'Sixty seconds.'

Hilton waited for a response that never came. 'Skip? Fifty. Skip, for fuck's sake. Thirty seconds.'

'I'm out,' said Riley.

*

There were around twenty-five people milling around at the ICP when Riley made it back there. About twenty too many. Kate Muraski intercepted him, a concerned look etched on her face. He gave her a minuscule shake of the head.

'Is it safe?' asked a tall, well-built man in a grey suit who was standing next to Liz. Riley ignored him and went over to the table where Hilton and Stock were sitting. 'You got that?' he asked Hilton, meaning his final communication.

'Yes.'

The grey suit strode over. 'Oscar Turnbull. I represent the owners. Is it safe?'

Riley turned. 'I didn't make it safe. It just didn't blow when I expected.'

'Can you make it safe?'

'It's definitely a Viper of some description,' said Riley, talking to Stock as much as Turnbull. 'You could see that on the camera feed?'

Stock nodded.

'When I lifted the cover off the square box on the top there were twenty-one switches. Three rows of seven. Only one of them was pointing down, a red one, the rest were up. Are you a betting man, Mr Turnbull?'

'The odd flutter. What's that got to do with it?'

'When a Viper is initially activated by flipping one of the switches, it activates a randomiser circuit. Like something from a fruit machine. It cycles through all twenty-one switches and makes one of them the "off" switch. And it's most likely not the one in the "down" position, which is the one most beginners would choose. The red one. The problem is, there is no way to tell which one of the twenty left is the active one that will shut the whole system down. What do you think of those odds?'

'So you're going to let it blow us up?'

Riley thought they were probably a safe distance away, but it paid to be cautious. There might, after all, be a secondary. 'Well, I suggest you all get out of here.'

Some of the observers didn't need telling twice. The crowd began to shrink rapidly.

'It might cause millions of pounds' worth of damage,' said Turnbull. 'We spoke to the architects—'

'Sell a goalkeeper or two,' suggested Riley. 'You've got about ten on your books.'

'Staff Sergeant,' admonished Liz. 'That is hardly the point.'

'No. The point is this: if that really is a Viper, which I believe it is, it is a modified version of something called the Harvey or the Harvey's casino bomb. It was planted in 1980. It contained eight triggers. The double wall trigger was the casing – two slabs of steel separated by rubber. Any drill would act as a bridge, closing a circuit. Even if you could make a hole, the next step was often to inject water at high pressure to try and disrupt the electronics.'

Riley was at risk of mansplaining and he could see his audience was getting impatient, but it was important that he conveyed how serious this was. When Turnbull made to interrupt him, he ploughed on. 'But this fucker had a float, like the one you find in a toilet bowl. If it rose up because of water, again it closed a circuit that was encased in a steel box to isolate it from the disrupter jets. The tilt trigger was very simple. A piece of foil wrapped around a plastic pipe. The foil was connected to a wire. If the bomb moved and the foil touched metal, the circuit was completed ... *boom*. The panel screws were holding back spring-loaded triggers. Undo the screws and the contacts closed. Do you want me to go on? It had a timer that could go from forty-five minutes to eight days. Rendering it safe involves a little bit more than: *which one do I cut, red or blue?*'

Riley waited for Turnbull to make his point, but he simply shook his head in dismay.

'What happened?' asked Liz, as if she didn't actually want an answer but felt compelled to put the question. 'At the Lake Tahoe casino?'

Stock answered. 'It blew up, is what happened. The FBI's best couldn't disarm it. Even today, it is set as a test on bomb-disposal courses around the world. Everybody fails. Everybody.'

'We always say it's the Kobayashi Maru of IEDs,' Riley explained. 'As in *Star Trek*. A no-win situation. But that's in the movies. The Viper is the more evil son of that bomb in Lake Tahoe and it's the real deal. It's concerned with just two things: causing maximum damage and killing anyone stupid enough to mess with it.'

'How big is this bomb?' Turnbull asked.

Riley shrugged. 'The original left a five storey-deep crater in the casino. It was close to a thousand pounds of TNT. I doubt this is that big. But I think we should all move out to the Met's ICP and let it do its worst.' The Met were outside, near the statue of Tony Adams.

'There's nothing to be done?' Liz asked, horrified at the thought.

Riley hesitated just a second too long. 'Not really.'

'Fuck it, Dom,' said Stock. 'I know you. You've got an idea.'

'I have. But shift the ICP to outside,' Riley said to Hilton. 'Or as far away as you can before you lose comms. Alex, any advice welcome, so patch yourself in. My next best guess is we've got just under forty-five minutes. If it hasn't gone at kick-off, it'll blow at half-time, I think, when everyone comes back inside for sand-wiches and a drink. They don't allow alcohol in the outside area.'

Riley looked to Liz for confirmation. She nodded and then asked: 'Is that a guess? About half-time?'

'Of course. From now on everything is a guess.' He turned to Stock. 'By the way, I've remembered how Captain Kirk solved the Kobayashi Maru.'

'Well, that's reassuring,' said Stock. 'And if you've got an idea, I'm coming in with you.'

'It's an OCD,' Riley reminded him.

'Shit, we've all got that,' said Stock, deliberately misunder-standing him. He started gathering his kit.

'Alex,' Riley said.

Stock looked up from his bag. 'Yeah?'

'You don't have to. One idiot is enough.'

'I know. But maybe between us we can make one whole brain cell.'

Riley laughed. 'Don't bank on it. But before you rush in like the fool you are, we need to start here. I want some strips of wood. This long. About this wide.'

'Behind the champagne bar,' said Turnbull, pointing across the acres of carpet. 'Over there. Lattice work. You can rip that off.'

'Good. Alex? Can you get me a dozen strips.'

The EXPO didn't need asking twice. He scooped up pliers and a screwdriver and jogged off towards the bar.

Muraski almost whispered her question in his ear. 'Dom,

do you know what you're doing? Or is this just bravado? Or a real OCD.'

Riley rummaged in his bag, found the battery-operated drill, a tape measure and a handful of screws. He put a length of det cord, battery, wire, pliers, two rolls of tapes and snips into his jacket pockets. 'We're about to find out, aren't we?

FORTY-SEVEN

Riley laughed to himself at the irony of it. He had often said that there was never a big digital clock ticking down in any EOD situation. That it was pure Hollywood. Timers from washing machines, dishwashers, DVDs, yes. But never a *Mission: Impossible*-style display. Well, he was wrong this time. In several places around the Emirates stadium giant digital clocks showed that, under normal conditions, there would have been eight minutes left, plus stoppage time. Had the bomb-maker factored that in? What was the most injury time given? Four minutes? Five, maybe? He hoped they had more margin than he had thought to take the Viper out.

'How did Kirk pass that test then? The Koba-whasit Maru?' asked Stock as they studied the device.

'You don't remember?'

'The name's Stock, not Spock.'

'He reprogrammed the computer before the test began.'

'That's cheating. I don't think we have that option.' Stock groaned. 'You going to tell me why we built a bit of garden trellis just now?'

'In a minute. Let me think if we have an alternative.'

Riley looked over the device one more time, wondering if he had this right. He was now convinced that Safi had wanted him to discover this bomb, no matter what the Russians had intended. Maybe Moe had been told to shout those clues. Safi wanted Riley to face the Viper, knowing he couldn't just walk away and let it blow without trying something.

Don't play the big man, Dom.

This time, he wasn't entirely sure who was speaking to him. Nick? His grandpa? Maybe it was Moe, from wherever he had landed. Whoever it was, it was good advice. But somehow this felt like unfinished business. Which, of course, the bomb-maker would have been banking on. That an ATO like him doesn't live like normal people, doesn't obey their rules, doesn't walk away from danger. Those who thought ATOs and EXPOs were a breed apart weren't far wrong. What you did most days out there in Afghan, it was beyond sane. And so was this. Which is why he needed to try and beat this bomb.

Because it's what we do.

He knew the voice now. *Yes, Nick, because it's what we do.*

'The FBI had the right instincts,' Riley said eventually. 'If you sever this upper box from the lower at the junction where they meet, you should cut all the connections to the charge. They used a shaped C-4 charge to beat the electrical impulses.'

'Nice idea. But it was booby-trapped, wasn't it? There was extra dynamite in the top box which the X-rays didn't pick up.'

'That's true,' said Riley. 'But I think they were in the right area. Hand me that thing.'

Stock passed over the frame that Riley had constructed from the woodwork of the bar. Riley slotted it over the switches.

'Fuck you doing?'

'So, this jig is designed to throw every switch at once into the off position.'

Stock looked at the jerry-rigged frame and shook his

head. 'Dom, I'm the reckless one here, remember? Even I wouldn't do that.'

'Which is why I want you to leave.'

'I can't do that. This is crazy. You're banking on the shut-down mechanism being faster than the initiation. That didn't work for the FBI.'

'You got a better idea?'

'We get out of here, let the fucker blow.'

'Not this time,' said Riley. 'You go. Now.'

'It's a bad move.'

'And I'm still going to try it.'

'Fucking up this bomb won't bring him back, you know.'

'Who?'

'Nick. Your mate. That's why you want to do it, isn't it? To beat the man who built the bomb that killed Nick. Well, he's dead, Dom. Safi is dead too, mate. He won't know fuck all about whether you render this safe or blow yourself to bite-sized pieces.'

Riley nodded his agreement. 'But I'll know.'

'Only if it works. Otherwise it's straight into the Big Black for you. *Operation Fucking Certain Death*. Sooner or later, that comes true.'

Riley spoke softly, his words carrying a plea for understanding. 'I have to try, Alex.'

Stock hesitated, then seemed to deflate a little, knowing he was defeated. 'Okay.' Then, 'Good luck, soldier.'

Stock held his hand out. Riley took it and Stock yanked him in towards him, swinging a fist at his head as he did so. Riley was shocked at the sudden ferocity, but instinct took over and he dipped back from the waist and felt the rush of air as the blow passed him by.

Stock shifted his weight from side to side, keeping Riley guessing. 'I am trying to save your life, Dom.'

'It isn't yours to save.'

Even before he had finished the sentence, Stock hunkered down and drove at him. Riley leaned in to take the force, letting some of his rage stiffen in his muscles. They collided with an explosion of grunts. Riley punched down onto the back of Stock's head and his knuckles burnt with the pain. Stock had him round the waist and forced him down onto the carpet. The beer-soaked smell of a thousand hospitality events rose up from it. Riley pulled at Stock's hair, got his face up and stabbed a finger into one of his eyes. Stock yelped, but didn't shift. A blow landed on Riley's ears and his head sang. This wasn't going how he envisaged it at all.

*

Kate Muraski was standing next to Hilton, who was trying to make sense of the confused sounds coming over his headset. One of the SO15 commanders came up behind them. 'What the hell is going on?' he demanded. Before Hilton could explain, he said: 'We have eyes on them from across the stadium and your two fucking idiots appear to be fighting.'

'Sir,' said Hilton, looking at the blurred camera feed. 'I think you're right.'

'Over what, for Christ's sake?'

'How to tackle the bomb?' offered Hilton, without any real conviction.

The commander put his fists onto the table and leaned in, a vein in his temple throbbing. 'Thirty more seconds and I'm going to send someone in to bang their heads together.'

'Sir.'

Hilton looked at Muraski, who asked: 'What the hell are they doing knocking seven kinds of shit out of each other?'

'From what I can tell, my skipper is trying to stop Riley killing himself.'

'For fuck's sake,' she said, pulling out her pistol and breaking into a sprint, so that Hilton only just caught the final word. 'Men.'

*

As Riley managed to flip Stock off him, the younger man rolled away and pushed himself upright. Riley lashed out and kicked his knee. There was a satisfying crack and Stock lost his balance and began to stumble backwards. Towards the bomb.

Riley moved as fast as he could ever remember moving, ignoring the pain from Stock's blows, springing to his feet and grabbing a handful of the EXPO's clothing just as he was about to fall into the Viper. They stood there for a few moments, breathing hard, aware of what they had almost done. 'Trembler device,' said Riley, welcoming the wave of icy calm now washing over him. 'We fall into that and we're toast.'

'Truce?' rasped Stock, looking over his shoulder at the row of switches.

'We'd better,' said Riley, his breath also coming hard. 'You were going to carry me out over your shoulder?'

'I hadn't thought that far.'

Riley made sure Stock was standing properly on his own two feet before he let go of him. Gingerly, they moved away from the machine and caught their breath for a moment.

'Shall we try moving your wooden piece of Meccano together?' asked Stock eventually. 'We might get a more even pressure that way.'

Riley nodded. 'If you insist. I'd rather it was just me testing my theory, though.'

Stock smiled. 'And let you get all the credit?'

Riley blew out his cheeks and released a stream of air. 'Okay. No more tricks, eh?' Stock shook his head. 'Right. I'll see you on the other side.'

They took their time positioning themselves. Riley knew the clocks around the ground were clicking towards the end of the theoretical first forty-five minutes' playing period. Half-time. There couldn't be long left before he discovered the hard way that he had been right.

Stock and Riley put their hands on either side of the jig. The Viper was against a wall, so they couldn't stand either side of it, which would have been the ideal placement. Instead it was like a four-handed piano piece: the trick was not to collide with each other.

Riley felt his confidence drain away. What if he was wrong? What if the bomber had anticipated this sort of move? Well, Riley probably wouldn't live to know much about it. Oblivion would be instantaneous. He began to sweat, as if he were back under the Afghan sun. He could smell the drains, the dust. Riley snorted a little to clear his sinuses.

'You okay?' Stock asked.

'You don't have to stay, Alex. It's death or glory and I'm not sure which one is waiting for us.'

Stock glanced at Riley and winked. 'Now he tells me.'

Riley looked at the jerry-rigged contraption he was gambling his life on. It was far from reassuring.

Fine time to get the yips, man.

Riley laughed to himself. He didn't have the yips, that sudden doubt in your own ability that blights sportspeople's performance. It was just that he was out of his comfort zone, beyond the usual drills and skills. He looked over his shoulder to one of the clocks. Half-time was a heartbeat away. Maybe oblivion, too.

'Ready?' Stock asked, worry creeping into his voice at Riley's hesitation.

Riley could hear his heart thumping in his ears, mixed with the sound of Stock's laboured breathing. Alex, too, must be wondering what the fuck they were doing there.

'You?' Riley asked.

'Right now? I'd rather get it over with.'

Riley felt his fears recede. It either worked or it didn't, and it was too late to stop now. 'On three, yes?'

'If you say so, boss.'

Riley made sure there was saliva in his mouth and coughed a little to clear his throat. 'Okay. One . . . two . . . THREE.'

As they pulled down on the makeshift rig, the switches all flicked position simultaneously. Each man closed their eyes and held their breath.

FORTY-EIGHT

The throwing of the switches initiated a powerful militarygrade mobile communication device within the Viper, designed to dial a number using multiple frequencies until it was put through. The relay phone, located outside the ground beyond the reach of the electronic counter-measures, then made another call. This one activated a second device containing Semtex.

The resulting explosion caused a plume of smoke that stretched into the night sky until it was invisible, carrying with it fragments of steel, glass, wood, and, of course, people. Mixed in with the human remains were large fragments of furniture, portraits and carpets.

The detonation, which could be heard clearly from five miles away, punched an enormous hole through the upper floors, puncturing the roof. A fire started immediately, growing greedily as it was fed by a surfeit of inflammable materials. The sky above the scene began to glow a devilish red.

A second, smaller, explosion wracked the frame of the fatally damaged building. A section of the gable roof creaked and gave way with a hideous crash, sending sparks to the heavens, like fireflies seeking paradise. Windows splintered with the sound of a gunshot. The trees nearby crackled as their new leaves shrivelled in the heat before some smaller twigs and branches caught fire. Soon, whole trees were engulfed, their skeletal forms consumed by flames, like victims of some arboreal witch trial. The heat ignited the fuel in the cars standing on the driveway and their plume of toxins coiled into the motherlode of smoke.

Within twenty minutes, before even the first of the fire engines arrived, the east wing of Dunston Hall, home to the Russian Vasily Kutsik, was no more and the west was just beginning its journey to ashes.

FORTY-NINE

They had screwed their eyes shut as the switches flipped. Now, slowly, they dared to open them. Their hands were still on the trellis, gripping it so hard their knuckles were white. 'We can probably let go now,' said Riley quietly.

They did so, backing cautiously away from the machine before looking at each other as if they had just found a winning lottery ticket. Riley realised he had been holding his breath so he sucked in a good lungful of air. Then they both gave a nervous laugh that was only a few steps away from hysteria.

'Fuck,' said Stock. 'We still alive?'

Riley ran a hand through his hair. It was sticky with dried sweat. He desperately needed a shower. But, Jesus, he was alive. 'Either that or heaven is really shite.'

'Jesus, I didn't think that would work.'

'Neither did I,' admitted Riley. 'But we've got to get out of here. Just in case. We'll let it soak for an hour or two, eh?'

Stock put an arm around Riley's shoulders. 'Fine with me, you mad fucker.'

A figure appeared at the glass and stepped inside. It was Kate Muraski, pistol at the ready, not quite believing what she was seeing.

'What are you two laughing at?' she asked, unable to keep the irritation from her voice. That caused hysteria in the pair, which annoyed her even more. 'Oh, grow up.'

Riley gulped back his laughter. 'Said the woman who has, apparently, come to shoot us.' He pointed to the pistol in her hand.

'I thought I might have to fire in the air to make you pay attention. Instead you've gone all *Women in Love* on me.'

Riley looked blankly at her.

'Is it safe?' she asked, pointing at the Viper.

'Yup,' said Stock. 'We did it. We beat the Kobayashi Maru.'

As if to give a lie to the ATO's premature boast, Riley heard the soft plop of a panel falling from the bottom of the Viper onto the carpet. Then, the whirr of an electrical motor, followed by the hiss of escaping gas, which all three of them registered.

'Jesus, fuck,' said Stock, taking a step towards the machine. 'What's that?'

'Gas! Get the fuck away from there, Alex.'

Muraski remained rooted to the spot, her jaw slack.

'Get out!' Riley yelled. 'Hold your breath.'

He grabbed Stock by the collar and pulled him away, using him to career into Muraski, who let out a cry. She dropped her pistol as Riley gathered them together and propelled them with all the driving power of a tighthead prop towards the partition. With a final heave he pushed them out onto the terrace and stepped back inside.

Before they could recover, Riley had slammed the doors shut and wrapped a length of det cord from his pocket around the handles, so that when Stock tried to prise them apart, they held firm. 'Dom, don't be stupid!'

'Get help. Now. You've been exposed.' Although God alone knew to what.

373

'No! Let me—' Stock began.

The sound was muffled because of the glass panels, but Riley clearly heard the splatter as Muraski was sick over the plastic seats. She gripped the back of one of them and dry-heaved several times. That answered one question: it was most likely a nerve agent.

'Shit!' yelled Stock. He stared through the partition at Riley, desperation etched on his face.

'Get her to the Met,' Riley shouted through the glass. 'They'll have antidotes.' Stock would know, but might have forgotten in his panic, that SO15 routinely carried syringes of atropine and pralidoxime, which helped mitigate the effects of the majority of nerve agents. 'Now, Alex.'

Alex hesitated, as if considering a solution to save Riley. But they'd had their one lucky break for the day.

'Move it, Alex. Or she'll die,' he pointed out grimly, feeling reality hit home: he might well have killed them all. 'And maybe you, too.'

Reluctantly, Stock put his arm around Muraski and half carried, half dragged her over the dividing wall. Riley took off his headset and killed the camera and microphone. He didn't want anyone witnessing what was about to happen.

Riley turned back to the Viper. He could feel his eyes smarting. Holding his breath was probably a waste of time, as whatever it was might well be absorbed through the skin and mucous membranes. Still, he took in a lungful close to the small gap where the two doors mated and strode across to the steel box. His eyes fell on the hose, curled next to the machine.

The hose.

Now he knew how this device worked. After all, gases like sarin were floor-huggers. Introduced from above, via a hose, the lethal fumes would quickly sink down through the hospitality space and kill anyone down there within minutes. Safi had built a different kind of Viper altogether, but Riley had called it in, and the Met had evacuated and sealed off the stadium, before they had had a chance to fully deploy it.

It took him several precious seconds to locate the conduit to the VIP on the floor box in the right-hand corner of the room, beneath the carpet. He ripped it back to give him full access. He was going to have to take a breath soon. His eyes were watering now, blurring his vision. He removed the various pieces of kit from his jacket, placed them next to the machine – even though his lungs were burning, it was important he was calm and steady, not panicked and fumbling – took off his jacket and shoved the sleeve down the hole, then ran gaffer tape over it. Better one room was contaminated than two.

Riley lay down, putting his left hand in to the bottom of the Viper to examine by touch what was sitting above the opening. There was a small prayer he kept repeating, although he doubted there was anyone to hear him. *Please God, let there not be an anti-handling device up there.*

Riley closed his eyes and imagined the 3-D layout of what he could feel in there, changing the neural messages from his sense of touch into images of wires, pipes and junction boxes. His brain was screaming for him to let some air into his lungs and, overriding all his conscious instructions, he let out a little puff of breath and sucked in poison in return.

Concentrate, pal.

His fingertips found the single nozzle that was issuing the gas. He followed it back to a flexible tube. He rolled back, grabbed the pliers where he had left them, and reached in and bent the tube back on itself, squeezing as hard as he could to crimp it. He used a cable tie to secure it in place. He hadn't stopped the flow – he could hear an electric motor protesting with a whine as it tried to push the gas past the obstruction – but he had severely reduced it. The lower half of the room, though, was still full of whatever the agent was. And he had taken in some of it when he could no longer hold his breath. Already he could feel a burning corrosion deep in his bronchi.

Riley knew he didn't have time to dwell on what was happening to his body. Instead, drills and skills on biohazards kicked in. He had to locate the pump and the valves that were involved in mixing what was very likely to be a binary system. He went back in.

Another small exhalation. More toxin taken in. The alternative was to pass out from lack of oxygen. No choice.

His fingers found the little cluster of leads that fed to the pump. There was no time for the pliers, or to worry about a secondary bomb linked to a collapsing circuit. He gripped and yanked at the wires, until he felt several come free. Waited.

The struggling motor stopped its whining. Done.

Riley rolled away from the machine and stood on wobbly legs. His stomach spasmed and he threw up the meagre amount of food inside it over the carpet. The specialist officers would be here soon in their . . . in their . . . what? What were they called? His mind was fogging up. Totally-Encapsulating Chemical Protective Suits, that was it. They should keep them safe.

But Riley, he was fucked.

His vision was tunnelling but his eyes fell on the Glock that Kate Muraski had dropped. He hoped she was okay. She couldn't have had that much exposure. And Alex, of course. He'd probably had about the same dose as her, maybe a little more of it, because he had been closer to the venting gas. They had a decent chance of survival. He blinked the pistol back into some sort of focus.

He remembered Nick, out in that culvert in Afghan after the IED had detonated, his body blown to shit, and the decision he made to end it before the suffering got any worse. Brave man. Riley's stomach cramped again, but there was nothing left to bring up. His mouth tasted of metal, as if he had been sucking coins. What was it? Sarin? Tabun? Some new neuro-crap created in a lab out in the Urals?

You'll never know, pal.

Riley stumbled over, picked up the gun, raised it and, without a moment's hesitation, pulled the trigger.

FIFTY

After being inoculated with a cocktail of drugs, Stock and Muraski were taken to a brace of directors' suites, where each was instructed to have a long, hot soapy shower. Specialist medics from the Defence Science Laboratory at Porton Down were on the way by helicopter to examine them. Sterile isolation rooms were being prepared at the Whittington Hospital, just in case.

Meanwhile, the VIP levels of Arsenal were in full decontamination mode. Techs from the Terrorism Command in high-spec haz-chem suits had forced their way into the box where Riley had decommissioned the weapon. Riley had been rushed to the Whittington, so they had been told, but there had been no word since.

It was only after an hour or so that they had discovered that there had been a secondary device after all. It had demolished the east wing of Dunston Hall, killing thirteen individuals, including Vasily Kutsik.

Muraski took another lengthy shower – the second since her exposure. Had the idea been to gas the dissident Russians in their box, with an explosion at the house as a back-up in case things went wrong at Arsenal? It was a WAG, but a decent one. Already *Russia Today* was reporting that terrorism in the UK had moved into a new phase. Russia was even offering specialists in chemical warfare and explosives to try and get to the bottom of the incidents. The cheeky fuckers.

Jamal dead and now Riley was either fighting for his life or dead as well. OCD. *Operation Certain Death*. No longer funny. It probably never had been.

She stepped out of the shower and towelled herself until her skin glowed red. Then she slipped on the robe and walked through to the living area, looking for the remote to turn on the gargantuan TV.

While she was searching, the phone on the writing desk rang. She hesitated for a moment and then crossed and picked it up with a shaking hand, knowing it would be about Riley.

*

When Kate Muraski knocked and entered his suite, Alex Stock was sitting on a lilac leather sofa, wrapped in a quilted silk dressing gown that made him look like Michael Douglas in that Liberace film. Like hers, his clothes had been bagged and removed by one of the suited haz-chem lads. He had reassured them both that if they had been fully contaminated, they would be dead by now.

Kate was holding a wooden tray with several objects wrapped in plastic bags on it. 'Your phones and wallet have been given the all clear,' she said, nodding at the collection she was holding.

'Great. Any news?' he asked.

Muraski looked as if she was trying to eat her own lips before she spoke. 'He's pretty bad. He shot out the fire suppression system and got drenched with water. That helped, apparently. But he still got a high level of exposure.'

Stock closed his eyes and thumped the cushion next to him. 'Idiot.'

379

'That idiot saved our lives.'

'That's why I am so pissed off with him. Had to play the big man.' He sounded angry, but there was moisture in his eyes. '*Fuck.* He should have just let the gas bloody run.'

'He couldn't do that, could he? That's not what you blokes are trained for. Walking away. Is it?' she demanded.

'No.' He gave a small cough, pulled a face and spat into a tissue. He examined it, but there was no blood. 'Something tastes off.'

Kate put a hand on his forehead. It seemed unnaturally hot.

'You okay?' she asked. 'You're a little flushed.'

'Yeah. Just a little nauseous. It could be the drugs. I could just be hungry.' They had been advised not to eat until the Porton Down specialists had finished with them.

'How come the Skripals survived bloody Novichok? But Dom's at death's door?'

'Nobody knows what the gas was. The trolley is still awaiting proper forensic dissection.'

'And Dunston Hall?'

'The real target, maybe,' she said. 'Maybe the whole bombing campaign was an act of obfuscation. You know there is a theory in my outfit that Salisbury was deliberately blatant to detract attention from several other assassinations of dissidents which received almost no publicity.'

'What a clusterfuck. You realise that Dunston Hall being blown up means there is still an active Russian team out there?'

'Yes,' she agreed. 'But we always knew that was a risk. Safi wasn't about to plant his own bomb from the grave, was he? Someone delivered the Viper here and, judging by the CCTV footage we have so far, it wasn't any Afghan. Someone also wired the Hall to blow.' Muraski paused for a second. 'Maybe now they've murdered the dissidents at Dunston they've got what they wanted. Time for a vacation. Lots of other cathedrals besides Salisbury to see.'

'You believe that?' Stock asked. 'That they'll just go away?'

'No. Not the Russians.' She sounded as if she wanted them to carry on, just so she could have the satisfaction of taking them down. Stock didn't blame her one bit.

Muraski eventually put the tray down on the coffee table and took a seat opposite him. 'I think they're going to cremate our clothes. The medics will be here in a minute to check us out again.' She pointed to the tray. 'As I say, they've been given the all-clear. We've been promised some new kit to wear soon.'

'As long as it's not the Arsenal away strip,' said Stock without thinking. 'Sorry, that's not funny.'

One of the phones on the tray vibrated in its plastic bag. 'I see the directors get a signal,' said Muraski.

'It's Dom's.'

'What?'

He pointed at the jiggling handset. 'That phone. It's Dom's. He gave it to me just before he went in the first time. You going to answer it?'

She did so. It was Riley's friend Scooby. She took a breath and told him the situation.

'Will he survive?'

'We don't know.'

'Oh, Christ, poor old Dom,' said Scooby

'Why?' Kate asked, scared of the reply.

'Because it might be better if he doesn't make it.'

EPILOGUE

Six days later

He liked it down there. It was warm and safe. He had come close to the surface on two or three occasions and he hadn't enjoyed the experience. The chill seemed to enter his very bones and there were voices, harsh and metallic. He had allowed himself to sink down once more, back into the depths, where he would be cossetted, as if he was in a second womb.

Then, without asking him, someone had pumped air into whatever he was wearing and he began to float upwards. Nothing he could do halted his progress. He tried to turn to face downwards, so he could use his feet to kick himself back to the deep, but he was locked in position. Riley surfaced into air that stank of chemicals. He felt himself shivering, the waters still around him freezing. He wanted to go back to the warmth. *Stop this.*

'Stop this!'

Riley was shocked by the sound of his own voice. It sounded strange and tinny, as if he was listening to a playback on a very cheap tape recorder, like the Philips one his grandparents . . .

A pain started in his chest as he remembered that Henry had gone.

He opened his eyes and the pain knifed into his brain. He shut them again.

'We'll turn the lights down,' someone said. 'There.' Riley waited a few moments and tried once more. Better. Still painful, but bearable. Just.

Riley took stock of his surroundings as his peripheral nerves came online and the phantom waters that had engulfed him receded. He was in a bed, propped up by several fat pillows. Wearing pyjamas. It was daylight outside. His was the only bed in the room. A line for fluid had been run into his hand, fed from a clear plastic bag of what could be saline. And now he was hot, not cold. There was a figure lurking at the foot of his bed, but he couldn't focus on him or her. He blinked until his vision cleared a little more. It was only then he realised he was surrounded by walls of plastic sheeting.

'Who are you?' he asked the hazy shape at the foot of the bed. 'Why is it so cold in here? Where the fuck am I?'

'I'll let your friends answer that.'

'What friends?'

Riley sensed the man leave and heard a door open and close.

Two more outlines appeared and then moved to either side of the bed. 'Hello, Dom.'

'Kate?'

'Yes.'

'How do you feel?' It was Oakham.

'Christ. What the hell …?' The sentence petered out into a croak. 'Water?'

'There's a tube for that just over your left shoulder.' He found it and sucked in a mouthful of fluid that tasted like chemicals.

'What's going on?' He waved the arm without tubes to indicate the tent. 'Am I contagious?'

383

'They don't think so,' said Muraski. 'It's just a precaution.'

Remember that joke the medics used to tell when they talked about biological warfare? This soldier goes to the regimental doctor with weird symptoms and the doctor tells him that he has been exposed to a potentially lethal agent. 'Don't worry,' says the doctor, 'we'll put you in quarantine and feed you pizza.' The soldier says: 'Pizza? Will that help?' 'No,' says the doc, 'but it's the only thing we can fit under the door.'

Yes, just the time for a side-splitter of a joke. It's all about timing, Nick. 'How long have I been in here?'

'Almost a week. You were put into an induced coma,' said Oakham. 'The experts thought it best. Give your body a chance to recover. You're in a specialist facility in Wiltshire. One of several built after the Salisbury poisonings.'

'I . . . How are you?' he asked Muraski.

'Me? Fine. Well, I had a few days of what I would imagine morning sickness is like. But that passed.'

'And how am I doing? And no bollocks, eh?'

'Some scarring on the lungs. Liver damage, but it's a resilient organ. Maybe a little neural damage, but they won't know till they've done tests.'

'Have Izzy or Ruby been in?'

'You're very lucky to be alive,' said Oakham, ignoring the question.

'Have I missed them?'

Oakham carried on like a runaway train. 'Dom, if you hadn't shot the sprinkler system on the ceiling in that box and doused yourself with water . . . well, we wouldn't be having this little chat. Did you know that formulation of sarin was soluble in water?'

'I have no idea,' he admitted. 'I suspected it was some form of sarin. I don't remember shooting any sprinklers. I recall picking up the gun.' But at that point it hadn't been the fire system he had thought about putting a bullet into. 'Now, listen. Enough of the bloody herogram stuff. What aren't you telling me?'

Oakham cleared his throat before answering. 'We believe your grandfather was murdered.'

'What?'

'All Six operatives, serving or retired, are given a full autopsy and toxicology report. Even ones as old as Henry. There were traces of a drug in his bloodstream. Plus they found a puncture mark. From a hypodermic. It was hidden beneath one of his nicotine patches. Could easily have been missed.'

'And my grandmother? She was in the house too.'

'We think she was a target as well. But she had locked herself in the basement to reboot a monitoring system. Apparently, the door insulated her from all sounds and, when bolted from the inside, was secure enough to resist any intruder.'

'That's true. But why? Why murder them?'

'We think they wanted them out of the way while they prepared the east wing. The Russian's place. As it happened, the death of Henry alone had the desired effect. People coming and going, nobody monitoring the CCTV at Dunston, Barbara deciding to spend the night in town. It all meant they had free rein.'

'Prepare it for what?' Riley asked.

'It seems that when you flicked the switches on the Viper it triggered an explosion that destroyed the east wing of Dunston Hall and much of the west, I am afraid. As I said, your grandmother wasn't on the estate, she was long gone. The Russians weren't so lucky. Kutsik and several of his friends died in the blast.'

'Christ.' He waited for more. None came.

Look at the body language, Dom. What aren't they telling you?

'And?' he asked. 'There's something else, yes? Why wouldn't you answer about Ruby and Izzy?'

There was movement and the plastic curtains parted with a tearing, Velcro-parting sound. As she pulled the sections apart, Riley could see Muraski clearly for the first time.

'Kate, what are you——?' Oakham began.

'As you said, it's just a precaution,' she snapped. 'I have to tell him.'

Even before they broke the news, Riley's stomach felt as if it had just been put into an express lift to hell. 'Tell me what?'

'Just after you had been taken to the Whittington, before you were transferred here, Scooby phoned.' Muraski stepped through the plastic shrouds and took his hand, squeezing it hard, pushing herself through this ordeal. 'There had been contact between his people and unknown actors in a house in Padstow.'

Riley felt as if he had been punched in the solar plexus. 'They're dead?' he gasped.

She shook her head. Her face was pained, as if each word she uttered physically hurt. 'One of the PPOs is dead. One seriously injured. They were unarmed. Their assailants were not.'

The express elevator arrived at its destination, right in the heart of that black vortex in his soul: it began to leak its poison into him. 'And Ruby? Izzy?'

A tear escaped from one eye, trickling down Muraski's cheek. 'They're still missing, Dom. We have no idea where they are.'

Riley ripped the covers back and swung his feet off the bed. He tore off the dressing holding the IV drip in his arm in place and yanked the needle from his arm. When he spoke, it was more an animal growl than human speech. 'Get me some clothes, you bastards. Now!'

AUTHOR'S NOTE

The Harvey's Resort/Viper bomb is based on a device used in a genuine case of blackmail against the casino in Lake Tahoe. The device was as fiendish as described here.

Every ATO knows the note that came with it:

Stern warning to the management and bomb squad:

Do not move or tilt this bomb, because the mechanism controlling the detonators in it will set it off at a movement of less than .01 of the open end of the Richter scale. Don't try to flood or gas the bomb. Do not try to take it apart. In other words, this bomb is so sensitive that the slightest movement either inside or outside will cause it to explode.

This bomb can never be disarmed or dismantled without causing an explosion. Not even by its creator. Only by proper instruction can it be moved to a safe place where it can be deliberately exploded. Only if you comply with my instructions will you learn how to move the bomb where it can be exploded safely.

If exploded in situ this bomb contains enough TNT to severely damage both Harvey's and Harrah's, across the street. That should give you an idea of the amount of TNT contained within this box. It is full of TNT. It is our advice to cordon off a minimum twelve hundred feet radius and remove all people from that area.

> *To get the information on how to move the device safely you must pay $3 million in unmarked $100 bills. You have 24 hours to comply. Instructions as to delivery are in a separate envelope. Any deviant from these instructions will leave your casino in shambles.*

(Extract from blackmail demand delivered with "The Machine" to Harvey's Casino.)

There are now several recognised ways of rendering that style of bomb safe (none of them involve a rig like Riley's), but at the request of the MoD and the Metropolitan Police's Counter Terrorism Command, the various solutions have not been detailed here.

Inverstone Lodge is based on Inverlair Lodge near Inverness, where washed-out SOE agents really were held for the duration of the Second World War. It was the inspiration for Patrick McGoohan's TV series *The Prisoner* and, in 1974, original script editor George Markstein wrote a novel called *The Cooler*, using Inverlair's wartime incarnation as a real-life version of The Village.

There is strong evidence that Mujahideen fighters from Afghanistan were trained in guerrilla warfare by ex-SAS instructors at secret camps in the UK, organised by MI6. One instructor explained that the three-week training courses involved various military activities, including the 'planning of operations, the use of explosives and the fire control of heavy weapons – mortars and artillery', 'how to attack aircraft and how to lay anti-aircraft ambushes aligned on the centre of a runway' and mounting 'anti-armour ambushes' (see the website markcurtis.info for the full story). However, Operation Homegrown is entirely fictional.

ACKNOWLEDGEMENTS

I am sat on a flight bound for Washington DC, staring out of the window of this Airbus A330 as Nova Scotia whizzes by beneath me. My mind takes me back to the offices of Simon & Schuster UK, sat there with the team, my agent and a blank notepad. Following the huge success of my biography *Painting the Sand*, writing fiction was the topic of conversation. It all seemed so surreal and feels like yesterday. That was a year ago, and once again I find myself here, another exciting journey, another book and something I certainly did not expect, but I haven't got here on my own. Success in this business does not come from the efforts of one, but from the team.

Firstly, Julian Alexander, my agent. Yet again, his calm reassuring advice has guided me through the unfamiliar terrain of fiction writing. His honest approach has been refreshing and couldn't be more appreciated.

Rob Ryan, a true gentleman and friend, a man that has taught me what it is to think outside of the box when writing. Hours have been spent laughing at some of the weirdest and most wonderful ideas you get when you put two guys from opposite worlds in one room together.

Bethan Jones, my editor, and the team at Simon & Schuster,

once again they have made this experience easy and exciting. Their continued efforts and attention to detail has been amazing.

My family and friends, their support has been unquestionable. I am rubbish at comms at the best of times, let alone when writing a book, but they have been there, patient and waiting in the sidelines.

Staff Sergeant Dom Riley will return in

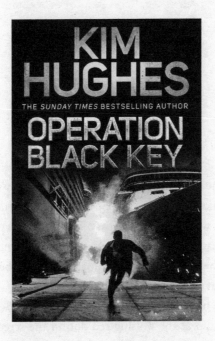

by *Sunday Times* bestselling author
and real life bomb-disposal expert

KIM HUGHES, GC

Turn the page to enjoy an early extract now . . .

ONE

'Target sighted. Cutting engine.'

Despite his near-whisper, Lieutenant James Varney's voice came over the speakers of the Special Boat Service's Mobile Command Centre truck with admirable clarity. The MCC was parked up on the pebbly beach near Herne Bay, the stretch of Kent coast where Varney and the men under his command had launched their Rigid Inflatable Boat on that night's training mission.

Inside the highly modified IVECO lorry, Staff Sergeant Dom Riley looked up at the pulsing red dot on the screen above the radio operator's head. This indicated the position of Varney's RIB, currently some six miles offshore, in the liminal zone where the Thames bled into the Channel. Back in the day, Riley had been out there himself, practising the same moves, pretending that hostiles had taken over the objective and had mined it, threatening to cripple the UK's vital maritime trade in and out of Tilbury. The fictitious target was one of the Maunsell Forts, Second World War-era structures that had once held anti-aircraft guns and now sat, decaying, forlorn and unloved, out in the estuary.

If he closed his eyes, Riley could picture the four units making up the fort, which had once been linked by long-rotted walkways.

Each sat on rust-streaked legs, standing like the aliens from *The War of the Worlds*, as if ready to stride ashore. With engines cut, the six SBS men would paddle the RIB through darkness – it was gone midnight, with March's new moon mostly obscured by clouds – to the largest of the four (there had once been five, but a careless Swedish ore transport had taken out one of the quintet). It was an unnerving approach for the men in the RIB, Riley knew. The metal giants groaned and creaked with the waves, as if they really were living, breathing entities. First time out it was, Riley had to admit, a spooky, sphincter-clenching sound.

Riley was in the truck purely as an observer, part of the MoD's new initiative to have more 'cross-fertilization' between regular and special forces, to see if they could learn from each other. It was his role these days. Observing. His army-appointed shrink had recommended 'light duties' for him. What kind of fucking light duties does an Ammunition Technical Officer do? You're either making bombs safe or teaching others how to do it. Not standing on the sidelines, just watching, like some military voyeur.

Apparently, though, since the disappearance of his wife and daughter ten months previously, he was too 'unstable' and 'volatile' to be trusted with a live device. It was bollocks. Yes, in between shouts he might have a short fuse, but once he was at work, confronted with a real fuse and a genuine threat, his focus was only on the job at hand. And he needed to focus on something else right now.

He had to admit, though, that his attention was wavering that night, ever since he had spoken to his grandmother, Barbara Clifford-Brown, on the phone. She had said, cagily, that she might have a tentative lead on what had happened to Izzy and Ruby, his missus (well, strictly speaking, ex-missus) and little girl. Riley had pushed her for more, but she said it would wait until they could speak in person. Barbara was once in MI6 and she had her own ways of doing things. She'd probably prefer to communicate through dead letter drops. Open phone lines were certainly an anathema.

Riley had arranged to see her in London the following day. He had to remember to steel himself for disappointment. With the army's unofficial blessing, he had followed plenty of leads over the past few months while on his reduced duties. All had ended in a heartbreaking cul-de-sac. Ruby and Izzy had been taken by persons unknown after a gun battle on the streets of Padstow, of all places, that left one bodyguard dead and another badly injured. The police and MI5 – involved because Riley had worked alongside them during a series of terrorist outrages – had also drawn a blank. So any feeling of cautious optimism about Barbara's call was cut with a low hum of anxiety that it would be another dead end.

'Approaching access ladder.'

James Varney again. Onboard he had two almost-qualified ATOs, which the SBS was desperately short of, thanks to threats to tankers in the Straits of Hormuz which required the bomb-disposal experts out there. The trainee ATOs were backed up in the RIB by a team of regular SBS 'swimmer-canoeists', too bulked up with body armour, stun grenades, night vision goggles and Colt C8s to do any actual swimming. In a real-world situation, their job would be to take out the 'X-Rays', enemy combatants or terrorists on the fort, clearing the way for the ATOs to perform their task of neutralizing any explosive devices. This time, at least, the IEDs were phoney, installed by a team of sappers from the Royal Engineers.

'Wish you were out there, Staff?' It was Joshua Kebede, the Special Boat Service Captain in charge of the exercise. He was from the outfit's specialist MCT – Maritime Counter-Terrorism – unit.

Riley drank the last of his now-cold coffee and binned it. 'What, freezing my nuts off in a blow-up boat in a fast-running chop, climbing some rusting ladder up into a dark, unsecured, rotting iron box that might actually fall into the bloody sea at any minute, while pretending to save the nation?' Riley waited a beat. 'Every time.'

Varney came back on. *'Hussein, Ricketts, you're on.'*

'Yes, Skip.'

'Liddy and Perring, you're covering.'

'Yes, Skip.'

Kebede and Riley turned to look at the MCC's speakers and waited for the next communication. No sound came for a while, apart from static and the odd electronic whistle. Riley was aware that the men out at sea had trained hard as a unit, so that most communication was by hand signals, nods and even winks. SBS men were tough fuckers for the most part, although Hussein and Ricketts, the ATOs, had been fast-tracked to bring the numbers up to strength. From what Riley could gather, the pair weren't as steel-hardened as the rest of the team. Yet.

Riley pictured them once again. If he had any sense, the bomb guy on point would be climbing gingerly, testing the rusted and pitted rungs and uprights of the ladder. It was a perfect place to leave a VOS, a Victim Operated Switch, a trip wire or pressure sensor, designed to detonate when a hand grabbed it or a boot sole pressed down on it.

'Hold it. Wire next to steel hatch.'

Riley nodded to Kebede. The ATO had found the first fake booby trap that the sappers would have put in place.

'False alarm. Clear. Checking rim of hatch.'

Good. By the book, thought Riley. The exercise was going smoothly. With a bit of luck he would make it home in the early hours to his 24-hour local and pick up a bottle. End the night as he normally did. At the bottom of that bottle. It was quiet and warm down there, with no nasty memories to taunt and prod him, a different world.

'*Nothing. Lifting hatch.*'

Riley heard it clang back with a noise that made him wince. Later, after the enquiry, he would discover that a plunger must have been placed on the floor where the rectangle of metal would drop. At the time, all Riley knew was that the command vehicle was filled with a roar that threatened to blow the speakers' cones apart.

A voice that might have been Varney's was just about audible over the racket. '*Fuck, fuck, fuck. Get out of here! Now!*' Then, a piercing, agonized scream, before comms went dead. Static filled the air. The red dot on the screen stopped pulsing and faded to black.

Riley sprinted along the length of the truck, throwing back the door, jumped down onto the beach and crunched rapidly towards the incoming tide that was hissing over the pebbles. He heard a new, terrible sound over the moan of the wind, a dreadful groaning, followed by the deep boom of another detonation. Then, Riley swore as he located the crimson glow on the horizon, like a beacon out at sea, marking the spot where good men were dying.

The horizon lit up with another flash, this one a searing white rather than red. As the rumble of the collapsing fort reached him, Riley heard Kebede approach and stand at his side, his breathing shallow and ragged. The man spoke for both of them when he asked: 'Fuckin' hell. What's gone wrong out there?'

It didn't require an answer, but Riley gave one anyway. 'Fuck knows.' Riley had no idea who or what could have caused this disaster out at sea. Nor could he possibly know that the events out there, many bleak miles from shore, would one day come back to screw up his life even further.

TWO

Helsinki. Three months later.

Dom Riley had to admit that he had been incarcerated in the cleanest prison cell he had ever seen. Not that he was an expert on prisons, apart from a few hours in an MI5 detention centre and a night in the glasshouse at Colchester, sleeping it off after a drunken night on the town. But nothing he had witnessed in person or on TV came close to the room in which he had been locked up. The walls were a pristine white and graffiti-free, there was a privacy screen of frosted glass in front of the toilet. The opaque texture matched that of the panes in the porthole windows, high on the rear wall. There was a bed with a duvet and (feather?) pillows, a desk, two chairs, and a comfy armchair. It was like he had been whisked off to a gaol built by that bloke from *Grand Designs*. Riley had no clear idea of why he was in this jarringly pristine Finnish prison. Espionage, the arresting SUPO officer had said.

Espionage?

What the fuck was he talking about? Riley had been following Barbara's lead, a painstakingly negotiated meeting with a Russian grandee, to establish if the abduction of his daughter and ex-wife was carried out by elements of the FSB or GRU or some other bunch of acronyms on British soil. Finland was not part of the deal. Just

397

a convenient place for a meet. Neutral territory. He was no threat to the security of the nation. It had taken a frustratingly extended period to set up the meet and now he was out of action, kept away from the hunt for Izzy and Ruby. *What a fuckin' waste of TIME.*

It was only after the final word bounced off the walls of the room that he realised he had blurted the sentence out loud. He filled his lungs. Breathed easy. Take stock, he thought. Be practical. Not the flake in Cell Nine.

The guys from *Suojelupoliisi* – the Finnish Security Intelligence Service aka SUPO – had ignored his protests. At least Riley still had on his own clothes, rather than an orange jumpsuit or whatever colour the Finns went for. They had, however, taken not only his shoelaces, but his boots, too. Probably because they realised they had steel toecaps. There was a steel sole insert, too. Not that either would offer much protection if you stepped on a proper IED, but they gave some psychological support. And steel toecaps came in very handy for arse-kicking anyone on the team who wasn't doing their job. Not that he had had a team for some time. He was still officially an ATO on light duties.

But that could change any moment he wished, he was sure. He had made a concerted effort to mislead, or at least misdirect, the army psychologists. To stay calm in their presence, no matter how much they probed about his missing wife and daughter or his friend Nick, who had died in Afghanistan, a victim of an IED. To put a plug in the vent of the hot lava of anger that boiled inside him, always threatening to blow. To make them think that PTSD wasn't an issue. It was like fooling a lie detector. However, Riley had to be careful not to be too remote and unemotional. What man wouldn't be disturbed and outraged by the disappearance of his family? It was a balancing act, and so far he reckoned he hadn't wobbled too much.

Although there had been one notable stumble. In the aftermath of the Maunsell Fort fiasco – which, appallingly, was a piece of hazing, a prank, gone horribly wrong – and when no blame was attached to Riley or Kebede, a goodwill tour of the US had been arranged for him. He had lasted a few days before the feeling of inadequacy hit him – how could he put up with PR shit when his family was missing? – and it ended with him standing up an attractive Puerto Rican woman from the New York and New Jersey Harbor Authority at The Aviary bar on the Upper West Side and flying home. She probably thought he saw the price of the cocktails and bailed. Not big or clever.

Now he was away from the shrinks, he could let all the fury rise to the surface. Possibly punch a wall or two. But he knew that would be a waste of energy and maybe his carpal bones. He needed to get home. He needed to find out if Barbara's tame Russian was on the level. For crying out loud, he just wanted Izzy and Ruby back. Alive. Was that too much to fucking ask?

The metal door opened and Riley glimpsed the two SUPO men who had arrested him before a long streak of piss in a sharp blue suit ducked into his cell. The newcomer straightened up and adjusted his tie while the door clanged shut behind him. He was thirty or so, with a blond fringe of floppy hair, and the bulletproof confidence of his class.

'Staff Sergeant Riley. I am George Hutton of the Embassy's Legal Affairs Department. Do you mind if I sit?'

'Be my guest.'

With some awkwardness, the newcomer folded his long limbs into the armchair and put his briefcase down next to him. It was like watching a leggy foal make itself comfortable. Riley waited until Hutton had finished unbuttoning his jacket and smoothing his tie before he asked: 'What is this bollocks? Who sent you? And can you get me out of here?'

Hutton opened his case with bony fingers that suggested he could have had a career as a concert pianist and took out a slim folder. 'So, Staff Sergeant Riley. In a bit of a pickle, eh?'

'Not really. The charge is espionage, for fuck's sake. I'm innocent.'

'Espionage and, additionally, compromising the security of the nation.'

'Like I said, it's bollocks. Do I look like a spy? I'm just here to try and get to the bottom of—'

Hutton had flicked open the folder and was peering down at it when he interrupted. 'What happened to your wife and daughter. I know. I also know that you met with a Russian operative—'

'Former operative.'

'Don't be naïve, Riley,' he snapped, the chummy demeanour evaporating like spit on a hot griddle. Riley took another look at him. High cheek bones with a face just the right side of gaunt, a wide mouth that didn't open when he smiled and eyes that were a startling green. When he spoke, you got a glimpse of teeth that were a shade too white.

'There is no such thing as a "former" or "Ex-" KGB man,' he said. 'Their loyalties and service has simply passed to its various successors.' That slit of a smile pulled across his face.

The penny dropped with a loud clatter. 'Legal Affairs? For fuck's sake. You're Six, aren't you?'

Hutton answered with a noncommittal wave of those preternaturally long fingers. 'And you have, um, associations with MI6's sister organisation across the river.'

He meant Five. 'I think "associations" is a bit strong. I helped them out some time back. And if you know that, then you know *I am not a spy.*'

'Well, let's see shall we? Can you start from the beginning?'

'Which beginning?' There were plenty to choose from.

Afghanistan. Nottingham. Scotland. The Emirates Stadium. *Padstow.*

'Your meeting with...'. Hutton allowed a flicker of distaste to show on his face. 'Colonel Brodsky.'

*

Dom Riley was not surprised that there was an Irish pub in Helsinki. They were everywhere in the world, as ubiquitous as Starbucks or Maccie Ds. He was taken aback, however, to learn that the Finnish capital could somehow support a dozen shamrock-and-stout establishments.

He was sitting in the latest addition to the list, Mary's Shebeen, situated not far from the Nordmann department store. Despite the name, it wasn't decorated like an illicit drinking den, but riffed on the classic Dublin pubs, plenty of dark wood, etched and stained glass, intimate snugs, signed hurling shirts and an ornate ceiling stained nicotine yellow in honour of the cigarette smoke it had never seen.

He was the sole occupant of a booth, distressed green leather under his arse and a ruinously expensive Jameson's in front of him. He took a sip of the whiskey, a few quids' worth by his reckoning. Part of him wanted to down it in one and order another. And then another. Numbing the higher centres of his brain, the ones that questioned the wisdom of meeting a man in an Irish pub in a foreign capital, a liaison that had taken weeks to set up, thanks to careful work by his grandmother, using the famous but mysterious 'back channels'. Helsinki was agreed as a venue because it was where the Russian said he felt safest. The UK was out of the question; he had history there, and he didn't want to be seen consorting with an agent of a foreign power on home soil. Finland, though, was acceptable to him.

Apart from the fact that Riley probably didn't have enough limit on his credit cards to drink himself unconscious at Helsinki prices, he had seen what alcohol had done to his mother's brain. He didn't want to inherit that particular family jewel.

Riley had been drinking pretty heavily before the incident at Fort Mansell. He had gone up a gear or two afterwards, while waiting for Barbara to put this meeting in Helsinki together. He knew full well the booze was a crutch, a tool designed to facilitate a retreat into a fantasy world. One where Izzy and Ruby were home and safe from harm, instead of . . .

No good ever came from that speculation. Plus he needed whatever wits he had left to deal with a retired KGB colonel. So, despite the temptation, Riley sipped.

There was a chance that the man he was meeting would have information on them. On who had taken them. They had been snatched in Cornwall, well over a year earlier. He felt constant guilt that it was his fault that they had been taken. That, because of his job and his history, Ruby had been kidnapped and . . .

No. They're alive. You know they're alive.

That was his old friend Nick, the ATO blown in half before his very eyes by an Afghan bomb, a less frequent visitor to his head these days. He was, at best, an unreliable source of information. Him being dead and all.

Yup. No wonder you need to see a shrink.

Riley flexed his left hand, trying to rid it of the pins and needles that sometimes invaded it. His body had recovered well from his exposure to a Sarin-like nerve agent during his last proper ATO assignment, but sometimes he got a neural reminder of just how lucky he had been.

He heard the squeak of the main door opening and the tap of a cane on the tiled floor. This could be his contact. But Riley didn't look. If it was his man, he'd make himself known. Riley was the amateur spy here. He would do well to remember that.

The metal ferrule on the cane tapped its way to the bar. A few minutes later a man of some bulk, dressed in an overcoat with a fur collar and a tall Homburg on his head, struggled into the booth, wheezing. In his left hand he held the walking stick and in the right was a pint of Guinness. A moustache of creamy foam was sitting on his top lip.

'I got the taste for the black stuff in London,' the man said, once he had recovered his breath, putting the cane on the seat next to him and wiping away the froth from his mouth with the back of his hand. 'Of course, not as good as you can get at the Toucan Bar in Soho, but perfectly acceptable. Dominic Riley, I assume?'

Riley hesitated a moment before answering. 'Yes. You must be Colonel Brodsky.' Riley had asked Barbara how he would know Brodsky, but she had assured him the man would find him.

Pavel Brodsky examined Riley carefully and Dom returned the favour. The Russian was moon-faced, with few wrinkles, but with eyebags you could store handfuls of change in. His turkey-wattle neck and veined hands betrayed his longevity. If Barbara was right, he had to be well into his eighties. 'Thank you for meeting with me.'

'I am on holiday. That's all this is. A short break from my little house in St Petersburg. A chance to see some Finnish art. I am a big fan of Jorma Hautala and of Helene Schjerfbeck, of course. And to drink a Guinness or two. Do you know there are a dozen Irish bars in Helsinki?' His English was excellent, with barely a trace of an accent.

'So I've heard, colonel.'

'Former colonel. And call me Pavel.' He took a hefty sip of his pint. 'You are a bomb disposal man, I hear.'

'We call them ATOs. Ammunition Technical Officers. But yes. Was one.' *Am one?*

'Afghanistan?'

Riley nodded.

'You are a brave man, then.'

He wasn't sure whether the Russian meant because of his role as a soldier neutralizing Improvised Explosive Devices or just because he'd been to Afghan. He had had no choice in the latter, and he was good at the former. 'I'm not sure bravery comes into it.'

'Perhaps not. But we have something in common, I suspect. We never want to see Afghanistan again.'

Riley was more ambivalent than that about the country – true, half the population seemed to want you dead, but it had a rugged beauty and simplicity that he sometimes missed. In terms of not wishing to revisit the places where so many comrades lost lives and limbs, though, that was a given. So he just gave another incline of his head.

The Russian's features softened and his shoulders relaxed. It was as if Riley had passed some test. 'How is Barbara? Well? Bearing up, as you say?'

Riley knew he meant since the death of his grandfather, Henry Clifford-Brown. Murdered, Riley and others suspected, by agents of the Russian state. But now wasn't the time to bring that up. There was a little dance to be done first.

'Coping. I suppose she is as well as can be expected. The loss of both her husband and her home hit her hard. But she has a flat in London now. And she's a tough old bird.'

Brodsky's substantial and wiry eyebrows twitched towards the brim of his Homburg. He took his hat off and placed it with the cane. 'I shouldn't let her hear you say that. She was quite a beauty in her day. But then I was handsome and dashing once.' He chortled to himself. 'Ah, Barbara. It was Henry I came across first, of course. In Bangkok. I met Barbara later, when Henry and she were in Moscow and Paris. And again in London. A remark-able woman.'

'She is.' It was only latterly he had begun to appreciate just how remarkable she was. On the outside, you only saw an elderly, slightly stooped woman with arthritic hands. If you could look into her past, you would find a very capable, very ruthless agent of Her Majesty's secret services. But enough of the skipping down memory lane, Riley thought. He needed to bring it back to the main purpose of his visit to the city. However, he was not the lead partner in this *pas de deux*. 'I'm grateful she got in touch and you agreed to help.'

'I am sorry about what happened to Henry. Death by lethal injection. Premeditated murder, I should say, given the way it was hidden under a nicotine patch. It was wrong. It was unnecessary.'

Unnecessary? Riley thought. But he didn't challenge him. Brodsky came from a world where murder was sometimes deemed very necessary indeed.

Brodsky sipped once more and fixed Riley with a stare that might have been threatening. It was certainly uncomfortably intense. 'And it was rogue elements within the state security apparatus. The killing of your grandfather was not officially sanctioned. I think perhaps you should look closer to home.'

Riley's mouth kicked into gear before he could stop it. The words came out as a growl. 'Rogue elements? Isn't that what you people always say when your schemes go south?'

The Russian's head moved from side to side as he considered this. 'There is some truth in that,' he eventually admitted. 'But it wasn't one of my schemes, you understand. The bombings. The murders. In my time such idiocy would have finished with a bullet in the back of the head.' He sounded like he missed the old days. 'Like your grandmother, I am retired. But like her, I keep some channels open.'

From inside the overcoat the Russian extracted a magazine-sized guide to Helsinki. He laid it on the table and slid it across. 'Can you put your telephone on the table, please? I want to be sure you are not recording this.'

Riley did as he was asked. Brodsky tapped the Home button to make sure it was off.

'Thank you. I'm assuming I don't have to frisk you?'

Riley opened his jacket. 'Be my guest.'

Brodsky nodded his satisfaction and tapped the magazine. 'In here is a piece of paper which contains all that I have discovered about the events leading up to the disappearance of your wife and daughter.'

'More than a year ago now,' Riley reminded him. 'Since then, nothing. No ransom demand. No blackmail attempts. No claims of responsibility.' Just the torture of silence.

'Once you have digested its contents, I would like you to dispose of the paper. By which I mean, I do not want it to leave this building. Understood?'

'Understood.' He was keen for the Russian to fuck off now and let him read the damn document.

Brodsky sensed his impatience, reached over and squeezed Riley's shoulder. 'Do not get your hopes up. It is not good news, I am afraid.'

Riley started to speak, but Brodsky raised a hand to silence him. He finished his pint and wiped his mouth for the final time. 'Tell Barbara if she ever wants to visit St Petersburg, she will be most welcome. I don't think she got across to the Hermitage when she was stationed in Moscow. It is a marvel.' He struggled to his feet and slid out of the booth, collecting hat and cane as he did so. 'I hope you find what you are looking for. I assure you, though, you have been searching in the wrong place.'

Riley felt a familiar fizz of anger and bottled it. 'So where is the right place?'

The Russian shrugged. 'That's not my job, son.'

It took a monumental force of will not to stand up and grab him by the throat. 'That doesn't help.'

A thin smile this time. 'I wish you luck, Dominic Riley. I know what it means to lose family.'

Riley found that no words would come. Not with a steady voice. He gave a nod as a farewell and Brodsky left, limping his way to the door. Riley would bet a fistful of roubles there was quite a story behind that gammy leg.

He waited a few minutes before he scooped up the guide and headed for the gents, only to be confronted with gender neutral toilets. All the cubicles were unoccupied, however, so he selected the farthest one and locked himself in. Then he flicked through the pages of the magazine until he found a single sheet of paper, with typed text on both sides. He had to read it several times before he could take it all in.

It had been called Operation *Reznya*. Carnage. An apt name. Its aim was to sow further confusion in the UK in the midst of the post-Brexit chaos. The public would begin to think society was breaking down, with bombing campaigns by the Muslim radicals, the far right and a resurgent IRA. As a bonus, the events would be a cover for taking out several Russian dissidents who had proved a thorn in Putin's side. It was instigated by something called Directorate 14, and given to the shadowy Unit 29155 for execution. The latter had managed to infiltrate two teams of three Russian agents into the UK completely undetected. One of them succeeded in recruiting a bomb-maker of Afghan origin, which was where Riley had come in, being an expert on that country's range of lethal devices.

According to the document, all of the Russian agents were

exfiltrated when Carnage was deemed to have run its course. In fact, there was a feeling it had overstepped the mark and the agents were reprimanded. What did 'reprimanded' mean in Putin's Russia? Nothing trivial, he hoped. Maybe one of Brodsky's bullets to the back of the skull.

The last sentence was handwritten, probably by Brodsky. *There is no evidence that any of the operatives had anything to do with the subsequent disappearance of Staff Sergeant Dominic Riley's wife and daughter.*

What the fuck? These were the guys who exposed him to a nerve agent, leaving him with pins and needles, slightly out-of-whack tastebuds and a liver running at eighty per cent capacity. And they had taken Izzy and Ruby as part of the whole sick undertaking. *No evidence?*

He read the sentence again. Bullshit is what it was. It was the 'rogue elements' nonsense all over again – blame anyone rather than take responsibility. He tore the page into confetti and flushed it away, dumping the magazine among the used paper towels on the way out.

**Don't miss the next explosive thriller featuring
Staff Sergeant Dom Riley.**

Available to order now.